THE BAREFOOT SHERIFF

RIDERS OF THE PURPLE SAGE
BOOK ONE

IRENE RADFORD

This book is dedicated to James Garner, Jack Kelly, and Roger Moore, the three Mavericks who gave me a deep love of Western television series and dominated the genre for generations. I fell in love with all of them.

CHAPTER 1

Columbia River Plateau 1871, early autumn

A SHARP PAIN sliced through my foot all the way to my knee. My balance slid askew as I fired my last bullet into the gut of the alien monster in front of me.

She stood almost as tall as me, clad only in purple skin and translucent wings. I knew her sex with only a glance. I rarely saw females in battle. They were often shamans, or witches. Deadly.

She wove the air with her three fingered, reptilian paws in a complicated pattern that I knew would cast a magical bolt of lightning likely to kill me. I let my sliding feet carry me to the ground, beneath the fading arrow of magic. It fizzled and dropped sparks right onto the small of my back.

Burning agony sliced across my waist nearly hip to hip.

I ignored it as I drew my belt knife and launched it directly into the single eye of my enemy. Humanity's enemy.

What my bullet through her heart didn't accomplish, the sharp blade did. The one-eyed witch died instantly, with her claws waving helplessly through the air.

I watched as her purple skin greyed and her almost translucent hair lost its lavender tinge. Her wing membranes crumpled into the rocky ground.

Never trust a one-eyed witch. They sometimes came back to life.

Or spinning purple spaceships brought reinforcements. Swarms rarely happened during daylight. Rescue ships waited until the darkest hours of the night.

This dead critter wouldn't rise again. The near-constant wind of the high desert plateau already began to scatter the remains into the scrub sagebrush.

"Dust to dust," I mumbled, the only prayer I remembered from before. Before my life became an endless battle with mundane weapons against arcane powers.

If I wanted the bounty for this swarm feasting on seven dead Indians courtesy of the U.S. Army, I had to act fast to harvest the spiral, hollow horn growing from the middle of her forehead. Males had straight horns.

A single mournful note escaped the horn. Sweet and melancholy, her death music tugged at my heart. I wanted to cry.

"Fuck it. I don't need the money."

$250 per horn, $1000 for the spiraled horn of a witch. I tore the horn free of flesh and bone. Unusual how easily it came away in a single piece.

The money added up fast. That only mattered if a Rider of the Purple Sage, the paranormal branch of the Pinkerton Agency, lived long enough to spend it.

I had a deadly reputation among my fellow agents. No one, human outlaw or alien, messed with Josie Blue. I'd spent six years in the field, longer than three-quarters of my comrades. Before that, I'd spent four years as a Union Army scout during the war.

I never talked about my life before that and tried not to think on it too often.

I figured I'd used up most of my luck. This should be my last mission. If I survived long enough to find safety, maybe a nice little town populated by people rather than the dead and dying carrion eaters littering the ground around me.

They didn't eat just any carrion though, never sheep.

These critters would pass up dead buffalo, deer, wolves, and cattle for a single taste of dead human.

I braced my left hand against my bleeding back as I heaved myself upright. Every muscle twitch sent fire through my veins and dimmed my vision. But I had to stand. Crouching on the ground made me vulnerable.

Elinore, my skewbald mare, nudged me gently beneath my arm. Gratefully, I accepted her assistance until I stood beside her. She'd worked hard defending me today. Her instincts and a little training, and she was as formidable a warrior as me. Her iron-shod feet and big teeth behind a half ton of weight inflicted as much damage as my two Colt .45s, Derringers in ankle holsters, a brace of knives, and a Spencer repeating rifle.

"You'll have a scar or two from this battle, my dear." I brushed her neck and nose with delicate fingertips. She hung her head, nearly as exhausted as me. Her saddle didn't sit straight on her back. Something was very wrong with my closest companion. My friend.

"Guess you aren't up to carrying me." I buried my nose in her mane.

She remained still as we both gathered the strength and courage to move.

"First things first." With one hand I dug a worn and stained shirt from my saddlebag. No water left in my canteen to dampen the cloth. Couldn't find the blame thing anyway. Then, still clinging to Elinore, with one hand and my teeth, I ripped the once fine cotton in half. I still needed the mare's strength to hold me upright, so I turned and rested my back and neck against her while I tied half the shirt around my waist. The pressure from my make-shift bandage gave me enough relief I could turn around and dab at Elinore's wounds with the other half.

Those alien horns were wicked sharp. They'd left some jagged cuts. But horse hide can be tough. The bleeding slowed already and would soon scab over.

I hoped my own wound would too.

"If you are ready, dear heart, we'd best get going. We need to find water. And food. It may be autumn, but that sun is still hot enough to kill us both. One foot in front of the other." We dragged ourselves along a twisted game trail that headed up toward a ridge. I'd be able to see for miles in every direction up there so I could choose a direction.

I hadn't had a human companion in a long time, to I talked to Elinore, and myself, and maybe the universe, just to hear my voice, make certain I could still use it.

If only this scrap of high desert offered shade from anything taller than a tumbleweed or rabbitbrush, I'd rest a while. No water either.

We had to keep going. One step at a time.

I CLUNG TIGHTLY to my saddle horn as I balanced on one foot and shook a single grain of sand loose from inside my boot. The blamed thing felt as big as Mount Hood and rubbed the ball of my foot. A blister had begun erupting a couple miles back and the sand finished the job.

Elinore's head drooped in search of a moist leaf on a tumbleweed or a blade of grass growing in the shade of a scraggly sagebrush.

I was here in the middle of nowhere without a whiff of civilization or other people for miles.

For now. I decided to reload my guns from the half-empty box in the saddlebag. One never knew who, or what hid behind a boulder.

We needed water.

Not even of a puff of cloud in the sky. Just a very long horizon as Elinore and I climbed to the ridge.

Agent Josie Blue, alone and broke, with only my beloved horse to talk to. I'd collected a small fortune in bounties for Pinkerton. What good did it amount to now?

I'd worn the boot soles thinner than paper. Every imperfection in my path felt like I walked on a bed of nails.

Holding the boot upside down, I shook it until my shoulders ached and my teeth rattled. Another fine bit of grit fell out. "Shit! Is that all it was?"

Then I examined my foot and found one slightly larger bit of sand embedded in my sock, right beside the hole in the sole that had grown bigger since this morning. I couldn't remember when or where I lost my hat. The rock in my boot came loose with only a little scraping from my broken and filthy fingernail.

My lower back protested the movement in one long jabbing burn. To relieve the pain, I pressed the muscles just above the bandaged slash that hadn't closed after three or four hours of walking. The ache dulled for a moment. For those few heartbeats I was free of the reminders of why I wandered alone, twenty miles beyond nowhere.

Then Elinore shifted her weight off her lame foot and the sun glinted off a metal piece of her tack. The blinding flash jabbed my eyes and an image I didn't want to remember jumped to the front of my mind.

Tangled body parts, none of them matching. Bright and festive clothing dulled with blood. So much blood. Too much blood. All the while a jaunty tune jangled my ears...

Elinore stood rock-solid-still once I adjusted my balance, despite the weight I leaned on my horse. "Good girl, Elinore. Good girl," I murmured to the skewbald mare.

Steadier on my own, I put my boot back on, taking the time to scan the landscape for threats. Almost surprised, I realized we'd reached the top of the ridge. A rutted road led north and south. Not much of a road, just packed dirt on either side of a ridge. Dry grass tried desperately to stay upright in the slight breeze. Still, it was a road, and roads led somewhere. Right to go north or left toward the south?

I shaded my eyes with one hand, still clinging to the saddle horn with the other. The fading sunlight glistened on a long strand of water, about twenty miles north of me, running east to west.

I replayed the last map I'd seen in my head. "What do you think, Elinore? Is that the Columbia River?"

The horse snorted and looked south.

"Follow the telegraph wires. If you say so, friend." I rubbed Elinore's ears and trudged a few more steps onto the road. Out of long habit I looked around, noting landmarks, not many of them. "Up we go, girl, and we'll reach the crest, then it will be downhill." I walked as I spoke to Elinore, keeping up a constant litany of meaningless words despite my dry throat and aching eyes.

Ten steps became fifteen. Damned drunken road builders! I stepped on a rock. Again. Flailed for balance and hopped in a half circle, inventing new curses each time a foot came in contact with the hot dust.

"Damnation on this Satan cursed land!" Blood and pus began oozing out of the raw skin beneath the now popped blister.

Heavy blackness dragged at my body and my mind. I needed to sit down. I needed water. I needed to sleep.

I needed to survive so I could report my findings to the Pinkertons: A spinning purple and gold generation ship, big, unusual to be seen in daylight, (make a note of the abnormality) descending to hover about ten feet above a dry creek bed. A hatch opened while the ship continued to spin. A dozen winged critters disgorged, they gathered in a single swarm before descending like an arrow shot from a crossbow into the heap of slaughtered bodies, singing their triumph. And then they began to feed as if starving, not saving any meat to take back to their mates on the retreating ship. The music stopped.

I'd lain in wait, having followed the troop of U.S. Army cavalry bent on eliminating the native tribes—the easy job. They left the harder job of eliminating the space aliens to the Pinkertons.

The spiral horn I'd collected would tell my superiors more than my written words. If I found a place to sit down long enough to write that report.

That meant I had to keep moving.

When I finally settled both feet on the ground, I assessed our location once again. The slight change in elevation gave me a clear view of...

"Blessed mother of God, it... it's a town!"

Not just a cluster of miner's huts, this was a real, if small, town with a livery stable, general store, three saloons—one more prosperous and cleaner looking than the other two—a bank, a jail, a tiny schoolhouse, a brick church at the far end, and wonder of wonders, a doctor's office and a millenary/dressmaker. And a post office with telegraph wires running cross country in a straight line toward the silver ribbon of a river.

We trudged another one hundred yards, each step harder than the last.

"We're here, Elinore. We're safe." For now. "I can get a new hat! You can rest that miserable foot of yours. And I can get my back fixed."

A warm whuff of air caressed my face. Elinore's breath smelled bitter, lacking moisture. A lot like the sour sandpaper in the back of my own throat.

"Only another few yards," I whispered to Elinore as I gathered her reins and led her to a nearby trough outside the split rail fence of the livery. I let her suck up a few swallows of clean water. Then I pushed her back to an open area inside the corral so I could dunk my head into the water. Elinore nudged my dripping braid, wanting more. Best not to let my friend be greedy with her water just now. Colic was never good.

I took the time to unbuckle the worn saddle and place it astride the nearest fence railing. The saddle blanket landed beside it. I didn't trust anyone else to do this essential chore.

Elinore shook herself from nose to tail and grunted her relief. Her muscles rippled, revealing prominent ribs. But Elinore rubbed her muzzle against my shoulder, nibbling on hairs that sprang free of my braid. I should probably get a haircut but pulling the chestnut mane into a tight braid was easier than letting shorter strands blow into my eyes and mouth.

"As long as you have your sense of humor, we'll be all right. You can have a little more water now."

Elinore stretched her rein to the limit to get to the trough and gulped.

I pulled her back, headed for the nearby pump where I cupped my hand to catch my own drink. Then I doused my head again to ease my aching brow and rest my dazzled eyes. The water slid down my throat like velvet. I could have drunk a gallon or more. But I cut myself off before fully satisfied. What's good for my horse was good for me too.

"How long you staying?" a squeaky-voiced teenaged boy asked from the open door of the livery stable. The sign above the doors proclaimed "Jed's". Then in smaller letters below, "Livery, Hour, Week, Month."

Four other horses stood about the corral, hip-shot and sleepy-eyed, two geldings and two mares. A single buckskin stallion patrolled a second corral, restlessly pacing the perimeter, lifting his muzzle to sniff and grunt at the mares.

My nose told me none of the female horses were in heat, including Elinore. Most people were sensitive enough to notice major changes in smells. I had trained myself to catch the slightest whisper of scent on the wind. Often that was my first clue of an enemy presence.

The grass within the enclosure had been eaten down to stubble and trampled into the dirt in both corrals. Useless for grazing purposes. The water troughs stood full and clear though. And there was good pasturage beyond the fence where five more mares and geldings grazed.

The sun was setting rapidly, changing the color of the sky from white to gold to dark grey. Not a cloud in sight to add some red or orange to the horizon. I had to squint and look at the ground lest metal tack reflected the slanting angle of the sun again. I couldn't afford more of a headache. Or another flash of memory.

"We'll be here at least a week," I replied to the boy, pushing away from Elinore's solid strength. I looked around and found brushes sitting neatly on a shelf just inside the wide, stable doors. Everything in its place. A neat barn meant a hostler who cared. Fodder should be

on the schedule soon. "We'll stay as long as Elinore needs to heal."
Even if that took a year or two. "You've served me well for ten years,
sweet lady. You deserve a good long rest." I let my mare return to the
trough for another short drink.

Unthinking, I grabbed a brush and began grooming my faithful
friend with long even strokes. A cloud of dust burst free of the white
and reddish-brown coat.

"I kin do that," the boy said, sounding sullen. "That's my job."

"I know. But Elinore here likes it when I groom her."

With one hand I reached into my trouser pocket for a coin, a
nickel seemed like a princely sum. I needed to make the few larger
pieces last a bit longer. I flipped it to the boy. He caught it unerringly.

"Elinore needs several more short drinks. Don't let her get greedy
for several more hours. She'll need a full measure of grain and hay.
And use her name. She'll respond to you courteously if you do. Otherwise, she'll ignore you. Or plant a hoof in your chest. She'll do the
same to that stud if he gets too close. And don't put Elinore inside.
She needs to be able to see the horizon and the night sky. Stables
spook her."

"Yes, sir."

I didn't have the energy to correct him.

Elinore shifted her weight from sore foot to sore foot. Her skin
rippled in discomfort.

The saddle had sat strangely because she hurt all over, starting
with her feet.

I ran the brush the length of her spine one more time and handed
it to the boy.

"You got a name, sir?"

"Yep. You got a blacksmith in town? I want to pull Elinore's shoes
and let her feet rest."

"Blacksmith walked away one night two year ago. Left all his tools
but he put out the fire in the forge. Pa put the tools in the tack shed. I
kin pull those shoes for you. Don't reckon I kin put 'em back though."

"Don't worry, I can shoe a horse if the forge is still intact. This a
quiet town?"

"Mostly."

"Anyone else go missing suddenly?" I stood beside my horse, my partner, too tired to move, afraid not to.

"Not that I kin recamember." The boy wouldn't meet my gaze.

"Bad marriage? Gambling debts? Too much drink?" There were a lot of reasons for a skilled craftsman to walk away from everything he owned and not take his most valuable possessions, his tools, with him. But only one reason came to mind. I looked at the ground again before I recalled the horrible images of ten years ago, and last week, and this morning.

"Didn't rightly hear why he left. Pa said Young George—his pa was Old George—weren't quite right in the head. Kept seeing flying purple things."

I stiffened. "Two years ago? Anyone else see anything strange?"

"Nah. Young George always saw strange things. Even as a kid. He reported a flying machine shaped like two saucers stuck together rim to rim."

No, no, no, no! Not now when I'm so tired I can't think.

"No one else ever saw anything, a'fore or since. Oh, and them saucers were purple too. Young George had a thing for purple."

Maybe, just maybe the menace had gone elsewhere until today. Two years was a long time to desert a thriving feeding ground.

"Who sells the best grub in town?" I couldn't accomplish anything on a starving belly and an exhausted and foot-sore horse.

"Rosie's. The saloon just beyond the post office. Her cook fixes up a great plate of rare beef, potatoes, and fresh greens."

"Rooms to rent there too?"

"Sometimes. Iff'n Rosie likes you."

"I'll be back in a bit. I'll tend to my horse's shoes then. I'm the only one who touches her feet. Understand?"

The boy nodded.

"You got a name?" I asked.

"Jed. Just like my pa."

"Thank you, Jed."

With that, I slung my saddlebags over my shoulder and added my rifle's scabbard to the bundle. I didn't need to check my holstered Colts, or the ammunition tucked into the loops of my gun belt. Their comforting weight and the ties around my thighs to keep them in place hadn't changed since I'd counted every bullet when I reloaded a mile back.

Later, when I had privacy, I'd go through my diary for entries around two years ago, see if Young George's disappearance was an isolated incident or part of a pattern.

"You never gave me your name, mister. What do I tell my pa about the new horse in the corral?

"Just call me Blue," I called back over my shoulder.

"*Blue?*" the boy gulped.

I turned to face him down.

His protuberant throat apple bobbed in his skinny throat. "Blue, the bounty hunter?"

"Check the tooling on the saddle cantle. If you find the flower of a purple sage, that's all you need to know."

CHAPTER 2

NEIL SANDERSON SCRUBBED his scarred face with his palms, not liking the figures quoted in the letter on his desk. He adjusted his spectacles, but still couldn't bring the outrageous numbers into focus.

Oh, the railroad companies were interested in building a spur line to Heller's Hole, named for Ralf Heller, the first owner of the defunct copper mine in Zilch Valley, but only if the local ranchers and business owners contributed toward the cost of such an enterprise. Not investment dollars, straight out funding of the construction costs, at three times what Neil knew the work would cost. Someone was making a whale of a lot of money. If he allowed it to go through.

Late Friday afternoon, and only a smattering of people in the bank. Nothing his teller, Martin Youngblood, couldn't handle alone in the next ten minutes. Then they could close up for the week.

Father would skin him alive if he found out that Neil had locked the doors even five minutes early.

But Father was in Portland, "courting" investors for the family bank. More likely drinking, gambling, and whoring from the comfort of his gentlemen's club. That was fine with Neil, as long as Father didn't bet the bank and lose. And Mother could pretend she knew nothing about her husband's activities as long as he didn't bring them home with him.

Since Neil came home from the war, Father had shown an increasing tendency to make rash and hasty decisions. Best he do it elsewhere. Neil had set up a gentleman's agreement with Father's cronies in Portland to keep him on a strict allowance.

"Useless to try to read between the lines of this letter when I can barely see," he muttered to himself. He'd had perfect vision until the first battle of Bull Run when a cannonball had dug into the churned turf thirty yards in front of him. The spraying dirt and debris had struck him in the face, taking most of the sight from his left eye and leaving his face a bloody mess.

His skin had healed—leaving a few pocks—but his vision had not. He'd found an expert lens grinder in Portland last spring. His new spectacles helped. But when he was tired and the sun had shifted away from the bank's windows, he had problems.

He'd spent the rest of the war in the paymaster's office, dealing with accounts and receipts. But he'd come home alive. That was more than he could say about a goodly number of friends and cousins.

Neatly folded, he tucked the railroaders' letter into his desk and locked it. Three more customers. He'd help Martin and they'd both quit earlier than expected.

"What?"

Three young men, two with distinctive fine silver blond hair, strangers all, none of them as old as twenty, shuffled in. They closed the front door, on this fine autumn evening, and flipped the open sign to "Closed". All three of them carried a Colt .45 aimed at the remaining customers and Martin. They didn't seem to notice Neil off to the side behind the tills with a half wall between his desk and the public.

The fine hairs on Neil's nape bristled. This was more than he could handle on his own.

"Open the safe and give us all the money and nobody gets hurt!" the first young man through the door yelled. Much too loudly. His hands shook as he raised his gun level with Martin's heart.

The locked drawer at the bottom right side of Neil's desk looked empty. Neil pressed a slight indentation on the base. The secret compartment was also empty. His father had the only other key. Why would he take Neil's service revolver to Portland?

Without thinking, or grabbing his smoke-colored spectacles to protect his eyes, from the sun, Neil dashed to the door, twisted the lock, yanked it open, and ran toward the center of town. He needed help. Fast. He needed a gun two minutes ago.

"Damnit, why didn't we hire a new sheriff last year!"

"THIS IS FAR ENOUGH," I said to myself. I fell more than dropped to the wooden sidewalk. Half a dozen people, mostly men, three women each with a hand looped through the arm of a man, milled about in the rapidly chilling twilight.

Three deep breaths and I had enough strength to yank off my boot, or what was left of it. I wiggled my toes, relishing a few moments of freedom and fresh air. Still, every bone in my body ached and sharp pain pounded behind my eyes. A moment more. One more moment. My belly growled disapproval of that notion.

"Food, bath, sleep. In that order. I'll consult the banker tomorrow, or maybe Monday. The local doc when I can." I held the boot ready to force my foot inside.

Another moment. I just need another moment.

A squinty-eyed man in a nice woolen suit ran out of the bank across the street—the only stone building in town; the church at the other end of town was made of red brick, the rest ramshackle wooden construction. Then he stopped in the middle of the street and stood, jaw agape and eyes wide in terror.

I squinted to bring the scene into better focus, and watched more carefully without changing my posture.

Five short and sharp explosions broke the quiet. All the people in the street froze in place. As one, they turned and faced the bank. A woman screamed, followed by the others.

Six more shots.

I sprang to my feet, a revolver in each hand, cocked and ready. One boot on, and one boot off I stalked across the dirt street.

"Don't go in there! They'll kill you!" The well-dressed man of about thirty years, wearing wire rimmed glasses, held up both hands, palms out. His sandy-brown hair flopped into his eyes. Pale splotches marred his skin. Scars. War souvenirs?

Another time and place and I might have found him attractive. No time for that now.

"Please don't go in there, all they want is money and they don't care who they shoot to get it." He grabbed my arm and tried to hold me back. "May I borrow your gun so I can deal with them?"

"Why didn't you stay inside and hand over some money?" I shook him off and kept walking. I don't give up my gun to anyone, even the few I know well and trust.

I kicked open the door with my booted foot and took two more steps.

A cold sheen of perspiration broke out across my brow and down my spine, inflaming the already burning open slash across my back. The same thing happened before every gunfight. All these bank robbers could do is kill me. The *things* I hunted for the Pinkertons, and the bounty could do so much worse.

One quick glance and I placed three boys, still in their late teens with a six-shooter each. Two with silver-gilt hair that tickled a memory. On the floor, three men; all bleeding, two writhing, one pasty white with too much blood pooling beneath him.

The white-haired boys began drooling and humming.

I thought I recognized the tune. But no. It varied away from the musical bridge. It had different origins.

The third bank robber held a young man by the throat, a gun to his temple. "Come any closer and I'll shoot him!" the dark-haired robber squeaked. His shoulders trembled.

The other two outlaws shifted their aim to me. They seemed less nervous than the other one. They would be responsible for the blood on the floor.

"Let this guy open the safe and you all live," said the guy with the gun to the teller's head.

"But... but... but I don't know the combination. Only Mr. Sanderson knows."

The robber's finger tightened on the trigger of his gun.

"I don't have time for this. Or the patience to deal with amateurs. By the authority invested in me by the Riders of the Purple Sage a division of the Pinkerton Agency, you are under arrest," I said by rote.

The men looked confused, but they all took aim on my gut. At least the nervous one no longer threatened the teller.

"You have been warned. One, two, three."

Right trigger, left, right. The three outlaws dropped in their tracks, blood blossoming on shoulders and thighs. The teller dropped too, but he merely crouched on all fours sobbing.

"I feel sorry for your mothers," I said, holstering my weapons. "They'll have the nursing chores."

"OH, MY GOD! YOU SHOT THEM!" the well-dressed man came up behind me. He threw his hand across his mouth and gulped, his throat apple continuing to work as he held back bile. "I was running for help when I heard the shots..."

"I am a duly authorized agent of..."

"I know. I heard you the first time. But you just shot them!"

His voice sounded educated, cultured. An east coast university, I guessed.

"They killed that man over there and wounded the other two. They threatened the teller and me. Self-defense is what I'll plead. Not a jury in the land will convict me. Now get out of my way. Call your sheriff if you must, but definitely call a doctor and the undertaker."

I holstered my pistols and turned to exit. "The boys aren't dead. Just passed out."

"Um... you're going to need this, I think." He held up my boot, peering at me over the tops of his glasses. The left eye didn't open all way and the right one blinked rapidly. The pale dents scattered across his face looked like scars, and not leftovers from a youth's pebbly skin.

I looked at my feet. The big toe on the left poked through a new hole in my sock, my last pair. My face flushed. Without looking at the man I grabbed the boot keeping my gaze down.

"I'm Neil Sanderson. My father owns this bank. And you are...?"

"Hungry, thirsty, filthy, and tired." I limped out to the sidewalk and retrieved my saddlebags and my rifle.

"SOMETHING STRANGE ABOUT THAT MAN," Neil muttered. Then he spotted the son of the general store owner through the still open bank door. "Fetch Doc Buchanan!" he called across the street. He hustled back inside.

First, he yanked his handkerchief out of his coat breast pocket and pressed it hard against the still bleeding wound in Zeb Smith's side, beneath his heart. The bleeding had slowed, thick and sluggish now. Not good.

The other two wounded men, a rancher who only came to town once a month, and Jed, the livery stable owner still writhed and moaned. Both gritted their teeth trying desperately not to appear weak and cowardly.

"Martin! Get some bandages."

That order was met with gulping sobs.

A quick look showed the young man trying to get his feet under him as he wiped his tear-streaked face with his sleeve. Too young to have served in the war, he'd probably never encountered violence of this magnitude before, not even a Saturday night when the da Foe boys came to town. Like Neil, Martin was good with numbers and much happier with his quiet job indoors than riding herd on cattle.

He'd probably never shot a weapon in his life.

Neil hoped the boy wouldn't have to learn to live with this sort of thing as a normal occurrence. "Move, Martin. Now. While these men are still alive."

Doc Buchanan slammed into the bank lobby, took one look at the carnage, and ordered someone outside to get stretchers. New worry lines showed on his face, making him look closer to sixty than the forty-five Neil knew him to be. The silver strands in his dark hair looked more prominent too.

"Stretchers, bandages, more hands! Now!" He'd served in the war too but had no visible wounds. Just experience.

His authoritative voice compelled Martin to move faster. In seconds he disappeared into the backroom and emerged with the white tablecloths Mother insisted Neil keep on hand for the rare occasion when he might offer tea and refreshments to a favored customer. Neil hadn't used them in over two years.

Then Martin looked around. When he didn't see any reduction in the amount of blood on the floor, he looked ready to dissolve into uselessness again.

"Start closing out your drawer, Martin. We need to make sure every single penny is accounted for," Neil said, sounding calmer than he felt. The boy needed something familiar to do. Something routine where he could measure progress with each coin and bill counted and written down.

Neil had only the unfamiliar chore of maintaining a constant pressure on Zeb's wound. He could do that. He had to do that. He had to ignore the blood on his cuffs and seeping into his boots. He didn't care that Mother would scold him for the mess. He had to keep pressure on that wound.

TWO HOURS LATER, Elinore was comfortable with her bare feet and chowing down on fresh grain and sweet hay. So, I sat at a small table in the back corner of the saloon, my unbooted feet propped up on an empty chair beside me. In this chair I had a clear line of sight to the door and the room.

I didn't have to look at the upright piano adjacent to my corner. I hadn't played an instrument—any instrument other than a mouth harp—in six years. That was at the end of the war, when Mr. Pinkerton and his assistant, Colonel Beauregard Martine from New Orleans—a southerner who fought for the Union—had taken me to a concert in Washington City. That was when Martine became Brotherton, and I joined him in the Riders of the Purple Sage. I wasn't their first recruit. But ever afterward I associated Mozart with the conspiracy to chase after paranormal miscreants and keep them secret from the general public.

I hummed the final sequence of *The Marriage of Figaro*, a joyful piece that brought the concert to the interval. *I used to enjoy singing almost as much as I loved playing.*

Did I dare play the rickety old instrument? The harp looked long enough to support proper strings.

"It hasn't been tuned in donkey's years. So, give up looking at it with the same kind of lust most of my customers look at my girls," Rosie the owner of the saloon, said, placing a full mug of beer before me, the foam frothing down the side in enticing tendrils.

"I'm losing my touch. I didn't see you walk across the room," I replied, releasing my grip on the revolver that never left my hip and shifting it to the beer mug.

"Because you were daydreaming about that there piano. Don't know anyone who can tune it, so you'll have to satisfy your lust for music some other way, dearie. Now what else can I get for you?"

"Nothing, Rosie. I haven't eaten so well in... donkey's years."

"Then savor every bite. Holler if you need more of anything." She patted my shoulder in easy familiarity and wandered away, warily watching the five cowhands playing cards at the table in front of the bar.

Slowly, I chewed a bite of rare roast beef, savoring every juicy morsel. I closed my eyes in bliss, then reached for my second beer, fingers clasping the handle of the glass mug unerringly. I drank deeply of the brew, not caring how bitter it tasted. It was wet.

I had time to relax and enjoy decent food. I'd lived, slept, and eaten rough for so long I'd almost forgotten what it felt like to savor a meal in safety and comfort.

And I'd longed to sing to someone other than Elinore.

Next, I forked a small, buttered potato into my mouth. It too tasted heavenly and made the beer seem a little sweeter.

Or maybe the unaccustomed alcohol numbed my tongue.

"Are you enjoying your meal?" Neil Sanderson asked. The banker. Bespeckled. Dressed like a gentleman.

I looked up and swallowed. "Very much." I turned my attention to the mess of greens slathered in bacon grease. No delicate way to eat them. So I used my table knife to cut them into ragged squares. I still had to slide my fork beneath each wad to get it into my mouth.

All those table manners Ma had drummed into me occasionally allowed me to make a play at civility.

"May I join you?"

"Chair's empty." I gestured toward the seat opposite me at the round table.

Neil Sanderson pulled the chair back so that he could sit. The scraping of the legs on the wooden floor jarred my ears. I winced, then forced my shoulders beneath my earlobes once more. I had to get over jumping and starting at every harsh noise. I'd need more than one night, or a month of nights, of good, *safe* sleep to desensitize my nerves.

I continued to eat, and drink. But the mug came up empty. I stared at it a long moment then lifted it in the direction of the bar. A few seconds later, Rosie appeared at my side with a new mug. She whisked away the empty and returned to her station by the bar.

Sanderson's gaze followed the middle-aged woman in her thread-bare sateen, rose-colored, off-the-shoulder gown.

I winced at the sheen of the fabric shimmering under kerosene lamps, remembering all too vividly the drape of fine silk on my fifteen-year-old body, the swish of the folds of my skirt as I walked, and the delicate green color that highlighted my chestnut hair and pale skin.

I mentally shook myself. Sun had brightened my hair with more blond streaks than red or brown. My face now looked leathery and tanned. As for the dress I'd worn to my older sister's wedding? An uncomfortable and useless frippery and waste of money. I'd only worn skirts once since then. Truth be told I hadn't encountered many occasions when they'd be appropriate. That concert in Washington City only required my cleanest Army scout uniform.

"Rosie never serves. She directs her girls to do it for her," Sanderson said.

"We like each other." She'd known that I was a woman upon first meeting, I didn't have to tell her. Or pretend otherwise. That endeared her to me.

I chewed the last of my roast beef, comfortably full and content. "Why are you here, Mr. Sanderson?" I looked longingly at the one bite of potato and two of the greens left on my plate. But I knew I dared not eat any more or I'd chuck it all up later.

"I'd like to make you an offer." Amazingly, Rosie appeared at his elbow with a short glass half full of amber liquid. Whisky, by the heady scent that wafted my way, very fine whisky at that. He took one small sip and nodded his approval to the saloon owner.

"You must be a regular," I said, longing for my own shot of the water of life. I'd best stick to beer tonight, save the whisky for another night when I wasn't so tired I'd likely fall asleep before the second sip.

"Only decent saloon in town. There are two others but not as clean, nor do they serve as fine a meal and drink. Cow hands with a greater need for horse-piss beer than food keep them operating."

"You aren't eating now."

"Mother's cook has a game pie waiting for me at home." He pulled an ordinary, steel pocket watch from his coat pocket, flipped it open with his thumb and frowned at it. "And I'm already late thanks to the attempted bank robbery. Oh, and thank you for your assistance, by the way." He pocketed his spectacles and turned to face me.

I got my first clear look at his cloudy blue eyes and nearly fell into deep lust.

"You could have locked the doors of the bank and gone home as soon as the bodies were hauled off, and not been late."

"Paperwork. I have to report the attempted robbery. And Doc

needed my assistance with the dead body. Now, after consultation with Doc, I want to offer you a job," he said, capturing my gaze.

I saw honesty in his eyes.

"What kind of job?" I took another deep swallow of beer, swishing it around my mouth before swallowing. Rosie must have guessed my fatigue and started watering the beer.

"Sheriff."

"Oh? Why do you want to replace your sheriff? Besides the fact that everyone else rushed to help you and the doctor, but I saw no one with a tin badge." I dropped my feet back to the floor, ready to stand quickly if I needed to, but my upper half leaned back, looking relaxed. Casual. Ready to assess my options. Or run like hell.

"We haven't had a sheriff in a while."

"Why?"

"The last one died about two years ago. We haven't seen a need to replace him until today."

"How'd he die?" I pulled my feet back beneath me, for better leverage, winced at the sudden pressure on the blisters that sat upon blisters, and leaned toward the man. *About two years ago.* Near the same time as the blacksmith going missing.

"Natural causes. He was sixty-seven. His heart gave out."

"You had a body to bury?"

"Of course. His headstone is in the town cemetery, with his body in a coffin buried beneath it. Why wouldn't it be there?"

"If you don't know, you are better off not knowing." I accepted his explanation with reservations. "Do you have the authority to hire a new sheriff?"

"Yes, I am the mayor, duly elected by the citizens of Heller's Hole."

I nodded. The idea of getting paid for staying in town while Elinore healed meant I wouldn't have to dip into my savings at the bank in Pendleton. I'd do that soon enough, if I lived that long.

On the other hand, I could consider this as an experiment at retirement. Out of one hundred Riders of the Purple Sage, I only knew of two or maybe three who had survived more than ten years. I'd lasted six, better than most.

"What is changing in town that you feel you need law enforcement? Besides the bank robbery by three inept youths with more greed than brains."

"We are in transition. A copper mine made us prosperous through the war. Then the lode grew thin. Richer mines opened elsewhere, closer to railroads. Old Mr. Heller shut down the mine and took his fortune to the city. Heard he died a few months back. Meanwhile the town nearly died. Now the officials have driven the golden spike somewhere out in Utah and the two coasts are connected by rail. The army has done a good job of eliminating raids on the trains by the Indians."

And nearly eliminated the tribes themselves, I thought, gritting my teeth. And every one of the massacres left carrion to feed the enemy. I didn't have to hunt for bounties, I merely followed the troops. My livelihood aside, if the U.S. Army didn't provide regular meals of dead bodies, the flying *things* would starve to death and the entire race would be eliminated.

I hoped.

"Regular trains run along the Columbia River, only twenty miles from here," Sanderson continued, unaware of my slide into a silent diatribe. "We can get livestock to the railhead in less than a week, without walking the beasts down to skin and bones."

I could see the market potential as clearly as he did. I hadn't touched my savings and investments in most of the years I'd worked as a bounty hunter, nor during the four years of the war when I led a squad of scouts behind enemy lines. Maybe this town offered a place to move some of my funds, settle down and live, rather than just survive.

"Our ranchers, the few that kept the town alive, suddenly have access to markets. But we need to build our herds now that the army isn't confiscating half of everything. We run both cattle and sheep around here, beef on the lower slopes of this little valley, sheep on the other side of the road on the upper slopes—never shall the twain meet." He gave me a cocky grin. "Breeding takes time. I'm currently negotiating to have a spur built from here to the railhead. By the time we negotiate and then build, the ranchers should have enough animals to make the expense worthwhile."

"Transition means change, newcomers, more money, opportunities, and… opportunists."

"Exactly. Those young bank robbers were unknown to me. Must have come in from the city, or the high hills where a few renegades try to glean a few more pennies from the mine. We need a sheriff. You are the most qualified man in town."

Should I correct him?

"Neil!" a middle-aged man called from the swinging doors. He looked about the room almost frantically. His gaze swung past Neil and me, then back to us jerkily. "Neil. Jed and Aaron are going to pull through, but Zeb is in bad shape. He wants to talk to you before…"

"Yes, Doc. I'm coming. Deathbed will and testament." The mayor downed the last of his whisky and shoved back his chair. He stiffened and paused only a moment while the whisky burned all the way to his stomach and then backwashed into a satisfied gasp. "Think about the job, Mr. Blue. You can find me at the bank in the morning, but I have to ride into the city before noon." He stalked out of the saloon with long strides.

"Doc?" I waved the newcomer over to my table.

"What can I do for you?" He hurried to my side, distractedly watching Sanderson leave.

"I need your services. When is convenient?"

"How urgent? Were you hurt in that fiasco at the bank?" He focused on me. "Matt Buchanan, by the way." He thrust out a hand in greeting.

"Josie Blue," I replied, shaking his hand. Firm, dry, no-nonsense grip. "I need your skills soon, but not this minute."

"My office, in an hour. No, make that an hour and a half. I have no idea how long Zeb will last."

"Good, I'll have time for a bath."

"Do that." And he left.

"You ready for that bath?" Rosie asked.

"When you have time to prepare it."

"I've got a boiler out back specifically for baths and laundry. Got three tubs on the upper floor. My girls will carry up the jugs of hot water now." She waved a gaudily clad girl in bright green and pink polished cotton over to clear the table. "Corner room, turn left at the top of the stairs. Got your own exit to the balcony. Had your bags taken up while you dealt with the livery stable."

"Thanks, Rosie. It looks like I'll be staying in town for a while. Add a nice tip to my bill."

"Sure thing, Sheriff."

CHAPTER 3

"Take another swig of whisky then bite down on this." Doc Buchanan slipped a piece of hard leather between my teeth.

I tried to obey. Really, I did, but the whisky made my brain fuzzier than my eyes. I stretched out, face down on his table, my back bared from butt crack to nape. My breastband pooled on the flat surface beneath me. I already breathed easier without the constriction.

I kind of knew what was coming and instinctively clenched my fists around the handles conveniently placed on either side of my head. The stretch across my shoulders urged me to adjust my hands, but...

"Are you keeping your true sex a secret for a reason?" Doc Buchanan asked at the same second he slashed a scalpel across the long, festering wound above my waist.

Freezing heat followed the blade through my skin. The slice went on forever. The whisky fumes vanished leaving behind blinding pain.

I gasped and spat out the leather strap, the better to scream away the red mist filling my vision.

"Go ahead and yell. The neighbors are used to it. They never question if I'm abusing my patients or my ladies." He chuckled.

"Don't make me laugh. Please," I ground out between gritted teeth.

"Are you done yet?" I dropped my forehead to the surgical table. A little of the uncomfortable stretch of my shoulders and neck eased. "I need to let go of these handles."

I'd draped my gun belt around the handles, within easy reach if anyone had the audacity to breach the privacy of this office. Shooting something right now seemed like a good idea. But it wouldn't make this surgery go any faster.

Damn it hurt. Every drop of poisonous goo sliding out of the slash burned my skin, but no longer ate at my innards and my sanity.

I needed this done. *Now.*

"So, tell me about the masculine disguise before you move." He pressed against the wound again. More ick spurted out.

"Left over from scouting for the Union army. My colonel knew but told me to keep it secret from my men. Now? Pinkerton doesn't care if I'm a man or a woman, so long as I do my job. It's just easier to ride and fight in trousers. So, I let people assume what they will. I'm tired of explaining." The removal of some of the infection left me too limp to resist the urge to babble aimlessly. The whisky anesthesia added to the looseness of my tongue. I barely felt him dabbing at his surgical incision with clean gauze.

"You know I won't tell anyone unless they ask." Doc Buchanan continued squeezing and wiping the wound. "Fewer will ask if you continue wearing the breast band."

"Fine." I gasped and bit back a curse as he poured a measure of raw whisky across the slash. "I can think of a better use for that bottle than cleansing an infected wound."

"I saved you a couple of swallows." He handed me the bottle.

I released the handles and arched upward so that I could drink. Instantly I regretted the movement. The skin around the gaping cut stretched awkwardly. New pain flared sharply from nape to hips.

Fuck the Goddamn monsters. I shouted a similar sentiment in Nez Perce and in Spanish. More words my mother never taught me spilled from my mouth. Ma's Chinese cook had taught me a few more but they burned even my ears.

"Drink up, then bite hard on the strap again, and hang on to the handles. You'll need to hold on tight, so you don't move while I cut again. Gotta lance the core of the wound a bit deeper."

I obeyed, concentrating on how many blond streaks the sun had added to my reddish-brown braid.

The touch of the blade felt cold for about three heartbeats.

Then the pain turned to pure fire more intense than the original cut.

Pride alone kept me from screaming. The leather was thick. I expected my teeth to break through the barrier any second. Sweat broke out on my back while my brow chilled, robbing my brain of blood. Blackness encroached from the sides.

The temperature inside the lightless cupboard rose to near suffocating. Sweat stained my pretty silk dress. I dared not move, or cry, or peek at the carnage outside...

The range war violated the unspoken rules. My family's enemies had shot up Sister's wedding banquet. Guests as well as the wedding party had come armed and shot back. I didn't know if anyone on either side survived. Except for me.

I forced my eyes open so the looming darkness wouldn't taunt me with yesterdays.... My eyes wouldn't stay open. Maybe Doc had slipped some laudanum into the whisky.

His cutting and probing continued long beyond the time I exhausted what little endurance I had left. Easier to just let myself faint.

"Aha!"

Doc's exclamation startled me back to consciousness. "Wh..." I swallowed deeply. My tongue felt thick and near useless. "What does that mean?"

"It means I found the source of your infection. Ever seen an insect like this?" He dangled a dead bug-like thing in front of my eyes. He held the thing, barely an inch long, by tweezers.

I gulped, trying not to pass out again from shock.

One large eye that nearly filled its forehead. A fluted horn, not spiraling, stuck out of the top of its forehead. Purple skin turning grey as death leached color from it. But the most telling feature was the scalloped bat wings stretched between the underarm and the knee.

And the mouth full of a double row of very sharp teeth fully formed, and lethal even in this embryo.

"My God. They've marked me."

MATT BUCHANAN, Doc to everyone in town because there was another Mathew who'd been there longer, held his patient down with just a little pressure on her shoulder. Good, the laudanum was taking effect. Perhaps he should have given her morphine.

"You don't understand! I've got to get out of town before they swarm and murder a whole lot of innocent people." She wriggled and pushed sluggishly.

"Getting up right now will only make things worse." He looked carefully at the gash across her back, just above her trim waist. Quite a contrast between the softly textured skin there and her strong shoulders and long legs. He had to remind himself that she was a patient, and not a desirable woman.

Rosie might welcome him tonight. If she wasn't available, rumor had it she'd brought a new girl in from the city who needed to gain experience with a gentle hand.

Doc Buchanan could do gentle when he needed to.

"We don't have much time. *They'll know!*" his patient protested.

"How long since they cut you and implanted their spawn?" He dropped the bug into a specimen jar and poured formaldehyde over it until it was covered. Strangest bug he'd ever seen. But he'd seen fully grown versions of this menace after the last cannon had fired at Gettysburg.

They made cleanup of the battlefield easier. Bountiful food made for a population explosion. By the end of war, hungry and growing youth didn't always wait until the wounded soldiers were dead before they began devouring flesh and bone, discarding only the uniforms and leather boots—with the feet still in them. He desperately wanted to sit and think through the ramifications of this bug implanted in a bounty hunter's back.

"Three days, maybe this morning. I can't remember. Time travels in leaps and bounds," Josie mumbled on a resigned sigh. She'd begun slurring her words. Then she yawned, letting her eyelids droop.

Good, she'd rest a little longer before bounding off of his surgical table.

"Josie Blue, or whatever your real name is, you are malnourished, dehydrated, and tired to the bone. You haven't got any fight left in you, which is why that embryo died instead of maturing. I don't think that's their usual method of spawning. Perhaps they planted it as a marker, a means of following you." He shrugged his shoulders. *Jaysus* he needed a drink. Not until he'd escorted this last patient to her bed.

"Maybe it's time for you to stay put for a while; rest and heal; then take a stand against the carrion eaters, with some local help. Heller's Hole can be a mighty restful town if you let it."

"Take a stand? Can't. Those buggers are always on the move. I've killed hundreds in a single battle, barely half of them. And they reproduce with a vengeance. There are always more of them!"

"But only twelve exited the huge generation ship this morning."

"Only twelve?" That would require some serious thought. "If you are fighting a hopeless cause, then another reason to stay put for a while."

"Not hopeless. Me and my comrades have driven them deeper and deeper into the frontier where there are fewer people for them to attack." Her hand fondled the gun belt, inching toward the grip of her .45. "They have to follow the army and clean up after they massacre the local tribes."

"At the moment I don't think you can walk further than Rosie's Saloon, across the street, let alone all the way to the livery stable. And from what I hear from Jed Junior, your horse would collapse under the weight of your saddle."

"Elinore is a good mare." Josie bit her lip and screwed her eyes shut. "Cutter Pine insisted I buy her because her splotches match my hair. Bad reason to buy a horse. But she turned into the best horse I could ever need." Then her shoulders relaxed, and her hand fell away from the butt of her revolver. "She deserves a rest."

Matt heaved a sigh. "Let me stitch you up a bit, then you can get some sleep. I recommend you don't get out of bed until noon on Monday."

"Can't waste daylight..."

"You're in town now. We have oil lanterns to light up the night. You'll let yourself sleep as long as you need. Maybe even sleep the clock around. Twice. Not much in this world won't wait until Monday."

"Elinore won't wait. I need to poultice her feet..." Josie drifted off into a drug induced sleep.

He bent over the ugly wound that would leave a nasty scar and inserted the first stitch. But his gaze kept jerking over to the dead bug, willing it not to revive.

CHAPTER 4

I DREAMED. I knew it was a dream defined by excruciatingly vivid detail. Too vivid to be real. Yet I couldn't wake up and separate myself from the course of action I knew must follow.

The whirling noise as the two purple saucers spun in opposite directions, rims touching, golden lights flashing. A hatch sliding to the side to reveal a doorway, then a ramp lowering. Twelve winged figures lined up inside the ship. That huge, huge ship that could house thousands of alien carrion eaters. Only twelve stepped free of the ship, wings extended. They caught air and....

Birdsong tickled my brain. If birds talked to each other with their melodious calls, then nothing dangerous lurked nearby. I could almost sing a harmony to those songs. Hum it if nothing else. My throat was still too dry to sing.

The raucous, deep throated croak of a raven added a bass note to the bird's symphony.

Not a carrion crow.

I was safe and could appreciate the natural music.

Song. Melodies... How badly out of tune was the old piano in the saloon?

The one-eyed creatures sang beautiful melodies in juvenile tenor tones through the single horn atop their heads. Never had I heard a mature bass note from them.

No aliens. No music too beautiful to be made by humans.

I was safe.

A rooster crowed. The light filtering into the room through blue and white gingham curtains spoke of morning well past dawn. That damn rooster crowed again. It must be a very territorial bird establishing his dominance over a flock.

In my mind, he'd just condemned himself to the stew pot.

I needed more sleep. Lots more sleep.

A deep gong reverberated through the wooden building.

In panicked disorientation, I flung off the sheet and light blanket that had comforted me all night.

"How long have I slept?" I sat on the edge of the bed and cradled my aching head in my hands while I figured out where and when I was.

Indoors. Warm. Comfortable. A gentle breeze fluttered the thin curtains.

"What day is it?" Nothing in the pretty room gave me a hint. A pretty bedstead with a solid wooden frame with nicely turned spindles, and a matching washstand. Tentative exploration told me that the water in the pitcher was still warm. My freshly washed hair had dried, with just a hint of a kink from my usual braid. My feet still hurt but someone had washed and darned my socks, both pair. That someone had also stripped off my filthy clothes and slipped a frilly night gown over my head. It barely reached my knees or covered my shoulders. The owner had broad shoulders and a deep bosom.

The place smelled of spilled beer, sawdust, and sex.

Rosie's Saloon.

A quick brush of the nightgown over my nether parts assured me that no one had taken advantage of me while I slept. Rosie herself, or her girls had taken care of me and respected my privacy.

I plucked at the sheer white cotton that didn't hide much of my body's secrets at all. "Frills and lace. Must be one of Rosie's."

I hadn't worn such a garment since I was... fifteen. When everything changed.

My stomach growled, yanking me away from distressing memories, and reminding me that I hadn't eaten anything since I'd devoured that wonderful roast beef dinner last night.

Only last night? From the intensity of the light I guessed that I'd missed my morning appointment with the mayor at the bank.

Oh, well, like Doc had said last night, not much wouldn't wait until Monday.

"I'd better go take care of Elinore."

My stomach nearly rebelled at its emptiness.

"Well, I guess some things won't wait. First up is breakfast." I wondered what Rosie offered her guests. A couple of eggs and toast would slide down mightily easy about now. Better than the stale crackers and jerked meat I usually ate while living rough. Best get dressed in whatever was left in my saddle bags. A clean shirt anyway in case the mending fairy hadn't had time to launder my trousers.

The mending fairy. My sister had called our nursery maid that when we were children. Less than two years older than me, Eva read stories about Brownies to me at bedtime. If the little pixies mended shoes, then why not socks and tears in clothing?

The sudden stab of grief at that thought didn't hurt as badly or last as long as I expected. Eva had been gone ten years now, along with her new husband and the rest of both of our families. And our rival clan, the Carons. A dispute over water rights had grown into a feud and all-out war within twenty years of staking land claims.

I was all that was left of either clan.

Perhaps the time had come to stop running away from those memories.

A quick rap on the door interrupted my search for fresh clothing. I twisted the knob. It refused to move. Then I discovered a key in the lock on my side. Half a turn released the mechanism.

Rosie had honored me in giving me control of who came and went into my room. Very unusual in a brothel.

On the other side of my door I found my denim trousers cleaned, patched at the knees, and folded neatly, along with both my shirts and my breast bands. The third shirt had become bandages. A patter of delicate footsteps told me the mending fairy had run away.

Moments later, I walked carefully down the grand staircase of the saloon. My socks tended to slip on the polished wooden steps. I carried my boots, unwilling yet to test the tenderness of my blistered feet.

"'Morning Sheriff," Rosie called from the large round table in the far left corner of the open room. Last night, I had chosen that table because I could watch the door as well as the bar and the other diners. And no one could approach from the back.

"Got any more of that coffee?" I asked my hostess as I took the chair beside her. The piano was behind me too. If I couldn't see it, it wouldn't demand that I play it. Ma had taught both Eva and I how to play and sing. The was the only activity that kept me off a horse, riding the fence line of our ranch and tending the cattle herds.

"Coffee and more," Rosie said, lifting one hand in signal to the plainly dressed girl hovering behind the bar. The polished cotton, off the shoulder gowns must wait until the place filled with male patrons later in the day. Rosie herself wore starched calico with a neat, crocheted collar. At home, Eva crocheted and tatted. I couldn't be bothered with the making or wearing of fine decoration. Useless items on the range.

The girl returned almost immediately balancing a tray with a china coffee pot, a sturdy off-white cup with matching saucer, and a plate overflowing with crisp bacon, lightly fried eggs, and four pieces of buttered toast—thick slices of fresh bread. A pot of real butter, not bacon grease, also graced the repast.

"Doc said to feed you up. He also left a jar of salve for your feet and your… other wound. You should use it twice a day until you can put your boots on easily." She poured coffee for both of us.

"Can't go bootless. Got to tend to my horse. She's in worse shape than I am."

"Doc warned me you'd say that. I found some house slippers that should fit you. The old sheriff left them behind when he passed."

"I can't wear house slippers out in the paddock."

"They're sturdy, with a good leather sole. No one will notice much. Too busy figuring out how many weapons you actually carry beyond the two Colts."

Life in a small town. Gossip spread faster than the wind could carry it.

"Any chance I can catch the mayor before he heads into the city?"

"Have to wait until he comes back tomorrow afternoon, or maybe the next day. Depends on how late his business keeps him in town."

I had to pause with a piece of bacon halfway to my mouth. If the man left town at noon he couldn't get to Pendleton before supper time. Too late on Saturday to conduct much business let alone ride back after dark.

"What day is this?"

"Sunday. Church is just letting out. We won't open until tomorrow."

"Elinore!" I pushed the chair back and jumped to my feet. Then I had to sit back down again, heavily, in a hurry at the sharp jabs of pain that ran from the balls of my feet, back to my heels, and then up my legs to my lower back. A wave of dizziness made the room spin. Pain took on new meaning and levels of agony.

"Easy, Sheriff. Take it easy, you're still on the mend. No need to worry about your mare. Neil Sanderson groomed her yesterday morning. Jed Junior took care of her yesterday evening and again this morning. Doc said to let you sleep. And he left a pot of foot salve for Elinore's feet and hocks to reduce any swelling. It's the same stuff he left for you, but in a bigger and uglier pot. We take care of our own here in Heller's Hole. Heaven knows no one else will."

"I only limped into town yester... a day ago."

"But you saved our bank and Neil says you're going to be our new sheriff. That makes you one of us. Like it or not." She finished her coffee and stood. "Now finish your breakfast. Plenty of time to deal with your horse and then meet my girls."

"The mending fairies?"

Rosie chuckled. "Yeah, those girls. They are happy to do for you."

"Why?"

"Just knowing you are in the corner room means the men behave better. Not one black eye or sprained wrist among them this morning. That's a first after a Saturday night in Heller's Hole. But then too, Mac da Foe didn't bring his boys into town. His youngest is nearing his sixteenth birthday. On that day, the whole lot of them will be here, all at the same time so they can watch young Rollie take his first woman."

"Might be time I tend to your piano," I said. "They say that music doth soothe the savage beast." But it might entice the swarming, purple carrion eaters as well.

~

"ROSIE TELLS me you're a dab hand with leatherwork," I said to Jed, the young stable hand. I carried my boots and wore the stiff leather house slippers. They might protect my feet from further damage, but just putting them on had hurt. Walking meant little steps and deep concentration.

Doc's salve helped. Some.

"I kin mend tack and patch saddles," Jed replied, keeping his eyes on the ground as a blush crept across his face.

I gave him the courtesy of not engaging his gaze. I needed to search out Elinore's place in the pasture. I squinted as a familiar silhouette lifted her head and whinnied a greeting. But the skewbald horse did not move from her place at the far end of the open field. The other mares and geldings grazed nearby.

"Fix these." I said as I thrust the boots at the boy.

"Ain't worked on boots 'afore." Jed protested. But he took the boots and turned them sole up to inspect the damage. "That's delicate work to cut and sew good soles."

"If you can mend and braid bridles and belts you can repair boots, seeing as there isn't a cobbler this side of Pendleton." I took care not to fall into the boy's uneducated vernacular. Speaking proper English had been drilled into Eva and me by nannies and governesses alike since I'd uttered my first words.

"Lotta work. Delicate work. It's gonna cost you," Jed replied.

"I figured that. An extra quarter for you if you have them done by nightfall."

Without waiting for a reply, I headed across the pasture, taking slow measured steps, seeking the softest spots in the dirt so as not to aggravate my raw foot wounds further.

I'd barely traversed half the field when I noticed that Elinore had not moved since her first greeting. Surely the mare would have recognized my voice and scent by now. We'd lived and worked close by each other's side since before the end of the war. She usually came to me in search of treats and scritches, and to check on my welfare. On this day when I didn't want to walk any further than I had to, my horse, my beloved companion, remained firmly in place at the far side of the field.

The soft chuckle of a creek tickled my awareness. I followed the line of the slight depression in the terrain east toward the mountains. Late in the dry season, mountain snow still fed the waterway.

And there stood Elinore, smack dab in the middle of the water. The mountain coolness splashed gently above her hocks.

"Does that feel good?" I asked. I kicked off the clumsy slippers and joined my friend in the creek. Soothing coolness caressed me from my toes to halfway to my knees. I wanted to sit on a nearby rock and lose myself in that blessed water.

I sensed Jed Junior approaching from behind me. He walked slowly, greeting each of the horses in the pasture.

Elinore had found a wide patch of sand, free of rocks, to stand on. I sought the extension of that soothing footing at my friend's head.

The horse butted my shoulder with her long nose, begging for pets and scratches behind her ears. She dribbled water from her mouth. Clearly, she'd drunk her fill and now simply needed to soothe the inflammation in her feet.

I sighed in relief as the cold water numbed some of my own pain. The shooting jolts along my nerves disappeared.

"Will you let me see your feet?" I asked Elinore, moving to her side and tapping her leg.

On command the horse lifted her left foreleg, bending it so that I could cradle the hoof in one palm. Free of iron shoes and accumulated dirt, the crack in the hoof showed clearly. I pressed lightly on the part that had started to go soft.

Yellow pus shot outward like a geyser. I ducked my face away, letting my clean shirt catch the brunt of the mess.

"Oh, my good Lord," Jed Junior gasped. He looked pale to the point of fainting.

Elinore jerked her foot out of my grasp. Cold water splashed my denim pants when the horse plopped her foot back into the comfort of the creek.

"Okay. You don't want it touched yet. But we've got to get rid of some of that pus to relieve the swelling and pressure." I tapped her foreleg again and she automatically lifted that foot. I grabbed it before she could think about it. A bit more pressure, more yellow pus, and soon the infection drained only blood.

Elinore would keep it clean in the creek.

"I'll leave it for now, my dear."

She reprimanded me with a side eye. My war mare who wasn't afraid of anything, did not approve.

"Looks like we are stuck in this Godforsaken town for a while. You'll need more time than I first thought." I stroked Elinore's muzzle with affection. She almost forgave me. Almost. "So, I might as well take the sheriff's job to keep you in hay and oats."

Elinore dipped her head and slurped up a bit of water.

"Speaking of hay and oats, sir," Jed Junior said from the embankment a few feet away. "Can you get her to eat?"

Alarmed, I looked him square in the eye. "She's not eating? She ate last night. Anything since?" Not good. Not good at all.

"Some oats and hay you fed her last night. This morning, she refused both until I put some honey in the oats. That she ate greedily. But she's not grazing at all. Normally all the horses love the sweet, fresh grass down here by the creek." The boy looked dejected, as if Elinore had insulted him by refusing his offerings.

"Then feed her oats and honey until her tummy settles. She's been eating as roughly as I have, and not satisfying her sweet tooth at all. And we'll need some Epsom salts to soak that abscess."

"Honey and oats are expensive, sir." Jed refused to look me in the eye. "Doc might have some Epsom salts. Don't know that Meg down at the general store carries that sort of thing."

"I'll hit up Doc for the salts when he gets back to his office. In the meantime, use the salve he left for us." I fished the pot out of my pocket and handed it to him. "Be lavish with it. I can afford the oats and honey. But I'll need to send a telegram to my bank in Pendleton." Damn. If I hadn't slept the clock around twice, I could have sent a letter with Neil Sanderson.

"Telegraph's closed until ten tomorrow morning," Jed replied. "Micah O'Toole at the post office only sends 'grams from ten to two on Monday, Wednesday, and Friday."

"What about incoming messages?" This town was pretty far out of touch with the modern world. What if the alien monsters attacked. I didn't have enough firepower to defend the entire town, especially the outlying farms and ranches.

"Oh, Mr. O'Toole will stop ever'thing to write down an incoming, but no one can pick it up until ten to two, Monday, Wednesday, or Friday."

I cursed and grumbled under my breath as I climbed out of the creek. The soft, moist grass felt like a velvet carpet under my damaged feet. The borrowed slippers looked like torture devices in comparison to the soothing water and supple blades of grass. I could probably use some of the salts and salve myself, unless Doc had mixed some into his lovely potion.

I frowned deeply as I contemplated my discarded socks and the hard-soled footwear.

"I've got some sheep's wool I could line those slippers with," Jed said.

I started to smile with renewed interest in the slippers. "This is cattle country, isn't it? Why do you have raw wool at the ready?"

"We got sheep around as well as cattle. Big spinning and weaving mill's gone in in Pendleton. They pay decent for wool."

"I've been out in the field too long," I mused. "I haven't actually been in town much these last few years." Closer to four years since I'd signed papers to officially separate from my trainer/partner Cutter Pine. I was safer well away from his headlong dashes into battle. Planning an attack took all the fun out of being a bounty hunter for him.

By that time, I had used up most of my anger and need for revenge. I easily saw the wisdom in choosing my field of battle and using the landscape to trap the monsters in a closed space. I also collected more of their single trumpet-like horns as proof of a kill than Cutter and turned them in for a higher bounty. A lot like the scalp taking one hundred fifty years ago. But I didn't feel guilty for collecting the trophies. The purple *things* weren't human—two arms, two legs, a head and torso. But their single eye and horn kept them from blending into the general populace. And their music.

I reckoned I had more money in the bank than Cutter. And I didn't have to split it with him.

I'd learned a lot about battle strategy, money management, and life in the Army. Cutter himself had taught me how to defend myself from bullies. He never expected me to turn those lessons back on him when we split.

I slogged out of the creek, reluctant to step out of the soothing water.

Elinore decided to stay put.

"Will you eat some fresh grass if I feed it to you?" I asked the horse.

Elinore had to think about that. Then she moved to the edge of the flowing water, where it barely covered her hoofs.

I plucked some of the lush grass and held it out to my companion and best friend. Elinore lipped it out of my hand. It disappeared quickly. She pushed at my hand, eager for more.

"So, you've decided you like it."

Elinore snorted and pushed at the outstretched hand with her muzzle.

"Well, I can't stay here all day," I said firmly. "I have letters to write and telegrams to compose." I plucked one more handful of grass and held it at my side, trying to tempt Elinore out of the water so she could graze on her own.

Elinore, an opinionated mare to begin with, reared her head and backed up a step. But only one step.

I stood my ground. "You want it, come and get it."

Elinore placed her front hoofs on the grass and snatched the fresh fodder from my palm. She started to back up again, thought better of it and began to graze, keeping her hind feet in the water.

"She'll do better now." I heaved a sigh of relief. "Okay, Jed, how long will it take you to line those slippers? I've got too many blisters and bruises to walk the town barefoot."

"Just a few minutes to stuff some raw wool in 'em. The boots will take longer to fix. Them's nearly gone. I kin patch the soles but the uppers are nearly spent as well." He hung his head, as if afraid of disappointing a customer. "If ye'r writing letters and such, might as well order new boots at the same time."

"Guess I'll have to. Elinore isn't going to heal very fast, and this town can't have a barefoot sheriff."

"You'll be needing another riding horse for a while too. I kin rent you one. Five dollars a month."

"I'll buy that roan gelding from you for ten."

"Nah, he makes us more money renting him to locals. He's mighty mellow."

"That's a lot of money for a placid horse that doesn't know his own mind. What about the stallion? Nice coloring and a good thick mane and tail. I might be willing to pay $7 for him." I studied the animal two fields away, separated from the mares by two high fences.

"Pa says the buckskin stallion ain't worth much. He's a trouble-maker even when the mares aren't in heat. We can't keep him much longer, eats his head off and tosses most every rider."

"We'll see about that. Is there someplace other than here I can stable him?" I surveyed the buckskin more critically, liking the depth of his chest and the length of his legs. His grass heavy belly needed some tightening. Most likely he'd been overfed and not ridden much. A few weeks under my care should sort out most of his problems.

"Nice and airy shed behind the sheriff's office, with a bit of paddock. And he's much better behaved if you ride him every day. I try, but don't have much time. He does take to schooling though, like he'd been trained well but refused to work after his previous owner sold him."

"He gets bored. I can see that. Is that stallion okay with you, Elinore?"

The mare snorted a reluctant agreement that almost sounded like "For now."

"Deal, Jed." I shook the boy's hand. "I'll have the money for you soon after I send those telegrams."

CHAPTER 5

DR. MATHEW BUCHANAN ripped off his neck scarf with a vicious jerk. He hated the thing. A gift from his wife when he went off to war eight years ago. Or was it ten? He didn't remember. Didn't want to.

The wife had disappeared when he returned home to Boston nearly five years later. Neither their neighbors, nor her family knew where she'd gone. One lonely widow had whispered that six months after he left, his wife had run off with a remittance man from England who had a title and a substantial allowance—as long as he stayed away from home and the scandal he'd left behind.

Doc hadn't heard from her since, and frankly, didn't care. He'd taken the next train west and halted briefly in Chicago. Conditions there reminded him too much of life in an army camp with not enough food to go around and the officers got most of it. He'd patched up wounds in men, women, and *children* from the hard work in the meat processing plants. After only a month, he took another train ride or three and a wagon train to keep him moving until he landed in Heller's Hole. And here he stayed. Normal ailments and farm accidents. Nothing exotic or *en masse* here. Just everyday living.

He contemplated burning the neckcloth, the last remnant of his civilized life in Boston. The only time he wore it was to church services Sunday mornings. Not that he believed in anything but his skill as a surgeon and the closest whisky bottle. The remnants of the once thriving town and parish expected him to show up every damn Sunday, drunk or sober. One fussy old biddy, Ethel Sanderson in fact, had told him she couldn't respect a man who didn't go to church every Sunday. She meant the little church that borrowed space in the schoolhouse, not the brick Catholic church, St. Agatha's, at the other end of town. A lot of Protestants still considered Catholics little more than pagan sorcerers.

The Reverend Zebedee Sanderpoole, of the Baptist persuasion, accepted him, counting heads and offerings as more important than hearts and faith. To make the contents of the offering plate stretch far enough to support him beyond his miserly pay as schoolmaster, he used the school building for his services and his office, so he didn't have to pay to build a proper church.

He left that endeavor to the Catholics who maintained their own brick building, left over from the pre-war mining heyday of the town. Basque sheepherders and Mexican ranch hands filled the pews there every Sunday. A few Anglos also showed up regularly, and the O'Tooles, all seven of them. They weren't welcome in the Protestant end of town.

Matt had attended too many Catholic rituals in Boston with the nearly forgotten wife and her Irish relatives. What was her name? Carol? Carolyn? No, Christine, called Cara by her family.

Harpy was a better description of her and her managing ways. The remittance man was welcome to her.

So, to burn the neckcloth or wash it? Once cleaned up it would make a mighty fine bandage or sling for the delectable new sheriff. He was certain Josie Blue was not the name given to her by her parents.

He glanced out the grimy window of his rooms behind the office/surgery and watched Josie Blue limp from the direction of the livery stable toward Rosie's. She stopped in front of the post office and glared at the sparkling clean window. She stepped up to the stoop and peered in. She wouldn't find much. O'Toole never, ever, even in an emergency opened his doors on Sunday. He was an old-fashioned Irish Catholic who never missed mass or worked on the Sabbath.

Then the sheriff shrugged and crossed the street to her new office.

"Well, Doc," he told himself. "Your patient needs food. She's far too skinny. And I need to inspect her wounds." He pocketed another small jar of salve and headed for the saloon. Rosie always closed on Sunday, but maybe he could cajole lunch from her, as long as he promised to share it with Josie.

NEIL SANDERSON ROSE from his knees to find the Catholic church in the city devoid of worshipers. A single priest snuffed the altar candles, making sure he bowed his head in reverence as he crossed from one side of the raised edifice to the other. Neil had indulged himself in extra moments of silent prayer, something he couldn't do at home where every one of his neighbors and customers considered Sunday morning services the social event of the week. Especially with his mother at his side. She'd demanded that the Reverend Zebedee Sanderpoole refrain from ringing the school bell at the conclusion of services so that she could better hear the conversations floating around her.

Neil had picked up an appreciation for the rituals of the Catholic faith while attending University in New Jersey. Then during the war, he'd found the gentle consolation of the priests in the hospital tent aided healing much more than hellfire and brimstone preaching of the Baptist chaplain. He didn't feel like his sins had brought on the wrath of God and inflicted his wounds. The Rebs had done that.

Now he scheduled meetings in the city with other bankers, lawyers, and investors on Monday mornings just so he could confess on Saturday and attend Mass on Sunday.

The anonymous priest finished his duties and walked sedately down the aisle until he stood at the end of Neil's pew, about the middle of the small church building. "Are you in need of assistance, sir?" the man asked.

"Not today, Father. Though, thank you for asking. Life is chaotic and I find a few moments of quiet contemplation helpful."

"Is the chaos your problem?"

"I try not to create or add to the noise of the modern world. But I am in a position where I mostly sort it out. That is easier if my mind has had a peaceful rest."

"Words of wisdom I wish more of my parishioners recognized." The man smiled.

Neil couldn't help but return the gesture. He sidled along the pew until he stood beside the cleric, a shorter man of middling years and the tanned and weathered face of someone who had spent decades in the saddle or on the field of battle. He held out his hand in greeting and introduced himself.

"Father Theo, rector of this parish," the man replied. "I arrived two weeks ago and look forward to providing an island of peace to any who need it."

Neil raised an eyebrow in question. "No last name?"

"No longer," Father Theo replied. "When I entered seminary, I cast aside much of the ugliness of my previous life."

"Neil Sanderson," he introduced himself. "From your posture, I guess that some of your previous life was spent in the army."

"Yes." The priest clamped his lips closed and a frown of anger, or distaste, marred his square features. It lasted only a heartbeat. Then his expression cleared, and serenity returned. "My housekeeper has prepared luncheon for me. Good-hearted soul that she is, she always presents far too much food, with many choices. I believe she thinks it her God-given duty to fatten me up, like a sacrificial lamb. There is more than enough food for two, if you'd care to join me. I'd be interested to hear what brings you to my humble church."

"Thank you, Father. I'd enjoy that." Instantly Neil put aside his plans to meet the law firm for an informal meal where they could parade their eligible daughters in front of him. "But first I must dispatch a note to some friends, apologizing for my rudeness in not appearing at their table. I'll see enough of them tomorrow at a business meeting." Without the giggling presence of their daughters.

"And Neil, if you can find it on your conscience, would you be willing to send me the occasional report on… anything unusual happening in Heller's Hole?"

What? Neil didn't remember having told the priest where he was from in their brief introduction.

"I've heard tales of strange purple and gold lights hovering over the desert. It may be left over effusions from the mining days. Or something else entirely. I'm told that occasionally a Rider of the Purple Sage, that's a division of the Pinkertons, will stop in a community in disguise to investigate."

I WRENCHED OPEN the single door to the shed behind the sheriff's office. Wide enough for a single horse and person to enter, the portal sagged into the dirt enough to make opening it a chore. I silently thanked Doc for the salve that allowed me to brace my feet and put some weight into moving the solid door. Inside I found enough room for the horse, and storage for hay bales in the loft. Further exploration revealed closed shelves for grooming brushes and other paraphernalia, hooks for hanging tack and even a saddle stand. I could patch the gaping hole in the roof where winter rains had rotted some of the planks.

A tiny, but tidy barn, not a mere shed.

What about the paddock?

The half-acre, fenced with sturdy posts and cross bars, had grown wild during the two years of disuse. Now, at the end of summer, the grass looked dry and parched. In a few weeks, the rains should come again and refresh the area nicely. The stallion could graze a bit to supplement his hay and oats. No honey for him, except as a rare treat while training him, until he lost that belly.

I delayed surveying the office by walking the rough-hewn fence line. A few posts wiggled when I leaned on them. A few splinters shed beneath my hand. Not enough to warrant replacing them. Just packing new dirt around them should solidify the line. Just in case that stallion took jumping into his tiny mind.

Not much else to see or do out here. If I did take the job as sheriff, I'd have to occupy the office space for an hour or so every day. The town needed to be able to find me. But, oh I hated the idea of sitting inside and writing reports. That part of my job as a bounty hunter, I left to the clerks in the office in the city. They'd always done an excellent job of turning my scribbled notes into readable tales.

I took a deep breath and faced the back door of the office that looked as big as the barn. Surprisingly the door yielded to a small amount of pressure, a little warped, but unlocked.

Strange.

A shiver ran the length of my spine as I wondered how many ghosts might have settled in this small building.

Someone, or something, did not want me here.

I'd never allowed a restless spirit to keep me away from my duty before. That poltergeist over in Idaho City was a slippery problem, but eventually ended up sobbing in a corner when she'd finished her teenaged tantrum. Restless spirits trapped between worlds couldn't inflict any worse pain or damage than did the alien predators I hunted for bounty.

Quickly, or as quickly as I could walk across the dusty plank flooring, I checked the glass-topped door that faced the street. The lock held. I swiped a finger across the grimy glass, rolling the wad of dirt between my fingers to test the texture. Mostly dust that clung together like matted cat's fur. No one had attempted to clean this place since long before the previous occupant had departed. I could discern only moving shadows along the street as folks returned home from the two churches, one at either end of town.

Was cleaning this place part of my new job? I didn't even know where to start other than resetting the barn door to open more easily.

As I turned around, the desk at the side of the single room grabbed my attention. Anyone sitting in the cane-backed swivel chair had a full view of the two barred cells and both doors. No privacy here. But there was a pump and a privy between the office and the barn. It didn't smell so I didn't think anyone had used it recently. I added a good dose of lime to the list of cleaning supplies I compiled in my head. And I'd probably have to prime the pump and hope the well beneath was still sweet.

Back to the desk, a good solid wooden thing my father would have approved of. Three deep drawers on either side of the knee hole, a center drawer, all empty, and a hook inside the knee hole sporting a set of open handcuffs on a hook to the left and a hefty ring with skeleton keys for the cells on the right. The cell doors stood open a half inch or so. I'd have to test those keys and locks before I had to make any arrests.

Nothing else. No evidence of secret compartments for gun storage —the glassed in, tall, and empty rifle case on the wall behind the desk offered space for three long barrels. The tiny key seemed to be on the ring with the cell keys. No papers or files on or in the desk. No wanted posters—those were pinned to the wall adjacent to the front door. Only a note on fine linen stationary suitable for invitations to tea or bank foreclosures inside the center drawer, anchored by a solitary door key.

I read the neat printing in fresh black ink.

Mr. Blue, you will find all previous reports and files at the bank. My assistant has directions to hand them over to you.
N. Sanderson.

My sense of unease that had lingered as a weight on my shoulders, fell away. Someone, at least, thought I belonged here.

I'd know for certain once I had sent my letters and telegrams in the morning.

For now, I needed to sit here and absorb the essence of the building. It hadn't welcomed me at first. But the building didn't know me. And I didn't know it. That would change. We'd see how we got on together before I fully committed to this town. And Neil Sanderson. He did have a lovely smile.

A knock on the front door and rattling of the glass within the frame roused me from my musings. I looked up and saw the shadowed silhouette of a man standing on the wooden sidewalk beneath the roof's overhang.

If he bothered to knock and test the lock, he couldn't mean me harm. And my revolvers rested easily on my hips. I felt naked and vulnerable without them. I pushed the chair back and crossed over to the door, key in hand. The lock worked easily, as if recently oiled.

"Can I help you?" I asked as I opened the door.

"I prescribed food and rest. I've brought the food," Doc said, holding up a basket covered in a blue gingham cloth, the same shade as the curtains in my room across the street at Rosie's.

CHAPTER 6

I smelled the crusted and fried pork chops inside the basket as Doc passed me, headed for the desk. He hadn't asked permission to enter, and I hadn't invited him in. But officially this was a public building. I didn't think I had the right to bar him entrance, even if I wanted to.

He had brought food, and it was getting on for suppertime, I thought. The old clock behind the desk had needed winding years ago. If it still worked. My appetite told me to welcome the meal, any meal, when I found it.

Or in this case, it found me.

"Come right in. Make yourself to home," I said, trying to mask my instinctive sarcasm.

I eyed the food as Doc withdrew each wrapped item from the basket. The pork chops came out first. I nearly leapt upon the meat. Domesticated pig beat dead rattler or prairie dogs any day.

With an effort I walked serenely behind the desk, as my governess had taught me and Eva, and took the chair, establishing my authority in this place before he could supplant me. The Army had taught me the politics of authority, how to establish it and how to maintain it.

Cutter Pine didn't like my attitude when we hooked up after the war. He might have rescued me and banished the aliens from my home—after they'd eaten my entire family, the wedding party, and our guests as well as the invading rival clan of Carons—and managed the business of death certificates, property sales, and changing my name, but I'd repaid the debt and then some. I was only fifteen when he found me hiding in the cupboard, sobbing, frightened, and confused.

By the time the war ended I was twenty and in full possession of my wits and confidence.

Doc frowned at me as if he understood my tactic and objected.

Then he smiled and produced jacket potatoes, fresh bread, a tub of butter, and a bowl of spiced apples.

Patiently I waited for him to bring forth plates and cutlery, as well as linen serviettes.

With each selection of food, my mouth watered. Sweet well water seemed the only thing needed to wash it all down.

I decided to let the water wait and dished up half of each serving. The first bite of pork was halfway to my mouth when Doc pulled forth, with a flourish, the final offering from the basket: a full bottle of rye whisky.

A sharp memory of the smooth, smokey, flavor hitting my tongue, a slow swallow, followed by a biting backwash flooded my mind and mouth at just the thought of the whisky. I could drink half the bottle and know the sweet oblivion of another couple of hours of sleep.

Too often Elinore had awakened me to impending danger when I was too muddle-headed to load a rifle let alone stir the campfire to life and light a torch. The aliens feared fire more than lead bullets. Without a Gatling, I couldn't load and fire my Spencer repeater fast enough to do more than keep the buggers at bay while I found fire.

But I also knew that luscious taste of the rye would leave me weak-limbed, headachy, and dry mouthed. In my early years of bounty hunting, Cutter had plied me with plentiful drink to help me forget my nightmares and open myself to his not so gentle loving care.

That was a different story, I didn't care to remember right now, only that I recognized Doc's ploy and didn't like it.

I'd spent years learning to have confidence in myself and not depend upon the needs and wants of someone, *anyone* else.

"I'll pass," I said, nodding to the bottle. "No cups here." I wanted water. Or tea. I wanted my wits about myself when I still had chores to do and letters to write, and an unknown town to protect.

"Will these do?" Doc asked. He held up two tin cups from the bottom of the basket.

"Thanks. I'll take one back to the pump to see if it's still works and the water isn't tainted." I rose and aimed toward the back door.

"Josie?" He grabbed me around the waist and held me tight as I passed him.

Alarm tensed my muscles and I rocked to my toes, ready to flee or pivot and deck him.

I swallowed my instinctive fear of strange men. "Doc, don't force me to handcuff you and stuff you into one of the cells with those filthy, rodent and insect infested mattresses."

His body stilled. I wondered how hard he had to think about it. The girls at Rosie's had confessed to me that Doc could be gentle when he had to.

That told me a lot about the man.

Still not enough to entice me.

"You know I can and will subdue you." My voice sounded flat to my own ears.

"Unfortunately, I do realize what you are capable of." He hung his head in disappointment even as he dropped his hand and allowed three inches of space to grow between us. Close enough to reassert himself if he dared.

I drew my knife from its belt sheath. "Try it again and I'll cut 'em off."

He blanched and added a full foot of space between us.

"I do believe you would do that. Nice to know that you have boundaries and where they are."

"If *I* decide I want sex with you, *I* will make the decision and let you know." I breathed deeply. Best to leave the door open a crack and let hope keep him from growing to resent me.

"Ah, Josie, don't be that way." He crept closer.

I lifted the ring of cell door keys from their hook beneath the desktop. A pair of handcuffs with their key still in the lock came with them. "I may strip you starkers, but it won't be so I can have my wicked way with you." Oh yes, Cutter had taught me a lot about life. "I'll just leave you to be found by whomever I hire to clean this place."

He blanched. "Josie, I am the town doctor. I need to retain some respect..."

"Then act like you deserve respect by giving some. And that goes for Rosie's girls as well. Remember I sleep in the corner room. The girls tell me you can be gentle. From now on, you have to. Every time. With every girl."

Quietly I loaded his plate and the bottle of whisky back into the basket, shoved it into his arms, pushed him out the door. The key fit nicely and turned easily. It worked on the back door as well.

Damnation! I'd forgotten to ask him for Epsom Salts.

FEELING ODDLY replete after a meal of fried chicken, mashed potatoes, and cooked diced carrots and turnips with lashings of sweet cream butter, Neil decided to walk through the city on his way back to his hotel. He had much to think on.

Father Theo had spent a good part of the last hour informing Neil about strange purple lights in the sky and wholesale slaughter of buffalo, cattle, horses, and yes (shudder) people that coincided with the events. Little was left of the victims. Their clothing, or in the case of domesticated horses, their tack. Large bones sometimes remained. Little else.

Except sheep. They seemed to escape the carnage unscathed.

Whatever ate the other beasts apparently didn't like the taste or texture of the oily wool that often grew two feet long. Not enough meat beneath and too much work to get through the coats.

Putting some physical distance between himself and the rectory allowed him to push aside some, not all, of his shuddering horror at the revelation. He couldn't remember anything in the Book of Revelation that mentioned demons eating the flesh of living beings while still on Earth.

The little he'd heard about the purple aliens suggested they ate only carrion, unless they were starving. It appeared they'd grown too numerous to survive on dead bodies alone. Sometimes they had to kill for their meat. Or coerce all too willing humans to kill for them.

By the time he reached his hotel he had convinced himself the stories were all Indian mystical nonsense.

But...

He had to pause on the front porch of the hotel and plunk into a wobbly old rocking chair, with peeling paint.

During the war, after a battle, he had the responsibility for totting up losses of men, ammunition, artillery, horses, and other supplies that had to be replenished. He had a feel for numbers, part of his training and education to follow his father into the banking business. Battle numbers did not always add up.

At first, he'd thought that the number of troops deployed, those reported dead, those injured, and those fit to return to duty never matched. He put down the errors as poor record keeping and generals inflating the number of troops and deflating the number of dead bodies.

At first the discrepancies numbered a few hundred men. He accounted their absence as men who had fled the scene and lost themselves in the wilderness, or "Out West" where strangers could make up a story, change their name, be accepted, and live out their lives in relative peace.

Josie Blue could have been one of them.

He added a stop at the Pinkerton's office to his list of business tomorrow.

As the war progressed the numbers of missing troops—even supply officers behind the scenes—multiplied exponentially.

If the force behind the purple lights cleaned up the carnage after each battle...

Without bodies, the generals did not have to report the exact number of deaths. Their reputations for winning with minimal losses, meaning corpses, enhanced their positions to whomever they reported to.

Neil grabbed his temples with both hands, hoping to stop or divert his looping and horrible thoughts.

Perhaps he should saddle up his horse and ride the hills until sunset. He changed his trajectory toward the stables behind the main street.

He wouldn't bother eating supper in the hotel dining room.

Halfway up the ridge, where the trail twisted back on itself and he faced the lowering sun that made shadows long and the air stilled as if waiting for the last gasp of sunlight, a purple glow that faded toward yellow and then white, lit up the crest of a foothill below Mt. Hood—a white crested landmark many miles to the west.

The glow held firm for the space of ten heartbeats then exploded upward in showers of sparks and rays, trying to mimic the dying sun.

A single solid shape, like two saucers stacked rim to rim, the bulging bases on top and bottom rose higher and began to spin. The top turned clockwise and the bottom counter to that. A single row of blinking lights circled at the joined rims. Purple, white, yellow, green, purple, then bright red, like a colored glass over a theater spotlight.

He shielded his eyes with his hand. When he looked up, the phenomenon had vanished. Only an after image remained in the center of his damaged eye.

Molly, his mare, remained placid, only flicking her ears toward the strange *thing*. Instinctively she knew that it was too far away to present danger.

If not for that single ear flick, Neil would have passed it off as a trick of his imagination and fuzzy vision.

But his eyesight in his right eye, the one spared from the dirty shrapnel at the first battle of Bull Run, had seen true.

He shuddered and turned his faithful mount back toward the snug stable at his hotel.

He knew better than to trust his damaged eye. The doctors had warned him that his imagination would fill in the gaps where his vision could not focus. The expert—genius—lens maker in Portland had sold him nice spectacles that gave back some of what he'd lost.

But this? The purple haze and spiking lights were entirely different in his experience. Surely, he could not have imagined it.

Could he ever trust himself again?

CHAPTER 7

I LAY in bed the next morning, staring at the darkness outside the window. Dawn had yet to glimmer on the horizon. I felt like I'd been watching for hours, though I was fairly certain that if I consulted my tin pocket watch only a few minutes had passed since something had brought me out of deep sleep to full awareness.

My eyes remained open of their own volition. Dreamland no longer beckoned me.

So, what had disturbed me?

Rosie's remained silent. The proprietress and her employees would likely sleep until nearly noon since they'd need to work late tonight. Even the cook and kitchen maids would not begin meal preparations before the sun rose fully above the ridgeline east of town.

Even the blasted rooster remained quiet.

So, what had awakened me?

Anxious now, I slid out of bed and into my clothes. Not for the first time I was grateful I'd given up feminine garb years ago. Trousers and shirt came to hand readily as well as my braces and belt—both were useful tools when living rough and frequently encountering outlaws as well as alien predators.

Barefoot, I approached the single window from the side so that I cast no shadow or revealed my presence by a flicker of movement. If I could see the outline of the window, then false dawn should be nearing.

The rooster had not crowed yet.

Nor had any of the other morning birds begun their songs.

Ah, there was the first trill…

Only the music was too sweet with multiple harmonies. Music that lifted my heart. A lilting rhythm that made my feet itch to dance in swirling patterns in the arms of a handsome man. Music I could lose my soul in.

I jerked myself out of the lulling trance and reached for my guns.

Grateful that Rosie had given me the corner room with its own private exit onto the rear balcony, I gently twisted the knob with my left hand while retaining a gun in my right. Keeping to the side, I opened the door a full hand width.

The music continued without interruption or pause.

The aliens weren't watching my room, just singing the end of the night and the beginning of day. In full harmony with alto notes and a soprano descant.

When I heard music like this in the field, only tenor and bass tones filled the air.

They must be close to their home for females to join the hymn of joy.

But where were they and how close?

I'd learned from Cutter on our first mission for the Riders of the Purple Sage that the trumpet calls of the aliens travelled long distances. I'd trained my ears to judge that distance by the volume of the ethereal music.

Three ridges and deep valleys to the west. Flatter land out there. Fewer trees to absorb and distort the sound. Still dark. The sun had to crest the closest ridge to the east before penetrating the gloom in the direction of the song.

Ah! The first spear of light shot up from behind that ridge. A line of pure golden sunshine ran along the line of hills.

The monsters would go to ground now and leave people alone. I'd only seen the males in daylight when they had corpses to feed upon. No one seemed to know what they did when not feeding. I'd never seen them unless they had a feast before them.

The great battles of the war had kept them on the east coast for years. But as the war eased and the battles moved westward, along with slaughter of the tribes, I had seen far too many of the purple aliens and heard their songs far too often to count.

Just to be sure none of the predators lingered in the vicinity, I slipped out the door and closed it quietly. Step by careful step, I prowled along the balcony encircling the saloon, then down the stairs to the plank sidewalk. Barefoot, I made little or no noise.

I holstered my gun when a farm wagon stopped at the back door of Rosie's and unloaded barrels of flour and open crates of greens into a fenced and lidded holding bin beside the back door. A few moments later a rancher brought hanging joints of beef, and a third wagon brought cured bacon and sausages with only a few barrels of pork chops. The last of the suppliers secured the four feet tall wooden fence and gate with the padlock left open for them.

They each tipped their hats to the new sheriff before driving off.

The growing daylight showed no hints of purple on the western horizon.

Hellers Hole, my town, remained safe for another day.

NEIL PACED the length of the boardwalk in front the boarding house that promised breakfast starting at seven. Another thirteen minutes according to the courthouse clock. He reset his polished steel pocket watch to match. No sense winding it again. He'd done that half an hour ago when he left his hotel. The dining room there didn't open until eight. How long could he linger over his breakfast before the Pinkerton offices opened at eight? His mouth watered over the thought of eggs, a rasher of bacon, and slabs of newly baked bread slathered with fresh churned butter and jam made from local seasonal fruit. Probably blackberries this time of year.

His stomach growled reminding him he hadn't eaten supper last night.

He hadn't slept well after spotting the purple lights to the west of town. Nor had he wanted to eat, knowing what kind of carnage had happened.

Soon after dawn painted the Columbia River gold he'd packed and repacked his saddlebags so he could leave town as soon as he finished his appointments in town. That depended upon when and if the railroad people got back to him. He'd delay long enough to have dinner with those men and depart in the morning, but no longer.

With the help of a sleepy-eyed night clerk at the hotel, he'd located the Pinkerton's office behind an unremarkable and unmarked wooden door beside the bank. Another, more pretentious door led to the public offices of the agency through the bank and a bevy of armed guards. Admission came only with an appointment after eleven in the morning.

The hotel clerk didn't know for certain, but thought an agent or supervisor or someone arrived at the private door soon after eight. He swore he'd seen a man in a great coat and a bowler with the brim pulled down to shadow his face enter the place at that time while the clerk walked home after working all night.

Neil planned to invade the anonymous office soon after it became occupied.

Ah, at last, plump Mrs. Murphy turned the closed sign over to open and unlocked her front door.

"Good morning, Mr. Neil. Heard you were in town yesterday. And I knew you'd be in need of breakfast early. You always keep rancher's hours, unlike most bankers and lawyers and such." She brushed her hands clean of flour on her apron—it might have been clean when she started baking bread this morning. Then she shook his hand vigorously. "Got your favorite scrambled eggs with bits of ham, fried potatoes..."

"And fresh bread with jam?" he finished for her.

"Blackberries my Jimmy picked yesterday, and I jammed up straight away."

"Don't suppose you saved some of the whole berries to serve up with fresh cream?"

"Yes, yes, I did, 'cause I expected you for breakfast."

Neil smiled and found his own way to the dining room to the left of the entry. The only boarder to join him was Indigo Martins, the school master at the local secondary school. A cadaverously thin man, he peered curiously over the tops of his wire rimmed spectacles. This gentleman had steered Neil toward the lens master in Portland.

"Snandason," the teacher slurred. He wasn't drunk. Apoplexy had hindered his speech and thickened his tongue about five years ago. Still he'd recovered enough to continue working as long as Mrs. Murphy took care to feed him and clean up after him.

"Martins. I'm hoping you have a student, gifted with numbers who can come work for me after the new year." Neil took the chair opposite his companion about halfway down the table. Neither man liked the end chair and the sense of presiding over Mrs. Murphy's home.

"Might vah 'ell send a youn' man to learn the bnk trade from you. Two actually." His speech began to clear as he continued. Sort of like brushing off the rust surrounding his throat. "Must decide best suited to life in the wilderness."

Neil swallowed his smile. "Heller's Hole is hardly the wilderness," he mumbled. "We hope to start work on a spur rail line next year. I am meeting with several potential investors while I'm in town. You might send both young men on a one month trial. Let me decide which of them is best suited to my bank."

"Good luck. Marvelous t'ese railwahs. Running a mainline through here 's contrib-ed greatly to t ton's pros-per-ity and ci-vil-iza..."

That took some deciphering. Neil let Martins ramble on in his disjointed manner about the marvels of technology while they both ate. The teacher nibbled his toast delicately, as if his mouth refused to open wide enough to take a proper mouthful.

The longcase clock at the base of the stairs ticked off the long minutes. Then as Neil nursed his third cup of coffee and his fingers twitched with nervousness, he heard the clock bong ominously the three quarter hour. He jumped to his feet and headed for the door before the time piece finished its announcement of the impending hour.

He walked rapidly toward the nearby Pinkerton's office, nodding to acquaintances and tipping his hat to friends. The town had come awake in the hour he'd dawdled over breakfast.

And there, the man in the great coat and bowler pulled low over his eyes stood, unlocking the wooden door. The day was proving quite warm—too warm for a woolen great coat. But then the bulk of the garment could hide a multitude of weapons. Mr. Josie Blue certainly concealed many of them in his clothing.

"Sir!" Neil called to him.

Immediately the man stood from his crouch over the lock. He looked around and narrowed his focus to Neil.

From what he could see of the man's dark eyes, they seemed to bore into his brain and soul with questions.

"Sir," Neil said more moderately as he came closer with measured steps. "May I have a word with you regarding one of your employees?"

"Depends upon the agent in question." The man held a key still in the lock, neither turning it nor disengaging.

"A Mr. Josie Blue turned up in Heller's Hole, about twenty miles southeast of here. His horse is lame, he lost his hat, and his boots nearly flopped apart, but his sidearms were loaded and ready. I've offered him the job of sheriff after he thwarted a bank robbery on Friday afternoon, right about closing time."

Neil rubbed his suddenly sweating palms on his own suit jacket, then offered a hand to the Pinkerton agent. "Neil Sanderson, mayor of Heller's Hole, and banker."

The agent shook his hand briefly then twisted the key in the door lock. "Brotherton. Robert Brotherton," he said as he pushed the door inward. "So, what kind of trouble has Josie Blue gotten into this time?" He pushed up his hat brim and surveyed Neil briefly, but thoroughly.

Oh, dear. Had he made a mistake in offering the job to Blue?

"None that I know of, other than needing a place to stay while his horse recovers. That may take some time."

Brotherton ushered Neil inside and up a narrow, enclosed staircase. At the top, a tiny landing gave the two men barely enough room for both of them to stand or breathe. Only one door, on the left, offered them escape. Returning the way they came, required too much contact, too closely for politeness' sake.

Brotherton fished a different key from his inner pocket and applied it to the lock. The door required a strong push to open, then much sidling and shuffling from both of them for the agent to get passed Neil to enter the office first.

Neil wasn't certain, but he thought he'd been frisked for weapons in that do-si-do. *I guess the best detectives in the world need to be careful.*

"What do you need to know about my agent?" Brotherton asked while hanging his coat and hat on a rack beside the door. He kept his back to Neil until he settled behind a massive oak desk that was covered with neatly stacked files. He ran a finger down the third pile to the right and rested it on one near the middle.

Neil took a moment to assess the man, ordinary height and build, nondescript features, unremarkable brown hair and mustache. Only his very dark eyes and penetrating gaze stood out. Otherwise, he might pass through a crowd totally unnoticed.

He'd met a man in the army with a similar gaze. Only then he'd been called Colonel Beauregard Martine from New Orleans.

Made him wonder if Josie Blue had another name before joining the Pinkertons. He knew who to ask.

"I took a ride last night, up on the ridge, saw a purple glow off to the west. Once before, about two years ago I saw something similar, the night our sheriff died of a heart attack and our blacksmith went missing."

"Hear anything unusual up on that ridge?" Brotherton freed that one file about an inch from the stack.

"Nothing unusual. I have a constant ringing in my ears left over from standing too close to a cannon ball when it landed in the dirt thirty feet in front of me. Most music clashes with the noise in my head and takes me back to the battlefield." He pointed to his spectacles and the pock marks on the left side of his face.

Enlightenment washed over him. *That* was why he preferred the quiet Catholic mass over the more raucous Baptist services. Instead of a pastor ranting at the top of his lungs but saying little of import, loud hymns, and an out-of-tune piano, he had to listen only to soft chanting by a priest who'd been taught to sing properly.

"I saw some action during the war too," Brotherton said softly. He offered the instant camaraderie of brothers-in-arms.

"First Bull Run, or Manassas as the locals called it, was my only battle. It was too much. When I recovered, the army put me in the payroll office. I truly am a banker more than a soldier."

"I was there. And three others before I took a bullet to my chest. Heart and lungs never the same. I too finished the war behind a desk." Brotherton didn't elaborate on what desk he had manned. He could have done anything from ordering supplies, to writing official dispatches, to managing intelligence. The Pinkertons were known for being excellent spies as well as bodyguards and detectives.

"So, can I trust Mr. Blue as our town sheriff?"

"Maybe. Check this account when you get home." He scratched some words and numbers on a piece of notepaper, folding it four times until it fit easily into a vest pocket and passed it to Neil.

Then he looked up and speared Neil with a piercing gaze. "Did you find a purple sage flower embossed on Elinore's saddle?"

He knew the mare's name! Not many men had such intimate association with co-workers.

"No, but the lad at the livery stable did and reported it to me."

"That's all you need to know. The emblem has to be earned."

CHAPTER 8

"Sorry, sir, I cain't fix your boots." Young Jed hung his head as he handed me the sorry excuses for footwear. "I patched 'em a bit, least wise you won't get no rocks in your socks, but there ain't 'nuf leather in the uppers to attach rightly to the soles."

"You did your best." I heaved a sigh. Those boots had served me well for years. Good thing I'd had Rosie trace my feet on a plain sheet of paper last night. I intended to mail it off to Pendleton to a boot-maker along with my other letters. "That's all I asked." I handed him a two-bit piece.

"Won't stop people calling you the barefoot sheriff." The boy cocked a grin at me, then quickly swallowed it when I frowned.

The delivery men this morning had been hard at work spreading gossip about the new sheriff.

"How's Elinore?" I decided a change of subject was in order.

"Still in the creek, but she ate good hay last night and the oats and honey you ordered this morning. That's expensive fodder, sir."

A polite way of saying I owed him money. I'd expected as much.

"How long will this cover her keep?" I handed him my last two greenbacks. Except for the emergency cash I'd had hidden in a secret pocket of my waistcoat, that would have to do until I got those telegrams off to my boss and the bank. I needed to stop at the milliner's as well. No one survived long out here in the middle of nowhere without a good hat.

In my mind, the emergency stash began evaporating.

Jed's eyes opened wide at the sight of so much cash. "That'll keep her a while. Pa will let you know when he comes back to work. He does all the bookkeeping and stuff. Ma says he had a good supper of chicken soup last night and should be up and about in a few days. That bank robber's bullet didn't hurt him as much as we thought. But he lost a lot of blood and needs good food. We been too long without rain and the chicken ain't layin' much."

I raised an eyebrow in skepticism. His excuse to make me feel sorry for him didn't work. But then, I wondered if I dared tell him to take Rosie's rooster...

"I'll talk to your pa when he's up and about. For now, I need to check on Elinore."

The roughness of the pasture beneath my feet felt worse today. The bedroom slippers wouldn't last long if I continued to wear them as shoes. I winced as I stepped on a pebble.

Elinore looked up at my approach and snuffled a greeting.

That was a good sign, even if she continued to soothe her feet in the cool water.

"Feeling better, Elinore?" I asked.

Elinore slurped up a bit of water and splashed some of it toward me with her wet and dripping muzzle.

As I approached, she snuffled my pockets. "You must be better if you are looking for treats. Don't worry, my girl, I won't ask you to move out of your creek until you're ready. Jed will brush you when I'm busy in town. And I'll check on you every day." I rubbed the horse's ears affectionately. "Now eat some grass. It's fresh and green here by the water."

Elinore obliged, having to move a few steps downstream to reach beyond the patch she'd already cropped short.

Satisfied that we both had taken solid steps on the road to healing, I ran my fingers through Elinore's mane. No need to untangle it, Jed had already groomed her. The boy must like Elinore above and beyond the money I had just given him.

A few steps down the boardwalk, I found the post office and telegraph station. The front door was unlocked, but Micah O'Toole, who had to be the middle aged postmaster with Irish red hair fading to auburn, bent over the clattering machine, copying down the code as rapidly as it clicked. He held up one hand, palm out, signaling that I had to be patient until he was free.

I'd never bothered to learn the code and had no idea if the message was as urgent as the man's frown suggested.

"You Josie Blue, the barefoot sheriff?" O'Toole asked with just a hint of an Irish accent. Obviously, he had not returned to the old country in many years.

Another sigh rose from my sore feet to my chest. "Yes."

"Got this telegram for you." He handed me the sheet of copy paper with his neat printing across the top. Sure enough, the short message was addressed to Josie Blue, the barefoot sheriff.

The name at the bottom explained it. Robert Brotherton might intimidate people with his terse words and crisp orders, but he had a sense of humor, much like Elinore.

"That'll be two bits..."

"You didn't have to leave the building to deliver it." I glared at O'Toole.

"Them's the rules."

The translated code on the very bottom left of the message indicated that Brotherton had paid for the delivery as well as the cost per word to send it.

I pointed to the initials. "SPD. Sender Paid Delivery."

O'Toole shrugged. "He might have paid. That's doesn't mean I'll see the money."

I slid a nickel across his high countertop but kept my finger on it until I'd read the telegram.

Heller's Hole c/o sheriff. Location confirmed. Courier dispatched with necessities.

"News travels fast around here for being the arse side of nowhere,"

I muttered releasing the coin. At least I'd have a refreshment of my funds by suppertime. Tomorrow at the latest. Depending on what time the courier left the city.

"Likely Mr. Neil talked to this man Brotherton. He's in the city today. Should be back in the bank tomorrow sometime."

"Let's hope so. He still hasn't sworn me in as sheriff or given me a tin star."

"That's okay. Got a message for Martin Youngblood, Mr. Neil's assistant, and teller. He'll take your oath and hand over your badge."

"Does Mr. Youngblood have the authority to do that?"

"Sure does. The telegram gives it to him, and I'll swear by it."

"The Barefoot Sheriff. I like it," Rosie said on a hearty laugh.

I scowled down upon the plump woman I'd dragooned into being witness to my swearing in. The boy at the bank had read the words associated with the office, voice quavering and hands shaking.

"I won't be barefoot long. I'm expecting some decent boots by courier this afternoon," I grumbled as I grabbed Rosie's arm and led her across the street and south two buildings to the... no, my, office.

"You must tell me your secret for such fast delivery. You only sent telegrams and letters this morning." Rosie paused at the entrance to the office to fiddle with my long braid. In resignation I flipped the thin plait over my left shoulder so that it hung straight down the center of my back. Then I adjusted the now fully visible tin star badge of office so that it hung straight on my leather vest. "If you insist upon dressing as a man, you should invest in some better waistcoats. This old leather thing is worn and getting ugly. I suggest some nice brocade, with double breasted buttons."

"I like sturdy and utilitarian..."

"Oh, bosh. You are settling down now and need to appear like you belong to the job. Belong here. I dictate fashion in this town, not that old biddy Ethel Sanderson, no matter what she might tell you, and I say you need waistcoats that make you easily identifiable and unique."

"I need people to respect me and my office, not admire my clothes."

"Your weapons will do that. Now listen to me and march right over to the milliner's and order some new clothes." The short and plump woman looked more like an exotic rooster with her feathered hat and hands clamped on her hips. Her mouth looked as stern as any school mistress.

"I need help cleaning my office before I order new clothes. Besides, I need to wait and see what my boss... my *friend* includes in his dispatch. Hopefully he remembers a good hat and boots." I wiggled my toes in the leather slippers. Definitely more comfortable than walking barefoot, and the sheep's wool padding Jed had added cushioned my bruised feet, but not at all practical. Especially if I brought the buckskin stallion to the paddock behind the office.

"I'll send Daisy and Jonquil over after they've eaten. They are on the rag this week and can't assume their regular duties for me. Put them to work, keep them from becoming lazy and getting fat. Their regular customers prefer them slim and young looking."

I grumbled some more. I hated that women had to resort to prostitution in order to keep themselves in bed and board, a fate I might have fallen into if Cutter Pine had not taken charge of me and my father's estate ten years ago. At least Rosie treated her girls well and protected them.

"They'll need mops and brooms and buckets and dust cloths just to get started. Oh, and I'll need to prime the pump out back. Yesterday I could barely move the pump handle for the rust build up."

"And who is going to pay for all this?" Rosie narrowed her eyes while she assessed the grimy state of the windows and then the footprints in the dust on the floor. She shuddered and batted away the foolhardy spider that dropped from the low ceiling onto her hat. When it hit the ground, the woman had no compunction about grinding it into dust with her well-shod heel.

At least she didn't run into the street screaming in horror.

That made me wonder just what the madame would do to a customer who dared break her rules.

~

"YOU REALIZE, Mr. Neil Sanderson, that your request is difficult, possibly unethical?" Ashley Q. Fondant Jr, Esq. said peering over the tops of his half glasses. The lawyer had worked for the Sandersons for at least five years, and his father had handled the family business for twenty years before that. Still, the man insisted on formal addresses. Neil's father was Mr. Sanderson, therefore Neil had to have his given name within the address.

"Yes, Ashley, I do." Neil had gone to primary school with this man, and they'd shared a room at a boarding house in Princeton while at University. Ashley had grown thick around his middle and looked as a prosperous man should. Neil had not.

When Neil had joined the army at the beginning of the war with good eyesight, Ashley had been rejected because of his need for corrective lenses. Now they both needed assistance seeing. "That very difficulty is why I come to you for help rather than an unknown judge in Portland. You know the situation and the people involved."

"Precisely. A judge might accuse me of a conflict of interest."

"You have a copy of my father's will."

"Yes. Both he and your mother consulted my father when you joined the army. They had no guarantee that you would survive."

"As did I."

"But you updated your will when you returned home, alive but slightly damaged."

"And my parents did not. My father insisted the clause 'in case of my incapacity to function as a banker due to accident or disease I grant complete control of my businesses to my wife. If she should not survive me, or likewise become incapacitated, my son, Lieutenant Neil Sanderson shall take control of said businesses.' Am I right, Ashley?"

"Yes. Incapacity is very hard to prove." He removed his spectacles and pinched the bridge of his nose. He'd always done that when he had a headache.

"But not impossible to prove." Neil had every intention of making his friend's headache worse until he got what he needed. "As for my father, I have had to hire a man to see to his needs. Jack Epps was the orderly who cared for me when I was in hospital after my injury." He waved his left hand vaguely in front of his face to remind Ashley of his wartime scars.

Ashley pinched the bridge of his nose harder and scrunched his eyes closed.

Neil rose from his comfortable Chesterfield chair and pulled the plush maroon drapes across a sparkling clean window to block the direct sunlight. That should offer enough relief of the headache to keep Ashley upright and not retreating to his bed.

"Jack, with the cooperation of my father's club manager, has done his best to prevent my father from betting, and losing, the bank, our home, and all of our investments in a game of cards, or wagering how many minutes late the next train will be. Once he bet on, and lost, how many raindrops would hit a designated spot on his hat brim while crossing the street."

Neil inhaled sharply at that memory. He'd covered the bet, but after that had placed serious restrictions on his father's allowance.

"Jack now informs me that Father only leaves his bed to go to a poker game, even if the game is with phantom players no one else can see. Most of the names mentioned are dead." The last came out in a rush. He had to say it all at once on a single exhale to get through it.

He'd learned a lot about life, and banking, and ranching from his father. He'd learned to give and accept love from his parent. Mother had always been cool toward him, doling out affection only on her birthday and special holidays if Neil and/or his father offered up an appropriately expensive gift.

"I need to bring him home. Father resists the trip. My mother is appalled that she must share the house with him again." He suspected that having a man in her overly perfumed, pink satin bed was the real issue, not Father's presence in the house.

Ashley nodded and made rapid notes in a bound notebook with lined yellow paper. "And your mother? Why is Aunt Ethel not capable of running the bank and the other businesses?"

"I question the rationality of her decisions."

Ashley looked up sharply and speared Neil with a questing gaze. The same look he used when he tore huge holes in Neil's logic in deciding to marry a girl of questionable lineage when they were eighteen and newly on their own.

Then Ash thought better of the movement and lowered his head again. He renewed the pinch on the bridge of his nose.

"Mother's life revolves around her church and managing the garden club, the music club, the women's club and other useless organizations that provide excuses to take tea together and eat overly sweet cakes."

Ashley nodded. His mother led a similar routine.

"Mother made friends with a new family who bought a small ranch at the edge of town. She gave them a strong recommendation for the bank to accept their loan application for operating expenses on their spread. At the time they seemed to have a firm grip on running the place at a small profit. I won't give you names for privacy reasons." Neil swallowed hard and wished for a glass of water. "Now they have switched from cattle to sheep and are turning a tidy profit. They make their payments on time, and in full. At first, mother pushed me to extend credit to them. But then they stopped coming to church. I suspect they attend Mass at the Catholic church. Mother has turned against them and demands I foreclose."

"That is neither rational, logical, nor legal," Ashley murmured.

"Mother is trying to make business decisions based upon her emotions and prejudices. To keep the bank operating at a profit to keep her in the latest fashion and bonbons, I need to remove her authority to act in my father's stead."

"Give me until tomorrow morning."

CHAPTER 9

"Have you found access to the attic?" Doc asked Josie from the doorjamb. The late afternoon sun streamed through the now clean and bright windows. Any chance of privacy had disappeared, along with his hopes of seduction.

Josie Blue wasn't just any woman who could be jumped upon. She'd grown up educated and sophisticated. No matter how rough her life had been these last ten years, she still needed to be courted and wooed. And he needed discretion. Like the mythical attic without windows and curious neighbors.

"What attic?" The barefoot sheriff, who was indeed barefoot today without even the leather slippers, poked her head above the desk. A smudge of dirt streaked her cheek and her nose, softening her stark and gaunt features.

He never thought he'd use the words cute and adorable to describe the haunted woman who dressed like a man.

"Rumor has it that the first sheriff, back around twenty-five years ago, hid a hoard of gold from California in the attic. He disappeared about five years later. We wondered why. The next sheriff wasn't interested in pursuing the rumor." Doc said. He stepped into the office and turned a full circle, admiring the cleaning job. Life had come back to the room, banishing any ghosts that lingered.

"I heard it was a treasure map leading to a Nez Perce horde of Spanish treasure," Jonquil said. She lugged in two buckets of water, presumably from the revived pump out back. She smiled prettily and walked with a light step, almost a different personality than when she swanned about the saloon wearing her tatty gown.

Ah, Jonquil, the lovely blonde who tickled his fancy with her wide-eyed and innocent act. She pretended to need stern direction. Rosie had told him she wouldn't be plying her usual trade this week at the saloon.

"What attic?" Josie repeated. She stood up to her full and impressive height. As tall as Doc, maybe an inch more.

"Come outside and look at the architecture," Doc invited. He retreated to the center of the street rather than stare at how her sweat-dampened shirt molded her slight curves. Still too skinny but she promised lush delights, if he could break through her resistance.

Josie followed him, wiping her face with a kerchief she moistened in the first of Jonquil's buckets.

"Look at the roof line," Doc pointed above the false front at the top of the first story. "It rises another eight feet at least above what should be the ceiling." Something else was off with the symmetry, but he couldn't place it, not with Josie distracting him.

"So, it does, so it does, Doc." Josie drummed her fingers on her thigh. She'd left off her weapons while she cleaned. "Why have you just noticed the anomaly?"

"Never had reason to look before." That was the truth. Looking up seemed a waste of time when all of his patients were down here at eye level.

"There would have to be a staircase, or at least a trap door," she replied. "Believe me, we've been all over this place. I washed down the ceilings above the cells myself. We've found nothing. I haven't even found evidence of a rat's nest or a snake. Just fleas and dust and one spider web."

"You're tall enough that you could reach the ceiling if you stood on the cot." Doc shifted his gaze from the roof to her face.

With one hand shading her eyes while she gazed upward, the sharpness of her nose and the pinch in her cheeks gave her a silhouette that could easily be mistaken for a man. A lot of his desire sank. He'd never liked men, though some of his fellow officers during the war had chased after the fresh-faced boys among the troops. They later confessed that they found the beardless recruits almost as good as a woman with her backside turned up when there were no women about.

"Sheriff, I think you'd best come see this," Daisy called from the office.

Doc didn't know this dark-eyed and dark-haired girl well. Her matter-of-fact, let's-get-this-over-with attitude didn't appeal to him. He found her more intriguing once, when she came to him as a patient with bruises and welts from a belt. She'd quickly squashed any lustful ideas with a hard slap and a threat to tell Rosie of his improper touch.

Josie stalked back into the office. Daisy pointed to the north wall, perpendicular to the cells. Yesterday the pale paneling had been covered in yellowed, outdated, and curling wanted posters.

"With the grime and the posters gone, there is a definite gap in the wood," Daisy said.

Josie ran a finger around the outline of a door. "Someone went to a great deal of trouble to hide this." She began pressing harder on both sides of the crack until a latch clicked on the top left-hand corner. High enough that only a tall man, or very tall woman, could reach it easily.

Doc did have to admire the stretch of her back muscles as they narrowed to her waist.

"Shall we see what secrets this old building hides?" Doc asked. He bowed gallantly and swept his arm toward the portal. "Ladies first."

"Let's hope all the vermin that should be all over the building aren't hiding up there," Josie huffed and eased her fingers into the widening gap. In a moment, she'd pried open the simple panel to reveal a landing and narrow stair leading upward, parallel to the wall.

Doc doubted plump Rosie, with her wide and flouncy skirts would fit.

"Let me get my weapons," Josie announced. She needed only a few long strides to return to her desk and retrieve her double holster with loaded revolvers. Then she was back before Doc could even consider preceding her up the hidden staircase. He didn't like the idea of encountering an angry rattler or hungry rat.

The wooden risers creaked. Dust filled the air. Spiders scurried away.

And Josie's shapely butt moving ahead of him enticed Doc.

He followed as closely as he dared.

They burst into an empty, low room lit by narrow slits under the roof's overhang and a single small window overlooking the back paddock. Heat created a miasma that made his vision waver.

Josie drew her right handgun.

They encountered only a brittle dried up corpse, skin darkened and stretched by natural mummification, laid out on the floor with arms and legs splayed and a spear piercing the chest where his heart should be. Fragments of once bright feathers and beads decorated the end of the spear.

Lines of chalk—no they were salt—outlined the mummy. From this angle, barely above eye level with the lines he could discern no pattern.

"Those bangles on the spear look more Romany than Indian," Josie said as she holstered her revolver. "The dead man must have killed someone important to them and shattered their list of sins and forbidden things."

She walked around the corpse, careful to avoid the salt on the floor, surveying it from all angles. Did she follow instinct or experience in keeping the lines intact?

"Damn," she muttered. "Damn, damn, damn! That's a salt circle. The Rom use them in their magic, to keep evil in. Best not to disturb the salt until we know for certain what's going on." Then she stepped over the line to examine the spear and its decorative bangles.

When she looked back at him, she held one of the desiccated feathers gingerly between her thumb and forefinger fingernails. "This is neither Nez Perce nor Romany."

Doc peered at it closely. A slight shift in the light caught a glint of iridescence in the straggly strands. Not a feather, but a ragged bit of wing membrane. A purple iridescent wing.

"I'VE BEEN afraid of this for a long time," I said, letting go of the foot long strand of feather that could have been torn from a very alien flying thing. It fluttered softly as it nestled back into the strands of a... a beaded votive offering to strange gods.

The corpse had a hole in his forehead. If it came from a gun, it had to be from a large bore weapon. Given the mummy's age and desiccation, I couldn't see any gunpowder residue to indicate range.

Someone really didn't like this guy.

I couldn't stare at the *thing* any longer. If I did, it would start moving in my imagination until it strangled me. And then ate me.

That brought me up short. Maybe this wasn't an ordinary person who dared cross the Rom.

A pile of neatly folded, very dusty clothing rested on the floor, in the far right hand corner. Must be the work of the Rom. I'd never known an Indian warrior to care so much for artifacts of a culture alien to their own.

Clothes. The aliens flew into battle naked. I'd never seen one outside of a hungry swarm. The lack of clothing while fighting might be a cultural thing.

Didn't the ancient Picts run into battle against the Romans wearing nothing but blue paint?

I desperately sought an alternative explanation for the strangeness of this corpse.

"What?" Doc asked. He bent forward examining the corpse

without touching it. But then he'd gone to medical school, dissected bodies, served in the Army and worked endlessly in hospital tents after battles. Carnage was nothing new to him.

Nor to me. I'd seen far too much since the night after Eva's wedding when both the bride's and the groom's family had gathered for a sumptuous meal at the ranch. They'd eaten their fill. Drunk too much champagne. Laughed and hugged and watched the groom kiss his bride at every chance, as if storing up memories and sensation before he headed off to war.

Ma and Dad had forbidden me champagne. And Ma sent me off to bed early. I was only fifteen and had no need to participate in the increasingly ribald jokes leading to an old-fashioned shivaree. According to her.

But me being *Me*, I never heeded orders well and curiosity demanded I observe everything, including the shivaree. I sneaked a glass of the sparkling wine and hid in a cupboard where the table linens were stored when not on the table.

My long legs didn't want to fold into the cramped space. I was already almost as tall as Dad and my uncles. My wide hoop skirt, (useless things) wouldn't fit. So, I'd left the door open a crack to let me breathe, and hear the adult party. A full yard of my mint green silk gown (Ma said it complimented my chestnut hair and hazel eyes) spilled out onto the floor. No one was looking for me.

I may have napped for a bit. My memory was fuzzy on that point. Everything else remained crystal clear in my mind.

A strange noise brought me awake.

The rival ranch owners, the Carons, had approached silently. Either that or no one had listened for them over the raucous din of the party. I had heard the distinctive click of someone cocking a six shooter… and then the explosion of ten weapons ranging from the deep roar of a shotgun to the lighter discharge of a Colt 45.

On the fringe of the crowd of the rival Caron clan I spotted a man I'd seen before. I didn't know him, but I knew I'd seen him before, on the ridge with binoculars watching the goings on at the ranch house as we prepared for the wedding. I spotted him as I rode out to check fences rather than participate in endless debate over which flower bundle went where.

In my cupboard, frightened beyond words, I held my hands over my ears and buried my face in my knees. The smell of my own sweat turned rancid within the tight confines of the cupboard.

When the noise abated and my breathing became too ragged to stay put, I had peeked out to find the entire wedding party sprawled in pools of blood. Gaping mouths and blankly staring eyes greeted me. Bright silk gowns and starched white shirts dripped blood.

I found Dad's figure first, at the head of table. He slumped in the armed chair, head on his chest, his bald spot in the center of his head, surrounded by coarse grey hair looked like it belonged on some ancient monk in one of Ma's books.

But our ranch was on the frontier. Defending our property was second nature. Dad's revolver still smoked from spent bullets. The other men also held long and short weapons, all discharged and empty.

At the doorway to the formal dining room and into the hall, all of the Carons sprawled, equally bloody and equally dead.

The feud over water rights was over.

I gulped back bile and blinked rapidly before I had the courage to move.

Then the real horror began.

It started with music. Gentle horns and soft strings. At first. I thought the wine had made me sleepy and I dreamed the bloody massacre. Music that beautiful could only come from heaven. Romance novels said that a bride would hear music like that on her wedding night...

I shook my head to banish the carnage that had come after the music. Flying purple things couldn't sing and eat at the same time.

"After an attack, the aliens disappear too quickly," I said quietly to Doc in the dust-free attic, so Jonquil and Daisy wouldn't hear. "They leave too many booted and bare footprints behind and scatter in dozens of different directions. Skilled hunters get confused trying to follow them. I've never seen them fly immediately after a feast. Maybe their bellies get too heavy for their wings to support them." Or they carried more than their own weight of bloody meat back to their nests.

I pressed my palms against my eyes, trying desperately to clear my vision and concentrate on the here and now. Behind my eyelids I saw only the face of the watcher on the ridge.

"Doc, can you turn that thing," I pointed to the corpse, "so I can see the spine and shoulder blades?"

"Why?" He sat back on his haunches and stared at me without moving to comply.

"I need to see if there are boney protrusions that might support folded wings." If he didn't shift the corpse, then I'd have to. I'd have to touch the thing anyway to wrap it in a shroud and send it to headquarters for expert examination. A report would not suffice this time.

That hole in the forehead was definitely not a bullet wound.

"Isn't that large hole in his forehead enough to convince you?" Doc kept his hand dangling between his knees. "I've seen these things in their native form plenty of times after a battle. But never in human form with vestigial alien traits."

"What if they aren't vestigial?" I gulped.

Doc stood abruptly and backed toward the stairs. "No!"

"What if they are shape changers and hide their alienage under hats and shirts and boots? Look at the feet! Three toes, like a bird, or a lizard."

"I am a scientist. Shape changing is impossible. There is no… proof." His voice dribbled away and his face blanched.

"I think we are staring at the proof. You have firm evidence that these things might very well be living among us, just waiting for the next range war or slaughter of Indians authorized by the U.S. Army. They only eat carrion but are not above manipulating humans into mass murder first." The watcher on the hill had been one of the purple aliens who ate dead humans. That was where I'd seen his face before.

CHAPTER 10

NEIL CHECKED his messenger bag to make sure the document he needed next lay within easy reach. He'd spent the entire day talking to important people. *Why do crises always come at the same time?* he asked himself. He'd dealt with the Pinkertons, his personal lawyer, the bank's lawyer, and a team of potential investors for the building of a railroad spur line into Heller's Hole.

Now he had scheduled an early dinner at the hotel with the railroad executives. He barely remembered their names and didn't care if he met them again.

They weren't the only railroad trying to build spur lines in the area. Just the only ones not too busy to discuss his proposal.

There had to be reasons they had time on their hands. They certainly weren't working at building railroads.

He descended the last few steps of the hotel's grand staircase, noting that the carpeted steps looked a little threadbare and faded. Business might be booming in Pendleton since the transcontinental rail line was completed two years ago, but travelers wanted accommodations in newer buildings mere steps from the train station instead of old-fashioned luxury at the center of town.

The grand hotel offered better food in a formal setting. They also guaranteed discretion among their wait staff. Anyone caught whispering gossip that originated in this hotel knew ahead of time that they'd have to leave town without a reference within hours.

Still, secrets got out, scandals were broadcast in the local newspapers, and business deals affected a company's value, up or down.

Tonight, he hoped word of his private deal, or lack thereof, with the railroad made it all the way back to Washington D.C. No wonder they had time to build his spur line, no one else would do business with them.

The maître d'hôtel seated him in a semi-private area where potted palms screened the table and chairs from outside view. "Thank you, Jenkins," Neil said as he accepted the printed menu of limited items.

"Very good, Mr. Sanderson. We are all happy to see you return to our establishment."

"And a fine hotel it is," Neil replied.

His fellow diners made their entrance within moments. They advertised the punctuality of their trains. At least they appeared to hold the same principles in their business practices.

When all were seated and hands had been shaken, Jenkins recited the day's special: beef nuggets sautéed in a new and exotic Russian sauce of sour cream, a soupçon of nutmeg, and mushrooms.

Neil ordered that. He'd learned that the French chef always paid extra attention to the special and left preparation of the normal selections to underlings.

Two glasses of excellent wine later, and feeling satisfied, if not overly full, Neil contemplated dessert and decided against it. His companions, however, could not resist the vanilla cake with rum raisin sauce. They were half asleep when Neil swallowed the last of his wine in a single gulp and pulled the envelope from his messenger bag.

"Gentlemen," he spoke resolutely.

Jenkins edged closer to eavesdrop, discretion be damned.

At least one man—not quite so portly as the other two—roused enough to open his eyes and stare at Neil suspiciously.

"I spoke with my investors this afternoon, and we are all agreed," he paused a moment while the railroad men smiled smugly. Then he placed the white envelope face down on the table between them. "If we must pay the full cost of building a spur line to Heller's Hole, then we will own it. Not you." He turned over the envelope to reveal his boldly printed "DENIED" in red ink in letters large enough to fill the entire width.

"But, but, but..." two of three men sputtered, spraying cake crumbs across the table.

Neil pretended not to notice.

"But you must lease the engines and freight cars from us." The third man said—the one who had been mostly awake when Neil pounced—pointing to his chest. "And we cannot in good conscience lease such valuable equipment to a line that was not built to our standards." He sat back against his straight chair, wine and cake ignored.

"Your proposed spur line is a dead end. You'll never recoup the cost," one of the others protested and calmly returned to his desert.

"Heller's Hole can become the gateway to the interior and the grain market developing there. The eastern seaboard is crowded, without enough fertile land to feed itself. *They* need the products we in the west can supply. I have investors eager to bring money to the project, but only if they can reap a share of the profits. Good evening, gentlemen."

Neil pushed his chair back and stood. The maître d'hôtel rushed to catch the chair and ease his change of position. "Secret?" he mouthed.

Neil shook his head. He wanted this gossip to spread.

"Jenkins, please put *my* meal on my bill. I'll be checking out after breakfast tomorrow morning."

"I NEED to hire a wagon to take the... um... bones to Pinkerton Headquarters tomorrow morning," I said between bites of mutton chops and buttered greens. My bare feet rested upon the chair opposite. My blisters had popped and left the skin raw and oozing.

Besides, if the locals, and my boss, the mayor, were going to call me "the barefoot sheriff" I might as well live up to the nickname. For now.

"I do not think it wise," Doc said from beside me. He ate his dinner less ravenously than I did. But then he had thirty pounds to lose, and I had twenty to gain.

"Why not get rid of the corpse now? Burn it and scatter the ashes far and wide," Doc said.

"He needs to be examined by experts," I insisted. "The sooner the better. Don't you think I'm up to the trip to Pendleton?" I dropped my feet to the floor with a wince, then planted my fork and knife firmly on the table with a loud clank that drew the attention of the other early diners at Rosie's.

"I would never question that," Doc replied mildly.

"But?"

"One: I do not like the idea of you driving a wagon, pulled by a horse you have never worked with, along a rutted and dangerously dipping road with unshod feet braced against the buckboard. You can barely walk as it is. And," he held up a hand, palm out, to quell my protest, "two: you've only been officially sheriff here for a day. Not good for you to desert your post for two full days of travel. Not without a very good reason."

"I have a very good reason."

"But not one you are willing to share with your citizenry. We do not want to start a panic among them about the aliens. Best they think the mummy we found is merely a wanderer who crawled into the attic to die. In which case, we'd ask Reverend Zebedee Sanderpoole to bury him in the local cemetery. Or perhaps Father Xavier, he's getting old enough to not notice discrepancies in the deceased."

"Better that than Daisy and Jonquil start whispering that we wouldn't let them into the attic because we found treasure." My whole body began to quake from the force of the laughter erupting from my gut. My mood brightened and my feet stopped hurting, for a moment.

I put them back up on the chair to keep them from hurting again, or the ooze from sticking to the floor as it dried. Prying them up again would cause more damage.

"What?" Doc riveted his gaze upon me.

"First time people would begin breaking *into* jail. By the droves." My laughter intensified until my eyes watered, and my breath came short and sharp.

A lady would never make a spectacle of herself so uproariously. My male disguise remained intact.

"Breaking into jail?" Doc mimicked my mirth.

I choked back my guffaws when Rosie marched over to our back corner table (quickly being recognized as *my* table). "Care to share the joke?" the madame asked.

I tried to swallow my laughter, but Rosie's stern countenance set me off again. I waved at Doc, hoping he had the self-control to speak. Or to find a reasonable explanation.

"We didn't find a treasure, but rumor alone is enough to make people try to break into jail rather than out of it," he gasped.

"Good one," Rosie said, pounding his back before he choked. "I'll tell the boys that and they'll know you are lying. So, what do we tell them?"

"We found a mummified corpse. Probably the first sheriff who committed suicide. Looks like he hung himself. The rope rotted and he dropped to the floor." I choked on the words, but a lack of breath sobered me.

"You are right, of course. What do we do with him?" she asked between giggles.

"I have a few patients I must see first thing in the morning," Doc said. "Then I will have a local rancher, who owes me a fair amount of money to lend me the use of his wagon and draft horse for the trip. I shall deliver our friend to the address of your choosing, Sheriff Blue, stay with friends that night, and return the next day."

"What did you do for him that he owes you such a big favor? Draft horses are too valuable to lend to just anyone for a trip like that."

"He broke his leg and the surgery to reset the compound fracture took nearly six hours. Then I kept his three small children in my apartment overnight until his wife got him settled and doused with pain medication. Those toddlers are more than a handful."

"You went above and beyond your duties as a doctor, and it's better for you to make this delivery. You can explain the anatomical details to Robert Brotherton better than I. You'd best take the spear with you. I know that the beads are Romany, or possibly Basque." That thought alone sobered me. If the latter was true, I knew the perpetrators. "I do not know which tribe or clan. Brotherton will know how to find out." There, a return to normal. A giggle or two still kept erupting.

"We are agreed then?" Doc pushed his plate aside and stood leaning his fists on the table.

"Agreed."

He took his well-worn hat from the rack between our table and the next one and plunked it upon his head.

"What? No proposition tonight?" I asked, laughing again.

"Not tonight, my dear. I bow to your wish to retain your masculine appearance, and for me to follow you upstairs would ruin both our reputations. My dear friend in Pendleton, Mrs. Murphy—a widow who owns a boarding house—will take care of me nicely. Now good night and sleep well. The salve I gave you should ease your feet enough to let you sleep." He bowed politely and exited. He burst into laughter again as he exited.

I smiled and finished my meal in quiet solitude.

TUESDAY MORNING, Neil guided his horse through the city traffic, pedestrian, wagon, and individual riders. The number of people in the city busily going about their day always surprised him. From one monthly trip to the next he figured the population had increased by several hundred.

He signed for a packet of papers at Ashley's office without seeing his old friend. Then continued his errands on the way out of town.

At the post office, he stopped to pick up any mail headed for

Heller's Hole. He had a formal arrangement to carry the mail when he was available. It saved the postmaster a lot of money to let him fill the job of a regular courier who came to town once a week, when he could. If he had more than five letters to deliver. The bank usually had that much, plus whatever missives the town's residents expected. Even when they didn't have a sheriff, the government sent "Wanted" posters. Sometimes Neil hung them in the bank. Not always.

Today, he noted a new packet sealed in a bundle, plus letters from various merchants in town addressed to J. Blue. None from the Pinkertons.

He had his own packet of letters from people he'd met during the war, or at university. Good reading during the long nights coming with the shift in seasons.

He tucked the mail safely into the saddle bag with his suit—properly folded by the hotel footman so he'd acquire fewer wrinkles.

The six-shooter on his hip added an uncomfortable weight, shifting his balance wrong for the saddle. But he figured it had become a necessity on the trail. With the increase in economic opportunities came opportunists, like the young bank robbers last Friday.

Mr. Blue had said that. It rang true.

Something about the young men who'd robbed the bank bothered him. Something more than the fine silver gilt hair of two of them. He knew, by sight, most everyone in town. The only family with similar coloring were the last hold-out miners working a trickle of copper ore at the original mine back in the hills. He hadn't seen them in town in a year or more. They didn't have enough money to make use of the bank and grew their own food. Once every three months or so one, and only one, of the men showed up with a saddlebag full of ore at the assay office—the general store with scales and other arcane equipment tucked into a corner and behind a partition. Rumor had it that the seam of copper had finally played out and the family moved on.

But those two boys...

Doc reported that a woman, with pale blond hair, not the white fly away locks of the boys, had retrieved them, promising that she would bring the boys back to town when the judge showed up. Doc did not know her.

Neil's musings had carried him several miles uphill. Now he needed to concentrate on his horse's footing on the narrow path. From droppings on the trail, he figured he followed two other riders moving much slower than himself. He knew this so-called road well. Another half mile and he should be able to pass the others where the hill plateaued for a hundred paces. He didn't feel like engaging in conversation with strangers today.

He had other things on his mind, like the ease and skill with which Josie Blue had shot, but not killed, the blond bank robbers. Doc had patched them up and sent them home with their mother—wherever their home was. They wouldn't be leaving the region in a hurry, not with those wounds, if the circuit judge chose to bring them to trial.

Certainly, a sheriff needed to be willing to use his weapons when needed. But the Pinkertons were known to try talking and negotiating first. Josie Blue had whipped out his guns and shot first, needing only seconds to assess the situation and shoot before the robbers could. He shot accurately, to cause a lot of pain and disable them, but not to kill them.

Was that a quality Neil *wanted* in a sheriff? What if those boys had been the sons of bank customers or local ranchers?

What if…

He'd run out of solitude and thinking time. The back side of a sturdy bay with black mane and tail, and the long legs and deep chest needed to travel long distances and still had enough wind to burst into a gallop when needed came into view. Then he noticed a sure-footed brown pack pony loaded with bulging packages. No speed from that beast.

Finally, a rider dressed in sturdy denim with a well-worn leather hat and a relaxed spine appeared.

Before Neil came within easy hailing distance, the man straightened, and his hands rested on the grips of his pistols. He dropped his reins, guiding the horse with balance and posture and knees. Man and mount worked together like a single being. He could well imagine

Josie Blue doing the same with Elinore, the faithful skewbald mare. The copper shield painted on one saddle bag confirmed his first notion that the man had sworn loyalty to the Pinkertons.

"Good day, sir," Neil called. "Nice weather. I think autumn is just around the corner." Pleasant conversation that didn't require engaging in anything personal.

The man grunted a reply, also noncommittal. But he didn't move his hands away from his weapons. The darkness of his skin contrasted sharply with the pale grips of those six shooters.

Neil tipped his hat. "Mind if I pass you? I'm in a bit of a hurry."

"Go on ahead. And let your barefoot sheriff know I got a late start, but I will deliver these packages soon as I can." He smiled, flashing a mouthful of misaligned but brightly white teeth contrasting with his café au lait skin. His face took on the caricature of a theater musicale.

Neil decided then and there to keep Mother at home for a few days to prevent her from running into the man and raising holy hell about demons of Satan invading *her* town.

Neil smiled inwardly. His fellow traveler let him know that he was expected and there would be consequences if he was waylaid.

His smile extended. The first time he'd met Josie Blue, the new sheriff wore only one boot and had a hole in his sock. Later when they spoke at Rosie's, the man had discarded both boots and socks while he propped his feet up on a chair. Barefoot indeed.

The Pinkerton agent riding beside him could only have adopted the sobriquet after talking to Robert Brotherton.

"I'll inform Sheriff Blue." He nodded briefly and eased his horse around the courier on the uphill side of the trail. "Do I need to give your name?"

"Nope. Blue knows I'm coming."

Neil didn't want to worry about the advisability of hiring Josie Blue. He really didn't. But the nagging feeling of a Pinkerton conspiracy built around him as he urged his horse into a trot. Was the agency planning on using Heller's Hole as a base of operations, taking possession and control of the town away from *him?* Would they welcome or shun the railway spur line?

He hoped they'd need the open line of communication to the city. Maybe they'd invest in the railroad.

But who could be the object of such conspiracy? If it existed. Josie Blue? Himself? Or the entire town of Heller's Hole?

To become an agent for Pinkerton, Blue had to take an oath to the agency. Some whispered that it was a blood oath. Did that supersede any oath he took as sheriff?

CHAPTER 11

Doc stood in the bed of a small farm wagon and hoisted old Ethan Aubry up by the armpits until he sat on the tailgate. From there the sixty-year-old rancher could scoot himself back far enough to rest his heavily bandaged right leg against a bed of pillows and blankets. His wife, Evelyn, stuffed padding beneath the leg indelicately.

"What did you do to him, this time, Doc?" she demanded, hands on hips and lips pursed in anger.

Or was it desperation?

"Bad enough we lost most of the day to his needing treatment. Now you're going to tell me he has to rest with his foot up. Tell me who's going to mind the fence line in the north pasture? And who's going to fix the chicken coop so's them coyotes can't git 'em? And who's going to weed the kitchen garden and harvest the apples that's just coming ripe?"

"I'm sorry, Mrs. Aubry. I'm sorry your son didn't come home from the war to help you. I drained the ulcer on Ethan's leg, and I packed it with a special moss. But if he doesn't rest and keep it elevated for a least a week, he's going to lose that leg. And you've got to bathe the wound every day, keep it clean so the infection doesn't spread. If either of you sees red streaks spreading from the area you have to bring him to me immediately."

Doc climbed over the side of the wagon and dropped to the dusty ground. "If you'd brought him to me when he first cut himself while sharpening a rusty blade, instead of waiting for the infection to latch on and not let go, then I might have saved him," he muttered under his breath. From his perspective the man *might* survive the winter. Evelyn would have to hire help or let one of her three married daughters move back in and have a son-in-law run the place.

But Ethan wouldn't allow that. The land should go to his son. He still hoped the boy would wander home after being missing in action for eight years.

Doc knew the boy was lost for good. The purple flying things made certain too many good men disappeared forever.

Evelyn's face sobered. The anger drained out of her as she fastened the buckboard closed and dragged her exhausted body to the driver's bench. Doc boosted her up and handed her the reins.

"Is it time, Doc?" Her voice held no hope.

"It's time to bring one or more of your daughters home."

"Jilly and Mike live in the city now. He's up for election to be judge. They won't come. They don't need to come. And Janey's Bill works for the railroad. A good job with regular money coming in. They won't want to give that up for a broken down ranch."

"What about Jasmine? Her baby is coming in about two months. She and Andy might appreciate your help with the little one, with half their land washed into the gully last winter. If he adds his few remaining acres to yours, you'd all have a big enough spread to make some real money once Mayor Neil Sanderson gets that railroad spur up and running."

"Andy never made a good decision in his life. How can we trust him to run the ranch properly?"

"You'll be there to advise him." He patted the woman's hand. "Now I've got to run. I have business in the city. But I'll be back tomorrow around supper time. I'll stop in to check on you and Ethan on my way back. Think about bringing Jasmine and Andy home. Think hard." He backed up so she could drive the wagon away.

Immediately, his mind turned to that errand in the city. He was already half an hour later than expected. Ethan's recurring illness had messed up more than the lives of his own family. A quick glance up the street to the sheriff's office showed Josie standing on the boardwalk, a hand shading her eyes as she looked southeast for the wagon that should take Doc into town.

Then she turned her attention to the north along the road coming into town. Finally, she turned her gaze toward Doc and shrugged her shoulders.

Doc grabbed his hat, coat, and satchel from just inside the door and hastened across the street. "What's wrong?" he asked from the doorway.

"WHERE IS HE?" I asked the air as I paced my office. Doc's intrusion barely registered in my mind.

"Where is who?" he replied, setting the satchel on the floor. "I know I'm late…"

"Not you, the Pinkerton courier. He should have been here last night."

"I might add that my wagon is also late. I doubt I'll make it to town before sunset…"

"Oh that. Found this note under the door this morning." I handed a folded piece of paper to Doc.

He opened it and glanced at the careful printing. "Well, I guess I won't be going to the city with your… evidence after all." Doc crumpled the scrap and stuffed it into his coat pocket.

"He's been dead and desiccated for twenty years. One more day won't matter," I said with a dismissive wave. Still, my fingers itched and my feet ached. I wanted to ride Elinore at a full gallop, but her feet were worse off than mine. Maybe if I just retired to the paddock and shot fast and furiously at random targets until I'd exhausted every weapon I owned...

"What I'm worried about is the Pinkerton courier. If he's still alive he's a day late." I winced as a sliver from the worn plank floor brushed against one of my blisters. Pain like a dull knife slash ran from my toe to my knee. The mending of the slash across my lower back hurt less. But the stitches tugged at the skin, reducing my range of motion.

Pain, like anger, or fear, was just something you lived with until it went away, or you did something about it.

"How many times have I told you to stay put and elevate your feet?" Doc roared.

He stalked toward me with fists balled and chin jutting.

I blinked rapidly in surprise. He might be a randy man who drank too much. But he'd always spoken mildly, even gently. I, Josie Blue, Pinkerton agent, bounty hunter, lone nomad, and dead shot, had no choice but to sit.

He glared at me, as fiercely as he'd spoken.

"I... I need to... ride out and make sure he is still alive," I protested, my voice soft, meek, and feminine. I hadn't been reduced to that state since I left Cutter Pine, out cold with two broken teeth and a jaw swelling as high as his eyes.

"Even if you could ride, Elinore isn't ready. Young Jed told me this morning he's still having trouble getting your horse out of the creek. She won't take kindly to carrying you barefoot."

"Barefoot? Me or her?" I quickly swallowed my smile at the image of riding my tacked-up mare without boots.

But if we were both barefoot and she bare backed?

Then I frowned at how much Elinore's feet hurt since she still preferred the creek to the pasture.

At least she was eating.

"I'll be buying the buckskin stallion as soon as the courier gets here with some cash, or bank drafts. I can ride him..."

"How far can you ride a barely broken horse barefoot? You know he's called Trouble for a reason."

"Further than you think. Jed Junior says he has had some schooling."

"Can you even walk down to the livery stable from here?"

"I must. It is my duty as a Pinkerton Agent and Rider of the Purple Sage to make sure the courier has not run afoul…"

"If he works for the Pinkertons, if he is trusted as a courier for them, then you and I both know he can take care of himself."

"You don't understand! If Brotherton telegraphed me that a courier had been dispatched, then he would have been on the road yesterday morning. He is nearly a full day late!" I spoke too loudly, out of fear. I knew it. I'd not felt fear for myself since Cutter rescued me after the aliens dispatched my family. But others were not as well trained as me. They couldn't smell the enemy creeping up from behind.

They couldn't outthink and outshoot the enemy like I could.

"Was he dispatched to the road, or to do a bunch of shopping for you? If he had to buy you new boots and a hat, maybe an entire new wardrobe, he'd be occupied all day. If he had to visit a bank, or two of them, then maybe he didn't start up the road until this morning." Doc looked up at the wall clock I'd wound and reset just this morning. The hands ticked over two o'clock and three minutes. "It's too late for me to leave for town now, But, if your man started the trip early this morning, he'll be here in about an hour. You can start worrying then. In the meantime, you are going to stay seated with your feet up. I'll check on Elinore. One less thing for you to worry and pace for." He grabbed his satchel and his hat and stomped out.

I sank into my chair and propped my bare feet on the desk, relieved that I didn't hurt, angry at myself for succumbing to weakness. The aliens left me no time to be weak.

NEIL SHIFTED UNCOMFORTABLY in his saddle. He didn't ride enough. After two days atop this horse—Molly, the mare he'd ridden home from the war, but only saddled for his monthly trips into the city—

plus the evening ride up to the ridge, every muscle in his body ached. He wanted nothing more than a hot bath, a good meal, and to sleep in his own bed.

His mother wouldn't give him the time and peace to do any of those things. He'd not get her signature on the documents he carried until he let her run out of arguments. And if he headed for Rosie's first? Mother would rail at him even longer.

He decided to talk to Doc first, get him to sign the testament of incompetence and not deal with his mother until the bank, the ranch, the house in town, and the investments were his, and his alone, to control.

Ah, there, just beyond this next rise, he could see the squat and square belfry atop the schoolhouse cum Baptist church. Almost home.

The horse perked her ears and lifted her head to better smell the livery stable, her home. Her friends would welcome her back to the pasture. He'd make sure Jed gave her grain along with her usual hay.

He pulled up beside the barn so he could unload his saddle bags. As he dismounted, he caught a glimpse of Blue, the barefoot sheriff, standing in the creek with Elinore. He'd cast off his coat and vest, wearing only a threadbare calico shirt and pants rolled up to the knees. The horse playfully splashed water at her companion. Blue bent over to gather water to splash back.

The damp shirt clung to his... her body.

No man would have such a firmly defined, nipped in waist spreading out and down to obviously feminine hips.

He needed to sit, dizzy with shock. He should let his mind catch up.

Neil's body twitched with delight, and longing. That banished his confusion.

So, this was Josie Blue's secret, the thing about him... er... her, that bothered him.

But why would she choose to deny her femininity?

She never corrected anyone who called her Mister.

He'd respect her choice for now. He needed a lot more information before he chose to reveal her secret.

His life just got more interesting, and more hopeful.

CHAPTER 12

I PACED. I didn't know what else to do. Daisy, Jonquil, and I had cleaned the office until we didn't know what else needed cleaning. A fresh dose of lime in the privy had robbed it of any leftover smell, even my most recent use of the place. The well water flowed clean through the pump. Not a flake of rust remained. It didn't taste sweet, like creek water, but it wasn't foul either.

I'd eaten some lunch—soup made from whatever Cook found left over in her kitchen at Rosie's—and sort-of-fresh bread and butter.

I had nothing left to do except pace.

The boardwalk outside had splinters that my feet did not appreci-ate. I tried the fleece-lined slippers. They had been thin when I first wore them. Now they offered less protection than two days ago.

"I am the Sheriff. I need to learn more about this town." I retrieved from the trash the wanted posters I'd pulled off the wall. A quick sort revealed that sixteen of the twenty offered minimal rewards for men I knew had died. One of them I'd shot myself when he tried to rob the chuck wagon cash box of a cattle drive. He'd been alive when I turned him over to the closest authorities, but later died trying to escape custody. Two posters were so old the criminals must be nearing one hundred years old and incapable of further criminal activity, if they still lived.

That left two who might go up on the wall. Jason Jacks didn't look much like his picture on the poster. He had grown much fatter and greyer than the chubby man portrayed. But the image and the reward were ten years old. Jacks had gotten meaner too. $500 for attempted armed robbery of a Wells Fargo coach was the least of his crimes. I had offered $5000 of my own money at the Pinkerton office for his capture or death. He'd started kidnapping and torturing young women and then demanding ransom money after he'd killed them. Not the most intelligent man. I hoped someone had captured or killed him. My reward for him had never been claimed as far as I knew.

So, I limped across the office to nail that poster to the wall, making sure to leave the door to the attic free of obstruction but still not openly visible.

When I returned to my desk, I reached for the pot of salve Doc had given me. It numbed the pain in my feet. At the same time, it numbed my feet from toe to ankle. Did I want to risk falling on my face because I couldn't find the floor?

I returned the little ceramic vessel to my desk drawer. The pink pot with flowers painted on the screw top reminded me of my sister's rouge. The memory stabbed my heart, not hard and painful as it had for nearly a decade. Now I found a bit of fondness as I traced the flower with a calloused fingertip. I closed the drawer on the pot and the memory.

I had only one wanted poster left. The one I'd saved for last.

Cutter Pine. My rescuer. My lover. We had joined the army together but assigned to separate units. He became my mentor and trainer during my first year with the Pinkertons after the war. I'd learned about guns and how to shoot them at my father's side, intending to become his ranch manager. I let Cutter believe I knew little. He didn't know about the four years I'd spent scouting enemy lines for the army—mostly on foot without the aid of a noisy horse. But he had coached me in training Elinore as my companion in the wilderness. Cow horses knew cattle, courier horses knew the fastest way between here and there, they didn't always know survival in strange situations.

Cutter Pine had nearly gotten me killed with his reckless abandon when we confronted danger.

He didn't work well as part of a team, something I'd learned leading my scouting party in the Army.

"I figured you'd gotten yourself killed by now," I whispered. I wanted to reach out and caress his handsome face on the poster. My mind filled in the missing details of dark hair, vivid blue eyes, thick beard shadow, and a small scar at the corner of his mouth where a remittance man in Colorado had punched him and his chunky signet ring had torn the sensitive flesh.

That was a bar fight I had nearly forgotten. I'd dressed myself in a nice gown with an immodest neckline, to please Cutter. The haughty Brit had claimed me as his own upon first sight. Cutter defended me. I could have taken down the man myself if the corset hadn't restricted my breathing and my body wasn't encumbered by yards and yards and yards of fabric and petticoats.

I wore the dress less that ten minutes before reverting to my usual trousers and calico shirt. I hadn't tried women's clothing since.

With rigid determination and self-control, I kept my hands in my lap as I read the details of the wanted poster. $10,000 reward, a king's ransom, for the capture or death of Cutter Pine for the crimes of... I choked. For the crimes of murdering a stagecoach driver and his guard, and grand theft of a mining company payroll in Nevada.

I didn't want to believe it. But I did.

"I'll wait to pin you on the wall until I've rested just a bit more," I told the poster, then slid it into the bottom right desk drawer.

The clock ticked over to three fifteen.

Footsteps pounded on the boardwalk.

The glass in the door rattled from a balled fist.

"Delivery for Sheriff Blue," a deep masculine voice called.

"Finally!" I said as I slowly rose from my chair, careful to equalize my weight on both feet so that neither hurt more than the other. "It's open," I called.

"Blue!" Lucian Whitmore greeted me, holding up a brown leather hat box with a blue ribbon around it, tied into a bow.

"You found a hat for me," I sighed in relief. The slight ache behind my eyes vanished with the knowledge that I'd no longer be squinting against the constant glare outside.

Some tiny bit of femininity deep inside me delighted at the idea of a new hat.

I grabbed the box by the handle on the top and thrust out my right hand to shake that of my friend. He bit off his riding glove and returned my greeting.

"Enough of that politeness. Give me a hug," Lucian proclaimed with his well-bred, educated English accent, similar to my mother's.

Gratefully, I melted into the tight embrace of my friend. The strength of his shoulders and upper arms infused me with warm memories of comradely evenings around a campfire, swapping stories, creating jokes, and outrageous puns, making stews out of freshly caught jack rabbits, or rattlesnake, and whatever supplies of flour and dried vegetables we could scrounge from our saddlebags.

Cutter Pine had been raised in the South before the war, with a minimal education, and had no liking for people of color. When forced by circumstance to patrol the wilderness with Lucian, he became surly and distant. He often retired to his bedroll, alone, before the evening was done.

I saw no difference made by skin color. Friends were few and far between in the wilderness. I cherished them all, black, white, brown, red, or yellow.

But not purple.

"What brings you to Heller's Hole in the back of beyond," I asked, limping back toward my desk, pointing to the uncomfortable straight-backed chair with the mostly intact cane bottom as an informal invitation for him to sit.

"Brotherton needed a courier. I was in the city. We both knew you'd be suspicious of a stranger and reject your packages as well as documents." He shrugged his black clad shoulders and took the offered seat, after he dusted it with his black handkerchief. "Now open my gift before you jump out of your skin with excitement."

He knew me well.

I obeyed. First, I caressed the leather box, top and bottom and all around the sides, an exquisite gift in itself with brass rivets connecting all of the various pieces, including a sturdy handle across the top and around the brass latch. Then I took my time untying the satin bow and ribbon.

"I can well imagine how anxious your family must have been Christmas morning when they could not take their turn opening a gift until you finished with yours," Lucian said on a yawn. But his dark eyes sparkled with joy.

"It's the only gift I've had in many years. Living rough in the field doesn't allow such luxuries," I replied, finally touching the latch.

"I know, *cher*. I know." His voice took on the lazy drawl of the New Orleans brothel where he'd been born. Fortunately, his white father had cared for him and his mother, keeping her as a cherished mistress for many years and given them his name. Then when Lucien was ten, he'd sent his son to school in England.

How he'd ended up in the far west working for the Pinkertons, I didn't know. That was a story for another long, fearful night sitting around a campfire, waiting for the enemy to strike.

To banish those thoughts, I applied gentle pressure to the latch and watched it pop open. Then I held my breath and lifted the lid.

Swaths of white tissue paper filled the top of the box, as any fine lady's hatbox should. Excited curiosity won over patience. I ploughed through the layers of protective paper to reveal the clean lines of a creamy white, Stetson. The finest hat ever made.

"It's beaver felt!" I said on a long exhale as I ran my fingers around the round, flat crown, and then the broad curved brim, luxuriating in the soft texture while appreciating the strong and tightly joined fabric. "It will last forever."

"As long as you don't lose it," Lucian said, laughing.

I coiled my long braid atop my head and placed the hat over it. The sun glare through the windows vanished, and my heavy hair stopped irritating my neck. My balance automatically shifted upright. "Ah," I sighed and leaned back in my chair. The chair back shifted with me.

"Don't fall asleep on me yet, Blue." Lucian jumped to his feet and shoved my chair straight up. "I have more boxes and bags for you that my pack pony surely wants me to dislodge from his overburdened back."

"More? I don't know if my poor heart can take that much excitement." I limped toward the door.

"Perhaps I should fetch one more box before we unload the rest." Lucian hastened ahead, pointedly not looking at my feet. "I can see now why they call you the barefoot sheriff." He pushed ahead of me and patted the noses of both his saddled mount and the pack horse, whose sides bulged with carefully roped together bundles. "Soon, my mates. I'll unburden you both soon," he murmured.

I studied the bays from the doorway under the shade of the overhang. One of Lucian's horses had a white streak running the length of his long nose, the other had a star. "Isn't that Blaze?" I pointed to the pack pony. "The horse you've been *riding* for the past three years."

He chuckled. "Yes, *cher*. And I will ride him again. No Name troublemaker is your new mount. I've been trying to teach him some manners on the long road up here."

"I've already purchased a No Name troublemaker stallion from the livery stable. He's been neglected and needs schooling more than that one does."

The starred gelding lifted his head, flicked his ears, and sniffed toward me long and hard. Then he turned his head away, no longer interested.

"He's looking back toward the livery stable like he'd rather be there, than here," I said. I'd considered venturing out of my office to exchange breaths with the gelding and get to know him. He'd made it clear that at least for now, his loyalty belonged elsewhere.

Maybe Elinore would show him differently. I wouldn't bring any mount into her herd without Elinore's approval.

"Boots!" Lucian proclaimed, holding up a pair of everyday riding and working boots with a low heel. No fancy tooling, just plain boots with a moderate point to the toe.

"Good boots?"

"Not the best. What was available on short notice. Custom boots coming."

"I sent off foot tracings with yesterday's mail," I said. "Perhaps they'll arrive in town before the bootmaker starts work on the order."

"Probably since I'm commissioned to take any mail back to the city tomorrow." Lucian inspected the still full packs. "But I brought stockings to fill in gaps and rough spots until the new footwear arrives." He held up another tissue wrapped package. "Finest cotton knit."

"Um... I have another... package for you to take to Brotherton. You're going to need to keep your packhorse." I led the way back into the office and aimed for the hidden door.

But I kept my hat on, too thrilled with it to hang it on the rack just yet.

NEIL HAD TAKEN the time to soothe his mother's histrionics, bathe, and change to clothing that didn't smell of horse and sweat and dust. Needing sane conversation and *good* food (Mother's cook pouted in her room refusing to cook until her employer calmed down and stopped changing her meal requests every five minutes) he wandered into Rosie's just as the sun set.

He paused a moment to watch the streaks of red and gold shoot through the gathering clouds. As the sky darkened to the east, he found himself holding his breath as he watched for hints of the circling purple lights he'd seen on the ridge outside the city.

The sky remained normal, holding its usual nighttime display of breathtaking red and gold beauty.

Pounding notes on the out-of-tune upright piano replaced the evening chorus of crickets and night birds. A wavering soprano tried to find a tune in the progression of chords.

He winced until his mind got used to the cacophony. Rising voices trying to speak above the... *music?*... gave him a bit of mental balance.

Gritting his teeth behind a welcoming smile, he pushed through the swinging doors. Not until the humid warmth of the interior engulfed him, did he remember that the equinox approached, and the air had begun to chill once daylight retreated. Soon his calico shirt and leather vest over denim trousers would not be enough protection against the elements.

"Mayor!" Rosie called to him from the big table in the back corner. She held up a pitcher of beer and an empty glass in invitation.

Neil nodded as he noted the faces gathered there.

Josie moved from the piano stool to her accustomed space, back to the corner walls where she could survey the entire room for trouble. The would-be soprano, Daffodil he thought, returned to the bar. Sheriff Blue immediately put her feet up on an adjacent chair, bare of course.

Neil chuckled inwardly at the soubriquet that had attached to her.

How could he ever have mistaken her for a man? Her long and narrow feet looked entirely too feminine and elegant to be encased in sturdy leather boots. Now that she'd had a few nights of rest and good food, she'd lost some of the gauntness of too many weeks of living rough. The planes and angles of her face had softened, never having endured a bristly beard or razor. In the right setting, with feminine clothes she'd be a right handsome woman. More striking than beautiful by modern conventions. But still, a woman who could charm a man with little artifice.

He found himself warming to the idea of working with her on a daily basis.

Sitting to Josie's left, Doc kept a strict six inches between his shoulder and hers. Clear evidence that the old horn dog had been put in his place. Had she used a right hook, or threatened him with a pistol or knife?

A lot had transpired since he'd left for the city last Saturday, three and a half days.

Then he noted the dark-skinned man he'd passed on the road

home sitting to Josie's right. He looked wary and alert with stiff posture leaning slightly forward and his gaze shifting constantly. Another Pinkerton observing the movements of everyone in the room. And likely listening for anyone above stairs or in the kitchen.

Slowly, Neil made his way toward the table where Sheriff Blue presided. He nodded and tipped his hat to the men who gathered at the close of the day. He knew them all.

They'd note who he talked to, where he sat, and how much he drank. Some would report back to his mother. Rosie and her girls would remain silent about all of their customers.

"Mister banker man," Josie said when he pulled out a chair and sat. 'Let me introduce you to Lucian Whitmore, an old friend."

The name Pinkerton didn't pass her lips.

"Pleased to meet you, sir." Whitmore stood and shook Neil's hand. "I believed you passed me on the road."

"Yes. Yes, I did."

"So, did you finish all your business in the city?" Doc asked.

"All of it, and a few personal errands."

"Are we getting that railroad spur?" Rosie asked, filling the empty glass on the table before him.

He took a long swig. Tea with Mother had done nothing to wash the trail dust out of his mouth. "We have hit an impasse there, Rosie. It looks like we will either have to find a different company to build it, or finance the construction and running of the line by ourselves."

"Oh." Doc's face fell. "We've tapped out all the investors we can find. That's a lot of money to pull out of the atmosphere."

"How much money?" Josie and Whitmore asked at the same time.

Neil considered the bare minimum needed against the paltry private funds available and added an additional forty percent to cover overruns and delays. He hadn't even considered the cost of an engine and freight cars.

He quoted the price, his voice barely above an embarrassed whisper.

"That's a lot of money," Doc said. "I don't know where we're going to find it."

Doc had put up a full quarter of the money needed. Neil had bought in with almost thirty percent. Mac da Foe had promised a hefty chunk but Neil didn't think he'd find the cash before the end of the year. All the rest had been dribs and drabs by the local folk, those who needed transportation the most.

Josie pulled a slim envelope out of her waistcoat interior pocket.

Neil hadn't noted the subtle charcoal grey garment embroidered with silvery rosettes. It suited her and the dignity of her job.

"Lucian brought me some interesting papers along with my new hat." She pointed to the pale Stetson hanging on the rack behind her, along with Whitmore's more battered black one.

"What kind of papers?" Neil sat straighter. His memory went back to his discussion with Brotherton. Now that he thought about it, the man had spoken of Josie with a note of affection as well as pride in his tones.

She slid the envelope across the table to him, without adjusting her posture. Those damaged feet apparently liked to remain elevated. "I'd like to open an account with your bank."

He opened the flap of the envelope. She'd broken the seal at some point, so he had no sense of violating her privacy.

"And I have a similar promissory note from our mutual employer," Whitmore said. "I've been assigned this region for my patrol route and am thinking about making this town my base of operations, maybe putting down some roots. Of course, any deposit I make to your bank will have to wait for my return to town in a few weeks."

Neil swallowed hard. He knew his eyes must be the size of saucers as he stared at the sum at the bottom of a long column of numerals. A quarter of the final figure would pay for the minimum amount he needed. If Whitmore contributed half that amount, the railroad spur line was a done deal. Heller's Hole would have easy transport of cattle, wool, and produce in exchange for manufactured goods, medicines, tools… and regular mail delivery.

"I'll have the paperwork ready for signatures first thing in the morning," he gasped, still staring at the letter with the Pinkerton letterhead.

"Bounty hunting for the Riders of the Purple Sage pays very well," Whitmore said, his white smile against his dark skin grew wider and spread to dominate his face.

"I wonder what Brotherton will pay for the mummy in my attic?" Josie said, hiding her smile behind a glass as she drank long and deep.

"What mummy?" Neil finally asked.

CHAPTER 13

SHIT! I screamed at myself.

That's what I got for dropping my guard because I was among *Friends*. And for drinking more than a single beer among *friends*.

My tongue got loose and my mind wandered.

In my agitation I slammed my glass hard against the tabletop and dropped my feet to the floor. The nearly scabbed over blisters opened again and sent knife slashes as high as my ankle.

It barely registered that yesterday the pain from inadvertent moves flew as high as my knee.

But the skin on my lower back pulled against Doc's neat stitches. I hadn't thought about that wound for hours. Walking delicately because of my feet kept me from jarring the more severe of my wounds.

I pressed hard against the muscle above the stitches, trying to hold everything in place and take the pressure off the incision.

Habit alone kept me upright. One did not give in to weakness in the field. That gave the enemy an advantage.

"What mummy?" Sanderson asked again. His hazel eyes seemed to penetrate my mind and disconnect it from my tongue.

"Doc?" I choked out, not sure what I needed to say.

"Lucian, you'd best show him," Doc said grabbing me by the arm and forcibly keeping me upright.

The pain was passing already. For the first time in ages, I'd continue to let people think I was in trouble so I didn't have to answer awkward questions. Fabricating stories around an almost truth was a skill Cutter had taught me early on.

"Is that wise?" Lucian asked. His words came out clipped and precise, and as English as if he'd just arrived from school in the old country.

"If he doesn't know already, he soon will. People talk to him more than me. And in this town, gossip is the only entertainment. It fuels society." He hauled me upright and eased me from behind the table, a barricade.

"Upstairs, Doc," Rosie ordered. "That way, the sheriff won't have to walk back here from your office after you finish whatever slicing and dicing you have to do." She came up on my other side, lending her strong arm in support. "I usually have to escort drunks and malcontents *down* the stairs rather than up," she muttered.

"I can walk," I said quietly out of the side of my mouth.

"No, you can't," Doc replied. "Let Lucian handle the mayor. He'll do it delicately after your little temper tantrum.

"Besides, this will give the town some more time to underestimate you," Rosie added.

"Underestimate me," I grumbled under my breath. "Good for a while. I'd rather they learn to fear me. Or respect me. Easier to keep order."

"Let them accept you first," Doc said. "They'll have so much fun speculating and spreading gossip, that by the time you need to earn their respect, with a touch of awe because of your expertise, you'll be a fixture in town, and they'll wonder what they did without you." He chuckled as he turned left on the landing, as if he knew all along precisely which room I'd started to call home.

NEIL FOLLOWED the Pinkerton agent up the narrow staircase between the walls of the sheriff's office. They each carried a lantern. Resident spiders fled before them. He heard no rustling or skittering of tiny rodent feet. Other than dust on the risers, he saw nothing to indicate a long time of neglect.

Outside an owl hooted and a coyote howled.

The town was alive while the two men scouted the darkness within.

"Have you known Blue long?" Neil asked. He didn't know how widely the sheriff had spread the knowledge of her sex and didn't want to release her secret if he didn't have to.

"A few years," Lucian replied. "We've fought beside each other often enough to know we trust each other. With our lives and our deaths."

Neil gulped and paused on the first step up. "What does that mean?"

"You were in the war?"

"Yes."

"Then you know about carrion eaters."

"Yes." Both the natural and the unnatural kind. And he never wanted to encounter either ever again.

"If one of us dies in the field, we respect each other enough to make certain we bury our dead deep enough, and cover them completely with a funerary cairn that nothing will disturb our graves."

Neil accepted that. "Good to know."

They climbed a few more of the steep and narrow steps. Only a glimmer of paler darkness at the top gave Neil the courage to keep moving upward. There was an end to this hidden stair.

"Why didn't I know about this secret attic?" he asked himself, not realizing he'd spoken aloud until he heard the words. "My father helped found this town," he added by way of explanation to the stranger above him.

"How old were you when he hired the first sheriff and built this office?" Whitmore countered.

Neil had to think about that. "About six. Mother and I lived in Portland prior to that. Father wanted to build and tame this mining town before he bought the ranch and moved us up here." They still lived in the town house and hired managers and hands for the property northeast of town.

He lost sight of Whitmore as he crested the passage and turned left into a larger space. The lantern seemed dimmer outside the tight confines of the stairwell.

"No need for you to know at that age," Whitmore said. "It may not have been walled off and secret at the time. My guess would be that the first sheriff lived up here."

"And the next sheriff walled it up to hide the dead body." Neil stepped into the low room. He felt like he needed to hunch his shoulders and duck his head to fit beneath the low, flat roof. His lantern helped him pick out the slit of a window that overlooked the paddock on the back side of the building.

Whitmore crouched beside the shadowy lump in the center of the floor. No furniture or discards littered the room. If it had been an apartment before being sealed off, no trace of the previous occupant remained. Whoever had left the unknown body up here intended it to remain here for a long time.

He smelled nothing of death or decay. Just dust. And salt. The natural dryness of the high desert would aid in the mummification process. He'd read enough about ancient Egypt to understand the process of deliberate preservation of bodies and how it differed from those found buried in the dry land.

Reluctantly, he set his lantern on the floor and knelt beside the corpse, careful not to smudge the salt line on the floor. The leathery skin and shrunken body robbed the man of identifying features, and his withered masculinity. Not that he'd recognize anyone from the time of his death. Six-year-olds tended to think strangers all looked alike unless there was something astoundingly different about them.

"Whoever laid him out, took his boots and hat," Whitmore said. "They also stripped him. Whether before or after death, I can't tell."

"Any jewelry or weapons?" Neil lifted his lantern again to get a wider circle of light.

"No. But the posture reminds me of something…"

"A diagram in an old college textbook… Leonardo Da Vinci I think." Neil mused. A wisp of fine, straight, white hair troubled him. Surely the man was not part of the clan of blond miners still living in the hills near the old copper works. Had anyone bothered to board up the opening after the veins of ore played out?

Or maybe…

His eyes shied away from the three toed lizard feet, and the suspicious hole at the top of his forehead. At least there were two eyes, making him less like the carrion feeders.

The moon rose enough to cast a glimmer through the glassless window, A silvery ray in a tight beam ended upon the mummy's head.

As his gaze moved, something odd in the color and texture of the floorboards caught his attention.

Silently he traced the white outline of the body to the lines forming five sharp angles surrounding the body.

Not just white chalk. Salt. Salt that both he and Whitmore instinctively avoided.

Atavistic fear filled him. What if…

"Whitmore." He gulped back hot bile. "I think we need to leave here. Now." He grabbed the neatly folded shirt from the pile in the corner and draped it across the single window, catching the fabric of nails hammered into the top corners of the frame. They might have originally anchored curtains.

Without waiting for his companion, he backed away, toward the stairs. Then he turned and ran downward, not caring if he stumbled and fell in the darkness.

"I'd rather die of a broken neck than whatever powers that *thing* wields."

"What? What did you see?" Whitmore breathed heavily behind him as they burst into the sheriff's office.

"There's a pentagram drawn on the floor inside a circle inside a square inside a triangle. The moon was about to illuminate the entire thing. I think the dead might reanimate if the moon hits it just right."

~

"WE CAN'T MOVE IT!" I whispered. My chin and hands trembled despite the numbing properties of the laudanum Doc had given me. My insides quivered and threatened to heave.

I flopped back onto my bed, not caring that the mound of pillows had scattered in disarray when I had abruptly sat up at Lucian's news.

"I don't like the idea of you working in the office with that *thing* staked out above you," Doc said. He fussed with the clasp on his bag, refusing to look me in the eye.

"It's been there a long time." Neil looked as shaken as I felt.

How could I work there knowing...?

"We have to leave it for now. The symbols surrounding it are the only things warding this town from the monsters," Lucian said calmly. He sat in the corner of my bedroom on a straight-backed chair. He kept his boots flat on the floor, ready to jump into action with a moment's notice.

Good habit for field agents. I should do the same.

If only my limbs didn't weigh more than Elinore. Each.

I drew in a deep breath to keep my mind from spinning out of control.

"Warding?" Neil looked puzzled. For all his fancy east coast education there were some things not taught in schools.

"You may be right." Doc sounded resigned. "I've lived in Heller's Hole for close on six years now. Not once in that time has there been a verified sighting of the monsters. We are just the right kind of place for them. So where are they?"

"Off the beaten track, limited communication with civilization, a scattered population... Who would notice if they swarmed and wiped us out?" Neil said quietly.

"They only feed on carrion," Lucian insisted.

"No, they don't," Neil and I said at the same time.

We looked at each other in wonder.

"That isn't… how do you know?" Lucian protested.

Doc looked skeptical as well. "In all the battles where I worked the surgeon's tent, not once did I see evidence of the one-eyed, one-horned, flying purple people eaters attacking a living person, unless they were already close to death. I dealt with plenty of wounded men. I watched at twilight as the aliens cleaned up a battlefield. I've even seen one of their purple ships flying in and out of those areas. But never have they attacked the living."

"There was a little-known battle in Texas, Santana Creek," Neil said. He stood slowly and began to pace, his hands worrying his dark blond hair.

"Never heard of it, and I've worked as a clerk in the records office," Lucian protested.

"Because the battle never happened." Neil sat. "I had to record the names of the dead. There were none, because no bodies were ever found on either side. A Confederate drummer boy managed to escape. He reported to a Union officer ten miles away that the night before, both sides were lined up and ready to fight a hopeless battle at dawn. Equal numbers. Equal armaments. Level ground. Neither had the advantage. Reinforcements for both sides were five days away. Both sides expected heavy losses, few to no survivors. During the night all the troops on both sides disappeared."

"And the drummer boy?" I asked quietly, not willing to disturb the near reverent quiet weighing heavily in the room. I felt for the boy. My own situation echoed his, the only survivor. I should have been at the battle site before the two sides met, counting people and weapons to report back to the reinforcements. But my corporal had fallen into a gopher hole and broken his ankle. My squad delayed moving forward until help arrived.

"The twelve-year-old ran at the first scream, watched a small band of the flying things descend and snap the necks of the men. They started on the outside and worked inward. In the darkness, the soldiers didn't notice their dead comrades until too late. The drummer boy was at a distance, so he noticed the pale golden glow around the bodies of the silent assassins. Only when the prey were all dead did a new wave of... aliens swoop in and devour the men, the officers, the camp followers, everyone. No one else escaped except him. No one wanted to believe him. But I read the report that accompanied the list of the dead. I had to strike their names from payroll, as if they never existed. General Sherman told me to bury the report, not notify the families, and never speak of it again."

CHAPTER 14

STUNNED SILENCE FILLED Sheriff Blue's bedroom. Doc wondered if she'd fallen asleep. But then she started mumbling as each of them relived their nightmarish memories.

They'd all held the secret of the monsters feasting on the dead too closely. Time they unburdened themselves. They all needed to share, find similarities, and figure out who in authority also held the secrets and might come to help the town of Heller's Hole should an emergency happen.

He'd start with the most troubled.

"You don't have to tell us everything, Sheriff Blue," Doc said quietly. He'd heard bits and pieces of her story as she wandered in and out of consciousness while he stitched up the wound across her back a few days ago.

The miniature purple flying thing implanted near her spine had been no bigger than a wasp and fully encapsulated in a thin membrane. Who knew how long she'd carried it. Maybe going back as far as her sister's wedding ten years ago.

He topped off her glass to keep her talking while Sanderson and Whitmore studied their own drinks, as if they could find answers, or wisdom, in the amber depths of the whiskey.

Doc tried to make sense of Josie's meandering tale. She'd only been fifteen at the time. Little more than a child. But being fifteen she'd sneaked several glasses of champagne, because she could. Then she'd crawled into a cupboard, thinking to listen to the increasingly ribald jokes and toasts, but fallen asleep instead.

That unplanned nap had probably saved her life.

"What time of day did the massacre occur?" Doc asked from the safety of ten years' time and the guarded corner room at Rosie's. He watched her down a good half of her whisky, then refilled her glass. Again.

"Sunset," she replied, barely above a whisper. "We'd had the wedding breakfast midmorning. The evening banquet was a farewell to all the men who'd enlisted and were due to report to duty a few days later. Everyone wanted to fight the goddamn rebs and be home in six weeks, end of the summer at the latest. Little did they know. Little did any of us know it would take four long years to bring them to an end to the war. Some still won't believe Lee actually surrendered to Grant. He turned over his sword for sharpening thinking the other general was a blacksmith."

A half-hearted chuckle rippled around the room. He was glad he'd banished Rosie soon after she'd put Josie to bed. The madame didn't need to know the sheriff's troubled history.

Knowing Rosie, she probably already did.

Doc did his best to banish the whisky fumes and remember the beginning of the story. Before, Josie had said the attack came during the wedding breakfast. An evening farewell banquet made more sense.

But first, the guests had to be dead because the aliens were still carrion eaters.

"What happened just before the attack, Josie?" He filled her glass, forfeiting his own portion of the whisky.

"Water rights feud. The Caron clan struck when they knew we'd all be gathered and half drunk. They sneaked in and shot everyone in one wave of," sniff, sob, "in one wave of blazing gunfire."

Doc didn't think a woman, a person, like Josie ever cried about anything, and never in public.

"They knew when to strike. One of the aliens had been watching the house. I saw him on the ridge. Then recognized him when they swarmed."

That was a new piece of information. Doc filed it away in the back of his mind for later examination.

"My family, the wedding party, were all armed," Josie continued. "Don't go anywhere, even somewhere safe, without a weapon at hand. No one left standing on either side," sob, sob. "Broke all the rules of engagement."

Where'd she learn that technical term? Obviously there was more to Sheriff Josie Blue than her lovely waist and luscious hips.

For the first time, in a very long time, Mathew Buchanan M.D. felt tenderness toward a woman, a need to enfold her with comfort and protection. Nothing sexual about it.

That shocked him, almost as much as the witch symbols warding the mummy in the attic.

"Sunset—twilight—makes more sense than full daylight," Sanderson mused.

"They took Josie's family before the war heated up and provided the monsters with plenty of carrion to fill their bellies. During the war, there were no sightings west of the Mississippi," Lucian added. "When I signed on with Pinkerton at the end of the war I followed the aliens west. I met Josie and Cutter Pine near Idaho Falls. Hunted with them for a while, until Cutter started going insane with his blood lust."

"Cutter... was always a little bit insane," Josie added. "More than a little bit."

"Who is Cutter?" Mayor Sandersen asked. "I've heard the name..."

"He rescued me from the cupboard after... after...." Josie gulped. "We went off to the war together. I became a scout. Don't know what he did. Pinkerton recruited us both, right after Appomattox. We followed the monsters together. Then I sent him back to Brotherton on his own." Josie clamped her mouth shut and turned her face away from the three men in her bedroom.

"Is he still alive?" Lucian asked. He looked around nervously, as if expecting the man to step out of the shadows.

"I haven't heard from or about him in over a year," Josie replied. "Maybe three years. There's a wanted poster for him in my office. Old one. Big reward. He shot a stagecoach driver during a robbery. You can ask Brotherton if it's still valid tomorrow when you deliver your report about the mummy in my attic."

"You're keeping... it?" Sanderson asked.

"No choice. We can't move the thing safely with those arcane wards in place. Brotherton will have to send his scientists here to measure and record and photograph it."

"Enough for now, gentlemen," Doc said, "Sheriff Blue needs rest and probably another stiff drink. Time to tackle this issue tomorrow."

She was already asleep, sitting up with her empty glass in hand.

Gently he pushed her back down into her nest of pillows.

DAWN TOOK its own sweet time in coming the next morning. My mind whirled and swirled with yesterday's events. I didn't like any of the probable outcomes of any course of action I considered. Chief among them that Robert Brotherton might dispatch Cutter Pine along with his scientists to study the mummy in the attic.

That would not happen if the wanted poster was still valid. While I truly believed Pine capable of murder, I knew the crime could have been part of an undercover operation. We Pinkertons were detectives for mundane crimes as well as paranormal ones.

Was Pine guilty as charged?

Did I really want to face that man yet? He'd been my savior, my mentor, and my first lover.

And nearly gotten me killed. Several times.

Every time he heedlessly rushed into battle felt like he'd abandoned me by leaving me alone and trapped to fight the enemy on my own.

I felt betrayed.

Before there was even a hint of night fading from black to grey I prowled the saloon, inside and out. In the strange half-light of the early hour, familiar furniture and hitching posts became looming monsters hiding in the deep shadows. The morning chill bit through my thin calico shirt and stabbed my bare feet. Autumn was definitely on its way.

In a bit, I'd pull on the soft, cotton stockings and test them against the almost healed blisters on my feet. Tender, new skin had covered the raw and bleeding spots. I thought I could stand the stockings pressing on the sore bits. Boots were still an unknown. But they were new and solid and cradled my feet when I'd tried them on yesterday. Lucian had found the bootmaker who had made my last footwear. He had an almost identical pair in stock.

Once the boots became comfortable, or at least more comfortable than the slippers I'd worn nearly through, I'd saddle up the stallion and teach him some manners. Then I'd move him to the paddock behind the office.

My office?

Not yet. Not until I eliminated the *thing in the attic.*

With the strange mummy complicating things, the ritualized nature of his positioning and the markings that contained it, strange frissons of primal fear coursed up and down my spine.

I boiled a cup of coffee and cradled my tin cup between my hands as I sipped at the thick brew, letting it warm me inside and out. As long as I didn't leave a mess in the kitchen, Cook made no objections to my early morning forays into the larder.

As usual, I watched the farmers and ranchers deliver supplies that kept the saloon running and offering the best food in town. The men tipped their hats to me. I returned the gesture with my new Stetson.

"Needs an eagle feather in that braided band!" called the dairyman as he set his can of fresh milk and a wheel of sharp cheese within the fenced holding platform.

"An eagle's feather?" I mused. "That would certainly be distinctive." But the native tribes in the area might object. They considered eagles sacred. Only chiefs, warriors proven in battle, were allowed to adorn their clothing and hair with such a wondrous and rare feather. "Well, I am a chief of the town's people and a proven warrior."

A tiny voice in the back of my mind, that sounded a lot like Cutter Pine in cadence and tone, whispered, *Do you really want to offend the Indians? You might need them as allies.*

"Right," I said aloud. "Time to test those boots and start riding. I need to check on neighbors and learn the lay of the land." All of it. Mummy or not. "Brotherton's scientists can't get here before tomorrow night. Lucian hasn't even left yet with reports and messages. If he could be pried out of Poppy's bed." The exotic brunette was the only dark-skinned girl employed by Rosie. Lucian had snagged her attentions early in the evening, and most likely joined her in her bed as soon as he left the meeting in my room.

Cook arrived and offered breakfast.

I agreed and gathered my tack while the bacon sizzled, and the flapjacks browned. Right afterward I'd test my new boots and the horse.

THE TOWN HAD JUST BEGUN to stir, merchants opening their doors, and people strolling out from their homes to complete errands. The horses at the livery stable began stomping and snorting as they looked for Jed Junior to break open a bale of hay and refresh the water in their troughs. Just to appreciate the aliveness of the town he called home, Neil paused a moment while he opened the back door of the bank with two keys for the double locks. He breathed in the cool air, the smell of breakfasts cooking, and the wind bringing the desert fragrance of sage and dust and a hint of moisture coming from the west. A cloud bank had begun to build over Mt. Hood. Perhaps the first autumnal rains would make it this far east tonight or tomorrow.

The clomp, clomp, clomp of horse hooves reverberated on the

packed dirt of the road. He looked up to see who of his neighbors headed down the street toward the south. Sheriff Blue of course. He saw first her white Stetson and the big buckskin stallion. She curbed the troublesome beast easily, moving with it, booted heels down and reins in a light, but controlling grip. Then he noted her new, double breasted waistcoat in tones of brown and gold. The tin star of her office displayed prominently over her heart on her fringed buckskin jacket, right in the middle of...

Best not let his thoughts stray there. He had to keep reminding himself that she still did not advertise her true sex.

I have too much work to do to think of such things," he reminded himself as he entered his bank. *His* bank at last.

Well, not quite his bank yet. He still needed Doc to visit with Mother and declare her incompetent to make crucial business decisions that could effect the financial health of the town.

He hoped that by the time Sheriff Blue returned from her ride he'd have organized all the papers for her to sign. Her personal accounts as well as her business investment. Only then could he write the letters necessary to begin building the railroad spur line into Heller's Hole with the options to extend the rails south to the next town and the next.

First things first. The moment his assistant entered he had a note ready to deliver to Doc requesting he visit Mother for morning coffee and question her closely.

"OF COURSE, the bank must foreclose on the Vulvich ranch!" Ethel Sanderson insisted, between sips of excellent coffee sweetened with fresh cream and turbinado sugar.

Doc savored his first swallow a long moment before replying. Neil's mother's cook prepared the best coffee in town. If today progressed as his friend the banker planned, he'd not likely be served in this house again.

"Mrs. Sanderson, Ivan Vulvich may be laid up with a putrid sore throat and lingering pneumonia, but he has two strong sons and three grandsons to work the land..."

"Nonsense. We must foreclose the loan now. They are late with their third quarter payment."

"Harvest season has begun. Their hay will bring good prices both here in town and the city." He took another sip of the excellent coffee, wondering if Rosie's cook could learn to make her own coffee this well.

"Not good enough. They can't harvest and sell the hay in time. The payment is late."

"There is also the matter of the double payment made last spring when they sold their wool to a big clothing manufacturer back east. Come spring and shearing season, they'll likely come close to paying off the loan."

"Presuming their sheep survive this coming winter. *My* ranch manager is preparing for a very harsh season. I see no signs of the Vulvich family making similar plans." Mrs. Sanderson set down the fragile bone china cup and saucer so she could place delicate jam tarts on her plate and nibble at them.

From the number of tarts on the platter, either the staff would have a hefty mid-morning meal, or Ethel would contribute to her own expanding waistline that could no longer be concealed by tightening her corset.

Doc surmised the latter. He grabbed three tarts himself, just so he'd have the joy of eating them before the town matron threw him out.

"When dealing with farmers and ranchers, timely loan payments have never been enforced. It's the nature of the business."

"That is of no consequence. Ivan Vulvich and his wife have always been pillars of the community. Their sons and daughters are prizes in the limited marriage market, though why Micha, the second son deserted proper behavior to marry that... that Nez Perce whore I do not know. For good, law abiding, *Christian* people we can overlook... certain discrepancies." She consumed another tart whole. Thankfully it filled her mouth so completely she couldn't speak for several long moments while she chewed.

Ah, the statement brought the conversation to the prime question in Neil's mind that he had suggested in his note to Doc.

"Christians? I was not aware…"

"They have deserted our church and become *Papists!*" his hostess shouted spraying crumbs hither, thither, and yon.

Doc gulped the last of his coffee and his second jam tart. He planted his feet flat on the floor, ready to flee.

"I have known many people who follow the old faith," he mumbled around the crumbs of his tart. "They are mostly good, God-fearing people, who respect our laws and harm no one."

"Don't be impertinent, Mathew Buchanan. You know as well as I do that *they* worship Satan and false idols. They are an insult to the entire community, and I will not have them taint my town!"

"Must I remind you that foreclosing on that family while there is still a reasonable assumption of repayment is illegal?"

He didn't want to mention that he'd been raised Roman Catholic by an Irish family in Boston until he went off to war. The horrors he saw there drove what little faith he had right out of his head and heart.

"That makes no difference. My family founded this town. My dowery funded the purchase of most of the property here. The law is what I say it is."

Enough said. Doc could sign a report of incompetency with a clear conscience. He quickly took his leave while seriously considering changing his Sunday morning church attendance. Heller's Hole might very well be a carbuncle on the arse of the state, but the quaint and sturdy Catholic Church, and Father Xavier, its gentle priest, seemed the one bright spot around.

CHAPTER 15

"Whoa, whoa, easy boy," I commanded the big buckskin stallion beneath me. It had taken me the better part of a week working with him on a long line to get this far.

I'd also doled out treats with a lavish hand when he behaved and withheld them when he asserted his very strong will.

"I know you've had training, and then been abandoned. You find it hard to trust any two-legger. I know. But you can trust me. I've written into my will plans to care for you and Elinore. Dead is the only reason I would abandon you."

He stamped and tightened the muscles of his back and a small hump formed beneath my seat as he shifted his back within the confines of the saddle. My hands remained passive, sensing how he chewed the bit and pulled against the reins. Then he tossed his head. Testing. Testing. We tested each other.

Elinore watched from the safe and comfortable creek. She flipped her ears and narrowed her eyes. Then she snorted at him and returned to grazing the sweet grass at the far edge of the streambed.

I could almost hear my companion and friend admonish the stallion for his bad behavior.

He settled, accepting my weight on his back and the confines of the bridle and bit.

"Easy, boy. That's it. You know how to do this."

He shook his head vigorously in one last attempt to have his way.

"Please don't give me any trouble," I whispered. He didn't want to relinquish control to a mere human.

I eased him into a gentle walk. An uneven gait. I tapped his sides softly, repeatedly with my legs as I urged him forward. I had to convince him that following my wishes was more fun than trying to unseat me. I kept him at an easy walk through the gate to the street and then south to the heart of town.

"I'm sheriff now and need to set a good example," I explained to my horse. Since intelligent Elinore had come into my life, I'd always talked to my mounts as if they were equals and partners. This guy cocked an ear as if listening.

"Good boy. We don't want people to get the idea they can race through town upsetting other animals and wagons. I am sworn to protect and serve, and therefore so are you."

That earned me another snort and vigorous shake of his head. I felt his muscles rippling with the need to run and burn off his belly fat.

I kept my sedate pace past the bank, tipping my hat to Neil Sanderson when he stepped out onto the boardwalk. Then I made myself peer at the windows of my office. The rising sun reflected back onto the street so that I could see nothing of the interior. The place looked quiet and empty. No ghosts or mummies walked during daylight. The office was safe for me and for the townsfolk. If I told myself that often enough, I might come to believe it.

Across the street, Rosie's looked equally quiet and empty. Only Cook stirred this early and she was occupied in the back of the building, no sign of activity out front. Doc's office and the brick Catholic church, St. Agatha's, came into view next. The Baptist church/schoolhouse building was back nearer the livery stable. I'd been too busy with Horse to notice activity there, though soon the town's few children would troop to the doors for their first lessons of the day.

"I can't keep calling you Horse. And I don't want to call you Trouble lest you feel obligated to live up to the name," I mused as we passed the last few buildings in town—mostly residences, neat and tidy but not overly large or grandiose. They probably belonged to merchants. I'd learn who lived in each of them soon enough. Then a grander home on the edge of town, set back from the road, came into view. "Probably our prosperous banker and mayor lives there."

From the gossip about Mrs. Sanderson, I expected nothing less than the white paint with maroon shutters and dark pink trim. The place looked sleepy, shuttered against the passing night. Yet I knew that Neil Sanderson had already risen and gone to work.

"Prosperous. Prospero!" I patted Horse between the ears as I said the name dragged out of some forgotten recess in my mind from a long-ago lesson. My governess at the time had been a great reader and tried desperately to instill her love of literature into me. My sister Eva had appreciated the books and stories. I took more interest in arithmetic and managerial skills. At the time, I hoped to take over the ranch and let Eva dance, dress in the latest fashions, and carry on witty conversations with prospective bridegrooms.

"Do you like that name, Prospero?" I asked the horse. "I think that man was an arrogant and demanding magician. You've certainly worked some magic on me, making me feel alive and well again."

The land opened up. I guided Prospero into a trot, and then when I could no longer see the town behind me, I gave him free rein.

He leapt into a full gallop, edging off the pounded dirt of the rutted road onto the rabbitbrush and safety of the plateau.

Wind threatened to rob me of my fine new hat, so I pulled the stampede chin strap tight and ducked my head.

Hardly necessary. Prospero hadn't been ridden or run in months and had lost some stamina. Less than a mile and he slowed back to an easy trot, shaking his head with... joy at the exercise, and gratitude toward me for allowing him the freedom to do what he needed to do.

A narrow track veered off the main road to our left. Out here, in the back of beyond, a track always led somewhere. Since this was the first such trail, I decided to follow it. "Time to meet the neighbors."

AND MEET the neighbors I did. The Russell family erupted from their tidy little house. I later learned their names, Ed and Vicky followed by Eddy, Mary, and Tom. The latter three each caught a sturdy range pony from the pasture out front, flung themselves onto the beasts' bare backs, and rode off toward town and the school. Only the oldest boy carried a book. The other two clutched slates.

I dismounted, taking a long look around as I did.

Vicky sat on the recently painted top step of her porch and sagged, her back curved and her head drooped. Ed stepped forward with an extended hand while he surveyed both me and Prospero. We exchanged names as we shook hands.

"I know that horse," Ed Russell stated, not moving toward the house or his beleaguered wife. "He threw me only time I tried to ride him."

"Prospero wanted to throw me too. I wouldn't let him. He's much better behaved after a few soft words, a treat, and a good ride," I replied.

I thought about extending the conversation, but my feet already felt swollen within the confines of my boots. "I'm the new sheriff." I pointed to the tin star pinned to the left shoulder of my leather coat. "Making the rounds, wondering if all is well out here." Only a mile or so out of town. Too close to help for serious criminals to pose much threat.

But the aliens? Were they so desperate that they'd attack this small family?

"Rustlers took the last of my cattle last week," Ed replied, scratching his patchy beard. "Scrawny and rangy critters. Not worth much. I'm keeping to sheep for now. No one steals sheep."

Sure enough, the sound of bleats and horns banging against the fence came from the back forty. One feisty ram didn't take to something in the movement of the other blobs of cream and black, too far away to make out much detail though.

"Too much work for thieves to keep them together, 'less they've got a good dog."

The floppy eared family mutt ambled toward us from the back of the house, tongue lolling. But his ears remained stiffly upright, and his eyes focused on me and my horse.

If he were here at the house, the sheep must be safe—the only danger coming from the ram's temper tantrum.

Still, warning tingles crawled up my back. Cattle thieves usually were looking for quick cash, to sell their ill-gotten gains to someone gathering a herd to drive to the railhead. Scrawny beasts, this time of year, were likely sick and not worth a plug nickel.

I held my hand out, palm up for the dog to sniff. He did so, then sat at my feet willing to accept a scratch between the ears. I did so and knew I'd made a friend.

"Are you certain they were rustlers and not a predator?"

"Only saw a cut fence line. No sight of hide nor hair of the cattle. Coyotes, wolves, and mountain lions usually leave the skull, hoofs, and horns." Russell shook his head in dismay. "Glad we got a sheriff around now, someone to report things to, maybe gather a posse to ride down the bastards."

"Ed, be polite and invite our guest in for coffee, maybe a bit of bread and butter. Haven't had time to bake up them apples you picked yesterday over at the Miller place. They ain't around anymore to object to the neighbors gathering apples from their neglected trees." Vicky stood slowly and turned to go back inside.

In profile, the reason for her listlessness became obvious in her rounded belly.

I hadn't been around pregnant women much to know how big she should be, but it looked to me like the woman was ready to explode. I wondered if I should ride hell bent for leather to notify Doc.

"Thanks for offering, Ma'am." I tipped my hat. "But I've too many people to see and miles to ride. Just stopped to introduce myself. You need me, you can send one of your children to my office with word."

Trying not to wince as I placed my foot in the stirrup, I mounted

Prospero. The horse seemed ready to run again now that he'd had a bit of a rest.

"Don't bother with the Miller place, just beyond that orchard you can see at the edge of my pasture, and across the road. House and home farm are down in the sheltered vale to the west. Got a nice creek for the family and to water the trees. Rarely freezes early so the fruit's not damaged before harvest. Nice set up. They packed up and left one night a month or so ago, without a word. Gossip at the general store says the bank was about to take the place back. Old man Sanderson is one mean bastard. Two days late with a payment and he forecloses. No notice. Nothing." Russell spat into the dirt.

"Interesting," I replied as I guided Prospero back the way we'd come.

"IF YOU EVER TOUCH HER in anger again, I'll have your hide!" I shouted at the grizzled war veteran on the porch of the next property I visited. I tossed his wickedly long Bowie across the dirt yard as I spoke.

The knife's bone grip looked well worn, but the blade itself had been recently honed to a razor's sharpness.

He still wore his Union Army threadbare uniform jacket with a corporal's two stripes sewn to the sleeves.

A once lovely, but now care-worn woman cringed in the shadows of the overhang, cradling her right arm against her chest.

"She's m'wife. I kin treat her as she deserves!" the short man who hadn't shaved or bathed in a year, at least, and with breath that smelled of stale whisky, shook his fist at me and the six shooter I aimed at his heart. He'd probably faced down enemy fire more menacing during the war, as evidenced by his peg leg and an eye made useless by scarring.

He might have a right to be angry at the world. That didn't mean he had to take it out on his young wife.

"Interfere with my rights again and I'll have the law on you!" he edged backward, not out of fear, but to put him closer to the double-barreled shotgun leaning against the clapboard wall of the single room cabin.

"In case you haven't noticed, I am the law," I announced. I took a step closer to the not old, but ancient looking man, putting myself between him and the now weeping woman.

She hadn't said a word, only screamed in pain when I was still at the other end of the open pasture that contained two dozen sleek and fat dairy cows. The man had twisted the woman's arm behind her back while holding a knife to her swollen belly.

I had heard the bone snap.

"Heard about you. The barefoot sheriff," he sneered. "How's a man who can't afford boots supposed to protect anyone, even hisself?"

I decided to ignore the insult. But I was mighty tired of being called the Barefoot Sheriff. "And as the law, I order you to harness up your wagon and take your *wife* to the doctor in town. I'll follow along to make sure you do."

My feet ached, swelling painfully inside the now too-tight confines of stiff boots. I longed to get off my feet. Maybe I'd ridden too far on my first day out. My beautiful new boots pinched my toes and rubbed my heels. And my back ached along the slash of the stitched-up wound. My own discomfort made me angrier than I cared to admit. This abusive farmer didn't help my mood or my temper.

"Cain't do that, Sheriff." He spat at her feet. "The ride into town will kill my babe." He looked too damn smug.

"And you cutting across her belly wouldn't do worse?" I muttered a few curses in Nez Perce, hoping he couldn't understand the insults behind the foreign words. *Damn!* He was an ignorant bully, taking out his own incompetence on his wife because she was weaker, vulnerable, and here.

I backed up two steps until I stood next to the woman. Then, still aiming my pistol at the man, reached down and released a smaller weapon from my ankle holster. This, I handed to the woman. "It's got two shots. Aim for his heart."

The woman trembled so badly she probably wouldn't hit anything she aimed at. But she might scare him enough to back off.

In the canny way of horses, Prospero shifted his body and attention from the trough beside the hitching post to the nearest patch of grass for grazing, out of line of sight from the angry man. The reins dangled near his feet and his training, which young Jed had told me about, meant he wouldn't wander far. The woman would have to work hard at shooting the horse rather than her husband.

"Now I'm going to set that break and splint it with some of that kindling you dropped when he hurt you. It's all I know how to do. You'll still need to see Doc Buchanan to make sure I do it right. Otherwise, you'll lose the use of that arm and won't be able to cook or clean or mind the chickens for that worthless piece of shit you call husband."

"Now wait a minute. I'm a good husband. I take care of her."

I glared him into submission.

"Most of the time. I wouldn't have hurt her, but Daisy's milk dried up overnight. I got orders to fill and not enough milk to fill them. I just got so angry I saw red. Nothing but a red haze thick enough to be the center of Hell. Had to lash out... at the first thing I saw." He hung his head in shame.

"What does a dry cow have to do with breaking your wife's arm? If you really take care of her, you'd not hurt her, not for love nor money nor to save your own life!"

The woman raised her pain-filled and tear-glazed eyes to me and nodded slightly. She knew what was going on. "It's just that his leg still hurts, even though it's not there anymore."

"So, he has to make sure you hurt too. Even to the point of killing you and the babe?"

I knew what a murderous rage felt like. I also knew that once started nothing stopped it short of being knocked unconscious. It had happened to me a time or six when I'd first started scouting for Colonel Martine. I didn't want to report the movements of the enemy, I needed to murder them all! They were as bad as the Caron clan who'd murdered my family, leaving them to be ravaged by the purple *things*.

The one-legged man suffered from the same ailment. He saw

nothing, heard nothing, felt nothing but the need to spill other people's blood when a fit of anger overcame him.

I muttered some more curses, in English this time, wanting him to hear the words ignorant and idiot.

"He allow you the dignity of a name of your own?" I asked, holstering my weapon and turning enough to glare at the man. He listed to the right, his wooden left leg probably chafed an improperly healed amputation.

"I... I'm Mariah and he's Josiah. Dayton," she whispered.

I had to strain to hear her. "You give that name a bad reputation," I snarled. Josiah was the name most people presumed I carried, rather than the Josephine entered in the family Bible. Josephine Louisa Baumgarten existed only on the official death certificate Cutter had issued when he helped me through the aftermath of the slaughter of my family.

I still didn't know how or why Cutter just happened to be passing by in time to rescue me from the claustrophobic cupboard.

Cutter had kept my real name alive only long enough for me to claim my inheritance and transfer everything to a series of banks from Seattle to San Francisco. After the war, Brotherton and his accountants had found ways to register all of my assets—including the Pinkerton-managed ranch—to Josie Blue.

"Are you ready, Mariah? This is going to hurt, but just for a bit."

The woman lifted wide and frightened eyes to meet mine and nodded.

"Bite down on this." I slid a piece of kindling between Mariah's teeth.

She nodded her acceptance of the coming pain.

I gritted my teeth, braced my aching feet and pulled sharply on Mariah's arm until it straightened fully, and the bones clicked into place.

Mariah screamed again and fired one bullet into the side of the house. She almost smiled in relief as her pain lessened.

"Now, are you going to take her to see the doc or am I going to haul her up to ride pillion behind me, Josiah?" Deftly, I tore two long strips of cloth from the hem of Mariah's apron and tied the make-shift splint in place.

Prospero placidly grazed on the grass outside the fence line.

"But the babe? She's but five months gone. Riding in the farm wagon will jostle it out of her," Josiah protested. "We tried a long time for that babe to catch…" His concern wiped a few of the winkles from his gaunt cheeks and brow. He looked closer in age to his wife now. Probably his own pain had aged his appearance. With a swallowed gasp I realized his hair and beard were almost as colorless as his pale eyes. He looked a lot like the mummy in my attic, with only a little more flesh clinging to his bones.

War did that to some men.

"Riding in your wagon will jostle her less than riding on my stallion. Take your pick. Walking four miles into town might kill you both."

"I'll hitch the wagon. Could… could you please gather some pillows and blankets to make Mariah comfortable, lessen the jolts?"

The man's anger had dissolved, and his humanity restored.

"Say, Sheriff Blue, ain't I seen you somewhere a'for. During the war?"

"Maybe."

"You was that crazy ass scout what tried to shoot a shavetail lieutenant in the balls when he tried to tell you how to track the rebs' passage down a straight ass road."

"Yeah, I did that a time or three."

War had done that to me.

CHAPTER 16

N<small>EIL</small> <small>TAPPED</small> his fingers on his desk in an irregular pattern. No rhythm, just taps.

He'd watched Josie ride out hours ago. Since then, Lucian had come by to sign an authorization for a new account. Doc had thrown a report on his desk validating that Mother was no longer fit to make business decisions. He did not linger. O'Toole had delivered a telegram that Father and Jack Epps, his caregiver, would leave Portland on the 10:00 train tomorrow or the next day. Expected to arrive in Pendleton by 3:00 PM that same day. They would spend the night, or three, in Pendleton depending upon Father's fatigue, and start for home the next morning. Typical. Neil suspected the delays depended upon the availability of a poker game.

The postmaster sat and wanted to gossip. Neil handed him three letters to be mailed, postage to be billed to the bank.

Neil was not looking forward to telling Mother about Doc's report or Father's return.

And still Josie did not ride back into town. This was her first ride since arriving last Friday, and her first on a new horse with a reputation for causing trouble.

His clerk, Martin had heard all about Josie Blue's attempts to settle the troublesome stallion. Gossip about her training sessions traveled through town faster than the wine.

Had the horse thrown her?

Had her wounds reopened and caused her too much pain to remount and return home?

Was she still alive?

He began to pace, neglecting his work and the customers lining up to do business with his teller. A few long steps took him outside, still in his shirtsleeves and hatless. He had to keep his eyes closed against the sun glare while he filled his lungs with fresh air. Still his innards bounced with anxiety.

The sheriff's office across the street already had the listless air of abandonment. All because Josie Blue was not there.

And she might have gotten into trouble with that fractious horse. And her old wounds. And her raw feet that had led her to the nickname of the Barefoot Sheriff.

He didn't need thought to direct his steps to the stable after he gathered his jacket, his hat, and his smoke-colored spectacles. And his small pistol, retrieved from home last night. Commandeering his own mare Molly that he kept stabled at the livery when he lived in town, he headed south in the direction Josie had traveled.

His bank and his mother could wait. He'd tend to them when he knew Josie was safe.

Now, those were thoughts he did not want to explore. Yet. Dealing with his mother would be more pleasant.

AHEAD OF ME on the road, I watched the Daytons pass the trail to the Russell place. There was nowhere else to turn off, or turn around the clumsy farm wagon, before reaching town. I let them go and retreated to the overgrown track that should lead me to the abandoned Miller place west of the road.

Ever since the Russells had mentioned their neighbors, something about the place intrigued me. The story of Neil's father evicting them for a late loan payment did not ring true.

Too easy to blame an absent banker than face the truth.

The heady scent of fermenting apples greeted me long before I caught sight of a building. Ed Russell had said they'd picked apples so they wouldn't rot and go to waste. Then the first few orchard trees came into view, limbs laden with bright red fruit. My mouth watered. I hadn't eaten or drunk since leaving town early this morning and it neared noon.

Prospero responded eagerly to my prodding and diverted our path to the first tree. He munched greedily at the fallen fruit, big teeth making easy work of chewing through the crunchy flesh. I picked two right off the tree from my place in the saddle. The first bite tasted like ambrosia, or fine wine, or all my worldly desires rolled into one mouthful.

I forgot my swelling feet and aching back for a few moments. I hadn't eaten fresh fruit in a very long time.

The rumbling in my belly warned me that too much would undue all the healing that half a week of good food and rest had done.

Reluctantly I steered Prospero away from the midday treat and back to the track.

No footprints or hoof marks showed on the dried mud of the road. The grass in the center above the wheel ruts and on the verge grew wild and had gone to seed. That didn't stop my greedy horse from grabbing a few mouthfuls along the route.

We crested a hill and finally saw the rusting tin roof of a structure. The house and barn stood beside each other in a disconnected L, nestled in a vale protected from wind and observation by orchards stretching into the distance.

The air around the place smelled... empty of human presence, or care, though a lot of love had gone into the design and building of the place. Bright geraniums, leggy and wilted had once graced the window boxes. Intact glass still gleamed in the many windows, their shutters open. A bench beside the front door still shone with years of polish. Worn leather boots stood upright beside the mud scraper.

No chickens scratched for bugs in the yard. Livestock did not call from the barn, off to my right and set at a right angle to the house.

I dismounted cautiously, hitching Prospero's reins around the porch railing.

I turned a full circle before mounting the steps. When working in the field I'd learned to extend all of my senses for watchers. Nothing. Not even ghosts. I heard birds twittering and crickets chirping. They'd be silent if humans or aliens invaded their territory.

I took the three steps up to the porch that ran the length of the home. Easy to imagine a family sitting out here of an evening, watching the sun set, letting a cool breeze fan their sunburned faces, and absorbing the wonderful contentment of completing a good day's work, and knowing this place, above all places on earth, this place was home.

A dull ache in my gut and in my head reminded me that I'd had that once. And I'd lost it all. Not only had the purple monsters robbed me of my family, I'd lost my home as well.

For nigh on ten years I felt like I didn't deserve to rebuild what had been taken from me.

In that moment, I fiercely craved a home.

Shaking off the reverie, I peeked in through the front windows. I couldn't see much because of the shady overhang. The door was unlocked when I tried it. Feeling only a little anxious at intruding on someone else's privacy, their home, I pushed open the door to reveal a long room with stone fireplaces on each end. Furniture made from rough branches, not planed planks, and polished with love and wear lay strewn about, as if thrown. Chairs upended, leather upholstery on the sofa ripped and the stuffing scattered. A large table upside down with tin plates and cups on the floor. Food and drink spilled about.

A pair of mice squeaked and ran off, carrying food in their cheek pouches. They were clear evidence that humans no longer dwelled here.

I shuddered at the implied violence of the chaotic furniture. With effort I suppressed the still vivid memory of the disrupted banquet ten years ago when my family had raised glasses of champagne in toast to newlywed Eva and her groom and all the other young men present who would soon go off to war in the east.

With a gulp to banish my tears, I followed the trail of destruction to the kitchen and a bedroom at the back of the house. A broken ladder should have invited me to a loft opening, probably to more sleeping space for children.

My God! Children had lived here.

I gulped and began the work I had trained for, all the while listening for a cautious or hesitant step. What had happened here?

A meal interrupted.

Anger fierce enough to demolish furniture.

People fled leaving a man's boots on the porch.

But no blood spilled.

I retreated to the barn. No sign of livestock. An open chicken coop, no horses or goats in the stalls inside.

Where had they all gone?

Who would know?

Neil Sanderson could tell me if he'd foreclosed and had the family run off. That didn't explain the boots.

Prospero whickered a question at me. I moved to his side, running my hands down the length of his neck, finger-combing his dark mane.

Questions plagued my mind. And still the place called to me, wanting to welcome me.

It needed a resident.

As if a house had a soul and intelligence.

Prospero soothingly rubbed his cheek along my face. Elinore would love this place with an open pasture and apples to gorge on. A creek chuckled behind the barn. The wind ruffled the strands of my hair that had come loose from my braid.

In the bright blue sky above, a hawk circled and screeched a welcome.

And then it shed a tail feather. The red and brown plume fluttered down lazily, exploring the air around me. It landed at my feet. Clean, pristine, elegant, a status symbol but not as prestigious or controversial as an eagle's plumage.

I bent to pick it up before it got dirty.

It fit elegantly into my hat band.

"Looks like we've found a home, Prospero."

CHAPTER 17

A FLASH of movement caught Neil's attention. He'd been studying the verge to the right and left of the road, seeking signs of disturbance, like Josie's body crumpled into lifelessness after being thrown by a horse known as Trouble.

He resisted the urge to draw his pistol and adjusted his hat brim instead. He squinted a bit to give him better focus on the cluster of brush to his right, near the drop off. His hat brim shaded his eyes enough to make out creamy hide with a dark mane and tail.

Then wisps of brown shone through the tree leaves lining the trail to the Miller place.

He held his breath a few more moments until he was certain Josie rode the big, rangy horse upright, and not slumped over.

"Halloo!" he called. Suddenly he felt lighter, and he breathed easier.

She jerked her attention in his direction while directing the horse to take the turn onto the road.

"Banker Neil Sanderson," she said. "Just the man I need to see." She tipped her hat, making sure he noted the long feather tucked into the braided band.

"Nice addition." He nodded to her. His gaze measured her from hat to… bare toes barely resting in the stirrups.

"My sheriff is barefoot again," he said, feeling deflated.

"Yeah, I wore the boots too long for the first time. They are in my saddle bag. But Prospero and I have reached an accord. He doesn't mind me taking control as long as I keep my balance in the saddle."

"Prospero?" He felt like an idiot parroting her. It seemed her day had been crammed full of events and he had a hard time catching up.

"He seems to like it, and it fits. Authoritative, arrogant, and powerful, but a sweetheart underneath, and very eager to please." She reached forward and patted his neck.

The horse lifted his head and cocked his ears, begging for more attention.

"Are you okay to ride him... like that?" He pointed to her feet—long and narrow, elegant feet. "I saw the Daytons drive into town, I could send them back with their wagon."

"Nope. You leave them be for now. I'm fine. Tell me about the Miller place while we ride back to town." She urged Prospero forward with a click of her tongue and a shift forward with her weight.

The horse obeyed her command.

What?

Neil had ridden the beast a couple of times. Or rather tried to. He'd dismounted and chosen another horse. Easier than fighting him every step of the way into the city.

"The Miller place?" Josie pulled him out of his disdainful contemplation.

"If I remember correctly, Prospero, the magician, was as much trouble as that horse. That's why he was exiled to an island." He turned Molly, his placid mare, around so he could ride beside the sheriff.

Josie laughed out loud.

He liked the sound of her laughter and the way she crinkled her nose when carefree.

"Oh, this guy will be trouble to anyone he doesn't like." She patted the horse's neck again.

"That would appear to be everyone but you. Should I start calling you Ariel?"

She laughed again. "I'm too tall to be a dainty sprite. Now about the Miller place. Why is it abandoned?"

"It is?" he asked in genuine surprise, half turning to look back toward the track. His hand itched to unholster his gun.

"Yes. Outside looks normal, tidy, well cared for but devoid of livestock, not even a chicken or a stray cat. Barn is empty too, except for a few rodents scurrying under the moldering hay. Inside is a wreck, broken furniture, and food left uneaten, as if their last meal was interrupted. Violently."

Memory of the strange mummy stretched out in the attic of the sheriff's office triggered his gag reflex. He choked down the bile. "Y... your conclusion?"

"Judging by your suddenly pale face, mine is the same as yours. An attack by the carnivorous aliens that leave nothing behind, not even blood. Sometimes they even eat the heavy bone of cattle skulls and their horns. Clothing and boots feed them too."

"You've dealt with them before." His voice sounded flat even to his own ears. Of course she had. They'd talked about it a few nights ago night.

"That's been my *job* for nigh on seven years. I've killed dozens at a time when they swarm. But they are growing bolder and more cunning." She gulped and blinked rapidly as if banishing tears.

"Still only males in a swarm. No females except a rare one-eyed witch."

Before he could reach out and touch her in compassion, she straightened and shook off her dire mood. "So, if the place is empty, why is it empty? And who owns it? The bank, I presume."

"I'll have to check the records, see the terms of their loan. Many of my customers borrow money to start a ranch or farm and keep it operating until harvest. When they have cash, they repay the loan and set up a new or extended one to carry through to the next year. If they've been gone less than a year, I have no reason to notice them until the loan is a month or more in arrears."

"It's harvest time. They should be picking apples by the bushel load so they can sell them and repay their loan. A lot of apples are going to waste..."

"I have to find their next-of-kin so that you, the sheriff, can notify them," he countered.

"Any reason I can't move in and start picking the apples, pressing them into cider... and learning to bake with them?"

"As sheriff, and my representative you can take charge of harvesting and selling any crops. I can't authorize you moving in." He had to stall, had to keep her in town a little longer. If she moved into the farmhouse, a mile and a half from town, he might never see her again.

"Can I trade the crops for livestock replacement? I'm thinking a laying hen should be worth a bushel of apples."

"Not yet." Think, think, think. "Not until we hear from next-of-kin, and I have authorization to sell." If only he could remember if the Millers had relatives in the area who might want to take over an orchard that was a going concern and making money.

His father had always handled that particular loan, even after he began spending months on end in Portland. Something about old Roy Miller—the father of the current owners—and Father had attended Willamette University in Salem together. And now Father was coming home. Would he demand to oversee the disposal of the property?

He would have five years ago as part of his plan to own the entire valley.

Or was that Mother's plan?

"Saturday night is coming up fast. I know that Rosie wants you staying at the saloon and keeping order."

Josie glared at him while she thought up a rebuttal.

He knew the moment she decided against continuing the argument. Her horse fidgeted and tried to turn back toward the farm. She winced as the stirrups chafed her feet.

Neil relaxed, knowing that his sheriff would stay in town a few more days at least.

"I suppose Brotherton will be sending his scientists to inspect our mummy any day now. I should stay in town at least until they leave," she said, adjusting her hat so the westering sun didn't penetrate beneath the brim. It also put a barrier between her and Neil. He couldn't see her face.

Might be for the best. Neil's eyes had gone beyond ache to near blindness. The smoke-colored spectacles did little to ease the pain. He closed his eyes, trusting his placid mare to find her own way home and not buck him off for the sin of inattention.

"Be grateful you can sleep at Rosie's and not in the office with that thing right above you," he mumbled, just to keep the conversation going.

"Do you happen to know if you have any Basque sheepherders in the area?" She pulled her bare feet free of the stirrups.

Proof positive that she wasn't healed enough to manage the orchard just yet.

"There is a clan working the high meadows to the southeast of town. They bring their flocks down for the winter. Come into town once in a while to stock up on supplies. Maybe attend Mass at the Catholic Church. Mostly keep to themselves. Why do you need Basque?"

"They know magic to keep the aliens away and cleanse the land after a massacre. Might be worth letting them winter at the Miller's place so they can remove any taint on the land."

DOC CLOSED his eyes and let his fingertips tell him about Mariah Dayton's broken arm. He found the break easily beneath the swelling. The tension in her entire body told him when he found the source of the pain. Ah, a second fracture, more likely a crack than an actual break, but still painful.

"Sheriff Blue did a good job. I'll just replace these twigs with flat splints. They're stronger and less likely to splinter. These linen bandages are less likely to fray and tear. But you'll still have to cradle the arm in a sling." Maybe he should wrap the sling so it kept the arm against her body. That would immobilize her and keep her husband from forcing himself on her. For a time.

"I'm also going to prescribe some laudanum for the pain. It will help you sleep too," he mumbled.

"Better you give it to him," she said with gritted teeth. "He needs it to keep his anger in check."

"Did he do this to you?" Doc asked. He kept wrapping the splints in place, adding an extra layer to protect her from bumping it.

She nodded, tears forming in her eyes. "He were such a gentle man 'afore the war."

Matt nodded in agreement. He hadn't known the couple when they were young and first courting. But men who'd suffered less than Josiah also exploded in murderous rages for no reason at all.

"Take the laudanum with a glass of milk to ease your stomach."

"Will it hurt my baby?" She cradled her belly with her free arm. "Josiah is most insistent I take nothing that might hurt it."

"Good advice. Drink the milk and give him the drug. He'll move slowly and not want to talk much for a while. But I think he'll be calmer and not so angry." He wished he could find a cure for men's inner turmoil. Maybe...

"Does Josiah like being a dairy farmer?"

"Not really. He wanted to be a baker, live in the city, and make fancy cakes and pies. But his daddy died and left Josiah the farm. He feels it's his duty to keep it running. We owe the bank more than the place is worth." Another tear leaked from the corner of her eye.

The late night conversation before Josie collapsed in pain ran through his mind in vivid detail. Both Josie and Lucian seemed eager to settle down on property of their own.

"With only one leg and one eye, Josiah either needs help with the cows, or he needs to move to the city and bake. Give me a couple of days. I might have a solution."

A series of gunshots exploded from the west side of town. Doc's ears hurt. Sweat streamed across his forehead and down his spine.

His stomach ached.

He hadn't reacted to violence this badly since... Gettysburg.

149

Because he knew that the aftermath would bring out the flying purple *things* that devoured corpses. And now it seemed they employed a squad of assassins that took down the living.

He dove across his patient to protect her from stray bullets.

Screams erupted from innocents from one end of town to the other.

Josiah stomped into the treatment room, fists clenched, His face turned beet red from his anger that he could not control his environment.

Logic caught Doc's mind and jerked him back to the situation. He had to act, not merely react. He had to hide his fears and confront the cause of violence before it escalated into an all-out shooting war.

"Stay here and stay down!" he commanded the Daytons. He grabbed his rifle from the upright cupboard where he kept surgical instruments, and stuffed a handful of bullets from his desk drawer into his trouser pockets. By the time he reached the boardwalk, he'd loaded and cocked his weapon.

The da Foe brothers, all six of them ranging in age from sixteen to thirty-five, from three different mothers, rode their skittish horses into town, flowing over the hilltop with weapons blazing at anything and everything.

Thankfully they were piss poor shots. Especially when drunk.

"A might early for the da Foes," Josiah said quietly. He looked longingly toward his wagon out front where he'd left his own rifle on the bench seat. "They don't usually break free of their da until Saturday. It's only Friday."

And then everything stopped and grew quiet. Doc felt as if he viewed the entire scene through a glass of water, or he'd wrapped a down comforter over his head.

His gaze didn't have to wander far to discover the cause.

Sheriff Blue stood in the middle of the street in front of her office, her two pistols aimed at the two da Foes at the head of the pack—the oldest and the youngest. Her big buckskin stallion ambled, back and forth from hitching post to hitching post, still saddled, as if he didn't know where to go.

"This is my town now and no one—absolutely no one—shoots it up!" Josie's voice held the tone and volume of a military man commanding green recruits.

The da Foe brothers milled about, trying to make a decision.

Josie might intimidate them.

If she wore boots.

The barefoot sheriff was, of course, barefoot.

CHAPTER 18

Keep them talking and you won't have to shoot another being today, I told myself.

"You won't shoot," the oldest of the lot sneered at me. He kept a tight hand on his reins, controlling his gelding by willpower alone. An ordinary horse lacking that extra spark of intelligence or personality to suit me, but more than willing to obey a firm rider. "Our daddy owns too much of this town."

I remembered a bit of conversation with Rosie. "Mac" MacKenzie da Foe owned hundreds of acres of range land, running thousands of head of cattle. No diversification, overgrazed land, constantly in debt. The only thing he seemed good at was breeding seven rowdy sons (his first two wives died in childbirth or shortly after birthing a second large baby) and raising them with an iron fist, not allowing them to learn the fine art of making a decision. Saturday nights he cut their leashes and let them run rough-shod through town.

Six men rode into town. But the gossip about Big Mac da Foe said seven sons, like some legend of old. So where was the seventh son?

Six were bad enough.

Rosie dreaded the night Rollie, the youngest, turned sixteen and his brothers supervised his introduction to the lovely arts her girls could teach the boy.

"And I police this town." I pulled the trigger of my left handgun, feeling the tension in the metal release, the vibrations coiling up my arm. I absorbed the recoil.

Maybe this was why the last sheriff hadn't been replaced. No one wanted the job of keeping the da Foes from over-running the entire town with guns blazing.

My bullet landed six inches in front of the gelding's left front hoof.

The horse reared. The eldest brother (I couldn't remember his name for love nor money because the girls at Rosie's refused to talk about him) fought to control the frightened beast with one hand while he tried to aim his own pistol.

In the meantime, a middle brother hoisted and aimed a bolt action Lee-Enfield .58 caliber. He hesitated while he adjusted his aim as his restive horse shifted side to side.

My bullet struck the barrel just in front of the bolt. The rifle fell to the ground with a clash of broken metal and splintered wood.

By the time the now useless rifle lay on the ground, the horse reared and screamed as if it had been shot. That brother lay on the ground, shaking his head and trying to pry himself to his knees. His arms seemed inadequate to take his weight. As soon as the horse, another gelding, had freed itself from his rider, it took off, cross country, away from danger.

"Now, each of you will take your weapons... all of your weapons," I kept my eye on bulging ankle holsters to make sure the da Foe brothers understood my ultimatum, "and lay them on my desk inside my office. You may then go about your business. You can retrieve your guns on the way out of town."

The youngest boy dismounted and grabbed his rifle from the saddle holster. "Hell, I don't need no gun to finish my business or celebrate my birthday." He hitched his pants up a notch.

"Come back here, Rollie!" the oldest brother roared. "You do as I say, when I say it!"

"Thank you, Rollie," I said, keeping my aim on the brother at the front of the phalanx. "Seems like you have more brains than all the others put together. Give my regards to Rosie. She's got more to teach you than your brothers can imagine." Like politeness and gentleness and respect.

Two other brothers dismounted and followed Rollie. That left two still atop their horses and one on the ground.

"Hey, Doc," I called to the shadow hovering near the medical office. "Got a new patient for you."

Blessedly, Doc hurried out his door, rifle in one hand, black bag in the other. He knelt beside the still addled brother, testing pulse and whatever doctors did to concussion patients.

I still didn't dare relax my stance or my aim. "You boys want to spend the night in my jail, without supper? Or company?"

One more da Foe slid off his mare and stalked toward the office. "I didn't come all this way to waste my time thinking about, but not having my Saffron, or going hungry," he muttered all the way to my office. His three younger brothers were just emerging and headed directly for Rosie's. "C'mon Jake or you'll miss all the fun."

That left just me and the eldest, and meanest, of the brothers.

I doubted I'd be able to talk him down from his temper tantrum. And I didn't want to add another gunshot victim to Doc's patient load.

"Be a waste of a good rifle if Sheriff Blue shot that Enfield out of your hands," Neil Sanderson said mildly, coming up behind me. He'd taken a moment to retrieve his regular spectacles and suit coat from the bank to make him look like the shrewd businessman he was. He fondled his six shooter like a lover, needing to shoot it. "Also be a pity if I have to foreclose on your daddy. The end of the month is coming up fast and I heard he hasn't sold enough cattle and hay to make his loan."

"You haven't got the balls..."

"I'll take pleasure in rounding up a posse and ousting all of you from the property," I added. I might not have balls, but I have the will and the gumption.

The eldest da Foe brother threw his rifle to the ground in front of him, turned his horse around and galloped toward home.

"He believed you," Neil said on a long exhale.

"I just hope he doesn't round up his own posse."

"You know he'll be back with the entire gang of ranch hands," Doc muttered as he helped both Mariah and Josiah to their feet, checking each for any further injuries.

They both appeared unscathed but shaken. Carefully he measured a quarter dose of laudanum for each of them in a tin cup with a goodly amount of water. He considered a dose for himself, then decided he needed his brains unaddled by the drug. He wouldn't dare drink at Rosie's later, not with the da Foe brothers in town. Most likely he'd spend the night patching up injuries from fist fights until well after Rosie closed down the bar.

"I heard tell that Old Mac ain't paid his boys for two months or more. They might not follow either him or Young Mac. Should've turned management over to Rollie two years ago and taken it away from Whitey. If you ask me that albino foreman ain't worth a shit." He spat onto the floor. "Rollie's the only one among them with any brains or head for figures," Josiah replied. He reached for his wife, and they held each other in a fierce hug that threatened her broken arm and his broken balance, barely stabilized by his ill-fitting wooden leg. But together they remained standing.

A good metaphor for the couple.

"I need to talk to Neil Sanderson. He's the one who will help you broker a deal to sell your land and get you to Pendleton where you can bake in one of the new hotels near the railroad."

"Do you think it's possible? Might we finally get free of the blasted dairy?" Josiah said, hands trembling where he clutched his wife.

"Maybe. Doc is good people. So's Mr. Neil. We can only hope," Mariah replied, letting her forehead rest against his.

They balanced each other.

Doc left the couple to work out today's differences in private. But he'd stay close enough to hear and intervene if either one of them went off the rails.

Carrying his Winchester cradled in his left elbow, he joined Neil and Josie in the middle of the street. He eyed the barefoot sheriff and frowned.

"I recommend you soak those feet in the creek with Elinore," he said sternly.

"Town needs her sitting at the bottom of the stairs at Rosie's with her Spenser at hand," Neil replied.

"I need to settle Prospero in his paddock, then I'll sit with Elinore a bit. Tell Rosie to water the drinks and serve them slow. I'll be there in time for supper, with my boots on and my weapons loaded." Josie hitched her gun belt, making certain it rested right where she wanted.

When she'd grabbed the big, troublesome stallion by the reins and led him behind the sheriff's office, Neil addressed Doc's proposal of settling Lucian on Josiah's dairy farm and then driving the couple to the city.

"I've contacts at the Grand, that will probably lead to a baking job somewhere for the boy," Neil replied. "I remember at the county fairs he always took blue ribbons for his pies and for decorating cakes. He's a real sculptor with fondant."

"What's fondant?" Doc asked. His attention shifted back to the Daytons now making their way toward their wagon and how lovingly Josiah helped Mariah into the back of the wagon, adjusting her pillows and blankets until she rested comfortably.

"Something fancy the bakers back east play with to make their cakes look elegant and... and different from just plain icing. Doesn't taste very good though."

"Just so long as we get him settled doing work that makes him feel good about himself. And soon."

"I'll get right on the paperwork. Got some things to check for Josie too."

They both winced and ducked as a howl of glee erupted from the saloon and a beer pitcher came flying through Rosie's front window.

"Anyone get hurt by da Foe flying bullets?" Josie asked.

"Not that I know of," Doc replied.

"Not one of them can shoot worth a darn," Neil added. "I'll ask around. The gossip mill will know before anyone comes to Doc for help."

"It's going to be a long day and longer night," Doc moaned. "I'll get my bag and set up near the door. No one gets in with a weapon and no one leaves until I check for and treat injuries."

"Good plan. I'll join you as soon as I close the bank."

"What about Sheriff Blue?" Doc asked.

"Sheriff Blue does what Sheriff Blue thinks best. But always remember that the horses come first."

"WELL, Elinore, Prospero seems to be settling in at the other paddock," I said, laying back on the grassy verge to the creek. I closed my eyes against the glare of the afternoon sun. Cold, mountain water soothed my feet.

Elinore splashed a little water in my direction.

Was that agreement or a plea for attention?

I decided to go with agreement since I had no intention of moving just yet.

"What do you think about moving to the old Miller place? It looks like there's enough pasture to keep you fat and sassy until you decide it's time to go out on patrol again."

Elinore shifted her feet slightly closer to the creek bank.

Through slitted eyes, I watched my friend for a ripple of skin or adjustment of her ears.

Instead, the horse grabbed a mouthful of hay that Jed Junior had left for her.

"You realize that if I buy that apple orchard, and live out there, I'd be a mile away from town and not available for emergencies."

Elinore rotated her ears at the word apple. She didn't have an opinion about the rest of the statement.

"Of course, if I convince a local Basque family, or even some

Romany to camp there for the winter, they can take care of the place, and you'd have their ponies to keep you company. I could come out most days, but make certain I stay in town on Friday and Saturday nights when things get wild at the local saloons." There were two others besides Rosie's. But they didn't have girls available so didn't attract rowdy men who came to town looking to burn away the loneliness and frustration of living on isolated farms and ranches.

"Speaking of rowdy saloons, I think I need to put my hat and boots on and get back to work keeping the peace around here. You ready to come out of the water yet?"

Elinore returned to the center of the creek and closed her eyes in bliss.

"Well as long as you are making that cold water your home, I guess we are both staying in Heller's Hole. Maybe the entire winter."

Maybe forever, a little voice in the back of my mind whispered.

"Tempting," I said to myself.

CHAPTER 19

"MIND IF I JOIN YOU?" Neil asked, even as he sat on the grass beside Josie Blue. Without waiting for her assent, he tugged off his own boots and plunked his feet into the creek.

Ah... that felt good.

He'd taken the time to change out of his business suit after closing the bank, thinking casual attire better suited to the rough evening he expected at Rosie's.

"Aren't we supposed to keep the da Foe boys under control tonight?"

"Only way to do that is add some of Doc's laudanum to their beer. He's mighty stingy with his drugs though. Told me one time he'd seen too many men injured during the war who became so dependent on opium that they couldn't function, long after their wounds healed. So now he only gives out small doses when needed and withholds a second dose as long as possible."

Josie nodded at his words. "I've seen the same thing."

"I looked up the Miller records." He pinched the bridge of his nose to help banish the headache after peering at his father's illegible scrawl for an hour.

"Can I buy the place?" She turned hope-filled eyes toward him.

They were nearly of a height sitting next to each other, shoulders within an inch of touching.

She looked so soft and vulnerable in the fading, golden light of the setting sun...

He yanked his attention away from her mouth and his desire to kiss her. Too soon.

The only other time in his life he'd felt so drawn to a woman had been during his university days when his cock ruled too many of his decisions.

And look how badly that turned out! He thought he'd been walking out with a shop girl, wanted to marry her, and bring her back home to meet his parents and settle...

Turned out she'd been selling her favors to two of his fellow students, and "married" three more with a fake judge and forged papers. Then she'd looted their bank accounts and left town.

He counted himself lucky that he'd been beguiled by the Army recruiter who promised glory and justice and a bunch of other patriotic nonsense. The girl hadn't waited for him to report for duty before she'd latched onto another wealthy student.

Out of long habit, he forced the low simmer of lust in his gut to behave.

But his gaze remained fixed on Josie's mouth, and their shoulders leaned towards each other until they rested together.

"If you are looking for a romance with another man—an illegal relationship I'll have to arrest you for—you had best look elsewhere," she said. Though her voice sounded grim and forbidding, the corners of her mouth quirked upwards.

"I know, Josephine Baumgarten."

She seemed to deflate as she slumped away. "I thought I'd buried that name long ago. I even have a death certificate. But that's in a stash of personal papers and a few mementos locked up in Brotherton's office."

"Never discount the resources of a snoopy banker. Turns out that Brotherton left one account in my bank in that name with Josie Blue as the account co-signer. In case you ever needed the cash. My father hid the records in the first place I looked for something out of the ordinary." His own laughter threatened to erupt.

Bending to the side to retrieve his left boot felt almost painful from the emptiness in his gut.

He'd liked the playfulness of the last few moments and now he'd lost it.

Forever?

"I've never denied my sex. It's... it's just too much work to correct people when they guess wrong." She bit her lip.

"Given your work for Pinkerton during and after the war, wearing trousers and riding astride are efficient. Do you miss your life before... before your family was massacred?"

"No."

That surprised him.

"I'd always planned to take over as foreman of my father's ranch. Wearing trousers, riding astride, and carrying a gun seems much more natural than wearing silk and lace and hooped petticoats."

He had trouble picturing her in such delicate and feminine attire.

"I really want to kiss you, Miss Blue." There. He'd said it. Out loud. Maybe now his innards would stop aching and twitching.

"Hold on to that feeling." She scrambled to her feet and picked up her own boots. By the time she'd straightened her back and turned toward the barn, Jed Junior had come within hailing distance.

Neil mumbled something rude under his breath, using words he hadn't considered since the war ended. His comment ended with "No fucking privacy..."

Josie chuckled. "That's my point. As long as this town presumes I'm male, and they won't accept me as sheriff or respect me if they know I'm a woman, we can't be seen as a couple."

"And I certainly can't take you home to meet my parents."

"I'll meet your mother in town one way or another. Probably in church come Sunday morning."

"Maybe sooner." He told her of his plans to remove his parents from managing the bank. "She'll probably show up on your doorstep demanding you arrest me."

"That might be fun." She eyed him up and down as he tugged his boots back on and stood up. "Right now, you'd better tell young Jed that the money I gave him earlier isn't counterfeit and my credit is good. I'll meet you at Rosie's in a few minutes." She raised her hand, palm up, and looked as if she meant to blow him a kiss, thought better of it and turned the gesture into a tip of her hat.

Neil's gut tightened. He had a chance with her. He just needed patience.

But he now couldn't quite understand how he, or any man in his right mind, could ever mistake her trim waist and nicely swelling hips for anything but feminine.

I SAT on the third step up from the saloon floor, tapping idly at the engraved stock of my trusty Spencer repeater rifle. My handguns lay on either side of me—easier to draw than from my holsters while seated. So far, the crowd remained loud, but tolerant. Doc had moved from the entrance to the most intense of the poker games dead center.

All the men had to do was look in my direction and much of their alcohol-induced rage dribbled out of them.

Good. I maintained peace tonight due to fear. Tales of how I'd shot a Winchester long barrel out of a man's hands had spread far and fast.

Soon I hoped quiet would come to the town out of respect—for me and for the law.

Barefoot once again, my heels raised and lowered in a restless dance to music only I could hear. The old piano was more a pain to play than to let the evening pass without music.

I allowed one man at a time to pass me on his way to meet one of the women draped over the upper railing when they weren't occupied elsewhere. Young Rollie—Roland Silas da Foe I'd heard his brothers tease him—was learning the delicate art of making love with Lily, the oldest of the women, at barely twenty-two. None of his brothers crowded into the room to watch. I knew that watching could easily rouse the men into more active participation. They wouldn't care if Lily agreed to the game or not. I cared to keep that tryst private.

I kept my attention moving restlessly so I wouldn't have to think about Neil Sanderson.

That almost kiss. His confession that he knew me and wanted me as a woman.

I knew I wanted him.

But he was a commitment kind of man.

What did I want from him? Just a short-term affair?

Or something longer, more permanent?

If I bought the Miller farm with its apples and lush pastures for horses, and maybe sheep... Both lucrative crops. That would require a kind of commitment.

My job as sheriff required a commitment.

My gut trembled with anticipation.

And dread.

Again and again, I returned my gaze to the out-of-tune piano. My fingers itched to play it. Long ago I'd found solace in music. I could pound and pound the keys, finding a common soul in Wagner's militaristic themes. Then the melodies of Mozart would make me smile. The mathematical precision and logic of Bach bored me.

I needed to play something.

If I could just play the damned waltz that ran through my inner ear repeatedly, maybe I could banish the tune I couldn't quite name...

Next time I needed to contact Brotherton I'd ask him to send a piano tuner.

I didn't dare take my attention away from the crowd. The da Foe brother presiding over the poker game at the big round table in the center of the room fiddled with his cards too often, too quickly. I couldn't see his cards from this position but had no doubt this wasn't the same hand he'd been dealt.

The volume of the conversation around the poker table rose by a factor of three. I came alert. The tune in my head vanished.

Doc straightened his spine in his chair across the table from the second oldest da Foe brother, hands resting lightly on the pile of chips in front of him. His cards displayed a royal flush for all to see.

"Cheater!" the da Foe screamed.

His brothers moved toward him, hands on empty holsters. Their guns were locked in my office, but they all carried knives and knotted fists.

I holstered one Colt, grabbed the other and rose to my bare feet and came down off the stairs. I handed the Spencer to Neil at one end of the bar. As all eyes focused on the poker game, I made no noise crossing the saloon floor to the big round table at the center.

One advantage to being the Barefoot Sheriff, boots clomped with a sound akin to authority. Tonight, I crept silently up on the impending fight.

"I do not cheat," Doc said. He did not raise his voice or push back his chair. He just sat in place guarding his chips.

"I'd think twice about throwing that punch," I whispered directly into da Foe's ear, the barrel of one handgun pressed firmly into the small of his back.

He whirled around, arm cocked, and fist clenched. I topped him in height by an inch. But he outweighed me by twenty pounds—most of that weight massed in solid muscle.

I raised my gun to his face as I widened my stance and flexed my knees. *I don't really want a fight tonight.*

He swayed slightly, trying to focus his eyes.

"Only three shots of whisky?" I said. My gaze swept the crowd.

Neil lounged against the bar, a mug of beer in his hand, my Spencer pointed downward. His first and only drink of the evening. Rosie maintained her place behind the bar where she habitually kept a shotgun.

"Are you going to concede the game, or spend the night in my haunted jail?" I asked. I didn't relax my stance or the aim of my Colt.

"H...h...haunted?" One of the younger da Foes gulped and laid his cards, face down.

"I confirmed an unexplained presence in the building the day the sheriff moved in," Doc said. Not exactly a lie.

I smiled slightly. "Want to test it? All you have to do is show me the ace of spades up your sleeve—the same card that tops Doc's spread."

"You accusing me of cheating?" da Foe shouted. His dominant right hand rose to shoulder height again and his fingers tightened against his palm. That punch would hurt. If I gave him the chance to throw it.

"Thank you, Cutter Pine," I muttered to myself. Just as my first partner in the Pinkerton's had taught me, I grabbed one of his wrists and twisted until he turned away from my cruel grip.

He fought me with the strength of his broad shoulders but didn't think to lash out with his foot. I pushed his arm up and up behind his back, throwing him off balance. I had just enough time to holster my remaining weapon and grab the other wrist.

"Sanderson, cuff him," I ordered.

Gingerly he pulled the dangling handcuffs from my hip pocket and fastened one of da Foe's wrists with the metal restraints. All without touching me.

With a deep sigh of exasperation, I released da Foe with one hand and attached the dangling cuff to his other.

Then I released my grip on his wrists, letting both his hands drop behind his back.

"Whichever da Foe you are, you are under arrest for cheating at cards, disturbing the peace, and attempted assault on an officer of the law." I grabbed his elbow and pushed him toward the exit.

"You might want your boots, Blue. It's started to rain," Sanderson called after me. He grinned at me, all knowing.

I paused at the door. "Not this time. But I would like my hat."

Doc produced it from the rack by the door and slammed it on my head at a rakish angle.

"Now you boys behave yourself while I'm out. I'll be back shortly."

"You... you're going to leave me alone in your *haunted* jail?"

"You bet your sweet patootie, Jasper da Foe. If you are still alive come morning, I'll let you run home to your daddy."

CHAPTER 20

"Good morning, sunshine," I sang out as I unlocked the back door of my office. Then I retrieved the breakfast tray (if you could call cold bacon, stale biscuits, questionable berry jam, and tepid, weak coffee breakfast) I'd carried over from Rosie's.

"Shut the fuck up!" a deep male voice, made deeper by a hangover, growled. "I finally get warm enough to sleep and you show up."

I glanced at the wood stove in the front corner beside my desk. Embers from the banked fire still glowed behind the grate.

"Why were you so cold—other than too much whisky clogging your brain?"

"Your damned ghost moaned and groaned and blew a frigid wind every time he passed over me."

I raised my eyebrows in speculation. "Eat your breakfast, Jasper. Then you can go home." I shoved the tray beneath the lowest cross bar of the cell, the slot designed for the exchange of food.

"You call that breakfast? Looks like shit to me," he shouted, rising to his feet from the thin pallet on the plank bench within the cell. Then he winced and pressed his fingertips into his temples and sat down again.

When I'd cleaned the office with Jonquil and Daisy, we'd beaten the mattresses free of dust and fleas. We'd seen no evidence of rodents. No need to soak them in carbolic soap and water. The mattress hadn't been the cause of his sleepless night.

I looked upward, wondering if the spirit of the mummy walked in the hours of darkness.

"Drink the coffee, Jasper. It will help the hangover." I pushed the tray deeper into the cell with the toe of my boot. "And watch your language. You are in town now and a degree of politeness is expected."

He frowned, thinking about it.

I guessed thinking might be too hard for him at the moment.

"You ain't barefoot. How come?" he mumbled eyeing the breakfast tray malevolently.

"It's daylight. The boots fit now."

"Like a warlock," he grumbled.

"At least try the coffee, you'll feel better." But it was so weak and cold he'd not aim to misbehave during future visits to town just to get good morning coffee.

"I'd feel nekkid without my boots."

I rolled my eyes. "That's okay out in the wild. Essential. I always slept with my boots on until I moved into town. Now I can do without when my feet hurt."

"Heard tell your name be Blue. Like Blue the bounty hunter. You him?"

"Maybe. Maybe not. I've done my share of bounty hunting. I've also done my share of rounding up outlaws. Now are you going to eat breakfast so I can turn you loose?"

He pulled the tin cup to his nose and sniffed. "You sure this is coffee?"

"That's what Rosie's cook told me." Though it was early enough Cook hadn't come in to work yet. I had scraped together yesterday's leftovers. I'd wait a bit for my own breakfast of hot, fresh food.

"Hey, these biscuits is good, got anymore?" Crumbs sprayed from Jasper's mouth as he spoke.

Buttermilk biscuits should be eaten hot and fresh with melting butter and fresh jam. Anything less was an insult to the mouth and stomach.

Strange. Before I landed in this nearly forgotten town, I'd have welcomed stale biscuits and cold bacon. While living rough I couldn't be choosy. Now after only a short time in town, I'd gotten used to good food and I'd had to loosen my belt a notch. Three weeks ago I'd had to add a notch to my belt just to keep my pants up.

Maybe I'd gotten too comfortable living in Heller's Hole.

"Your horse is in my paddock, out the back door. He's been fed and watered. You'll have to saddle him yourself." I reached for the cell keys beneath my desk and released him. "Now get out of here, and tell your daddy, Whitey and your brothers that there's a new sheriff in town who believes in peace, order, and the law."

"What about my gun?"

He gobbled the last biscuit and the bacon, stood, hitched his pants and exited his cell, looking almost normal. But his eyes squinted like the hangover headache lingered.

I unlocked the long gun case behind me and picked a rifle at random. The rest of the da Foe brothers had not awakened yet to retrieve their own weapons.

"That ain't mine, it belongs to Micah."

"Which one is yours?" I edged sideways to block his access to the weapons, not liking the way his eyes riveted on the rifles. My free hand rested casually on my pistol grip—I could live in town without boots but felt truly naked without the gun belt resting on my hips. He'd not get far if he tried to grab an unloaded gun and try to shoot me. Despite the friendly chatter, he was still a da Foe brother trained by a ruthless daddy to be a troublemaker.

I saw the moment logic kicked his brain into order by the way he held his shoulders. Tension in the cords of his neck sagged.

"The one on the end. The one with my initials inlaid into the stock in silver. JMdF."

I grabbed it by the barrel and handed it to him. "I unloaded all of them last night while you slept off your drunk. They will stay unloaded while in town—every time you come to town."

"I'll tell Whitey... er... Daddy. He ain't gonna like it, but I'll tell him."

"And that ranch manager he likes so much better than his own sons." That last was a guess, piecing together bits of gossip.

Jaspar da Foe winced.

I'd struck paydirt.

YOUNG ROLLIE WAS the next da Foe to wander into my office. He looked bright and chipper, moving with a new fluid grace with a smile on his face. Unlike his brothers, he'd not indulged in liquor last night. After only one beer, he'd allowed Lily to escort him upstairs and no one had seen him since. Until now.

"Come for your guns, Roland?" He was a man now and deserved a proper name instead of a childish nickname.

"Yes, sir," he replied politely, something I hadn't expected of any da Foe. He scrutinized the office intently, noting the empty cell, the wanted posters, the banked fire, and finally me and my desk.

"Everything up to your standards?" I sat in my chair and leaned back, making sure I was between him and the gun case.

"Um... yes sir. ...um you seem like an educated man."

"I consider myself so." I'd outgrown my governess when I turned fifteen and Eva became engaged. Thankfully she'd moved on to another ranch in the area and missed the family massacre. Her absence didn't mean I'd outgrown learning. The last book I'd read before that awful day was Blackstone's law. I needed to know more about water rights in order to counter the Carons.

"Do you... um... have any books around you aren't reading?"

That startled me. Of all the things the boy could ask for, books were the last thing I expected. "You could probably benefit from a session with my copy of Blackstone's Law so you understand why I locked up your brother and confiscated your guns. I'll need it back though."

His eyes widened in awe. "You'd really lend me that book?" He sounded as reverent as if I'd offered the Bible. He'd have to get *that* book from somewhere else.

"If you give me your word of honor to return it to me when you've read it cover to cover, or bought your own copy. I know someone in Pendleton who could find a copy for you."

"Oh, wow, Blackstone will be better than Tennyson's poems or Shakespeare!"

This time I opened my eyes wide in awe. "Where'd you get Tennyson or Shakespeare?" I'd borrowed the first from Lucian. The second came from Brotherton—when he was still Colonel Martine during the war.

"Thomas Edgerton, he's the circuit lawyer who comes to town once a month or so. He slips me books when he can. Daddy doesn't approve of books."

"Does your daddy know how to read?"

Rollie shook his head.

That explained a lot. "Does he know numbers?"

"Sorta. Mostly he leaves that stuff to the ranch manager, Whitey. Lately Mac Junior's been doing the accounts. He yells and shouts a lot at the manager."

"So, it would not be hard to believe the manager has been stealing money from the ranch."

Rollie hung his head and looked out the window rather than comment on his assertion.

"Embezzlement is a crime. Get me some evidence and I can arrest the man to face the circuit judge when he comes through."

"Yes, sir!" Rollie replied with great enthusiasm. "Now about that book?"

I unlocked and opened the middle drawer on the left, where I'd stashed the valuable law reference.

"I promise I won't bend the pages or spill anything on it," he whispered reverently. "I need to learn the difference between evidence and hearsay."

I handed him the book. "And Rollie," I called to him as he absently grabbed his own rifle from the rack, eyes glued to the book. "You can stop by and chat anytime. We'll talk about the law, or poetry, or whatever crosses your mind."

"Yes sir. You'd be easier to talk to than the school master. All Sanderpoole wants to talk about is the Bible and who has the most money in town."

"That would be Mr. Sanderson."

"You'd think. But Rosie actually has more."

Now that was interesting. I figured I'd made an ally.

Rollie left, already reading the fat law book. He left his guns in my case.

As Rollie left, a flurry of movement in the street alerted me that a finely dressed woman stalked toward my office from the bank. Anger drove her deliberate steps more than concern for her delicate walking boots—designed for city board walks rather than the rain-soddened streets of Hellers Hole.

Last night the first of the autumnal storms had sent rivulets of mud downhill towards the valleys to the west of us and the three creeks that fed the town from mountain runoff had flooded and filled several fishponds. Elinore stood in murky water almost up to her belly and she loved it.

Unlike the woman who stormed my office with all guns to bear. She frowned deeply every time a bit of slurry squirted out from her delicate boots. Heaven help any raindrop that evaded the umbrella, held over her by a more sensibly clad servant, and plopped on her hat brim.

Mrs. Sanderson was about to descend upon me.

Before breakfast.

I watched the woman crossing the street. She strode purposefully, despite the offending mud and rain. Her plaid gown in shades of gold, brown, and rust with a tiny bit of green trim might have been fashionable six years ago when fabric shortages at the end of the war had dictated narrower skirts. But a three-year-old magazine I'd seen in a general store in a one-saloon town two years ago would have called passé the flat skirt front with a few graceful crosswise drapes and a slight bustle.

The saloon of that wide spot in the road took up three-quarters of the building—no bigger than my entire office with the two jail cells. One corner offered a few basic supplies of food staples, tack, and tools. The other corner hosted the post office. A mail courier wandered through every fortnight or so. I had needed to file a report with Brotherton back in Pendleton at least two hundred miles away. I could ride there faster than mail it. The telegraph hadn't reached that far yet. But lo and behold, on the counter next to the till lay a fashion magazine—well drawings and a few diagrams of pattern pieces. An honest-to-God magazine, well thumbed, with curling corners, but contact with the outside world.

Mrs. Sanderson's gown looked newer than the magazine with nary a shiny spot or mended seam or missing button down the bodice. She probably didn't need a bustle frame or padding based on the upthrust of her corset and thick waistline. Rosie's girls in their polished cotton, off-the-shoulder gowns looked more recently fashionable than the second wealthiest woman in town, the dictator of moral behavior (based upon church attendance), and fashion.

To keep all that clean and dry, a tall, spare woman of indeterminate years with black curly hair and café au lait skin, wearing a simple wool dress with a man's great coat to keep her warm, carried a sturdy black umbrella for Mrs. Sanderson, but not herself. Chances were, the woman had been a slave ten years ago, before the war ended all that. Supposedly.

I debated with myself a few moments. Should I greet Mrs. Sanderson at the door and welcome her? Or should I take up a position of authority behind my desk?

I remained at the desk, but stood respectfully.

Yes, I had lived rough and mostly alone for a long time, but I did remember a few manners from my life before....

"Good morning. Mrs. Sanderson, I believe?" I greeted my visitor. I did not approach the woman and offer to shake her hand.

"Sheriff Blue." The woman swept aside her skirt and perched on the edge of the straight-backed visitor's chair. She nodded graciously that I had permission to sit.

Her maid stayed outside. At least the woman had the roof over-hang and a sturdy bonnet to shield her from the elements. Probably one of Mrs. Sanderson's cast-offs, judging by the bedraggled feathers drooping from the band.

Damn. I had wanted to watch the maid's expressions for clues about what Mrs. Sanderson really felt and what she said to manipulate my sympathy.

I sat and made a show of wiggling around and getting comfortable. "What can I do for you, Mrs. Sanderson?"

Ethel Sanderson crinkled her snub nose. "This place smells like dust. Old dust. Heavily salted. Don't you ever clean?"

"Smells like carbolic soap to me," I replied, sniffing.

"Well, your sensibilities must not be as refined as mine." She waved her fingers dismissively beneath her nose.

A frisson of alarm climbed my spine. Had my crew disturbed something around the mummy in the attic? I hoped not. Given the degree of magic encasing it, any disruption of the spells could trigger... something.

"You must arrest my son."

I leaned forward and rested my forearms on the desk, as if surprised. "On what charges?"

"He's trying to discredit me before the entire town! A town I helped his father build." She fell backward from her perch on the edge of the chair, flapping a weak hand against her ample bosom and gasping for breath.

I ignored her vaporous act. "Shall I call your maid? Does she carry smelling salts in her pockets?" Great big pockets designed for a man in that voluminous coat. The servant probably needed a man's coat to cover her tall and sturdy frame.

Mrs. Sanderson narrowed her eyes in speculation, then straightened her posture. The tightness of her corset had to make that semi-collapse murderously uncomfortable. And there was more than a hint of murder in her gaze.

"Are your son's accusations true?" I frantically searched my brain for any information I might have acquired. Pinkerton liked his agents to be familiar with the law and kept an extensive library of legal texts in each of their offices. I had found reading them a decent way to pass the long hours beside a lonely campfire with no one to talk to but Elinore.

"Of course they aren't! I am perfectly capable of making business decision based on the good of the community as a whole." Mrs. Sanderson nearly shouted. Her voice rose to a shriek, easily heard by her maid standing beside the door outside the office. She jerked her head around in reaction to the strident tone.

A good lawyer had the beginnings of a case with those two statements.

"Did Neil Sanderson make those accusations in pubic?"

Neil's mother pursed her lips in a thin, tight line.

I waited her out. I had hints of the source of the problem from Neil's point of view. I could only guess at the woman's perspective. Old people often lost good judgement in dribs and dabs, slow enough that no one noticed until they did or said something terribly wrong.

But Ethel Sanderson did not look that old. Her skin remained smooth, other than a few crinkles around her eyes, from squinting against bright sunlight, she might be only in her late forties—if she'd given birth to Neil when only eighteen, as debutantes often did. Even if she'd waited until her early thirties to have her one and only child, she'd only be sixty or so.

Still...

"Not in public. No. Neil remained discreet. He had papers delivered by Mr. O'Toole declaring me unfit and removing my minority share in the bank from my control. He has not said a word to me. Why, just now, he left the bank by the back door rather than speak to me. Doesn't he realize how he has humiliated me? Doesn't he know how this will diminish my leadership role in this town?" Her voice rose toward shrieking again.

I waited until she rose and began pacing, pounding the desktop with her first as she spoke each phrase.

"Until Mr. Neil Sanderson speaks his accusations in public, I have no legal reason to arrest him. This sounds like a family squabble to me. You must work it out between yourselves."

"My word should be enough!" She stopped pacing and lifted her chin in authoritative defiance. "That is your job."

"No, ma'am." I stood and faced the woman squarely. I topped her by half a head. Another thing Cutter Pine had taught me was how to intimidate without saying much. "My job is to uphold the law for the safety and protection of this town."

"Then arrest my son for fostering unsafe practices."

"How has he endangered this town?"

"By encouraging malcontents to attend that... that other church."

"However you dislike the Catholic church, the Constitution of the United States guarantees that no one religion shall be favored over another." I couldn't remember the exact wording, but Brotherton had drilled into each of us agents to not allow difference in religion to excuse crimes.

"They are Satanists who sacrifice babies and drink their blood!"

I bit my cheeks. "You may believe that. I have no evidence to support that as fact." Arguing with her would not change the woman's mind. "Now, I suggest you go and *talk* to your son. That is the only way you can settle this matter. I cannot arrest Mayor Sanderson without something more real than imagined slights."

I sat back down, fished a logbook and ledger—both blank—from the drawers and began idly doodling and listing meaningless numbers. When I lifted my gaze again, the maid was ushering Mrs. Sanderson out the door.

CHAPTER 21

Neil watched his mother's buggy travel north from the bank. He figured she was headed for the schoolhouse. Reverend Zebedee Sanderpoole taught eight or nine students during the week and opened the building as his Baptist church on Sunday mornings. The town paid his rent on the two rooms in the back for him to live.

So far, the town, and he as mayor, had turned a blind eye to him hosting the church there. So far. But what did Reverend Zebedee Sanderpoole do with the offering money he collected? Neil had seen no evidence of the money, or his teaching salary going toward anything except possibly his food. Most of the time he ate with parishioners, never showing his face at Rosie's or the other two saloons in town. His private rooms did not boast a stove suitable for cooking, only for heating in winter. And the town provided his firewood.

Come Sunday morning, Neil guessed the sermon would center on honoring your parents. Or perhaps becoming wary of trusting strangers. He'd best plan to attend the service rather than sneaking off to the Catholic church. Perhaps he should attend evensong tonight for a half hour of peace and quiet.

If any of the students' parents objected to his mother disrupting class time, he'd have a legal reason to confine her to the house. He hoped that Rachel, the maid, could keep her under lock and key, if not control.

He always had the option of sending Mother to the ranch to live. With his father when the old man arrived.

At the moment, his primary concern was to keep his mother out of the bank business.

Just as he finished processing two loan extensions, neither of which concerned the Miller orchards, he watched through his wide window O'Toole hasten from the post office to the Sheriff's office.

Time to leave boring paperwork and find out what drove the postmaster to hurry above and beyond his normal stately pace.

"THEY AREN'T COMING TODAY," Postmaster O'Toole said. His slight Irish accent tilted the last word upward, turning every statement into a question.

"Thank you for delivering this so promptly," I replied, ignoring the way he rubbed his thumb against his fingers in his not-so-subtle request for payment. "Mr. Brotherton paid extra for you to deliver it."

"Postmaster in Pendleton collects the money. I don't."

I stood from my desk, collected the telegram envelope, tucking it into my waistcoat pocket—royal blue and silver with silver buttons today—and marched toward the door, which I held open for O'Toole to exit.

I found Mayor Sanderson in the doorway, hand raised to knock on the glass.

My heart stuttered twice before settling back into its normal rhythm. *Damn*, I did not need the distraction of... of his presence right now.

"Do I need to remind you, O'Toole, that anything you read and translate in a telegram is strictly confidential?"

The tall and lanky man with thinning fair hair frowned, his lips pursed so tightly they almost disappeared. He shook his head and stalked out. His shoulder brushed against Neil's, but he walked on, not acknowledging that he had nearly knocked over the man.

"Good day, Mr. O'Toole," Neil called, politely.

"The same goes for you too," I snarled. "Sheriff's business is confidential."

"Confidential or disappointing?" Neil moved inward and stood beside the guest chair, waiting for me to resume my seat before sitting himself. He had pretty manners. But his politeness nearly shouted his acknowledgement that I was female.

I sat down anyway, propped my elbows on the desk and my head in my hands. "What am I supposed to do with... you know?" I lifted one elbow in the vague direction of the staircase and the attic.

"Does the telegram suggest when Brotherton's scientists and photographers will be here?" Thankfully he kept his tone bland and centered on the facts.

An outpouring of emotion wouldn't help right now.

"No. He's waiting to gather his experts." I flung the missive, still in its envelope toward him. It fluttered and landed on the floor before he could grab it.

I didn't try to decipher the expression on his face as he leaned over and gathered up the telegram and the envelope, now separated.

Slowly and patiently, he smoothed out the paper across his knee, adjusted his spectacles and peered closely at the printing.

Who knew that spectacles could appear so... attractive?

After a moment, Neil placed the paper face down on my desk, removed his spectacles. and folded them into their case. Then he pinched the bridge of his nose, hard, until his knuckles turned white.

I wondered if his mother ever noticed this habitual movement as a reaction to something that needed careful thought and took it as a signal to cease her diatribes.

"Well, I do not believe we should move the corpse until this psychic medium expert arrives from Portland," he said from beneath his hand where he still pinched the inner corners of his eyes.

"Do you have a headache?" I asked. The sun was hidden today by a thick layer of leaking clouds, so the bright light could not have triggered his sensitivity. I opened the bottom drawer of the desk and withdrew the mostly full flask that sat atop the false panel hiding additional weaponry. "I resisted this when your mother left." I handed the precious silver vessel to him. "I never carry this in the field in case I damage or lose it. Lucian brought it to me from my stash of personal items in Brotherton's keeping."

He studied the smooth lines and crisp engraving on the slightly curved inner side. "Eugene Evan Baumgarten," he murmured.

"It's all I have left of him."

"Then I drink a toast to your father." He raised the flask in salute and swallowed deeply of the ghastly brew.

An astonished gasp exited his mouth upon a waft of whisky fumes. His throat apple bobbed as he tried, without success, to speak.

"That's the worst whisky I could find in Rosie's collection. Startles me out of my doldrums and doesn't tempt me to overindulge."

He nodded, mouth still open, not quite daring to speak yet.

"So, I guess we sit tight and pretend our friend upstairs doesn't exist," Neil finally choked out.

"For now, that's as good a plan as any. Do you have news about the Miller place?"

"They have made no loan payments this year. The first of October they will be officially in arrears. I then have ninety days to foreclose and another ninety days to sell the land, stock, and homestead at auction."

"In the meantime, all those beautiful apples will fall to the ground and rot." Suddenly my mouth watered for the taste of a fresh apple, and apple pie, and apple butter and... and apple cider.

"I will ride out this afternoon and inspect the place. If it is indeed deserted, I can appoint a steward to tend to the harvest and prevent vandalism. The money from the sale of the crops goes into a trust against continuing debt."

"The harvest should have begun weeks ago. With this rain I believe you'll lose a good bit of it..." I mused out loud.

Neil grinned, the lines around his eyes relaxing as the whisky kicked in. "Ride out with me and we'll see if we can recruit the neighbors into harvesting the trees and taking half the apples plus the windfalls in payment," he said, his smile widening. "If we take sacks to fill, maybe Cook can be persuaded to bake pies for tonight's dinner."

His expression lightened. In the diffused morning sunlight filtering through the back windows, he looked positively handsome.

~

AN HOUR LATER, Neil and Josie rode through the drizzle that tapered off to occasional, widely scattered drops. Both of their horses seemed eager to stretch their legs and cover the mile and a half to the Miller's drive quickly.

Prospero seemed to remember the journey, or at least the apple treats at the end of the road.

Josie dismounted first, giving Neil the opportunity to admire her long legs and daydream.

She plucked two apples from the closest tree and divided them in half with her belt knife—shorter and more utilitarian than the Bowie she'd tucked into a calf sheath. Her horse lipped the fruit from the palm of her hand. She handed the second apple to Neil to share with his horse. Her half disappeared into Prospero before she had a chance to nibble more than two bites for herself.

"No more." She tapped her horse on the nose. "You are too greedy and will end up with a belly ache before we get home."

"You talk to that beast as if he understands you," Neil said, pushing Molly away from the tempting tree.

Remembered Bible stories from his childhood flooded him with guilt for succumbing to his own temptations... Wait, those were sermons by a series of pastors about the sinful nature of man. Fire and brimstone. Etc. etc. etc. He hadn't believed them since he'd left his mother's household to go to boarding school back east during his early teens. Now, when Ethel Sanderson pressured him to attend church services with her, he tuned out the pastor and added bank figures in his head.

"Do you smell smoke?" Josie asked. She took off her fine white Stetson as if the brim blocked her nose as well as shielding her eyes.

"Smoke?" Neil's first glance went to the chimney of the house. It looked clear and the scent on the breeze was faint.

"A small and distant campfire." She gathered Prospero's reins and walked him southeast toward the next field of apples. Greener fruit here, a different variety from the sweet and red ones on the north side of the property, and the yellow ones that ripened across the road.

He followed her, keeping a tighter rein on Molly.

They walked through seemingly endless aisles of overgrown trees. Even he could see that they needed pruning and the fruit was sparse on this side. Details were fuzzy. His damaged eyes picked out green, shapeless leaves and apples, and grey-brown wood. Nothing more specific.

The sweet smell of burning wood grew stronger. More light filtered through the thick branches.

Josie halted a few yards before a small clearing. All he could make out were five huge boulders—each the size of a one room cabin—in an almost circle. What lay beyond remained a mystery.

"Hey there!" Josie called.

A wide, masculine face with a broad nose and weathered skin popped above the closest stone. Impossible to tell his age. He reached a scarred hand with a missing index finger to adjust the brim of his hat. He called back a few words that Neil could not understand.

Josie bowed and answered him with similar words. A greeting in a foreign language?

"Come Neil Sanderson, we have been welcomed to rest by the fire of friends. May I present Esteban Shallook, master sheepherder of his clan."

"Basque?" Neil asked quietly.

"Yes. I have met them before. I know a few words of their language but not enough to carry on a conversation."

"Welcome, friend of Master Blue!" the shepherd called in accented English. Not a Spanish or French lilt, something entirely different. "Come, sit. Share your news."

Five men, ranging from very old with white hair and more wrinkles than features, to a lad in his mid-teens, stood up from a series of stumps where they'd perched. Seven stumps seemed empty. A flash of color and movement revealed women huddled between two of the boulders, heads bowed, in similar ages to the men. They clung to each other for protection from strangers.

"Thank you for the hospitality of your fire," Neil replied, nodding to each of the men. Always a safe response, no matter the language or culture. "I have met a few wandering Romany, but never before your people."

"Many outsiders confuse us for the Rom because we keep to ourselves and have dark hair and eyes. But we are not alike," Esteban replied, resuming his seat. This seemed to be a signal for all the men to sit and the women to retreat further. Apparently, the men did not consider Josie to belong to the female contingent.

"Do you camp here often?" Josie asked, accepting a tin cup of black coffee and a cigarette. She took one small puff and passed the stub to the man beside her.

He took a long puff and passed it to Neil. He pretended to breathe in his own share of the smoke and quickly passed it on, not daring to cough out the bitter weed. Not tobacco. Something sort of sweet and acrid at the same time.

"Mistress Miller and her husband invite us every year. We help with the harvest. Come spring, the husband helps us with the shearing. We share food and news, help each other, protect each other. But his year they do not come to welcome us."

"The house is empty," Josie replied.

All the men crossed themselves and held out their fists, index and smallest finger extended—near universal wards of protection.

"Then a misfortune has truly befallen the family. And us."

"Sheriff Blue is my steward for this land," Neil said, slowly, thinking through his options as he spoke. "I am the banker for the Millers." He truly hoped these nomads understood the concept of banks and loans and such. "The sheriff has the authority to welcome or ban you. Whatever seems best all around."

"Friend Esteban," Josie replied, "I welcome you to stay as long as you need, to help me protect the land. Help yourself to the harvest and sell what you can in town. Half the money to you and half to my friend Neil Sanderson for the bank."

"We will stay until winter sends us to the lowlands. Perhaps return in the spring on our way to higher pastures."

"Very good. We thank you for your hospitality." She stood and bowed low to him.

Neil mimicked her actions, making certain not to spill any of the black as midnight coffee when he set down the cup. He hadn't dared take a drink, and neither had Josie.

"We will fill our sacks with the red apples, across the drive, and leave you in peace."

"I will send my boy on our fastest pony if we hear any special music," Esteban said, staring into his coffee cup. "But this valley is protected. We do not usually hear music here that is not of our own making."

Josie nodded and led her horse back toward the orchard.

CHAPTER 22

I DRAGGED my attention away from the way Neil's dark blond hair curled around his ears, exposing his strong jawline and the way his mouth quirked upward. He glanced at me, and his grin widened a tiny bit. Just enough to reveal his lighter mood.

Warmth and contentment filled my chest, making breathing in the damp air easier.

We'd had a companionable day gathering apples. His hand brushed mine, my shoulder bumped his. Our fingers touched and tingled as we passed food from the picnic basket back and forth. We laughed and talked, easy and comfortable in each other's company.

Darker clouds loomed on the western horizon. We'd have heavier rain tonight. For now, I could glory in the shaft of sunlight that shot from beneath the gloomy layer and lighted the road into town.

My town.

Our town.

A quick search did not show any strange horses or wagons hitched in front of my office. True to his word, Brotherton had not sent any agents or scientists ahead to deal with the mummy in the attic.

But I did spot Ethel Sanderson's buggy parked in front of the bank.

Pedestrians seemed to have deserted the boardwalk and all of the businesses looked closed for the day.

"Oh shit!" Neil said. He didn't look embarrassed at his strong language.

"It's been hours since she confronted me this morning," I said, wondering what kind mischief the portly matron could have worked while we laughed and joked and got to know each other better.

"I hope she hasn't been preventing my clerk from working," Neil growled.

"Do you need me to help intervene?" I dismounted in front of the saloon and deposited my sack of apples on the doorstep. Then I reached up to take his load.

"She's *my* mother. I'll deal with her. But you might fetch Doc." He dismounted too and took a moment to breathe deeply. "Thank you for today." He brushed my hand and led Molly toward the bank.

I stood watching him for a brief moment, dimly aware that Jonquil had taken the apples inside.

"You ungrateful miscreant, you are no better than your wastrel father," Ethel Sanderson screamed loud enough for the entire town to hear. "Without me you wouldn't have a bank to inherit!"

Time to fetch Doc and his lifesaving vials of sedatives.

"Might need morphine to calm her down."

DOC STOOD on the boardwalk in front of his office, staring at the black bag he clutched so tightly he couldn't feel his fingers. *God, I need a drink.*

He'd had to administer laudanum to Ethel Sanderson twice to subdue her raging screams and pummeling fists. Neil had feared apoplexy, and rightly so.

The town matriarch did not take challenges to her authority lightly. With her face bright red, her heart racing, and stumbling gait, Doc had used every bit of charm and persuasion to get her calm enough to pour the cloudy liquid down her throat. He was ready to resort to an injection of morphine when Rachel, the maid, had reminded Ethel that without having to worry about the bank business, she'd have more time to devote to her garden club, her church duties, and her charitable works. The people of Heller's Hole would still look to her out of respect for who she was rather than how many loans she influenced.

"Bless Rachel," Doc muttered as he managed to remember to unlock the door and walk inside out of the rain.

If ever he deserved a dose of Rosie's fine brandy, savored in front of a friendly fire in the hearth, it was now. After the drink put him in a mellow glow, he'd seek out Jonquil with her soft and gentle arms holding him. Not Jonquil. She was too delicate and fragile. Maybe nurturing and comforting Lily. She'd make a fine mother someday.

He dropped his bag, not caring if he broke anything inside, turned around and headed for the saloon. Lights blazed from the windows, and he heard voices and laughter, but not the raucous din of a Saturday night. This was just a quiet Thursday. Maybe Lucian had returned and would be receptive to buying out the Daytons.

A delicate waft of cinnamon and baking apples tickled his nose. What was this? Apple pie?

He couldn't remember the last time he had baked apple anything.

He hastened his footsteps, the day's alarums and hysterics almost forgotten.

Life in Heller's Hole could be right nice some nights.

FRIDAY MORNING DAWNED bright and inviting. Even the rooster crowing his head off didn't bother me. Much.

I'd asked questions and now understood that the presence of a rooster among the flock of jabbering hens encouraged the laying of eggs for breakfast and Cook had them for baking.

My feet didn't hurt. Putting on my boots brought nary a wince. My feet, with the help of Doc's balm and Epsom salts, healed at a regular rate. Elinore needed more time. As long as I had Prospero to ride, giving my mare the time she needed to become sound again eased my mind about my new position as Sheriff.

"I'm riding out again today," I told Cook when I stood in her kitchen (this might be Rosie's Saloon, but it was Cook's kitchen) and requested breakfast, whatever she chose to prepare for me. Stale bread dipped in a frothy mixture of eggs and milk and cinnamon and then fried to perfection sounded wonderful to me. She topped it all with the last of the fresh blackberries and a dusting of sugar.

I took the plate from her gratefully.

"Don't suppose you'd like to ride east and check on my nephew and his family?" the plump, middle-aged woman asked.

"For you, Cook, I'll ride a new direction. I need to get to know the lay of the land and the neighbors."

"My name is Maisie Downes. But Cook will do. It's what I do and who I am."

"Thank you, Cook Maisie Downes. You let me know if anyone bothers you or pilfers your larder."

"Don' mind pilfering, as long as it doesn't get out of bounds. Outright theft I'll let you know."

With that, I took my breakfast to the main room with the pot of coffee.

An hour later found me in the saddle and wandering the back trails in and out of Heller's Hole.

By noon I was back in the office with my feet up, boots off, and savoring a large slab of apple pie—fresh from Cook's oven with a chunk of sharp yellow cheese and a flask of tea. Real tea, brewed perfectly. I hadn't had tea this good or refreshing since... since Ma died.

Satisfied with my new life, I studied the newest round of wanted posters that came in the mail. Cutter Pine still topped the list. The reward for his capture alive remained at the king's ransom of $5000. The amount offered for proof of his death dropped to $100. Barely worth the risk of confronting him.

Someone wanted that man alive. Why?

I roused from my musing when two big shadows darkened my open door.

A dark-haired man of middling height doffed his utilitarian brown leather hat. He stepped forward on slightly bowed skinny legs. His massive shoulders blocked the light coming in through the half window of the door. The sun had darked his face and carved deep lines around his eyes and pulled his mouth into a near permanent frown. He could be anywhere from forty to sixty years of age. Two six shooters rested easily in their hip holsters.

He looked like a man who lived in the saddle and wrestled cows for a living.

Behind him stood a younger man, of equal height but much fairer coloring. His hair was so light the sun seemed to pass right through it.

A shiver of apprehension climbed my spine.

The two men approached me side by side glancing toward each other in silent communication.

I stood, politely, keeping the desk between us. "What can I do for you? I'm Sheriff Blue." I offered my hand for a shake, like men do when greeting a stranger.

"McKenzie da Foe," the darker man said. He shook my hand briefly, weakly, then slid the straight chair right in front of the desk and sat, facing me squarely. His hands remained by his sides.

When I looked to the fairer man, eyebrows raised in question, he stepped behind Mac da Foe and kept his mouth shut.

"From town gossip, I gather that your companion, Mr. da Foe, is your former foreman and now your financial advisor. Aren't you going to introduce us?"

"My boys tell me that you ran them out of town for letting off a little steam in a bit of innocent fun." He completely ignored my request for an introduction. Why did he need this white-haired man to remain anonymous?

"Shooting guns in the middle of town is not innocent by any definition. It endangers the people and property of my town."

"This is my town, Sheriff Blue." He half-stood as his face reddened in anger.

"Is it?"

Both Mac da Foe and his unnamed companion stared at me blankly, as if I'd challenged his notion that the sun came up this morning.

"What do you mean by that! I'm the biggest landowner around. The law in this town is what I say."

I leaned back and crossed my arms. "I know at least three people who own more of this town than you. And now that Oregon is a State that sided with the Union forces during the war, their laws say the town belongs to *ALL* of the property owners, administered by their elected officials."

Damn, I'd given Rollie my one and only law book. I couldn't open the pages and show this blowhard the precise text.

"We'll see about that," Mac snarled. "My boys will come to town when they want and shoot whatever and whoever they choose."

"When any of your sons or hands come to town, I expect them to deposit their weapons here, where I can lock them up. And anyone who starts a fight or cheats at cards will be locked up as well." I stood, signaling the end of the interview.

That night, and the next remained quiet in town. No sign of the da Foes. They didn't even come to church—either church—on Sunday, I knew because I attended both since they didn't meet at the same time.

We all breathed a little easier come Monday morning.

But I sensed a wariness among the town folk as we went about our business and waited for Saturday night to come around again.

CHAPTER 23

MONDAY MORNING both Elinore and Prospero were off their feed, just when I thought my mare was healing and the stallion should be restless enough for a good gallop. They both shied from small, unexpected noises. My dawn patrol of the delivery wagons behind Rosie's showed me similar wary behavior of the big draft horses. The ranchers and farmers took care never to be alone. They crowded together, unloading at the same time and jostling each other in their hurry to be elsewhere.

The chill wind presaging the next storm bit through my buckskin jacket with unusual keenness. I thought about returning to my room at Rosie's to don my long johns beneath my usual trousers and calico shirt.

Cook clung to her bed until after nine. No one else was up yet, but I was hungry. I made myself coffee and scrambled some eggs with a bit of onion and ham—I remembered a few basic lessons from Ma's kitchen and could cobble together a few things over a campfire. I sliced and toasted the remains of yesterday's loaf to round out the meal. I'd have loved some jam and butter on the toast but had to make do with bacon grease. It did not serve a person well to rummage through Cook's pantry and misplace items. I valued my hide more than tasty treats.

With nothing else to occupy me in the semi-darkness, I put my boots on, grateful for their warmth, and began to walk the town.

Lights came on in the general store and the proprietor turned the "closed" sign around to "open." The millinery remained dark and closed. So did the bank. Neil usually came in early to do whatever bankers do before opening. Not even a lamp shone in the back office —hidden and rarely accessible to the public.

A single light shone inside the Catholic Church and I detected some movement within. Father Xavier always performed his rituals at dawn, usually alone. This morning, he opened the front door wide in a welcoming gesture. I tipped my hat to him and continued my patrol.

If the priest was up and about, the Baptist minister/schoolmaster should be too. Soon, the children would arrive in a boisterous burst of energy before they had to settle down to a boring day of lessons. I followed the Russell children on their half-wild, unsaddled ponies toward the schoolhouse and the livery just beyond. As we neared the end of town, the ponies crossed the street and picked their way in a wide berth around the school building, making their way toward the livery and the safety of their herd. Elinore stood at the open gate instead of in the creek. She took a broad stance, ears forward, lip curled above her teeth, a warning snarl and rearing feet in the offing.

I mimicked her attitude, making certain I closed the gate after the last pony entered the paddock. The Russell children dismounted with their books and slates and luncheon basket. They stood in a line facing the school, still and wary, reluctant to move. They edged behind me, arms around each other, placing the youngest of them in the middle.

Animals sense things normal humans can neither see nor hear. For their fears to bleed over to children was unusual.

Now I was worried.

NEIL LINGERED in bed long after dawn. Every time he tried to throw off his covers and move his legs, wave after wave of panic sent him shivering back beneath the protection of a sheet, two wool blankets and a quilted coverlet.

He couldn't bury his head deep enough.

If he closed his eyes, his mind replayed images of the aftermath of battle. Ten-year-old memories that returned in frightening detail.

"I am stronger than this!" he said, cooly, flatly, not giving way to the need to hide once more.

Resolutely he dragged on yesterday's clothing, merely draping his tie around his neck rather than make the supreme effort of knotting it correctly. Shoes presented a serious problem in tying them, so he opted for his riding boots and walked out of the house, one step in front of the other.

He couldn't even think about breakfast without gagging.

As he walked into town, wave after wave of anxiety swept through him. He really wanted to turn around and walk—or run—away.

He persevered until he reached the front door of the bank. As he took a deep breath for the strength to insert his key into the lock, he looked right and left for whatever peered over his shoulder and made his arm so heavy he could hardly lift it to the level of the lock.

Down the street, to the north, he saw Josie standing by the gate to the livery. Elinore stood beside her, and three children huddled behind them, inside the paddock.

They all stared at the schoolhouse across the street from them. Unnaturally still, as if turned to stone, or facing terror.

He couldn't see the white clapboard building with the squat bell tower from this angle, but he knew the source of his malaise was there.

"A few more steps. If I walk a few more steps I can stand beside Josie. She'll make everything right," he told himself.

He wished he'd brought a firearm.

～

SOMETHING MOVED near the door of the school, beneath the small, square porch. I squinted my eyes to focus my vision.

A lump, vaguely man-shaped lay prone on the weathered boards. The sound of his whimpering reached me.

"Who?"

"That's the Reverend Sanderpoole, our teacher," whispered the oldest Russell boy. He and his siblings crouched behind the water trough.

Something clicked inside my memory, like the lifting of a door latch.

Demonic *things* could not cross water. The filled trough might protect them.

A quick look confirmed that all of the horses had deserted their meadow and now stood either in the creek or beyond it. Elinore had probably lipped open the gate latch to let them run free of whatever frightened them.

Then I noticed Neil approaching as if wading through thick water. He looked a mess, shirt buttoned crookedly, vest open, jacket and hat missing. He wore good sturdy riding boots. But he minced his steps as if his feet hurt.

I instantly breathed easier knowing I was not alone.

"Protect the children," I ordered, handing him one of my pistols. "I'm going to get the teacher to safety."

He nodded agreement.

One step forward. Then another and another. Elinore plodded behind me. Good girl. Her need to protect me outweighed her own injuries and pain.

My breathing grew heavier, but I persevered until I climbed the three steps of the porch and stood over the minister.

"Have mercy," he pleaded banging his forehead against the boards. "I've done nothing to hurt you!"

The front door to the schoolroom stood ajar about an inch.

If we dealt with something eldritch that was more than enough space to loose a hoard of demons.

Oh, I'd read all of the Pinkerton tomes on demonology, witches, and magic. The Riders of the Purple Sage had been formed to control them until the purple aliens demanded all of our attention.

But reading and understanding are not the same.

I grabbed Sanderpoole's shirt collar and hauled the man to his feet. With hair standing in spikes, heavy beard shadow, and bloodshot eyes, he looked more unkempt than Neil.

"Whatever this is, it should not manifest within a church," I said forcing the reverend down the steps.

"W... w... what?" his jaw hung open and his eyes refused to focus.

"Sanctified space. Any ordained minister should know that."

"I never bothered. Didn't seem necessary to a true believer."

"Maybe, maybe not." With an extra shove between his shoulder blades, I got him back across the street to the relative safety behind the water trough.

"Neil, can you get some holy water, incense, and bells from Father Xavier?"

His eyes cleared from their mindless stare. "Of course!"

I needn't have bothered asking, for the intrepid little priest with a bald pate, wearing a black robe and a colorful stola about his shoulders strode toward us bearing a chalice with a flat lid atop it and swinging an ornate, smoking, silver ball on a long chain. A long rope of wooden beads, each bead as big as a man's thumb and the decade beads twice that size, and a carved crucifix hung from his belt. He mumbled prayers with every step.

He'd come armed as best he knew how. Better armed than me in this case.

Guns didn't work very well against supernatural forces. The tiny spark that ignited the gunpowder wasn't enough fire to overcome spirits.

Father Xavier handed the chain for the smoking ball of incense to Neil and lifted the carved wooden cross from his rosary to his lips and kissed it before brandishing it before him like a torch. I took the chalice. No bells though. I wondered if we'd have the time and opportunity to ring the school bell.

Shoulder to shoulder we marched across the street, through the schoolyard, and up the porch steps. We paused only a heartbeat while I kicked the door the rest of the way open, careful not to spill a precious drop of the Holy Water.

A black wall of impenetrable murk greeted us. Waves of despair and grief washed over me.

All I wanted to do was curl up on the floor and bury my head in my arms. All my sins rose up in my memory. Every wrong, every bad thought, every life I'd taken right down to the fly I'd swatted this morning.

"Shade of one who was wronged, I banish you!" Father Xavier shouted. He began swinging his rosary around and around like a lasso. The wooden beads clacked together with a regular rhythm. A different kind of bell.

I should have known the short priest would think of everything.

The murk withdrew a bit.

Before I could think, Father Xavier touched my shoulder and pointed toward the core of blackness.

I counted to three while the spirit gathered all of its power within itself.

"Our Father who art in Heaven," I chanted the only prayer I knew, drilled into me by my beloved, protective mother.

With a single fortifying breathe I flung the holy water, chalice and all, into the heart of the darkness.

Neil followed suit with the incense.

The spirit bellowed in pain and anger. It rushed toward us, its wrath a suffocating blanket.

Neil collapsed.

CHAPTER 24

Neil felt the strength drain out of his body. Dizziness overwhelmed him. He had to get his head down.

Had to.

His knees hit the floor with a thud. The sound came from somewhere else. He didn't really hear it, or feel it, just knew it had happened.

He tried to brace himself with his hands. The command from his mind to his hands failed.

Utterly.

Nothing but a failure.

Caught up in arithmetic.

Can't shoot a gun or rope a cow.

Too concerned with numbers to think for yourself!

Run on home and hide behind your mama's skirts.

I need your body to live again so just go away.

He recognized the voice behind the sneering insults from his childhood in this very building.

Judd MacKenzie da Foe.

Third and largely forgotten son of Mac da Foe. The same age as Neil. He'd died from a broken neck when he leaned out too far from the belfry while throwing desiccated cow turds at the old school-master and his fellow students out in the yard. Neil remembered his scream of terror as he fell.

And then nothing but the snap of bones and air whooshing from his lungs.

The taunts settled in Neil's heart like a hard and unbreakable hickory nut.

"No!" Josie cried.

He felt her kneel beside him and lift his head and chest against her. Cradling him.

Banishing the cold of the dead spirit.

Infusing him with her own strength.

Loving him.

In his mind, he saw her will become a hammer. His own determination to live long, active, prosperous, happily with her grabbed the hammer and slammed it against the near unbreakable nut.

Shell and shriveled meat of the nut shattered and spread far and wide, out of him.

Outside his chest, the pieces began gathering together, forming, coalescing into something sinister and ugly.

"Judd MacKenzie da Foe, you were a bully twenty years ago. You are still a worthless bully. I succeeded in life. You never accomplished anything but generating disgust. Begone!"

Father Xavier tossed his lasso of a rosary and roped the nasty spirit. It struggled, bucking and twisting until the priest managed to ignite a lucifer on the sole of his sandal and throw the living flame into the heart of the malevolent spirit.

Another wild shriek of defiance.

The fire gained fuel from the decrepit being.

A plea for mercy.

A whimper of despair.

And it was gone.

The roaring flames winked out.

Nothing left but a pile of ash.

~

WHEN NEIL STIRRED and he opened his eyes to gaze into mine, a great weight lifted from my chest. I could breathe again.

He twisted his body and braced his feet as if to rise from the floor and away from my embrace.

"Josie, I can stand," he said, hoarsely, as if the spirit had shredded his throat when he expelled it.

"Give yourself a moment to gather your strength and your wits." I'd never bothered with such niceties for myself. But I wanted to linger with my arms about him.

"I learned something, Josie, when Judd tried to take command of my body."

"You said a few words, he was a bully in life and was trying to be one in death."

"Yes." This time I let him scramble to his feet, needing only a little help from me. I kept a hand under his elbow and my other around his waist. He squeezed me gently before asserting control. "Judd was only joined with me for a few moments, but he had a great deal of wrath propelling him. He has been confined in the belfry for twenty years. Ever since he fell from there and broke his neck. Something about a web of magic mastering his ability to do harm when all he wanted in life, and death, was to take revenge upon those who suppressed his need to control everything, specifically his father Mac da Foe, and everyone around him, like his six brothers. The magic confining him had control over him, and he hated that."

"What allowed him to break free now?" I stayed close to him, ready to catch him if he stumbled.

While we spoke in low tones, Father Xavier gathered his equipment and peeked through the open door. "All of the children have gathered. Sanderpoole is still cowering and hiding his head beneath his arms. Coward." He almost spat the last words, something I didn't think he did often.

"Can you see to the children, escort them home if they need?" I asked. Anything to prolong this bit of privacy with Neil. And to gain precious information.

"All I ask is that you give me a few hours notice before I have to perform a nuptial mass." He closed the door behind him, testing the latch twice to make certain it held.

No comment about how the priest knew I was female.

Perhaps Neil had spoken in confession.

When the priest had left, closing the door behind him, Neil turned to face me. "I think we disturbed something when we found the mummy in your attic. Either that or the magic is breaking down because of the passage of years," he said, resting his forehead against mine.

A moment of weakness?

Maybe he needed to keep our discussion from traveling further.

Or perhaps, like me, he cherished the brief moments without prying eyes.

"We don't have much time." Not for us, or for the protection of the town. "I need to send another telegram to Brotherton, urging speed in sending his experts."

"We never have much time," he whispered as he placed his hands on either side of my face and lowered his lips to mine.

Gentle at first. Almost tentative. I returned his caress, matching him in intensity.

And then passion overcame us both at the same time. I grew greedy for him. Our hands explored shoulders and arms, backs, and....

We clung to each other cherishing each moment, letting our growing love for each other to spill out and enfold us together.

Raised voices and stomping footsteps on the porch finally broke us apart. We stood several inches apart. Without him, I felt chilled to the bone. And yet... and yet a hard knot of cold distance between my heart and the rest of the world cracked.

I wasn't alone any longer. I needn't push people aside anymore. My heart no longer needed protection. I could share it freely again. As I had with my sister and my parents. I now had Neil.

~

"Sit still, Mayor Sanderson!" Doc roared at his newest patient.

"I don't need your poking and prodding of my person," the mayor snarled back at him. "The malevolent ghost left me unscathed."

"I believe they are called poltergeists," Doc replied, trying to contain his anger at being awakened out of a restless sleep by Sheriff Blue. Too early. Much too early in the morning. "And otherworldly spirits can wreak havoc on your innards. Wrestled with them a time or two back in Boston."

"I'd rather be from Boston than live there!" Neil retorted, his voice raising to match Doc's.

"I'll have you know I attended Harvard Medical School, the finest..."

"And I attended Princeton..."

"The fact that you two are arguing about petty schoolboy rivalries makes it clear that you both have been affected by the malign spirit of Judd MacKenzie da Foe," Josie yelled at them both from the outer room, where she waited impatiently for Doc to finish his examination.

Doc forced his anger down. He had to approach each patient calmly, with his eyes and ears open to subtle clues to the source of the ailment. He took a deep breath and felt the lingering heaviness from a night of strange and troubling dreams fade away.

Another deep breath for good measure and he grabbed Neil's arm to test his pulse at his wrist then again at his neck.

Neil only struggled against his touch for a heartbeat or six before he too took a deep cleansing breath and allowed Doc to examine him.

"Josie has that rare ability to spread a circle of calm around her. Helps her to deal with rowdy cowboys and outlaws," Doc muttered.

"Yeah, she does."

"So, tell me about the poltergeist."

He listened to the tale, more for the tone of Neil's voice and the tension in his body.

"So, the ghost you banished was the missing seventh son of Mac da

Foe that everyone knows about, but no one talks about. They only remember that there should be seven sons, but only six come to town." He backed away from Neil and made a couple of notes in his journal.

"The only people who know about him are those who've been in town more than twenty years." Neil shook his head to clear it of the last bits of confusion.

"You're free to go. The bully didn't do you any lasting harm. But if you find your mind going blank or anything weird about your vision, then come right back here without delay." He gestured his friend off the examining table.

Neil's gaze immediately turned toward the outer room. His features softened.

"So, that's what's really bothering you," he muttered. He should have expected it. And then there was the gentle way she'd half carried Neil into the office, her shoulder beneath his and her fingers gripping the confused patient about his waist, clutching with anxiety. More than anxiety, love.

A bubble of disappointment burst inside Doc. Oh, well. Josie was too young and domineering for him, anyway. But he sincerely wished he could have bedded her just once before she settled upon a good man like Neil.

"Your turn, Sheriff Blue," he called to her. "Gotta make sure that bully didn't leave behind any ectoplasmic residue in you either."

"Judd didn't come near me. He only invaded Neil, and then only briefly. Now come along, Mr. Mayor. We need to find a new school-master and see if Sanderpoole is sane enough to get himself back to the city or if one of us needs to drive him."

"I'll drive him," Doc replied. "I don't think Sanderpoole has ever been sane enough to take himself anywhere." And he'd have a chance to spend some time with the widow Murphy to console himself.

DAYS PASSED as my town shook off the gloom of having a poltergeist in their midst. Careful questioning led me to believe no one remembered poor old Judd because no one wanted to remember him. Not even his father and six remaining brothers.

Prospero and I patrolled every morning, and I spent the afternoons in the office, or in Rosie's. The townsfolk knew where to find me. They greeted me with a friendly wave or tip of the hat when we passed each other.

By Thursday of that week, I was bored, but oddly content, because Neil and I—though never alone—spent a part of each day together, talking, sharing our thoughts, and falling deeper in love while discussing plans for finding a new schoolmaster.

And I'd heard nothing more from Brotherton or Lucian.

After another good meal of roasted chicken and new potatoes, I, barefoot again, took a last turn around the saloon, making certain no trouble simmered among the patrons. Mostly just the town folk, winding down with a beer before heading home to supper.

I heaved a big sigh, grateful for the peace and quiet, unlike what Neil must be facing at home.

Last week, Neil and I had heard Ethel's screams within the bank from the gateway of his house when returning from the Miller orchards. Apparently, Ethel's efforts to close the bank and intimidate the customers had failed.

Neil was faced with the necessity of getting her home. I had offered to help carry the woman, but Doc and Neil waved me off. The aging town matriarch needed familiarity, not strangers.

With the saloon quiet, and my tummy full of apple pie, I retired to my corner room with a book, and a chance to put my feet up—not so swollen as the night before.

Elinore and I both healed, but slowly. By next week I should be able to keep my boots on for an entire day.

Would Elinore ever have sound feet again?

The small coal fire in the franklin stove gave off just enough warmth to make the room comfortable and cozy against the wet and windy night. My eyelids grew heavy. I had to reread the next para-graph of the dime novel in my hands to make any sense of it...

Deep, sorrowful weeping invaded my dreams. My shoulders shook with sobs. My innards ached with pain.

Not real pain. I'd always known the burning tears came from grief and fear when this dream took over.

Why pain?

A soft knock on my door roused me the rest of the way from the too familiar and unwelcome nightmare.

I slammed my feet against the floor and sat up straight. My gun belt and knife sheath came to my hands readily from where I'd draped them over the spindle post of my bed. I grabbed them and unlocked the door, meeting my guest with a drawn pistol.

"Easy, Sheriff. Easy," Doc said, holding out his hands palms up. He wore only his trousers held up by twisted braces, and an undershirt.

Jonquil cowered behind him, eyes red, body shaking, and tears still leaking.

I pushed aside the solid presence of Doc, and grabbed Jonquil's arm, dragging her inward. "Who did this to you?" I glared at Doc, having heard enough rumors among the girls about how rough he liked his sex.

But he could be gentle too, when needed.

Jonquil winced and moaned, staring at her arm rather than look me in the eye.

I wrapped my free arm around the girl's shoulders, taking note of her torn chemise and the way she hunched over her belly.

"Not me," Doc protested in his most professional voice.

"Then who?"

"Get the girl inside and out of sight," Rosie hissed, appearing soundlessly behind Doc. She looked over her shoulders, in both direc-tions while pushing Doc and herself inside. Her nightgown sat crookedly on her shoulders.

"What is going on?" I asked. I leaned out my doorway and looked all around. The gallery was empty with lights showing beneath closed doors in only three other rooms. The saloon beyond the railing looked dark and deserted. Though I heard the wind howling and the rain pounding on the roof, the outer doors were tightly closed and locked against drafts seeking entrance.

"Please explain." I made a point of closing my door quietly and locking it against intruders.

"A stranger lingered long over his dinner and expensive whiskey," Rosie began.

"He drank more than half of the bottle," Doc added.

"I knew he'd have to stay the night," Rosie continued. "So I gave him one of the single rooms, right below this one."

There were three small rooms tucked away in the back corner, set up just so men could sleep off some of their drunk. Alone.

"The stranger took a shine to Jonquil and dragged her along with him. I tried to separate them, but he twisted her arm behind him," Doc said.

"We figured he was too far gone in his drunk to do much of anything... So, Doc and I retired to my rooms on the other side of the building." Now Rosie wept, dabbing her eyes with a lace edged handkerchief.

"Her screams of terror woke you, as they did me," I said flatly.

"He was beating her with his belt." Doc's statement carried a deep underlying anger.

"I slugged his jaw and felled him long enough to get Josie out of there and up here." Rosie looked pleased with herself.

"She was cowering in the corner, all hunched, covering her neck and face with her hands."

"Self-protection," I muttered. "Take care of her, and keep her in this room. I'll be back."

I opened the door again and found Cutter Pine, the man who had rescued me from the massacre of my family, and my first partner with the Pinkertons. He fell into the room, shoulder first, as if he'd been running at the door, ready to break it down.

Of course, he came to *my* town now that the magic web of protection was breaking down. A man as bloodthirsty as he probably couldn't find the town until now.

"I should have known." I ground my teeth with anger. "I thought I taught you a lesson the night I wrestled your belt from you and turned it against you."

"Ah, Josie my love, don't be like that. You know you liked it." He slurred his words as if he hadn't had hours to sleep off the liquor.

In response I kneed his balls, then slammed his throat with the side of my hand as he slumped over his injuries. He reared back gasping for breath and clutching himself.

I cocked my pistol.

CHAPTER 25

"Don't do it, Sheriff!" Doc's voice penetrated my delight in watching Cutter Pine writhe in pain on the floor.

Then I noticed where I pointed my gun, and how Doc hunched over his own midsection. I wanted to chuckle. Any man within shouting distance would cringe. Best I change my aim. What part of him would hurt enough to teach him a lesson without killing him?

Even as I debated my options, Cutter's moans and uncontrolled movements took on a different quality. I'd caught him in enough lies over the years to notice the different tone of his wails and moans. He no longer pulled his legs to his chest to protect himself in a fetal crouch. No. This man prepared to get his knees under him to rise in one swift and graceful movement.

My knee hadn't connected as solidly as I could have wished. He shouldn't hurt this badly for so long.

I shifted position so I was no longer in line with any trajectory he could muster.

"Right hand or left?" I asked him, moving my aim a little higher. He was no longer clutching his vulnerable nether parts. "I know you can shoot and rope with either hand. I can too. But you always reach first with your right."

His eyes widened in horror. "You'd... you'd... they'll fire me!"

No need to wonder who "they" might be. I used to answer to the same organization. Now I answered to Neil Sanderson and this town. I wanted Neil Sanderson, mayor of Heller's Hole, to keep me employed as Sheriff. I *wanted* our growing relationship to grow even more. I considered Brotherton and the Pinkerton agency as resources more than employers.

Interesting.

"Hand me my cuffs, please." I held out my left hand in the vague direction of my gunbelt on the bedstead. "I have a wanted poster in my office with your name and likeness on it, Cutter Pine."

"That was revoked!" Cutter yelled loud enough to wake half the house. "I was infiltrating the Murphy Gang and needed them to think I was wanted just like them until I could take them down and arrest the leaders."

"Then why in Hell did they offer $100, a respectable sum, for you dead, but $5000 for you if alive?" I snapped the cuffs on him behind his back and hauled him to his feet, nearly dislocating his shoulders, and mine, in the process. He was a big man.

"An incentive to keep me alive until Brotherton could intervene." He smiled and the lines around his eyes softened. "I always figured you'd be the one to rescue me and we could celebrate..."

"Or the rewards came from an outraged father who wants revenge for what you did to an innocent girl."

"NO. No. No. You know I only take my belt to prostitutes who disobey. And I pay for the privilege."

"Not on my watch, Cutter Pine. You are going to spend some time getting to know my least comfortable, and haunted jail cell until I get confirmation from Brotherton that for once you are telling the truth."

"Tomorrow's Friday. Our postmaster doesn't always work the telegraph on Fridays," Rosie said, a smile twitching the corners of her mouth at her convincing lie. "Sometimes he doesn't even open the Post Office on Fridays. Might be Monday, or Tuesday before he gets to it."

"Plenty of time for you to get to know my ghost," I said, turning Cutter Pine around to face the door. "Now march."

"Wait, wait, wait. I need my boots and my saddlebags." He shifted his weight to his heels to stall his steps.

I rammed my knee into the backs of his legs, making him stumble forward. He'd taught me that trick ten years ago. My father had taught it to me five years earlier when we'd first discussed me becoming foreman of the family ranch.

"Someone will bring you your things in the morning, with your breakfast, after I make sure you have no other weapons on you."

"My belt…" He tried to grab his waistband and hike up his denim trousers.

"I'm keeping that as evidence, in case Jonquil decides to press charges."

The girl's weeping started anew. "I… can't do that. He paid… he paid, and I have to let him do as he wishes." She collapsed to her knees, shoulders shuddering uncontrollably.

"There are limits," I protested.

"But my stepdaddy sold me to Rosie and he said… he said…"

"Wait just a goldarned moment." I shoved Cutter into the corner where he stumbled over the rocking chair with the patchwork quilt cushions. He'd not get by me while I finished this conversation. "That is slavery!" I shouted at Rosie. "Slavery is illegal now. We fought a goddamned war to end it."

"I know that," Rosie defended herself, settling hands on hips, and straightening her spine. For a moment she almost didn't need a corset. "I paid that bastard $5 to get rid of him and protect this girl. He brought her to me in worse condition than she is now, broken and bleeding—inside and out. I saved her life, but I don't own her. She can leave any time she wants."

"Except that now that she's a soiled dove, no one will give her a job as anything else and she'd starve."

I turned my attention back to Cutter Pine. "We'll deal with this later! Right now, I need to get this piece of garbage locked up."

"But my boots. I can't walk across that cold and muddy street without my boots!"

"Why not? I do it all the time. Don't tell me that the great and mighty Cutter Pine isn't as tough as me. Time was, you'd die first. I can help you do that by the way."

"Good morning, sunshine," I sang out as I entered the office by the back door. Prospero tried to follow me. "Go eat your breakfast, you over-sized puppy dog." I slammed the door on the horse's nose. He had too much curiosity, or interest in the apple slices in my pocket, for his own good. And mine. Almost as bad as Elinore.

I wondered how long my mare needed to recover before she lipped open pasture gates again and started following me around town, with or without a bridle.

My cheerful greeting was met with a snarl worthy of a caged wolf. Cutter paced his tiny cell ferociously.

Disappointment curled in my gut. I'd hoped to waken him with a raging hangover.

I should have known better. Cutter Pine never had a hangover, and rarely needed more than a few hours sleep. That helped make him an excellent agent for the Pinkertons.

"Where's *my* breakfast?" His lip curled revealing his very sharp and prominent eyeteeth.

"Always feed your horse first." I smiled sunnily.

"I taught you that."

"No, my father did. And your breakfast will be here after Cook comes to work."

"And when will that be?" He gripped the cell bars and shook them. They didn't budge but his arm and neck muscles bulged.

"Don't know for sure. No one else over at Rosie's is awake before noon, so there isn't much call for breakfast before then."

"What about you? I presume you ate. But you can't be bothered with sharing." His tones grew louder and angrier. That didn't bode well for either of us.

He didn't need to know that I'd prepared my own breakfast. I'd been learning from Maisey Downes.

"Did my ghost keep you awake?"

"There's no such thing as ghosts."

"But there are other monsters that will bother you to the end of your days, wanting revenge." I remembered a wolf who could have been Were who had attacked us after Cutter had murdered his mate...

I thought about the poltergeist I'd help banish just a few days ago.

I moved to unlock the front door, having spotted Jonquil walking across the street with a tray clutched in both hands. She walked strangely, taking short steps that listed to the left. Even from across the street, I could see the livid bruise around her right eye spreading down to her jaw.

I took the tray from her. "Come in, Jonquil. Let's show Mr. Pine his handiwork. In the ten years I've known him, he's never stuck around long enough to see how much damage he causes, or lives he ruins. You'll be out of work for weeks. Did he break your jaw?"

"Doc says no. But that man over there loosened three teeth. I'll be sore enough I don't want to eat much." She was too skinny as it was. She hung her head, her usually bright blonde hair hanging lank and limp. Defeated.

"Tell Cook I said to feed you applesauce from my apples. And maybe crumble some crisp bacon into it. And maybe some hot tea with honey. Hold the cup against the bruise while it's still warm. And if there's any ice left, wrap a kerchief around a clump of it and hold that atop the worst of the pain."

"When did you become 'nice'?" Cutter spat.

"I always was nice to *people*. I only unleash my anger toward flying aliens who eat carrion, and coerce *people* to create their preferred food." I inspected his breakfast. Rosie had provided just what the sheriff ordered for prisoners of the worst kind: cold gravy over stale, and slightly burned biscuits, with black coffee strong enough to eat a spoon if I dared stir it, guaranteed to eat holes in his stomach.

I shoved the tray beneath the cell door, noting that the fork was weak and warmed. Even if Cutter Pine managed to keep it, he wouldn't be able to use it to pick the lock.

"Want to tell me why you are here, in my town, beating up *my* friends?" I sat in my chair and put my booted feet atop the desk, seemingly relaxed and eager to chat.

Cutter snarled at me again.

"Better eat up. Never know if anyone will remember to feed you come suppertime, especially if I get called out on sheriff's business."

"I heard that Brotherton is sending a scientist and a photographer this way. Thought I'd check out what you are hiding in the attic, see if it points me toward the next swarm of the enemy." He swallowed a forkful of soggy biscuit and grimaced.

"Interesting," I replied. "Any idea when Brotherton's people will arrive? If they're coming. You could be making it up. I mean, why should you tell the truth if a lie suits you better?"

Movement in the street caught my attention. Neil Sanderson walked past my office, headed toward his bank. He tipped his hat as he passed the window but did not pause or try to enter.

I'd give him a few moments to settle in at his desk before accosting him.

"Eat up, Pine. I've got work to do and I need to return your tray, and the cutlery before I can leave you alone for more than ten seconds."

"WHAT HAPPENED LAST NIGHT?" Neil demanded of his clerk the moment the boy poked his nose in the bank. He knew Martin lived with his mother above the general store next door to the sheriff's office and could watch most activity in town through the apartment's one window.

Martin shrugged as he donned his work apron and green visor.

Neither was necessary. He didn't deal with dirty or messy or even dusty things, nor did he work under strong overhead light and need to shade his eyes. But the "uniform" separated a low-ranking employee from the more elite banker.

Mother's idea. "Martin, I'm instituting a new policy. You run this place as much as I do. Keep your jacket and tie on, lose the apron and visor. And as of last Monday you are earning an extra fifty cents a week."

The boy's eyes widened in surprise. "Th… thank you, sir."

"You've earned it. Now tell me why the sheriff is in the office so early and there appeared to be a shadow in one of the jail cells." He wished he could have discerned more when he walked past. The windows were sparkling clean and the sun angle hadn't blinded him. Still, he could only see silhouettes—he'd never mistake Josie for anyone else.

"Heard some shouting after midnight," Martin admitted, setting out his money drawer key, notepad and pencil, as well as the shallow tub of wax that kept his fingers nimble and able to separate bills that wanted to stick together. "I didn't bother getting up to see what the fuss was about. It didn't wake Mama."

The bell over the front door jangled, demanding his attention. Martin looked up with a smile to greet a customer. Neil took a moment to assess the customer.

Josie.

The world brightened a bit.

Morning sun broke through the light cloud cover and turned her chestnut braid into a molten gold halo.

He hastily stood. Before he could come around his desk to greet her, she approached with a no nonsense determined thrust of her chin.

"As your steward for the Miller property, do I have the authority to appoint a live-in caretaker?"

"Yes, I believe so. I've sent letters and a telegram to Mrs. Miller's brother. He's listed as next-of-kin on the loan application. But I haven't had time to hear back." He gestured to the chair in front of his desk and waited for her to sit before dropping into his own high-backed swivel chair.

Her posture remained stiff as she leaned slightly forward in... eagerness?

This was not going to be the casual invitation for them to review the property once more. Alone. Beside each other.

Private.

"What do you have in mind?" he asked. Best he get his thoughts away from finding special moments of privacy with her.

"One of Rosie's girls got beat up last night. Seriously injured. Two broken ribs. She can hardly breathe. Bad bruising around an eye and he loosed three teeth in her jaw."

Neil winced. He'd lived with his weakened eyes, blinding headaches, and light sensitivity for almost ten years. He still had not accustomed himself to the disability. Could still feel the pain of turf and shrapnel penetrating...

Don't think of it. Don't relive it. Don't succumb.

Whatever you do, do not try to remember the beautiful music created by the carrion eaters after a battle but before the hideous feasting began. Do not dwell on it. Think instead of the simple hymns and chants of the Mass.

He repeated the phrases a priest had taught him.

"Prostitutes get paid..."

"She doesn't want to be a prostitute. Never did. Her stepfather *sold* her to Rosie after raping and beating her to insensibility. That's slavery. Illegal. Though Rosie claims she paid the man money to protect the girl, and make the man go away. Forever."

"But she has nowhere to go, no way to support herself," he mused. "Women are still legally the property of the man who has guardianship or custody." Not that any man would survive trying to impose his will on Josie. Then her first question brightened his thoughts.

"Exactly. I can't save all the girls, but I can grant a kind of sanctuary to Jonquil. Esteban and his people will protect her at the Miller place. They are very protective of their women."

"I noticed. The women did not mingle with us."

"Women have more rights among their people than in our 'civilization.' Any man who trespasses on a woman under Basque protection is usually never seen again. If anyone stumbles upon scattered bones many years later, how he died can't be determined."

Again, Neil cringed just thinking about that fate. Though some men might deserve it.

"What about the man who beat Jonquil? I noticed a shadow in your jail cell when I walked by this morning."

"Cutter Pine. An old acquaintance. Wanted poster on my wall for him. I'm stalling before I send a telegram requesting confirmation of the bounty."

"Is Jonquil capable of managing the orchard?"

"I know that she's good at cleaning and mending. She should manage to put the house in order and make it comfortable again. I'll have to ask if she can cook, or grow, harvest, and preserve her own vegetables.

"Then do that. I'll authorize her occupation of the property as long as she maintains it. We've already talked to the Basque about tending the orchard. Shall we ride out there this afternoon and talk to them about protecting the girl?"

Josie's smile lit up her eyes. "Thank you. And we can't keep calling her Jonquil. I presume she had another name before... she started working for Rosie."

"All the girls take a floral name when they come under Rosie's care. Her beautiful garden, she calls them." He forced himself to keep smiling. He had a chance to spend some time alone with Josie! He'd dwell on that rather than the reminder that Rosie's "garden" were not officially slaves. But they might as well be, even if they got paid for their "Work." How much did they get paid? Enough to save some for their retirement?

How old—or young—would they be when they did retire from their work?

Before he could muse further on the problem of what to do with aging prostitutes, O'Toole charged into the bank, somewhat breathless, with telltale yellow envelopes clutched in his fist.

"Oh, good, you're both here. One for each of you." He handed one to Neil and one to Josie, then blatantly peered over their shoulders as they opened and read the missives, even though he knew the contents from transcribing them.

"Looks like you can buy the Miller place any time you want, Sheriff Blue. Mrs. Miller's brother—whose name, oddly, is also Miller —tells me to sell the place or burn it down. Sister and her children safe," Neil said. Interesting. Only a few days turn around. No questions about money. No interest in the place at all. And Mrs. Miller did not take her husband's name. But he'd signed the farm loan as Miller. Coincidence or did he take her name?

Why would he do that?

"We will have visitors from the city late this afternoon," Josie added, refolding her telegram and tucking it into her waistcoat pocket.

"This Brotherton, who sends you telegrams marked urgent, is he someone important?" O'Toole asked, his long face showing more vitality than usual. As Postmaster he should show some degree of discretion.

But if he did, Neil's mother and her friends would have no source of gossip to keep them occupied and out of the bank's business.

"Mr. Brotherton is someone important," Josie replied flatly. "I have to send my own telegram, then we'd best ride out and inspect the Miller place before I plunk down money for it."

She donned her hat and marched out with only a nod to Neil. "Coming O'Toole? I believe you are the only person in town authorized to operate your telegraph machine."

And then she was gone, and the bank seemed bigger and emptier than usual.

CHAPTER 26

"You up to a bit of a walk, Elinore?" I asked my mare.

Elinore ignored me, continuing to graze the lush grass that had sprung up after yesterday's rain. At least she'd wandered out of the creek.

I bent and lifted one fore foot to inspect the hoof and soft frog. Elinore didn't flinch or try to withdraw from my gentle touch.

Who knew what she'd do if *someone else* tried to touch her feet.

"Looks healed to me, Elinore." I put the hoof down gently, not totally convinced my horse had had enough time to grow sound again. Three weeks? Or was it four? I couldn't quite remember how long I'd called this town home.

There could easily be some tiny bits of grit trapped in there. "But I can still count your ribs. And mine for that matter. I think you can skip the trip to our new home."

Jed Junior had already caught her twice trying to lip open the pasture gate and follow me. He'd caught her easily and led her back to the creek. So far.

My horse was smart and learned from her mistakes and human routines.

Elinore reared up her head and tossed her mane at the word *home*.

"Yes dear, I've decided to put down some roots. But I can't pay out good money on the farm unless you approve. We've been together too long to take a chance on you not liking the place."

Elinore snorted and started walking, slowly toward the gate.

I watched her stride carefully. Still a bit of a limp on the left hind leg. "You are staying here, Elinore. For today anyway."

"Hey, Sheriff Blue," young Jed called me from the barn. "I think it's time you found a new stable for Elinore."

"What's she done now?"

"Tried to jump the fence by the gate after I jammed the lock with a worn-out hoof file. She couldn't build up enough speed or height to clear it. This time."

I closed my eyes and pinched the top of my nose. "When?"

"This morning just after breakfast when you checked on her. I had to lasso her and haul her back to the creek. I think she's done being alone. But her feet aren't sound yet."

"At least she's out of the creek."

I PULLED the last strap of a travois harness tight around Elinore's shoulders. "If you insist upon coming, you are going to earn your keep," I said, slapping her neck affectionately.

Elinore did not protest the fit of the harness (we'd done this before with injured comrades) nor the empty burlap bags I piled on top of the sled. She'd carry the bulk of the weight on her shoulders, not her back. It should be easier for her to haul the weight of the apples I planned on retrieving.

Elinore did give Prospero the side-eye as he pranced proudly around *his* paddock, showing off my riding saddle that used to be Elinore's exclusively, and his extreme masculinity. Elinore turned away from the stallion. If he approached her now, she'd likely plant a hoof in his chest.

"I sure as hell hope you two will learn to get along," I muttered.

"Why can't I go with you?" Jonquil asked. She kept glancing over her shoulder toward my office where Cutter Pine was still ensconced in the jail cell. She stood in the back doorway, neither inside nor out, ready to slam the door closed and run should Pine escape.

Last night he'd kicked a hole in the wall between the two cells. And got his foot stuck in the narrow space between the bars. Each cell was completely encased. The slabs of plywood offered a modicum of privacy should I ever have two prisoners. When I discovered him sprawled on the floor with his foot in the wall all the way up to his knee, I'd freed him by the simple expedient of removing his boot.

I was tempted to keep the boot out of his reach. That might, or might not keep him inside.

Hours later, he growled so loudly I could hear him from the hitching rail outside the barn. He sounded like a caged and hungry wolf. Not the first time I had made that association.

Maybe he was one of the legendary werewolves, or a skin walker who took the form of a wolf.

Maybe the uncanny creatures were just a myth to explain away human fears.

"You ready to tell me your real name yet?" I asked Jonquil.

Jonquil hung her head, blonde curls falling forward to mask her face.

"Your ribs are still hurting you." I had helped her bind them with linen strips this morning. "Riding or walking, will hurt you too much. Stay in your room, or help Cook. Just stay out of the saloon. You aren't working yet."

"Rosie will kick me out if I don't earn my keep."

"If all goes well today, I'll have a place for you to stay before Monday, if you tell me your real name."

"Stepdaddy will find me if I tell. His punishments make Cutter Pine's look like love taps."

"I doubt your stepfather cares any more. He got paid for you."

"But... but he said..."

"He lied. He just wanted you to fear him, to continue to fear him for the rest of your life. He thrives on inflicting fear."

That described more than one man I'd encountered over my years as a Pinkerton. One of those men lived just outside of town.

The purple aliens sometimes left one witness alive while they fed on the dead. That witness knew the fate that awaited them. Their fear would make them sweat. A cold, pungent, odiferous sweat that humans could smell yards away. Who knew how strongly the odor affected the carrion eaters. Did they find it pleasurable? Or if the witness's heart gave out and he died, did his meat taste sweeter?

I couldn't dwell on that now. I had hope for a future here in Heller's Hole with a job, and a new home, and a pasture for Elinore with plenty of apples to keep her happy.

And Neil.

A quick check of the sky told me that the sun approached noon and the dark clouds building to the west would dump rain on us tonight, ruining any windfall apples Esteban had not picked up yet. I strapped a picnic basket to the travois. Elinore sidled a bit under the additional weight.

"See, I told you, you aren't ready to travel with me yet." I scratched along my horse's cheeks and under her chin.

Elinore closed her eyes in bliss, then butted her head into my chest begging for more scratching.

"Two miles each way. That's all I ask of you, my friend."

"Back home on the farm, I rode bareback all the time," Jonquil said, a note of persuasion, or maybe seduction, creeping into her voice.

"Good to know. I've seen how well you can clean and mend. What about cooking and taking care of a kitchen garden?" I prodded.

"Everyday. I milked the goats and made cheese too." Now she sounded eager, and hopeful.

A bubble of warmth grew in my middle that I could offer hope to at least one of the soiled doves.

"I baked the apple pies for Cook when you brought the first load of 'em over."

My mouth watered in remembrance of the sweet/tart confection with just a trace of cinnamon. Smells and tastes that would warm any man's cockles.

Or soothe the aching emptiness of a lonely woman.

"You'll ride out to the orchard with me next time, if you tell me your name. You aren't fit to ride yet after what Cutter Pine did to you." I glared in the direction of his cell as if I could burn holes in the walls. Maybe burn down the whole building and the mummy in the attic as well.

"Now scoot back to Rosie and rest those ribs and your loose teeth. I've work to do before my guests arrive later today."

"Is Brotherton finally coming to set you straight?" Pine yelled. Of course he'd been listening to our conversation. "I'm not a wanted man!"

"You don't know the people coming, and you don't want to know why!" I yelled back at him.

I caught Prospero's reins on his next circuit of the paddock, grabbed Elinore's leading rein, though she'd follow me nicely, and mounted, ready to meet Neil in front of the bank.

Neil. One of the many reasons I looked forward to staying in Heller's Hole.

ON THE ROAD toward the Miller place—soon to be referred to as Blue's Hollow, according to Josie's written offer to buy the place— Neil noted at least three wagon loads of apples and other produce headed toward town. He didn't recognize any of the drivers. Drivers only, no families. Tomorrow afternoon, Saturday, had become an impromptu market day in Heller's Hole. Families from outlying farms and ranches brought their produce and livestock into town for sale, and to pick up supplies. They stayed overnight, camping in their wagons or staying with friends, attended church services on Sunday morning and drove home—almost as many Catholics as Baptists. Though a handprinted sign on the schoolhouse door proclaimed that classes and services had been canceled until further notice.

The widow Nelson had recently started renting rooms and providing breakfast to "respectable" families or traders in her rambling five-bedroom home. The warm accommodations might extend the market a few extra weeks into autumn. He wished the widow well. She needed the money, and the town needed the commerce. Market days brought more and more people from further away to trade.

He could almost smell prosperity on the wind.

"Are those drivers part of Esteban's family?" he asked Josie when she paused to allow Elinore to catch up to them. That horse needed a good long rest at the Miller place. The more time Josie spent at the orchard, the more time he could spend with Josie, away from prying eyes in town.

"I'm not certain. Those aren't Basque wagons. Maybe some of the locals are taking advantage of the offer to harvest and split the money." She shrugged and dismounted, her attention on the travois harness and how it rested on Elinore's shoulders. She ran her fingers beneath the straps, checking for chafing.

Neil surveyed the terrain. Only a few more yards to the turnoff on the right. The orchards were nestled into a small valley, sheltered by the ridge road above. A snug setting, hidden from view on the road. If you didn't know where to look, the overgrowth obscured all traces of the place.

Josie had surmised that the purple flying things could feast there and no one would know. Higher up, the equally obscure mining camp —if there was anything left there—was also hidden from view by outcroppings. Perhaps he should ask Brotherton's people to investigate. He refused to think that Josie's loyalty might lie first with Brotherton and the Pinkerton Agency rather than to Heller's Hole and *him*.

They made their way slowly down the drive with Josie hanging on to the tail end of the travois as a brake, to keep it from slamming into Elinore's hind end. The skewbald mare stepped more sprightly without the dead weight behind her.

All three horses caught the heady scent of ripening apples at the same time and lifted their heads, nostrils working.

Josie kept a tight rein on Prospero to keep him from bolting into the orderly line of trees.

They made it all the way to the house without too much trouble. But the big stallion pawed the ground restlessly. Neil guided Molly toward the first line of trees. All of the fruit had been harvested from the low hanging branches. He had to stand in the stirrups to find three bright red orbs of fruit.

Back at the hitching rail, Josie split each apple in half and let the horses nibble from her hand. Lunch dispatched in short order, they began nuzzling her pockets to see if she'd secreted more treats.

She hadn't. They soon gave up.

"Let's get our own lunch over by the creek. Then we can take a quick tour of the house and barn," she said, looking up at Neil with a bright smile.

"Sounds like a plan."

He mimicked her actions in loosening Molly's saddle cinch and leading her to an enclosed paddock with lush grass and filled troughs. Clean water. Esteban and his people took their responsibilities seriously.

When the two saddle horses had settled, Josie unhitched Elinore from the travois and encouraged her to join the mounts. The mare made no protest, but she still favored her left hind hoof. She hadn't when they set out from town less than half an hour ago.

"Something is different," Josie said, wrinkling her nose and turning a full circle in search of whatever disturbed her.

Neil couldn't see anything strange. All he heard was silence. The birds had stopped singing. Even the near constant buzz of insects seemed muted. But off in the distance he thought maybe he heard a light musical note drifting and shifting on the light breeze.

"Maybe Esteban and his people have done some cleaning in their clearing besides harvesting the apples and refreshing the water troughs," Neil offered.

The soft tune he might have heard faded to nothing. Probably his ears playing tricks on him. Again.

As secluded as this farm was, he didn't trust anywhere out of doors to be fully private. And they needed privacy for him to reach out and hold her hand.

Or kiss her. And he desperately wanted to kiss her. Their one moment of shared intimacy after banishing the poltergeist took place too long ago and didn't last long enough.

"We talk to Esteban after we eat and before we go inside."

She ignored the silent stretching of his hand toward hers.

I DELIBERATELY STEPPED upon a dry branch lying on the ground just outside the circle of large boulders that sheltered the Basque encampment. The resulting crack filled the space.

Beside me, Neil startled, then settled down.

We'd eaten lightly, more interested in smiling at each other shyly than ingesting the hand pies stuffed with shredded mutton and the apples we'd picked.

"Never creep silently up on a friend," I said aloud.

He nodded, just as one of the young Basque men, carrying a rifle, stepped away from the shadow of the nearest boulder. He waited silently.

"Josie Blue and Neil Sanderson to see Esteban," I called out.

Moments later, Neil and I took seats on the same rocks we'd sat on the last time we visited Esteban.

"My friend, I have a request of a delicate nature."

"I am intrigued." The Basque patriarch put down his cup and fixed his gaze on me.

"I know you do not approve of women living alone."

He raised his eyebrows. "Not all women, Josie Blue."

Heat flushed my face. I nodded, having no response to the almost accusation.

"I am grateful for the protection you granted me those few times we encountered each other in the wild," I replied.

Esteban threw back his head and laughed long and hard. "It is more like you offered protection to my clan. We value you, dear friend, for who you are, not for what you should be."

Much to my surprise, Esteban took my hand and raised it to his lips, a kiss as light as a butterfly.

At the same time, Neil clasped my other hand possessively.

I jerked my arms, reclaiming my hands and my identity. Neil frowned. Esteban loosed one of his body shaking laughs.

"The point of this journey, Esteban Shallook, is that I wish to offer shelter and protection to a fragile woman who is alone and vulnerable. If she stays in the house here, will you see that she is not molested?"

"What will she do here? If we come to an agreement?"

"You want something in return," Neil said. He twisted off his spectacles, let them dangle between his knees, flipping them in circles by the bow.

"Smart man," Esteban said bringing his tea mug to his lips. But he did not drink. "A fragile woman, alone and vulnerable. She is not worth much in your society. Yet you go to a lot of trouble to protect her. She has hidden value you wish protected."

"All women should be protected," the young sentinel remarked. "They are the givers of life. Without women, men would be no more. Women are more closely tied to Mother Earth than we men can ever be. I say we look out for the girl."

"So be it!" Esteban proclaimed. "We will watch over your girl, and protect her from marauders. And if the singers come to this vale again, we will bring her within the sanctity of these great stones."

"And your payment for this great service?" Neil prompted. He replaced his spectacles with one hand twisting the wire frame until the ear and nose pieces settled firmly.

"What are you offering, Neil?" A niggle of suspicion grew cold in my belly. "You may not give him my money."

"Money?" Esteban exploded. "You would insult us with money?"

"That is what satisfies my bank customers."

"Your customers? White men value pieces of printed paper or metal circles. Money means little to the people of the Basque. We earn the few coins that buy us coffee and salt and the things the earth does not give us."

"I recognize that, friend Esteban. I offer instead, the use of this pasture for as long as you choose," Neil said.

"Wait a minute, you are bargaining with *my land*," I protested. The lump of ice in my gut spread through my veins to freeze my toes and my fingertips.

Then heat jolted through me like a bolt of lightning. *My land*? My money? When had I ever cared about possessions and wages before? Sure, I hunted aliens and outlaws for the bounty. But... but...

"It's not your land yet, Sheriff Blue. No money has exchanged hands, no papers have been signed. The land, the apples, the barn and sheds, and the house too still belong to the bank. And I'll write it into the sales agreement that Esteban and his clan have the right to camp here whenever they want. Exchanges of labor to be negotiated each year."

"That sounds reasonable." Too reasonable. I was mad and wanted to stay mad. Damn it all! He had no right to deflate my righteous anger.

Silent glares from both men cooled my emotions. Too many emotions and questions and motives still churned within me.

No logic or practicality. I reacted to both men with my possessiveness.

I breathed deeply. Three times. The emotions no longer controlled me. Heading into a confrontation full of anger led to disaster. I'd learned that long ago. Cutter Pine threw himself into battle against the aliens too often fueled by anger. Thinking ahead, studying the terrain, and planning were as alien to him as the purple flying things.

"Okay, I need to survey the house, the barn, and the sheds before I agree to buy this place and settle in my housekeeper." I stood and dusted off my pants with my bare palms. "One of my dreams is to buy a piano and bring real music back to this valley, and not just the heavenly tunes created by our worst enemies. Music makes a home."

Without waiting for a reply, I strode off in the direction of the house and paddock. "I wonder if Elinore likes this place."

"If you feel like this place can be your home, then I'm sure Elinore will approve. The bond between you is strong. But I think your mare might be ready to retire from the rough life you two have lived," Neil said, coming up beside me.

He stayed close enough for our arms to brush each other.

I waited until we were out of sight and earshot of the Basque encampment to entwine my fingers with his.

CHAPTER 27

ELINORE STOOD in the creek behind the barn, munching at the fresh watercress along the edges of the slow-moving water. Prospero grazed near-by, right next to Molly.

The gate to the paddock gaped open.

I approached the small herd cautiously, nodding in satisfaction that none of the mounts startled or moved away. Elinore would not wander far. Prospero seemed to have decided to stay close to her.

I smiled at the joy of future foals from these two. My finger sought the silky hawk feather tucked into my hat band. Omens coming together. The home I thought stolen from me began to take shape right before my eyes.

And Molly? Neil's mare edged closer to Prospero with every mouthful of grass.

"Who would dare turn them out?" Neil surged forward, ready to grab Molly's bridle.

"Esteban and his family would have chased away any intruders." I grabbed his elbow to hold him back. "I believe Elinore lipped open the gate latch. She's done it before."

"She leads the herd now?" Neil rocked back on his heels.

"Like any wise female, my Elinore nudges the stallion in the direction she wants him to go, but letting him think it's all his idea," I replied.

"Is that what you do?"

I laughed and turned to face him. It would be so easy to frame his face with my hands and kiss him. Or drag him into the house to make use of one of the bedrooms...

"That's the way of horses if the herd is lucky enough to have an opinionated and smart lead mare, and a wise stallion. He's deferring to her greater experience. But notice, he's holding his ground on dry land and keeping his females safely behind him. He may be grazing—never waste an opportunity to eat—while he lifts his head frequently and sniffs the air for anything new or out of place."

"Does this mean I need to sell you my horse as well as the farm?"

"Only if you want to. If she helps keep my horses happy, I'll board her in the paddock behind my office."

I wandered over toward the barn and lifted the heavy crossbar away from the double doors. Neil helped me lift the wooden beam and let it hang on the left-hand support. Together we pulled the doors outward, letting light and air to infiltrate the building.

A waft of dust flew outward. It smelled of desiccated hay, akin to the odor that lingered in the attic with the mummy.

A sleek and lean tabby cat with a wriggling mouse in its mouth darted from one stall across to another.

"Three stalls to a side, two of them wide enough for small wagons, a tack room, and hay storage above," I itemized my first observations.

"Anything look out of place to you?" Neil asked.

"The wagons are gone, along with any livestock. Looks like one of the stalls was given over to goats, judging by the wire mesh front and the old droppings. No sign of the animals."

"And the cat has taken over another pen," Neil mused, peering over the enclosure.

I joined him, marveling at the five kittens snagging bits of the now dead mouse. Their eyes were open and the tabby's teats seemed to have shrunk. They were close to being kicked out of the nest she'd made in the straw with bits of rags to soften the surface.

"We always had barn cats when I was little. I even sneaked a kitten into my room to keep as a pet. Our housekeeper threw a fit. Papa let me keep it. He had a hunting dog that also helped herd the cows. So why shouldn't I have a companion too?"

Neil smiled and slung his arm across my back, pulling me close. "Mother would never allow me to have a pet. The kitchen cat made her sneeze. It stayed in the kitchen with our cook and caught mice regularly. Eventually Mother agreed the creature earned its keep, but it was never allowed to stray into the front of the house or upstairs."

We stood there for long moments just watching the animals as they ate and then curled up for a nap, close to their mama but no longer nursing.

Eventually, by mutual agreement, we ambled out of the barn, closed it up again—that cross bar seemed unusually heavy, a true deterrent to intruders—and headed toward the house.

At the door I tugged off my boots, grateful for the cooling and sense of freedom, I wiggled my toes as I entered the building. No sense in tracking in more dirt. Inside, the plank floor looked freshly mopped, the dishes that had been strewn about had been washed and stacked neatly on the sideboard.

"Esteban's family have tidied up," I said. The braided rag rug was back in place beneath the table, and all the chairs righted.

"Have they been busy, or is someone living here in secret?" Neil whispered.

STEP BY STEP through the eerily quiet house Neil kept looking over his shoulder, certain someone, or something watched them. He crept a little closer to Josie, uncertain if he was trying to protect this woman, or if she protected him.

"It's too quiet. Neither a floorboard creaking, nor a whistle of wind through a crack in the walls," she said quietly.

Neil opened all of the cupboards in the kitchen, and on the sideboard. All full of everyday utensils and linen.

"A typical farmhouse that started as a single room cabin and then grew with family and prosperity. They put most of their time and resources into the land first. And then the house as they could afford it. From the bank records, I think Mrs. Miller inherited the orchard from her now deceased father. Her brother got a larger property south of here. The trees had matured by then and began making a profit right away."

Even as he spoke, he noted the rough wooden walls here in the kitchen where it had all started. The room ran the full width of the house with a large woodburning stove, sink with a pump, and a curtained off pantry that was big enough for a bedroom. A folded up army cot stood in the far corner, out of the way but close enough to still be useful. The kitchen was large with room for the family to gather around the worktable or sit beside a separate hearth. With that knowledge, he found the seam in the floor and the ceiling where the front of the house was added.

"There's a loft." Josie pointed to the ladder beside the door to the rest of the house. A lot of color drained from her face. "Children," she whispered.

"It's where they slept. Mrs. Miller's brother said that she and the children are safe." So, Josie had some maternal sentiments after all. He'd wondered.

She gulped and nodded.

"Want me to go up first?" He swallowed heavily. Memories of the grisly finds in the attic of the sheriff's office paralyzed his feet. He really didn't want to climb that ladder into the unknown. But he had to hold up gentlemanly standards. He had worked hard to bring civilization to this town and manners were a part of it.

"I'll go first," Josie said, firming her chin and adjusting her gun belt.

Neil had no doubt that she'd have her weapons drawn, aimed, and cocked in the blink of an eye. Some of his nervousness faded. Some. Not all.

Her bootless feet made no sound as she climbed upward, sniffing and peering all around.

All too soon her head disappeared into the dark square of an opening, then her shoulders and torso. She paused and twisted.

"I wish I had better light," she said aloud. "But it looks clear. Come on up." She moved up the last few steps, leaving him room to climb.

He took a deep fortifying breath and began his own ascent. By the time he'd reached the top of the ladder, above the floor level so he only had to step sideways off the ladder to reach the room, she had pulled back calico curtains and lit the area with sunshine.

"Two rooms, one each side of the ladder." She pointed toward walls right and left of the small landing with open curtains instead of a door, and the windows at one end, under the apex of the roof.

They stepped into the left-hand room, above half the kitchen and the pantry. The other room occupied an almost equal amount of space above the rest of the kitchen. The front of the house, with the chimney and hearth was only a single story. But the field stone chimney formed part of the front wall of this second story.

"Three small beds for the children here, all neatly made," he said, just to break the silence. "Boxes for their clothing. Empty."

"A bigger bed in here," Josie added from the entry to the other room.

Neil crossed to her side and peered inward, almost reluctant to invade the privacy of the parents.

Josie stiffened and inched backward.

"Someone slept here." She pointed to the rumpled blankets.

As usual, Doc Buchanan sat by the front window of the doctor's office with his feet on the sill and his chair tipped back on two legs. His eyes drifted closed in the cloudy afternoon light.

Sunset came earlier every day. As the light brightened briefly below the clouds, touching the horizon, he made a note of the time on the big pendulum clock.

Five thirty-six. Yesterday the sun had dropped to the edge of the horizon at five thirty-seven.

Yep. Autumn had come.

He hadn't seen a patient all day. Everyone in town seemed in the pink of health. Or they were too busy with harvest or driving herds down from the mountain pastures into the sheltered valleys.

A brief flash of lightning off to the west lit the street for a moment with a too-white eeriness. When his eyes cleared from the dazzle, hints of purple and orange lingered along the base of the clouds.

He dropped his feet and rocked forward.

That uncanny purple reminded him of the aftermath of Gettysburg. That hadn't been his first observance of the one-horned flying aliens. But it was the first time he'd heard their music. A lovely, yet majestic tune. Each alien blasted a single note. Together they made a beautiful bass choir, as if they guided all the souls toward heaven.

He had seen enough hell during the war to lose any faith he had left in God and heaven.

Then the aliens descended in a swarm to devour the dead bodies.

They only feasted after sunset. Their music signaled the loss of light and the time to begin eating, not some spiritual experience.

Doc hurried to his partially open door and leaned out to listen. No music. That must have come from his memories, or his imagination. He didn't like the uncanny quiet. It seemed the world paused with bated breath, waiting for the real music.

If it came, it was too far away to stand out above the clatter of horse hooves and the creak of wagons straining up the last grade before entering town.

The first raindrops plopped along the ruts in the road just as Lucian appeared atop his horse down by the livery stable. A host of wagons and outriders followed him.

"You made good time!" Doc called to the Pinkerton cavalcade.

Lucian tipped his hat and continued on to the hitching rail in front of the sheriff's office. "Is Blue in?" he asked as Doc hurried across the street.

"Haven't seen the sheriff since afore noon. Some messiness south of town. Rode out with the banker," Doc replied a little breathless as he spotted the woman driving the first wagon. Nicely plump, in her forties. Make that early forties, with jet black hair falling free of a tight bun at her nape and wearing a black, veiled bonnet, and an equally dark day gown with leather gloves. Her Mediterranean olive skin stood out as paler than her garb, but shadowed enough to remain out of focus.

He thought some of the shadows about her face resolved into a black velvet patch over her right eye. His scientific curiosity engaged, wondering why. Did he have a cure for an infection? Or must he resign himself to a missing eye that he could not cure?

She looked like an amorphous spirit come to haunt the town.

She must be the medium come to lay the spirit of the mummy to rest and cleanse the attic of any residual magic.

His entire body quivered with excitement as he drank in the sight of her lush body. Tingles in his fingers and down his spine responded to her lingering aura of magic. Eye patch be damned. He had the impression she was the most beautiful woman he'd seen in many a long year.

His imagination filled in all the right details.

Might be time to start thinking about settling down with one woman, and one woman only.

I USHERED Neil ahead of me as we fled the house. The dwelling was too open for a person to find a hiding place, so I knew in my mind that the place was empty.

But my senses knew the sanctity of a private home had been violated by more than just Neil and me.

Time had gotten away from us. Dark clouds gathered to the west, blocking the setting sun. Strange colors boiled along the horizon as the sunset lit the underside of the clouds.

"Storm coming," the young Basque sentinel said. He adjusted and tightened the travois harness around Elinore's shoulders.

Elinore had allowed him to touch her?

But then the Basque sometimes had strange magic with animals.

They commanded dogs to control an entire flock of sheep with just a whistle. Their horses stood guard, alerting the men to anyone or anything approaching. So Elinore agreed with them when it came time to leave the soothingly cool waters of the creek and get ready to go home.

The other two horses stood by, saddles set and bridles dangling over the hitching rail, ready to return to the shelter of a stable and the rest of the herd.

"Papa says you need to be on your way now." The young man hoisted two burlap sacks of apples onto the travois. Four were already loaded. He must have stopped to adjust the harness when Elinore told him that four were too many.

"I only brought five sacks." I counted them again and noted the brand names printed on the rough fabric. "And those are not the sacks I brought."

"We exchanged your sacks for the apples we've already harvested. You need to be on your way."

Neil held my boots out. He'd already donned his own.

I debated with myself for three heartbeats. My feet still hurt, but the urgency in the young man's words and posture told me I might need to protect my feet if we had to run from… the coming rain or anything else that began prowling at sunset.

"There are signs that someone slept in the house," I said as I sat on the stoop and tugged on my boots. A little tight but not terribly binding.

The young man stilled, his face blank while he considered a lie.

The Basque did not lie. Their culture forbade it.

"Mr. Miller came back. He said he's an outlaw now and needed shelter for one night. He left before dawn." The words sounded flat, devoid of emotion, or opinion.

"Why did your father not mention this earlier?" Neil asked, grabbing Molly's reins and checking the cinches. "If Mr. Miller comes back, it won't be safe for… for your friend, Sheriff Blue," Neil said.

"Papa keeps his own counsel. Mr. Miller owned the house. No reason to keep him out."

"But you will have reason to keep him away from my friend. Your Papa promised to protect and honor her," I said, insistent and as authoritative as I knew how to be.

"And Miller will not own the place after Sheriff Blue signs some papers and some money changes hands when we get back to town," Neil added.

"So, Miller doesn't threaten us at the moment. Thank you for your help with the horses and the apples. We'll be on our way now." I didn't meet the boy's gaze as I mounted, but Neil and I shared a glance, of one mind to mount and be on our way.

Prospero pranced, eager to be on the road.

I didn't dare give him his head. We had to stay close to Elinore, hindered by the travois and her healing unshod hooves, and protect her from anything menacing that prowled about.

CHAPTER 28

RAIN BEGAN FALLING in earnest by the time they reached the end of the Miller's drive. Neil kept pushing Josie to keep movie forward rather than stop every few strides to check on Elinore.

They'd almost reached town when the dirt road became a quagmire, slowing even Prospero and his big feet and broad chest. Molly sensed the verge was safer for her dainty hooves than the road and kept veering to the side where Neil had to constantly duck beneath sodden tree limbs or risk being swept to the ground

Now Elinore had bogged down, and Josie needed help getting her moving again.

He dismounted and squelched through the mud to the center of the road.

He closed his eyes, breathed deeply and heaved one pole at the lower end of the travois. Up two inches and three more to the right out of the rut in the road. Rain spattered his spectacles, further blurring his sight. He'd done it! Elinore could now walk straight and drag her middling load along the high spot in the center of the road rather than through either of the ruts that were fast becoming rivers.

Good thing he'd changed out of city clothes before they began this day's adventure. He almost didn't mind being soaked to the skin. Getting away from his desk and spending time with Josie made it worth the discomfort.

"Ready to go," he called to Josie, who held Elinore's bridle and spoke soothing words to the horse.

Just how much language did the skewbald mare understand? He knew Elinore to be extremely intelligent for a horse. But Josie's bond with her was strong. For all he knew, they communicated telepathically.

Josie tugged on the bridle to get the mare moving. Elinore plodded forward. Prospero danced anxiously at the end of the rein Josie held loosely.

"Let's go!" Neil hastened toward Molly and mounted as quickly as the mud allowed. Josie continued walking beside Elinore, easily matching her pace.

"Mount up, Josie," Neil ordered, as he'd speak to his assistant, more an order than a suggestion.

"It's only a few hundred more yards to town," she replied, looping the stallion's reins around his saddle horn. She checked to make certain Prospero followed. He kept pace with Josie, occasionally nudging Elinore to keep her from faltering.

They made a sorry-looking troupe when they reached the crest in the road at the south edge of town.

Neil thought he saw a flicker of a heavy drape across the front window of his home. Mother must have awoken from her drug-induced sleep. He wondered how much laudanum would linger in her system by the time he returned home tonight. With any luck, Rachel would dose her again so he could evade her tirades. He considered again the advisability of moving Mother to the ranch five miles west of town, where she couldn't cause him much trouble.

But no. That would be cruel, to deprive her of company and gossip and a sense of control over at least the pastor, if they found a new one, and her friends. Did she know that Sanderpoole had deserted the school/church and locked himself in a windowless room at the boarding house until an aging and recently retired ranch hand had volunteered to take him to Pendleton? Besides, the ranch was better suited to Neil's father, who should return with his man Jack Epps tomorrow. Or maybe the next day. Traveling with the old man was a slow and tedious business requiring several days of rest at each stage of the journey.

Movement closer to the center of town drew his attention. "Damn, I can't see who, or what is going on," he muttered. Between the rain and his fuzzy vision he was vulnerable. He didn't like that feeling. If he had a dry bit of clothing he'd try to clean the glass lenses. His damp shirt or leather vest would only smear the water, further exasperating his vision. Maybe he should stay inside the bank next time Josie suggested they ride out.

But then he'd lose one of the few opportunities to spend time alone with her.

"I think that's Lucian," Josie replied.

Sensing home, Prospero trotted forward. But then his head reared up and his nostrils widened as he smelled strangers.

"Easy, boy," Josie soothed the big stallion. Then she clipped a leading rein on Elinore and threw herself onto Prospero's back. He didn't need a touch from her heels to surge forward.

Elinore could only follow. And she didn't like it.

If she were a mule, she'd probably park her hind end in the mud and bray loudly, refusing to budge.

Neil chuckled to himself at the image and grabbed the leading rein away from Josie as he came abreast of Elinore. "Go ahead and we'll approach at a more stately speed. Meet you at Rosie's where we'll deposit the apples." He waved the sheriff on and continued forward at a pace more suitable to Elinore and her sore feet.

"Didn't Josie tell you that it was too early for you to come with us?" he asked the horse.

She shook her head, flinging water drops hither and yon.

He couldn't get much wetter.

~

As soon as I knew that Neil had delivered the apples and Young Jed came running from the livery stable to deal with the horses, leading all three to the paddock behind the sheriff's office, I focused all of my attention on the newcomers. Doc's gentle attention to the sole female in the group barely registered. One less person for me to deal with.

Lucian stepped forward. "Do you have a key?" He held out his palm as if he expected me to hand it over.

"Yes." I squelched my way to the door and unlocked it myself.

My town. My office. My key.

Lucian frowned, as if I'd usurped his authority. He might lead this gaggle of Pinkerton operatives, he'd worked for the agency during the war, three years longer than me. He had no place in Hellers Hole. Yet.

As much as I trusted him with my life, his companions were unknown. Brotherton had not revealed their names, only their specialties in his telegram.

Inside the office, I discarded my boots and placed them neatly before the banked fire in the stove. An imperative finger pointed at Lucian's feet demanding he, and the others do the same. Even the woman in layers and layers of fluffy black that disguised her figure, posture, and face, needed to shed muddy footwear.

Lucian held the single visitor's chair for the woman. She left her concealing veil in place. If she moved more than an eyelash to look around, I couldn't tell. She must be the psychic medium Brotherton swore could safely cleanse the attic of magic and mummies.

Movement in my peripheral vision told me that the five men still outside split up. Three hefted luggage from their wagon and headed across the street to Rosie's. The remaining two awkwardly removed boxes that were long enough to require both of them to slide free of the wagon.

"About time y'all showed up," Cutter said, yawning. He slowly stood from the jail cot and stretched his limbs. "Let me out of here, Lucian, so I can teach Blue a lesson in manners."

Lucian paused in placing his hat on the rack beside the stove. He looked at me with eyebrows raised in question.

"I have a wanted poster with his name and face on it. I also have witness statements and my own testimony of his assault and battery, and maybe attempted murder. No one, not even his almighty self, Allan Pinkerton, gets away with that in *my* town." I leaned back in my chair, crossing my arms. I wasn't about to budge until I had introductions, and Lucian knew that.

"So, your first loyalty is to this town, not the Riders of the Purple Sage?"

I didn't have to think about it. A month ago I would have. I nodded and sat straighter as two of the men who'd arrived with Lucian wrestled a long piece of equipment, covered in protective black canvas through the door.

The covering around the bulky square at the top slipped revealing a single eye affixed to a black box. I recoiled a bit until I realized the men transported a camera and not one of the alien monsters I had hunted so diligently. I'd seen men working a camera before. They managed to capture amazing images of camp life and battlefields during the war. And some of the fancier wanted posters featured photographs of the outlaws rather than hand drawn likenesses. I thought the former were more accurate.

"Upstairs," Lucian directed them. "We'll talk later, Blue. Brotherton said he won't accept your resignation. You could have told me about that letter you had me transport."

"Brotherton doesn't have a choice. I quit. The letter was just a formality."

"If you aren't employed by the agency, then you have no place in this investigation." He started to turn away. Did his frown convey disappointment?

"My office. My discovery. My investigation." I stood and hastened to the wall, pressing on the spot between two wanted posters that released the latch to the stairwell.

I climbed the stairs slowly, giving the camera men time to follow with their burden. "I really don't want to be up here with you," I whispered to the mummy. "But I'll be damned if I turn this investigation over to another."

Other than a few footprints in the dust, I didn't notice anything amiss. The whisper of magic surrounding the corpse drifted around, stirred by the faint breeze creeping around the one small window in the western wall. No one had disturbed the corpse for twenty-five years. Why would they now?

"You should probably bring up some lanterns, Lucian. There isn't a lot of light for the camera to work."

The first of the photographers emerged from the stairwell, a spindly, ginger-haired man who didn't look strong enough to manipulate his awkward equipment. He gasped and swallowed heavily. His throat apple bobbed in his skinny neck. "I've seen worse after a battle during the war," he muttered and continued upward.

His companion kept his eyes on his feet. "Glad you warned me," he said when he finally looked at the object they needed to capture on film.

Only then did I realize he was such an ordinary man, medium brown hair, tanned face and hands, brown clothing and boots, that should I pass him on the street, I'd have no reason to notice him.

The perfect criminal, or Pinkerton agent, a man no one would remember.

Cutter Pine was just the opposite.

I hadn't heard back if Pine was still wanted. Knowing O'Toole's aversion to work, I doubted I'd get a message until morning, even if it came through.

On the other hand, O'Toole provided much gossip to the town. If he noted the newcomers, he'd high-tail it across the street within seconds of receiving the telegram.

"Please take special care in getting the artifacts and the lines defining the enclosure of the magic," I said, pointing to the outermost geometric figure.

"Yeah, Madame Glissen downstairs told us the same thing," Ginger replied, as he began extending the collapsible legs of the camera. "Twenty miles over rough roads in the same wagon listening to Mistress Wagging Tongue expound about the spiritual nature of the fresh blossoms and greening of dead grasses is enough to drive a man more insane than these loathsome creatures." Ginger adjusted his lens for a closeup of the three-toed lizard feet of my mummy.

The light bar flashed, nearly blinding me.

They reset the mechanisms and moved the camera for the next shot in only seconds. This must be the newest innovation. Brotherton, or more likely Pinkerton himself, demanded the most modern equipment available, even out here in the back of beyond.

"Strange," I mused while they worked, rapidly and efficiently. "Madame Glissen hasn't spoken a word since I joined you."

The cameramen shrugged and continued their work.

They needed only a few more minutes before the scientists replaced them. The camera exited and was replaced by magnifiers and an array of equipment for gathering and studying samples.

"Monsieur Lucian!" Madame Glissen called up the stairwell about five minutes later. She spoke in an accent unlike anything I had ever heard, a mixture of several European mother tongues, plus hints of... not Asian but something equally foreign. "The time has come. I require escort up these precarious stairs."

"You guys done?" Lucian asked the scientists, their gazes glued to magnifying glasses. At the moment they studied the minute differences in the glass beads, dried flowers, and woven grasses of the talisman atop the spear.

"Done enough for her to start work. My orders are to note and draw everything she does. She won't allow a camera near her—says it will capture her soul."

"There isn't a lot of room to move around," Lucian said, backing up until he banged his head on the eaves.

"We'll make do." The lead scientist, a man in his fifties with gray in his mustache and at his temples looked at me pointedly.

"I can make myself small." I decided to stand my ground. If I left the room, Lucian would find a way to exclude me all together.

Lucian looked at me skeptically since I stood half a head taller than either of the scientists and eye to eye to him.

To prove my point I ducked my head and crouched down in the far corner above where my desk would sit on the ground floor.

Wait a second! I measured the attic room with my gaze and compared it to my memory of my office space.

"We're missing about six feet of space up here. And the ceiling slopes way too steeply considering the roof is flat." I began a careful inspection of the beams that gave the illusion of the raw planks and supports of the roof, looking for signs of a trap door.

Lucian's gaze followed mine. "There should be access to the roof, in case of fire, or a leak," he said.

"The slope is really only on the front side. The back is nearly flat." I knocked on each plank, listening to the quality of the emptiness.

The place was well built and still sturdy after twenty-five years of neglect. All of the joins remained neat and flush, no gaps, nor warps.

"Monsieur Lucian! I am waiting."

"You go," I said, pausing when my knocks reverberated with a different tone. I grabbed the lantern Lucian had left at the top of the stairwell and held it high and to my right while I knocked again on a plank to my left. The lead scientist lit a burner beneath a glass beaker, adding enough light that just for a moment I spotted a line across the plank where there shouldn't be a join.

Another burner flare for a second and I spotted the right angles marking a trap door. No signs of a handle or hinges. Must be another pressure latch like on the door to the stairwell.

I reached up and my fingertips brushed the sensitive corner easily. Scientist number one was considered a normal sized man and he probably couldn't reach the ceiling here. A faint double click told me I'd disengaged the lock, then reengaged it. I pushed harder. A louder click and the two feet square section of ceiling dropped along with a cloud of dust and the naked body of a man with a single purple horn and half extended wings. A single sheet of paper with blank ink scrawled across it fluttered to the floor.

Flat, lifeless eyes stared at me.

"Doc! Get your ass up here, pronto," Josie called.

Doc didn't even have to think about pushing Madame Glissen aside and bounding up the stairs, two at a time. "What?"

His eyes went first to the old mummy, still lying spread-eagled on the floor with the chalk inscribed pentagram within a square within a triangle within a circle. Nothing had changed except the number of footprints scuffing the dust around the ritual ground.

The scientist lit two lucifers in rapid succession, leaving Doc's vision light-dazzled. But for an instant he'd seen something he hoped never to see again.

As soon as his eyes cleared, his gaze took in Josie's pale face and her defensive stance. Her eyes fixed upon a new corpse, sprawling ungainly from a trap door in the ceiling, half in and half out, one arm and one foot caught in the opening, all of his shrunken privates on full display.

"Don't touch him!" he ordered Josie. The dead man's mouth and nose were full of congealing, vividly red blood. It had dribbled down his chin but had stopped flowing.

Some exotic poisons had come into the region in the last few years with the influx of Chinese railroad workers and their tyrannical overseers.

He had no idea if the dead skin would retain whatever killed him or not.

"We've got to get him out of the way. We're losing the light," Lucian said. The fearless Pinkerton agent pressed himself against the far wall, beside the only window.

"What is going on up there? I must know before I study the magic involved," Madame Glissen demanded.

Doc still had not learned her first name or her origins. Patients, especially women, usually talked to him easily, revealing all of their secrets. Not this lady. He decided to ignore her. Another body with similar anatomic mutations to the mummy, complicated things enormously.

"Lucian, please find me some work gloves. Thick ones." He took the lantern from Josie and shoved her aside so he could get a better look at the corpse.

"My gloves are in the bottom left drawer of my desk," Josie said.

Lucian nodded abruptly and left with hasty steps. Within moments he returned but remained on the stairs with only his head visible above the flooring. He thrust the gloves into Doc's hands and withdrew again.

At least he blocked the stairwell to Madame Glissen. If she had true psychic medium abilities she might help. As a scientist, Doc doubted it.

"I'm taller than you, Doc. Give me the gloves and I'll lift him free," Josie said.

She only topped him by an inch, but she was stronger and leaner than he. He studied the angles and trajectory a moment and passed off the gloves to her. "You'll have better leverage than me," he agreed.

"I'll help," Lucian said, reluctantly. He mounted the last few steps, pulling on his own thick gloves, designed to protect hands from hauling reins of troublesome horses, or clearing brush or whatever hard work he fell into.

"Mighty tight quarters up here," Lucian grumbled. "But given the nature of the beast, I think we'd best not take him downstairs for examination, until we know who and what he is."

"Agreed," Doc said and replaced Lucian on the stairs, but high enough to see the entire area clearly.

With the two tall, and strong, Pinkertons pushing and lifting the body, they had it down and lain flat on the floor up against where the sloping ceiling almost met the floor. No one could stand upright within four feet.

"Can we get a blanket or something to cover this guy. Give him some dignity in death?" he asked. "Or so we don't have to look at him."

"There's a blanket in the empty cell," Josie said. She obviously was not giving ground to anyone in this investigation.

Lucian disappeared again.

"I saw a body like this after Shiloh," Doc said. His voice sounded choked and hesitant to his own ears. "The alien had finished feeding and was shifting back to his human form to make an escape. Halfway through, he was vulnerable, and a dying Reb soldier shot him with his last bullet and his dying breath. This guy looks like he's in the same stage of transformation. And he's fresh. Hasn't been dead long."

"He made certain the monsters wouldn't defile his body," Josie replied.

CHAPTER 29

THE ATTIC ROOM suddenly became too close, too small. Not enough air circulated. I needed to open a window. The one behind the temporary chemistry laboratory was blocked and sealed shut.

Any sense of territoriality about the mummy and the investigation vanished in my need for air.

"I thought I could do this." I pushed Doc and Lucian aside and stomped down the stairs. A dash to the back door and I flung it open, gathering great gulps of air.

"Dead bodies in confined spaces will do that to a person," Cutter Pine quipped. "Let me outta here and I'll help."

I stared over my shoulder at him. He'd stretched out on his bed again, arms crossed beneath his head. The pose showed off his still lean and well-muscled body.

Not tempting in the least.

"We used to do this all the time." I caught sight of Madame Glissen's black draperies disappearing into the stairwell. Good riddance.

"But every dead alien we encountered was outside. Strange how they seem to steal the air when inside, even after they stop breathing."

"Stopped breathing," I muttered. "When did this new corpse stop breathing?" Doc had said something about not long dead.

"Did you hear anything last night, Cutter?"

"Just some thumps and bumps on the roof. Figured it was squirrels, or owls chasing the squirrels. Nothing came close to me, so I dismissed it and went back to sleep." He yawned. "Leave the back door open for a bit. I'm starting to smell. Haven't bathed in a while."

I complied, agreeing with him as I stepped into the paddock. I'd best take the time to check on the horses.

Prospero greeted me with a whicker as he munched his evening hay. Jed Junior must have taken Elinore and Molly back to the livery.

Spotting the ladder propped up against the back side of the building gave me an idea. "Thumps and bumps on the roof. Someone climbed up there last night. Or today while I was at Blue's Hollow." I didn't recall having seen the ladder when I saddled Prospero before noon. But then I hadn't been looking for the ladder or much else. All my attention had been on my stallion who was anxious to be out and about and proved a handful just to get him tacked up.

The rain had let up a bit, but the paddock was still awash with mud.

"Where are you going?" Cutter demanded as I retrieved my boots by the fire. He stood from his bed and clung to the cell bars, rattling them uselessly. They didn't budge. This place was too well built.

"I'm going to investigate your thumps and bumps," I replied, tugging the left boot into place. Because of the deep but no longer painful blister and swelling, I needed to tug and shift and wiggle my foot more than usual, just to get the footwear on.

"At least you aren't going barefoot again."

"You heard about that."

"Yeah. Had to come to town and investigate." He smirked.

"Since when does investigating require beating up prostitutes because you like inflicting pain? You used to be able to control yourself, when you needed to."

I stood, shook each foot in turn to settle the boots and returned to the paddock.

"Blue! Take me with you, please. I'm going crazy cooped up here." Cutter shook the cell bars again.

They didn't wiggle in the least.

I smiled to myself and proceeded to figure out what had happened last night, or earlier today. Whichever.

I needed a dozen steps, squelching through the mud to get the ladder positioned where I could secure it. Slowly I climbed, cursing every step that slid along the ladder rungs. Each time the side of my foot slid into the side supports I cursed, choosing a few words in the harsh patois of the Canadian fur traders to match similar epithets in Nez Perce.

My fingers grew cold and then numb. "Just what we need, another storm front. This is supposed to be the high desert plateau!"

But if the ridges and hollows of this terrain didn't trap moisture and entice storms to linger, the local farmers and ranchers wouldn't have a hope of producing a crop of anything, let alone the lovely apples in Blue's Hollow.

I persevered, knowing that some answers were hidden in the office roof.

At last, I stood on the top rail of the ladder, with my torso draped over the slight overhang across the back of the building. I leaned over, bracing myself with both hands and swung my right leg up until my knee balanced the rest of me. Then, with arms and shoulders shaking from the tension and precarious balance, I swung the other leg up until I found secure positions for all four of my limbs. An ungainly maneuver. But I didn't care if someone watched my lack of grace. I was up where I needed to be, and I still had my boots on.

Crawling toward the center, I took note of just how flat the roof was. No sign of a slope all the way to the false front that faced the street. The roof remained flat as I crawled to the irregular but solid wooden decoration, using it to haul myself upright. From there I surveyed the town and surrounds from a different perspective. Someone had built that triangular hidden space into the attic for a reason.

In my mind I pictured the attic space, taking my bearings from the window in the back wall. "Wish I'd thought to bring a measuring stick." That was one tool I didn't need while riding patrol in the wastelands. During my weeks in town, I hadn't needed one either. Who besides the milliner would have one?

This was Friday. I'd limped into town several weeks ago, the longest I'd stayed in *any* town in years. I felt like I'd known these people for a lifetime. And yet I didn't know them at all. Some I'd never met. Like the naked, half transformed corpse in the room below. Would anyone recognize him?

I inched a few feet beyond what I judged to be the center of the roof.

With eyes and fingertips, I searched the planks for imperfect joins or seams where they shouldn't be. Whoever had constructed this building knew how to do it right.

There! Right where I thought it should be, I found the trap door, with a rusty ring to pull it up. No padlock. A quick twist of the ring and the latch underneath released. I shifted my feet for leverage and opened the door. Along the inside of the opening, I found a narrow ledge with a metal pole I could tug upright to fit into a convenient slot in the door and brace it open.

This was no afterthought of a design idea. The hatch was planned from the beginning of construction. I sat back on my haunches, thinking, puzzling.

Twenty-five years ago, when people still worked the mines and the town prospered, Neil's father had hired a sheriff, and this office came into being.

If anyone but the builders knew about the hidden space, no one else went looking for it.

The sheriff had disappeared within a few years and a new one replaced him.

The attic remained hidden as well as this triangular hiding place. Presumably the mummy was either the first sheriff, or had been captured by him, and ritualistically laid out with magic.

Why?

Both the mummy and the newly discovered dead body had alien origins.

But there had never been an incursion or a sighting of the aliens within fifteen miles in any direction away from town in the last twenty-five years.

Most of the inhabitants were blissfully unaware of the monsters.

I had to get back to the attic and stop the removal of the enemy.

The fastest route was down, through the triangle.

No ladder. But in the uncertain light from the still open trap door into the attic and from my own rooftop entrance, I thought I only had to drop a few feet.

I sat and moved both feet forward, letting them dangle over the opening. A quick scoot forward and the square doorway hit the back of my knees. I flipped around and braced my arms and shoulders to take my weight. My feet waved about, seeking a purchase.

Not there. I must be over the deepest part of the room.

A deep breath and gritted teeth for courage and I dropped the last two feet with a loud thump that reverberated along my spine.

The top of my head remained level with the opening, but I could see the other trap door. Doc had left it open after Lucian and I had removed the body.

Shouts of startlement greeted me from below. I had only a few moments to look around before Doc's bulky frame blocked the light.

Neat stacks of old straw and twigs nearly filled the place. It looked like nesting material for large birds of prey. A square of white paper sat atop the closest pile. I grabbed the entire folded missive and stuffed it inside my waistcoat just as Doc's hand grabbed my ankle and yanked me toward the opening.

Neil barely noticed the papers Martin put in front of him for a signature. All his focus remained on the bustle of activity across the street in the Sheriff's office.

He had greeted the fine carriage Jack Epps, his father's caregiver, had rented to transport the old man. The sight of his parent's thick mane of white hair, sallow skin that sagged on face and hands, and the murkiness of his once bright and curious gaze left Neil unsettled. He'd sent the carriage on to the house. As they drove south the quarter mile, his father's quavering voice drifted back to him. "Where are we? Why did we come here?" he'd asked three times in the short distance.

"Not much chance of hearing about your memory of the first sheriff in town and what happened to him. You can barely remember who you are." Neil shook his head and returned to his desk.

He knew he should return home to help his father settle in, but wondered what good he could do. He looked back to his desk calendar and noted that he'd last seen his father more than a year ago. Sanderson Sr. had been energetic and talkative at the time, but claimed he needed the milder climate of Portland in the Willamette Valley rather than the harsh winter on the high plateau.

Among the cavalcade of wagons and riders that had come with Josie's fellow investigators from the Pinkertons, had been several ranch families come to town for supplies, church services, and socialization. Rosie's should be hopping tonight. But then the saloon usually grew boisterous and busy on Friday and Saturday night.

The presence of the Pinkertons would only add to that.

Then he spotted Josie on the roof of her office peeking over the false front quickly and dropping back behind it.

What was she up to? They'd discovered the mummy in the attic, not on the roof.

"Curiosity killed the cat." He shoved back his chair and hastened toward the front door, grabbing his hat along the way.

"Satisfaction brought it back!" Martin called after him.

"Maybe."

Light drizzle did not penetrate the sturdy wool of his coat, or his hat. But his boots still sloshed through a slurry of mud. His feet were decidedly wet and cold by the time he mounted the boardwalk beneath the overhang. An easy decision to pull them off and leave them just inside the door, as Josie usually did. If she wore boots at all.

"Who are you and what's going on?" the man in the jail cell pleaded. He clung to the vertical bars, trying to shake them loose.

"Don't know," Neil answered.

He moved, unerringly to the gaping door to the attic.

"You've been here before."

"A few times," Neil said and stopped short to listen. A loud thump reverberated through the building.

"I'm Cutter Pine. I'm one of them and I need to know what's going on upstairs."

"If you are in that cell, then Sheriff Blue has a damned fine reason for putting you there." Neil leaned his head into the stairwell and peered upward.

"If he's in that jail cell, he needs to stay there," Postmaster O'Toole said coming into the office. He held a telegram in his fist, waving it about. "Hey, where's Sheriff Blue?"

"I think the sheriff is in the attic with the newcomers," Neil replied, careful not to assign a gender to her.

"This building has an attic?" O'Toole stood in place, staring at the ceiling. "Never knew that and I've been in town ten years."

"Apparently, that's not long enough." Neil grabbed the telegram and started climbing. He was halfway up before he remembered to explain to O'Toole, "I'll take this to Sheriff Blue."

Lucian blocked the entry into the room. Beyond him stood the woman clothed in swaths of black, including a disguising veil. Neil wondered just how much she could see through the layers of netting.

Doc stood halfway along the room, feet just outside the outermost chalk and salt line of the ritual markings surrounding the mummy. His hands reached up through the ceiling, clutched a booted foot.

Neil recognized the foot, narrower than most men's. "Sheriff Blue, what are you doing up there?" he called.

That might explain why she'd been sneaking around the roof.

"O'Toole just delivered a telegram for you," he added.

"Coming," Josie sang out. "Um... Doc, if you don't mind, I'd rather have Lucian or Neil help me down. They are younger and stronger than you."

As much as Neil wanted to jump to rescue her, more for the opportunity to hold her than any sense of chivalry, or confidence in his physical strength, he thought better of it.

"After you," he waved Lucian over to stand beneath the trap door.

"This might take both of us. Josie Blue is tall and muscular," the swarthy-skinned Pinkerton agent said as he positioned himself directly below Josie's dangling feet.

Doc reluctantly let go of Josie's foot and backed away to the far end of the room, pointedly not looking at another corpse pushed into the narrow space where the sloping ceiling met the wall.

"What's going on here?" Neil mimicked Lucian in placing one hand on Josie's foot and the other behind her knee.

Together they eased her down until she sat on the edge of the square trap. He couldn't see much inside the space, only that another door through the roof to the outside had been left open.

"Um… Sheriff Blue, you might want to close the roof access door, so we don't develop leaks." His bank owned the building and leased it to the city. He'd be responsible for necessary repairs.

"Yeah. I guess so. Be right back." She withdrew into the dark space. Moments later, the room grew dimmer, and he heard a slap of wood against wood and the grind of metal twisting against metal. Then Josie's feet reappeared in the opening.

Hauling her down became a simple matter of leverage and balance. Thank goodness she was tall and only had to drop a few inches once she'd completely cleared the trap. She even managed to push the thing closed and latch it once her feet rested firmly on the plank flooring.

She didn't linger beside her two rescuers, but marched around the chalk lines and grabbed the other woman (the psychic medium Brotherton had promised to send?) and blew out the lit match she held against a stick of incense. "I can't allow you to break the magic protecting this sacrifice."

Sacrifice? Neil gulped.

A CHAOS of voices erupted around me. I wanted to plug my ears with my fingertips but needed both hands to restrain Madame Glissen.

"I must free the tortured soul of this man!" she screamed, throwing back her layers of veils to reveal a pale olive-toned face with worry lines radiating around her eyes and mouth. She placed her hand over her eye covered by a black velvet patch.

"Never trust a one-eyed witch," Lucian said quietly.

I doubted anyone else heard him. In my mind I echoed the old superstition that agents whispered to each other before heading into unknown dangers.

"We need to return to my office to discuss this," I announced to everyone crowding the room. "All of us."

"Erm… Sheriff Blue, you might want to read this telegram first." Neil thrust the flimsy paper into my hands. Fortunately, I stood right by the single window.

I needed only a moment to absorb the message from Brotherton.

DETAIN CP AT ALL COSTS. DO NOT TRUST HIM.

"This changes things. I presume O'Toole is waiting for an answer?" I asked Neil.

"I left him downstairs. Don't know if he returned to the Post Office or not."

One thing I'd learned in my weeks of living in Heller's Hole, the postmaster was a lazy gossip. Learning something new and interesting was the only reason he'd leave his office. Letters he couldn't open without getting caught so he handed them over to the recipient promptly, hoping they'd linger and discuss the contents in front of him. Telegrams he already knew the information because he had transcribed them from his arcane machine. Now he needed to watch my reaction to the news and have something to talk about.

"Doc, can we use your office for a private discussion?"

"My pleasure." He bowed slightly and gestured toward the stairwell.

"Out. All of you." I did my best to corral and usher out everyone who had invaded this space. I had to push Madame Glissen to keep her from scuffing the chalk marks or snagging one of the talismans dangling from the spear still standing upright and piercing the mummy's heart.

CHAPTER 30

"THIS IS ADDRESSED TO YOU, Mr. Sanderson," I said the moment Doc closed the door behind us. I pulled the wad of folded papers from my waistcoat. The movement pushed aside the loose fabric that disguised my breast. His gaze felt as if he burned away all of my clothing.

A blush crept upward from my belly to the top of my head.

Heat flashed between us. I truly hoped we could be together soon. Very soon.

I was beyond caring who did and did not know my true gender. The town would have to get used to it eventually. I'd just hoped for a little more time to earn their respect as a sheriff before they had to get used to a female sheriff.

"What is it?" Neil asked, accepting the pages from my hand. Our fingertips brushed and renewed desire awakened.

We all stood in a circle around Doc's examining table, no chance for privacy. Lucian and Doc each kept a hand on my arms to keep me from running back to the magic puzzle of the mummy and the wards around it.

They knew me too well. When Pinkerton recruited me, he appealed to my sense of curiosity with words like "mysteries" and "Detective work."

"I don't know what it is, but I grabbed it from the secret room just before Doc pulled me out." I mentioned mysteries and puzzles.

Neil was standing next to me but he kept the papers folded and close to his chest so I couldn't read them. There had been another page that fluttered down with the corpse. Had anyone bothered to read it?

Slowly Neil opened the pages and scanned the top half of the first one.

"What is hidden in that room?" Lucian asked. He stood on Neil's other side and blatantly peered cross wise at the writing.

"Nesting material for a very large bird of prey," I replied. "Old hay and twigs. Clumps of sheep wool. Maybe the mummy—if he was the original sheriff—slept up there." I gave up angling my neck at an awkward angle trying to read. Neil would tell me the contents that I needed to know. Soon I hoped.

I took a deep breath and closed my eyes, remembering every detail committed to memory in just a brief glance. The army had trained me well as a scout. The Pinkertons had deepened my observation skills.

"I think that the symbols around the mummy, and the talismans tied to the spear form a ward to keep the alien monsters away from town. That is why it is important not to disturb them, no matter how much you want to, Madame Glissen. If that is your real name." I stared at the psychic, daring her to protest.

Madame removed her veils and returned the intimidation.

Never trust a one-eyed witch.

My skin prickled at the idea of facing down the nemesis of all Pinkerton agents.

"This letter may answer many of your questions," Neil interrupted. "It was penned by Samuel Cooper, he's the circuit lawyer who comes through town once a month and deals with property transfers, wills, and other such stuff. His visits mostly coincide with the circuit judge in case we have any criminal cases. We haven't for a couple of years."

"Nice to know," I replied. Brotherton had told me that trouble followed me because I always found some when other agents hadn't.

"Cooper explains that he transcribes the oral instructions for Marv Miller who is illiterate."

"Miller? As in Miller's Orchard, the property owner I'm buying from?" I moved behind Neil to read over his shoulder. Curiosity burned through me as hot as Neil's lustful gaze. "Cooper can also claim lawyer-client confidentiality, which is why no one knows anything about the orchard being abandoned."

"I only caught a glimpse of the new corpse," Doc said. "But aside from the obvious alien features, and the purple cast to his skin, he could very well be Miller. I only saw him a few times when he brought his wife and children into town. The only memorable thing about him was his very fine and very white hair."

"He only came to the bank once, to sign papers when he and Belinda inherited the orchard, and the mortgage ten years ago. I was home briefly from school before joining the army at the start of the war. Miller signed with an X. Belinda did the rest, but as a woman she legally couldn't sign on her own. I don't know that I'd recognize Marvin Miller again," Neil explained. "Except for the nearly translucent white hair."

I kept reading, half listening to the men describe Miller. "He gives instructions for Neil Sanderson, banker and mayor, to sell the acreage and all remaining structures and livestock on behalf of Belinda and the children should anything untoward happen to him. So, I can still buy the place." I breathed a little deeper knowing that we'd eliminated one problem.

"At the bottom of the page, Miller says 'Tell my wife I love her and that I tried to deny the urges and appetites of my kin. I truly tried to satisfy myself with beef—rare or raw—but my breeding and my family culture demanded I succumb. The shaman—the only one of them left—is most persuasive. He convinced me of my duty to him and our ancestors. So I joined a band of my kin at the old mine."

The lead scientist leaned forward eagerly, (the other two waited outside) the two cameramen gagged, and stepped back from the circle. They worked for the Pinkertons so must know about the alien monsters.

"Not a word of this to anyone other than Brotherton!" I ordered. "Especially do not talk of this to Cutter Pine. I don't know what he did to earn Brotherton's wrath but keeping him in ignorance seems prudent." Then I gestured to them to take their equipment and leave.

"I need a deputy to keep an eye on things while I'm tied up," I muttered. "You want the job, Lucian?"

He shook his head vigorously.

"The rest of the letter seems to be an explanation about the alien biology and how half-breeds occur," Neil said.

That brought everyone in the room to a halt. They didn't shuffle their feet or flutter their hands. Doc barely breathed. Until he grabbed the papers away from Neil and began reading. His eyes tracked the printing rapidly.

"Full blood aliens can't shape-change. They implant an embryo—that's the beginning stages of a baby developing—into an open wound of a human. The wound remains raw, looks infected, but most men won't have it seen to. It's not manly to give in to a little bit of blood and pus." He paused long enough to shake his head. "That explains the wound in your back, Sheriff Blue. I lanced it, removed the dead embryo, and stitched you up."

"I can't do my job with an alien horn slash that won't close," I recited my thoughts as I worked through the process, my mind spinning faster than my words. "The infection and the pain wore me down to the point I had to seek help. You were the closest, Doc."

"Miller goes on to explain that the implantation is risky and most of the embryos die within a day or two," Doc explained. "They had better luck with the process on other planets—my God they truly do spring from other worlds! But those embryos that survive emerge about three months later, fully formed, sentient, and hungry. During gestation they absorb enough human traits to thrive and grow to adulthood with the ability to switch between forms."

"That must be how they colonize new places to live, by blending in until they swarm," Neil added.

"So why is the mummy in the attic and why is he circled with magic to keep the rest of his kind away from town," I continued, speaking my thoughts rather than hiding them.

"And who performed the ritual?" Lucian asked. "Some of it looks like the Voudon practices I saw in New Orleans."

We all turned our attention toward Madame Glissen.

Doc BRISTLED with indignation that the woman he'd just found as his one true soulmate—based upon love at first sight, if he believed in such things—came under scrutiny from two of the best investigative minds in the country. How dare they?

He drew her closer to him with a gentle hand on her arm, needing to protect her at all costs.

She resisted and shook him off.

Deep disappointment weighed heavily upon his shoulders and down into his gut.

"My mother cast that spell," Madame said proudly.

"Why?" Josie snapped back at her.

Madame pursed her lips and refused to speak. She did not drop her intense and penetrating gaze.

Doc needed to break the tension between the two women. How? They both knew their own minds and had convinced themselves they were in the right. As a doctor, he knew how to placate hysterical patients. This was different.

"Perhaps this discussion would go down better over a meal?" Neil suggested. He retrieved the distasteful papers from Josie and tucked them into his inside jacket pocket. "Shall we retire to Rosie's? I believe she should have apple pie again and Cook does a splendid job with the spices." He gestured toward the door and began moving in that direction as if herding them all out of this office.

"I will need help moving Marv Miller's body so I can do a postmortem. We know from his letter that he probably committed suicide by poison. Is there anyone in town who can positively identify the body?"

"The Russells might." Josie said. "They are the closest neighbors to one of the orchards, the trees planted on the north side of the road anyway,". She seemed all too eager to retire to a good hot meal.

Doc wasn't certain he could eat after the day's grisly revelations. But he needed to stay close to Madame.

Damn, he didn't even know her given name.

He hung back from Neil's herding efforts and signaled Lucian to linger as well.

"Does Madame have a first name?" he asked quietly.

"Neither she, nor Brotherton enlightened me," Lucian replied.

"Should we be concerned?" Doc asked. Now that the woman had moved out of his line of sight, some of his protective instincts faded. Was it merely proximity to her that fueled his need to love and care for her? If so, she was a one-eyed witch for sure.

Never trust a one-eyed witch. He'd heard that superstition before. Back east somewhere.

"I'm always concerned. To my knowledge Brotherton hired her based upon reputation. I don't think he'd ever met her before he sent us on our way this morning. I do know that we had to stop her wagon seven times on the journey so that she could stretch her aching bones. She spent a lot of time inspecting the road ahead and the tracks running away from the road for something she wouldn't talk about. But she talked about everything else endlessly and repeatedly." Lucian's clipped English accent took on the drawl and French lilt of his native New Orleans.

Not a good sign for a Pinkerton agent who was always observant, alert, and in control.

MUCH TO MY SURPRISE, I found the upright piano at Rosie's in pieces spread out on a white sheet that covered a large square of sawdust-littered plank floor. Rosie herself stood squarely, hands on ample hips, a wide stance, and lips pursed in disapproval. A man with his head deep inside the middle of the musical instrument, hummed to himself. I recognized the notes as part of a scale.

He must have come in one of the Pinkerton wagons.

On second look, the white sheet—Rosie was well known for having pristine sheets on all of the beds upstairs—showed dirt and dust smudges in the shape of felt covered hammers and coiled wires where pieces from inside the piano had rested. Now, I presumed, those pieces were back inside and the few remaining outside were damaged beyond repair.

"Ma'am, I vill haf to replace one more string," the man said, his German accent muffled by the cabinetry of the musical instrument. "Dis one vill stretch no more." He held up a long wire in his right hand.

I could tell by the amount of rust on the "string" that it had seen better days. The amount of rust that flaked off and fluttered to the floor at his touch revealed only more rust with no hint of the original wire.

"Anot'er two dollar."

Shudders of anticipation ran up and down my spine. I forgot all about the revelations in Marv Miller's letter. I dismissed Madame Glissen, and the two half-breed corpses in my attic.

"I'll pay for it," I said. The music of my youth ran through my mind. Chopin. Mozart. Even some Bach. My fingers itched to caress the ivory and ebony keys, to make the music and the instrument a part of me. Ma had a baby grand piano, much nicer than this beaten up old upright.

I forgot the tantalizing aroma of baking apples with cinnamon and sugar.

"May I play it yet?" I asked the tuner, keeping my hands in my pockets to prevent me from caressing notes from the piano until given permission.

"Not yet," the man said, ducking inside the stained case.

He made short work of attaching a new string. It shone with the metal alloy glinting in the lantern light. Then he rapped a tuning fork on the top of the cabinet and listened as he plucked the string.

"Play zee high G-sharp."

Not a request.

I obeyed. "It's flat."

"Ov course it is." He struck the tuning fork again, held it to his ear and twisted something. "Again."

I played the note. And then, because I could no longer keep my hands off the keys, I played the G-sharp major chord, repeated it an octave above and below. A full three octave scale in the same key followed.

"Enuff!" the tuner shouted. He made one more adjustment. "I have tuned this ancient piece of junk in the classical mode. Is best for the strings. If you insist upon modern popular garbage, you vill haf to wait for the strings to settle and go flat. I vill not tune it so." With that, he closed up the cabinet and began packing his tools. Each went into a pocket on a long roll of sturdy cloth. The precious tuning fork received an extra wrap of soft, silk velvet protection before inclusion with the rest of his equipment.

"What about your discards?" Rosie brushed the edge of the soiled sheet with the toe of her satin slipper.

"Into zee midden," the tuner replied on a huff. "Is criminal to neglect a pianoforte so horribly."

"Haven't had anyone play the thing until Sheriff Blue came to town. Now I suppose I'll have to hire someone to play it," Rosie grumbled. "You want an extra job, Josie?"

"I'll play it for free." I pulled up the rolling stool, adjusted the height to suit my long legs and sat down, hands poised to pound a crashing chord from a Handel piece. Automatically my right foot reached for the pedal.

Then I thought better of it and yanked off my boots. "Much better," I proclaimed, wiggling my toes. "The barefoot sheriff has found one more reason to stay in town."

Off to my right, Neil, Doc, and Lucian took seats at the big round table in my corner. I thought Madame and the cameramen joined them. The three scientists in tweed and city shoes, sat at the adjacent table, heads bent together in arcane conversation.

I didn't care what they talked about. All I knew was that I had a piano and music back in my life.

A few scales followed by a few testing chords and some half-remembered exercises flew from my fingers without thought. Once the notes floated free of the dormant instrument, I knew how to play them all. No time to linger with the essential warm up of my brain and fingers. I had to find the music bubbling in my soul.

The Brahms Lullaby, one of the first pieces I'd learned to play, floated through the saloon. The normal clatter and chatter of a Friday night quieted. Another childish Mozart piece.

Then a Chopin waltz.

In my peripheral vision I sensed couples dancing, Lucian and Poppy flew past me, circling the scattered tables.

I found a rousing polka newly arrived from Vienna that I'd played for my sister's wedding. Doc persuaded Rosie to join him in the frolicking dance. Madame Glissen refused Neil's offer, but three of the girls approached him eagerly.

Dancing must be a rare treat.

As I pulled piece after piece out of my memory, another tune tantalized my mind. A note here. A chord there. A melody line formed around my left hand accompaniment.

"Where did that come from?" I whispered to the piano. My right hand drifted away from the melody I had been playing and took up the accompaniment.

The new tune, simple and unadorned along the bass clef, kept pulsing through my mind, compelling, lush, and... and spiritual.

Longing. Loneliness. Homesick to the point of breaking my heart. I'd felt all that. I'd lived with the emptiness in my soul since... since my family had been ripped away from me.

Not a hymn I'd learned as a child.

Something I'd heard more recently.

A tune I shared with... the monsters. Aliens who'd been driven from home after home across the stars, looking for a place they could belong.

But they could never belong... anywhere as long as they fed upon people.

My voice wanted to join, a husky alto bordering on tenor to complement the bass line.

The world faded away.

I knew only the heavenly music and the note of bright hope that melody reached for. Like the promise of a better place free of pain after death.

CHAPTER 31

"SHERIFF BLUE." Neil interrupted Josie's music when she paused. He needed to keep her attention until she mastered her tears.

Madame Glissen still struggled with hers.

"What is that tune? I've never heard it before." He thought he had a reasonably thorough knowledge of music, gained from his years at boarding school and university. His mother had taught him the rudiments of piano, but he hadn't pursued it, and her knowledge was also rudimentary.

"I... I don't know. I heard it once, but I can't place where or when."

"Time to eat, Sheriff. As much as we've enjoyed your music, you need sustenance, and we haven't finished our discussion," Doc said, pulling out a chair for her between his own and Neil's, the one against the wall so no one could sneak up on her. His eyes too looked a bit moist.

The swelling crowd of patrons objected loudly to the cessation of music.

Josie flexed her hands as if preparing a new chord and then stopped, massaging her palms and fingers. "I think I've had enough for one night after not playing for too many years."

"Come back tomorrow!" several men called, raising their frothing mugs of beer to her.

"You cannot... you have no right to play that music," Madame Glissen stammered as she gulped and dashed away her tears with a black handkerchief. The black lace edging and embroidered monogram completed the theme of her somber clothing.

"Why?" Neil asked. He couldn't help the sharpness of his tone.

"Because it will not release the soul trapped in the body of the mummy," she whispered, leaning across the table to keep the conversation private. "That music will only drive it deeper into the building itself, an irrevocable part of the fabric."

"Is it the soul of the mummy or the magic lines encasing it that traps him?" Neil, too, leaned over the table. But he made sure the Pinkerton party of scientists one table overheard him.

"Is it the mummy, or the magic that protects this town from attack?" Josie asked. She'd come out of her music-induced trance and swallowed half her beer in one gulp. No trace of tears reddened her eyes or splotched her face.

He'd never seen her indulge in alcohol so deeply.

"I do not know," Madame Glissen met Josie's gaze with her own sternness. "I do know that if you try to remove the mummy for study without releasing the magic, the trapped soul will wreak vengeance with fire, flood, earthquake, and tornado on the entire region."

Neil felt the blood drain from his face. The top of his head would lift free of his body at any moment.

"I watched my mother create that magic, followed her through the ritual, as did my brother—you know him as Esteban. I know him as a powerful sorcerer, if only he would use his magic."

Neil and Josie looked at each other in surprise. "He is so mild-mannered, so down-to-earth and practical," Neil protested.

"Now, perhaps, he presents that face to the world. But in our youth, he lusted for magical power. He was set to overtake our mother. He could have ruled all men he saw. He could have retaken our homeland from the Spanish and French and kept them away from our birthright."

"What changed him?" Josie asked. "I have known your brother for many years. He has never spoken of a homeland, but lived the life of a wanderer..."

"Like you, Sheriff. Perhaps you recognize that in each other. My people are doomed to wander if we cannot live in the mountains of our ancestors."

"The Esteban I know has never exhibited the least touch of magic other than his ability to connect with animals. He is the only person my horse will allow to ride her other than me," Josie insisted.

"I do not know what drives him *now*. Like many of the native tribes, our men undertake a vision quest when they come of an age to take a bride. Five days and five nights he wandered in the wilderness. Just when we despaired that he might never return to our family, he appeared out of nowhere in our midst, much changed in posture, a deeper voice, a softer vision when he looked to the horizon, and much wisdom in dealing with people and sheep." Now the woman hung her head and refused to look at them.

That sounded like the man Neil had met camped among the circle of house-sized boulders.

"Does he know how to deal with the mummy?" he asked. "I don't like the idea of it residing in the attic. I have considered burning the building and putting up a new Sheriff's Office with more room for cells, desks for a deputy or two, and perhaps living space above."

"I like your idea, of a larger office and jail, and the apartment," Josie chimed in. "But we have to consider fire spreading to the build-ings on either side, and Prospero's paddock and barn. Then again, I don't want to share space with the dead."

"There may be a way..." Madame said. "I must speak with my brother."

"NEIL, A MOMENT," I said, touching his arm as the group began dispersing after dinner.

The warmth of his body felt incredibly comforting beneath my hand. I wanted nothing more than to invite him to walk me to my room and linger…

But he had responsibilities to his family, and I planned to ride to Esteban's encampment as soon as it was light enough to see the road.

And neither one of us could afford the scandal of any open affection.

So, I led him to the boardwalk outside. The flickering light of an oil lantern inside the jail seemed the only sign of life. Rosie had promised to send dinner to the prisoner. Perhaps the deliverer lingered to chat with Cutter Pine. He could be ever so charming when he wanted something.

Right now, he wanted out.

For now, I decided to wait and watch while I asked Neil an important question.

He led me to a bench beside the door, put there for men to discard very muddy or messy boots before entering the saloon. Not everyone did. But enough did that cleaning the floors was less arduous.

"What do you need?" Neil asked, awaiting me to sit first.

I did so, rather than have him linger too long for us to be seen and start the whispers around town.

"The boys who tried to rob the bank that first day I came to town…"

"They survived. Doc turned them over to their families, extracting the promise they would appear next time the circuit judge comes through."

"I'm glad I didn't kill them," I sighed. One less burden to carry. "But what struck me at the time was the whiter than white hair of one of them."

"And his younger brother has blonde hair, but not quite the almost translucent strands. He's a little darker." He sat heavily beside me, as if his knees gave out. He leaned to his right until our shoulders touched.

I found I needed his solidity to keep my teeth from chattering as my mind worked through new horrors.

"You said something the other day about a few Finnish people living up at the old mine, eking out a living from played-out veins of metal. What if those families aren't from Finland but from... from another planet, from outer space?"

"There haven't been any attacks by the aliens in living memory in this town. Marvin's letter showed just how strong is the compulsion for them to feed on carrion. We'd have heard about an attack like that."

"The army has a policy of wiping out the local tribes who do not voluntarily give up their lands and their lives. Our own military provides the aliens with enough carrion for a small colony to feed upon. How often do Army officers report their kills to us 'civilized' folk? How many kills do they report to their superiors in Washington City?"

"Just like the war," he said flatly. "But the military presence is sparse around here. I doubt they've massacred very many Indians in this region."

"So, the aliens who cling to their old ways and old food source don't live close to Heller's Hole, the town or the close ranches and farms."

"But they might linger around the mine, the original Heller's Hole. They, like Marv, might be trying to wean themselves off of a carrion diet, trying to find a way to stay on this planet after being massacred and kicked off every place they've tried to make a home."

"If that's the case, then the magic wards around the mummy might no longer be needed. Let's burn it down. With or without Madame's help. We can control the burn to isolate it to the sheriff's office."

A SCRATCHING outside my private entrance to the back balcony woke me from a sound sleep. Thinking it might be Neil, I jumped out of my bed without my gun.

Instead, I found Rollie da Foe crouched beneath the railing. Enough light spilled out of adjacent bedrooms to show his shadowy form and he kept low enough to avoid an obvious silhouette.

"S...sheriff, I need to talk to you," he whispered.

I had to strain to hear his words. "P...p...please may I come in?" He sounded chilled, and the pale outline of his hands shook.

I held the door open for him as I stepped closer to where I'd draped my gun belt around a bed spindle.

Fortunately, I wore a flannel dressing robe over a sturdy and plain nightshirt that many men would not be ashamed to wear. I presented a not exactly feminine form to him.

"What?" I asked as I gestured to the rocking chair beside the banked fire. The stove still emitted enough heat to soothe him.

In the dim light I saw bruising around his eye and a gash along his cheek.

"Who did that to you?" I found a clean wash rag and poured some cool water from the pitcher over it. Then I handed it to him.

He pressed it eagerly to his eye.

"Daddy. Who else?"

"Have you run away for good, or just to tell me something?"

"Daddy is gathering all the hands. I don't know where he got the cash to pay them, otherwise, none of them will show up." He paused to swallow deeply. He stared at his feet rather than meet my gaze.

"Go on." A lot of people came to town today with the Pinkertons. Some from outlying ranches might have had their cash for supplies stolen on their way toward the protection of the wagon train.

"I... I finished the book you let me borrow. It's in my saddlebag. I'd like to borrow it again sometime soon. Some of the information is dense and the language weird."

"Rollie, what do you truly need to talk to me about?" I knelt in from of him, examining his hurts with delicate fingering. Superficial, but he probably had a headache and needed rest.

"I... I hate defying him."

"Family loyalty is a good thing, but I think your daddy may have overstepped the bounds. What did you say to rile his temper?"

"He... he and Sam Iamn, he used to be our foreman until Mac Junior took over, decided to take back the town. They are riding in tomorrow about sunset with every hand and outlaw they can find. He's pulling rifles and bullets out of storage and rounding up the

271

meanest horses he can. He's also handing out raw whisky right outta the still."

"I figured he'd do that soon enough. But it's nice to know when."

"I told him he couldn't do it. I showed him the pages in your book about civil disobedience." His shoulders shook with barely suppressed sobs. "I'm sorry, but he tore the book outta my hands and some of the pages tore. I'm really, really sorry. Books are precious and he had no right to do that."

My heart ached for the boy. "The book is replaceable. I'm touched that you care so much about it."

He gulped and leaned back in the chair, handing me the now warm wash rag.

"You need rest. There's a couple of single rooms downstairs with cots and a washstand. You can stay there." The rooms had been empty when I locked up. "What about your horse?"

"I hope you don't mind, I turned him out in your paddock. If Daddy comes looking for me, the livery is the first place he'll look. He hates lawmen so much he'd never dream that I might hide near the jail."

"I'll check on him, once we get you settled."

I'd also patrol the town and leave notes beneath the doors at the bank, and Doc's office, and Lucian's room. I was going to need some help.

"You've had a measure of oats and three handfuls of sweet grass. Now settle down," I ordered Prospero.

The big stallion snorted at me and shifted anxiously from foot to foot while I smoothed the blanket down the length of his spine. He accepted the blanket, knowing the saddle would follow and we'd ride soon.

"I'll get all the wrinkles out, so they don't rub," I soothed him, testing every inch of the thick weaving for signs of wear or trapped thorns or sharp twigs.

He busied himself with slurping up a long drink of fresh water and prancing, anxious for a good long run, yet wanting more breakfast before.

"One would think the horse intelligent enough to talk back to you," a sultry female voice interrupted my ministrations.

"He is, Madame Glissen," I replied. "He doesn't use words, but he tells me what he needs and his opinion of everything I do."

A quick glance while fastening straps and adjusting buckles told me that the witch had donned a leather, split riding skirt, flat-topped hat with a chin strap, and boots. She looked graceful and elegant even with her short, voluptuous figure. I didn't think I would look half so good in that getup.

She shivered a bit and removed a short frock coat from her bulging saddle bag. It didn't look warm enough or sturdy enough to ward off the damp, morning chill.

I trusted my buckskin jacket to keep me warm and mostly dry. The fringe along the sleeves and across my upper back would catch the drizzle and channel it away from my body.

"You took off your eye patch," I noted.

"It helps me focus my inner vision." The older woman shrugged. Then she mounted the ordinary livery stable bay horse she had led down the street.

"Champ's a good gelding. Sure-footed and doesn't startle," I noted. Over the last week, Elinore had introduced me to all the horses in the stable and given her opinion of each.

I was glad now that Elinore had treated Champ with indifference but approved of Prospero as long as he kept his distance, until she was ready.

"So Young Jed told me. He had to hold back a curious skewbald mare who wanted to come along. I suspect that horse has become bored with the stable and seeks new pasturage."

"At least you seem to know how to ride," I muttered to hide my smile at the description of Elinore. If all went well today, I'd give her new pasturage. "Why have you invited yourself to ride with me?"

"You go to visit my brother. It is time I stretch forth an olive branch to my family."

"Just don't get in my way. I have serious questions about the magical wards around my mummy and no time to waste on family reunions. Which get emotional and messy." I affixed the stampede strap to my hat and anchored it firmly. I added a long pin with a plain silver knob through the hat into my coiled braid atop my head. Knowing what Prospero wanted to do, I needed both precautions to keep from losing my fine new Stetson.

Hat secure and boots snug but comfortable, I swung onto my horse and gathered the reins. "Keep up or you'll never find Esteban's campsite." With a touch of my heels and a shift of posture, I gave Prospero his head.

The big stallion didn't need more encouragement. He needed only a few long strides to shift from a walk to a full-on gallop.

I felt through my seat and thighs the horse's joy at running free. His dark mane blew in the wind, and he spread his tail in a wide plume. I laughed out loud, glorying in the freedom.

This horse was meant to run, and I wondered if I should enter him in any of the local races come summer. Any gathering of people at a fair, or market day prompted horse owners to challenge others, especially from the local tribes, to test the fleetness of their favorite mount.

After a mile, I finally curbed Prospero and took control of the reins. "Easy boy, easy," I crooned to him. "No sense in having you winded and too tired to escape if we need to when we get there."

As if he understood my reasoning, Prospero eased back into a trot, and then a walk. "Elinore is a touch more responsive than you, my boy, but you are faster," I admitted. But only because Elinore was more than a mile back in town and couldn't hear me.

"That is quite a horse, Sheriff. One would think my people bred him," Madame Glissen said coming up beside me. Her hat lay across her shoulders, held in place by the long chin strap. The wind had played havoc with her sleek chignon, loose tendrils draped across her cheek.

My hat remained firmly in place.

And her placid gelding lagged a bit, breathing hard.

I smiled with contentment that I'd had the wisdom to pass on purchasing Champ. I wanted, needed, the stallion with fire in his heart and wings on his heels.

"How do you know Brotherton?" I asked, just before the silence between us grew heavy. The reunion business would wait a bit. I needed information first, then I'd let the emotions play out.

"From before the war. He had a different name then."

"So did we all," I muttered. For the first time in a long time, my gut didn't rip apart at the memory of *why* I'd changed my name and signed over my inheritance to Pinkerton control. Why I'd let Cutter Pine make all my decisions for me those first few weeks when I was still in shock and over-full of grief.

"What ghost did you raise for Robert Brotherton, known as Beauregard Martine back then?" I didn't know when he'd become a colonel in the U.S. Army, only that he'd worked with Allan Pinkerton from the beginning of the detective agency.

"You know him well."

Not a question.

"I've known him a long time. No one knows him well."

"Perhaps because he still mourns his wife, and I failed to communicate with her spirit. She passed beyond the veil, content that she'd lived her life well and loved him without reservation even though their last words were in anger. So instead of apologizing to her and expressing his own love for her, he must search endlessly for the outlaw gang that murdered her." Madame lowered her head and used her right hand to make an arcane gesture.

"That explains a lot," I muttered. "I'm surprised he trusted you with this case if you failed him before."

"The séance was not a total failure. It rarely is in a cemetery."

An otherworldly chill climbed my spine and set my teeth to chattering. I clenched them tightly to keep my fears to myself.

"How many ghosts did you raise?" I asked, once I had control of myself.

"Seven that lingered more than a few seconds."

"Hopefully those who dissipated have gone to their final rest rather than linger in this world."

"Hopefully. Martine saw them and understood. I am a true psychic medium. I did not make contact with his beloved because she was no longer there. I did not fail."

"Those seven ghosts...?"

"Much work. Many exhausting spells. Each took a turn using Martine's body and voice to pass along a message and then they too passed beyond the veil. He knows the breadth of my talents."

"That explains even more about Robert Brotherton," I agreed.

We traversed the last curve before the drive to the orchard. I reined in Prospero and held out a hand to stop Madame.

"What? Is there danger?" she whispered.

"No. Before we approach your brother, my friend Esteban, I have to know if your presence will be welcomed or shunned, or violent?" The man I knew never resorted to violence unless defending himself and his family. An estranged family member might provoke him.

She looked toward a distant horizon only she could see for a long moment of silence. "I do not know. When we separated, many years ago, we both felt much anger."

CHAPTER 32

"Not so hard!" Jonquil squeaked as Doc pressed upon her ribs with what he thought was a gentle touch.

He stepped back from the examining table, keeping a keen eye on her skin tones. Paler than usual with her fair coloring. Dark circles around her eyes and her slender frame had become gaunt after only a few days since Cutter Pine had attacked her.

"You remind me of Sheriff Blue in the way you hide your pain until someone actually puts pressure on your wounds." He gestured for her to jump down from the table and take a seat in the straight-backed chair. Again, he watched her movements as she gingerly grasped the edge of his rolling instrument cart and lowered herself.

"Rosie asked me this morning if I'm ready to return to work." She choked on a sob. "I don't think I'll ever be ready to face a man again. Except for you, Doc. You've always been gentle with me."

Doc's chest swelled a bit at the adoration in her gaze.

But he'd not hurt her. Not in any way. No matter how much he longed to bury himself in her soft and loving nature. But those blue eyes and golden hair reminded him of stained-glass windows in a church in Boston that depicted a lovely angel blessing the children.

"You know that Sheriff Blue can take you away from this life, give you sanctuary and peace. You won't ever have to return to Rosie's." He studied his hands rather than challenge her gaze.

"But she'll only do it if I tell her my name." A single tear leaked from her eye. "He'll find me and kill me if I tell."

"Sheriff Blue might ride off in a tearing rage and confront him. She'd win that battle." All the girls at Rosie's knew the truth about Josie Blue and seemed more than willing to protect her secret, that wasn't truly secret anymore.

"She might not. He's terrible mean toward trespassers. And he considers everything he sees as his property."

"I won't tell the Sheriff unless she needs to know in order to protect other women. You know you can trust me. It's part of being a doctor. I can't tell anyone what you say without your permission." He knew other physicians who violated that trust all the time. He'd only done it once, during the war, when a lieutenant needed to know that his sergeant was likely to go into a killing rage and turn on his own men and he hadn't finished his need to wreak havoc when the battle was ended. Or in the middle of the night when he woke from a nightmare and needed to murder someone. Anyone.

"My mama called me Jane," she whispered. "Plain and simple."

"That's a start. What was your daddy's name?"

Her head reared up and her eyes flitted back and forth, looking for a way to flee, or a place to hide.

"I... I don't know, only that he died when I was real young. Never knew him or his name."

"Your mother remarried soon after?" Probably to a man who would give her a home and food to put on the table.

"I guess."

"Did you ever call her new husband 'Daddy'?"

Jane shook her head.

"Let's try something easy. How old are you?"

"You know that. I'll be eighteen next month."

That meant that her stepfather had raped and beaten her and then sold her to Rosie when she was barely fifteen. Had he turned her over to his older sons to use before throwing her away?

"What happened to your mother?"

"She died giving birth to...*that* man's son."

That meant her half-brother was no more than sixteen, seventeen at most.

The blood drained from Doc's head and darkness encroached on his peripheral vision. He knew of only one sixteen-year-old boy whose mother had died in childbirth within fifty miles of town. Rollie da Foe, son of Mac da Foe and his third wife. He'd taken a fourth wife, but she hadn't given birth to any children that he knew of.

"I'll tell Sheriff Blue your given name and convince her to take you somewhere your stepfather will never find you." He hoped the Basque shepherds who had promised to protect her out at the orchard had enough magic to keep Mac da Foe away from his stepdaughter.

A DIFFERENT MAN than last time stood guard at the entrance to the stone circle. Older, broader, grimmer. He held a rifle across his body, finger on the trigger of his aged single shot—maybe custom made. I didn't recognize the maker. I'd never seen this clan wield firearms. That didn't mean they didn't have them. They had to have a way to protect their flocks from wolves and other predators.

"Tell Esteban that Sheriff Josie Blue is here to see him," I announced loudly, hoping I'd balanced authority and submission in my voice. Then I dismounted but kept Prospero's reins short and taut.

"You did not tell him that I'm here," Madame Glissen said in a harsh whisper that I'm certain carried deep into the circle. She stayed atop her horse.

"I will speak with Sheriff Blue, not with this other person," Esteban said, coming up behind us. He too carried a rifle, over his shoulder, muzzle pointed away from us. But his finger rested within the trigger guard.

Something had changed since yesterday.

"Very well. Can we retire within the sacred circle?"

"You may. *She* may not." He walked up to face me, only glancing once to the side to make certain Madame did not try to approach him.

"Esteban, *brother*, I would have peace between us." Madame dismounted but did not reach to touch him. She stood as stalwart as my friend.

"Sheriff Blue, please tell this woman she is not welcome here."

"Fine. I didn't invite her. She came of her own volition. You two can settle your differences, or fight it out, later. I need information first."

Esteban gestured toward the opening between two stones. The gap seemed narrower than yesterday. Prospero would not fit.

Reluctantly I dropped the reins and let him graze on the lush grass within the shade of the apple trees. Not many windfalls or ripening fruit within his reach. He'd not overindulge. Some kind of shivery extra sense told me to leave my Spencer repeating rifle snug in its sheath on the saddle.

I still had my six guns holstered at my hips, the knives in my ankle holsters and numerous fighting tricks at my disposal. Why I'd brought the extra weapons to visit an old friend, I could not tell. It had just seemed right when I dressed this morning.

Inside the circle, a solitary guard awaited us. He too carried his rifle across his body, ready to swing it in the direction of any perceived danger. The rest of the clan had disappeared, including their wagons that doubled as living quarters.

I whirled to face Esteban. I had not seen him standing in a long time. Usually we shared tea and his oddly flavored smokes while seated. Memory of his intimidating height—half a head above me—wide shoulders, and broad face with a large nose and full lips made me feel small and insignificant.

My pride reared up and stiffened my spine. I stood taller than most men. My weapons were part of my personality. I'd taken down rampaging outlaws and ravenous alien monsters. Esteban Shallook, my *friend*, did not scare me into backing down.

"Your sister tells me that you were part of the ritual that set the magical wards at the center of this town. A ritual that involved the dead body of a man who was half purple alien," I accused him.

He did not blink, did not blush or back down in the least. But he did nod.

"She also tells me that you became a formidable sorcerer after your vision quest."

He held my gaze but gestured the sentry to withdraw.

I didn't dare glance behind me to see how far he retreated. If he retreated. I hoped that showed enough trust in the man before me that he'd return the favor and speak honestly.

"You have heard truth. I do not practice my magic anymore. I have seen what terrible destruction I can wield. And I know the cost of such power."

Good enough for me. I didn't truly want to know what he had endured.

"I want only information today. Can we remove the body without breaking the protection of the wards?"

"No."

"What if we burn the place down, body and magic intact?"

He paused a long moment, his eyes glazed as he turned his focus inward.

"Perhaps."

"There's an unspoken 'but' in there."

"The one-eyed witch who cast the spell must be present."

Madame Glissen wore an eye patch to make her a one-eyed witch. She was present at the spell casting. Did that qualify?

"Your mother."

"She died a decade ago. She worked too much magic in her short time on this earth and it near blinded her when young. She always wore an eye patch, since before my birth. Then as she continued to work strong magic, it drained the life from her."

Outside the circle, Madame gasped in shock. If she spoke or protested, I couldn't hear her. All my attention was nailed on my old friend. He suddenly looked much older.

"You and your sister were there. Observers. Perhaps participants or tools." Over my years in the wilderness, I'd gathered a lot of odd bits and pieces of knowledge. Somehow, I'd missed out on ceremonial magic. I knew of it. I didn't know much about it. Shamans and priests rarely talked about it, let alone admit that it existed.

"I will not work with that woman. She is a traitor to our people. The corpse and the wards must remain in place."

~

Defeat!

He would not help me.

I didn't like defeat in any form. Usually defeat meant death at the hands of an enemy.

Failure!

I didn't like that idea any better. At least failure, or retreat, meant I would live to fight another day.

Prospero eluded my grasp when I reached for his reins. He'd finished grazing and meandered toward the creek for a good long drink, ignoring my pleas and then my orders to return to town.

"He knows what you need better than you do," Madame Glissen said. She led her horse in my wake.

"You did not confront your brother." I distracted myself with finger combing Prospero's mane. He needed another good brushing. He was the kind of horse who would always need more grooming. His coloring and his temperament would always lead him to making messes of himself, and for his herd.

"The son of my mother has made his wishes clear. I must absent myself from the ritual."

"Why? What did you do to earn his wrath?" Not much made Esteban angry. He tended to laugh and find ways to circumvent confrontations. I'd seen him walk away from a fight, sacrificing pride to maintain the peace.

"I married out of the tribe. I cheated on my husband in favor of another, better lover. I bore two children to a third man whom I did not marry. I speak my mind and do not listen to him. Name a sin, I have committed it."

"Have you killed?"

"In self-defense. I have stolen food to stay alive. I disdain my brother's gods. In fact, I do not embrace any god or goddess. Name a sin, I have them all on my conscience."

"You and I have much in common—except the marriage and children part. I have the additional sin of dressing and acting as a man. Yet he embraces me as a friend but shuns you."

"I commune with the dead but refused to raise our mother's ghost so that he could say *'Forgive me.'* one last time. He says the words in his prayers, but I doubt he means them."

I sat on the grass beside the creek, needing a few moments of quiet to think. And think again.

"I am surprised you found the stairway leading to the attic," Madame said, joining me on the grassy bank.

She tucked her feet beneath her skirt, staying as far as she could away from the gently flowing water. The recent rain had swollen its width and depth.

I considered yanking off my boots and bathing my feet in the water.

"We included the door in the illusion of... nothingness," she continued. "For twenty-five years no one noticed the crevice in the wall or the extra height of the building disguising the space below. No one. And yet, you come to town and you find everything that we so carefully hid."

She sounded almost like she accused me of having hidden talents.

"I explored the place. It has been my job for a long time to crawl into dark places and measure every inch to make sure there are no hidey holes. Outlaws create clever disguises for places to hide their stolen goods and evidence of crimes."

"Even you should not have found the attic. Other sheriffs and gossips have been just as nosey as you, Sheriff Blue."

She let a moment of silence linger. I startled when she finally broke it. "If you do not have Basque magic in your soul as my brother and I do to help you see through our illusions, then the spell is fading. The protections we set will not hold much longer. You must wait a bit longer, but you will be able to take the mummy away for study in a few months. Maybe a year."

I'd thought much the same when Cutter Pine showed up.

"Before then I need to protect my town from the flying purple things that make music so heavenly I swear they are inspired by angels."

I did not need to know why Esteban needed forgiveness from his mother.

I did need to know what could be done about the mummy in my attic, besides waiting.

Other than my own comfort, what would I gain by ridding my office of the remains of a half-breed monster?

Leaving him in place gained the protection of the town and the outlying regions from the human carrion eaters. For a time.

Today was Saturday, the night when rowdy cowboys came to town to drink and whore and shoot their weapons at anything that moved. Angry men. Men who carried anger within them for no good reasons and made other people feel pain in order to ease their inner turmoil. Mac da Foe.

Once before the monsters had used angry men to shoot up the gathering of my family to create carrion for their feasting.

Saturday night.

Mac da Foe had reason in his own mind to create chaos and death in my town. Or did all of that come from the white-haired foreman, financial advisor, and mind controller who always stood at his shoulder?

Could they breach the wards surrounding the mummy? Had that protection faded enough for Mac and his men to ride into town shooting at anything that moved and leave a trail of dead in his wake? Could the aliens follow that trail beneath the crumbling wards?

Why had Marv Miller succumbed to his dietary lust now, after a lifetime of suppression? Had the wards broken down more than

Madame Glissen suggested? Or was he part of the consequences of an alien living within the precinct of the wards for too long?

A sudden flash of memory made my heart skip a beat. Last month, my last battle against the aliens, only twelve warriors had burst from the innards of a huge generation ship. Not a smaller shuttle designed for hundreds, or thousands, of inhabitants. But only a dozen came that day. Other than the one-eyed witch with a spiral horn, I'd dispatched the *small* raiding party with little trouble.

Had the magical wards affected their numbers? Or something else?

Marv Miller apparently had had little contact with his people until recently. He'd succumbed to the influence of a shaman who needed his people to return to the old ways.

"Ask yourself what the wards do to humans who are vulnerable to manipulation," Madame Glissen whispered, as if she'd read my mind.

"Esteban, can I take your sister's place in the ritual to burn down the sheriff's office but leave the wards in place?" I called to the man whom I knew watched me from the shadows close by. Don't ask me how I knew, but I sensed him, or heard him breathe, or just knew him well enough that he would not leave me alone with his sister. He used shadows well to conceal himself. Perhaps he held the essence of the shadows in his heart.

"The cost of working big magic carries too much pain," he whispered back to me.

"A better question for you: do the wards feed men's anger and bloodlust as they dissipate?"

Esteban stepped free of the shadows.

"We did not think about the possible backlash of putting up the wards. We reacted only to the menace of encroaching aliens. MacKenzie da Foe remained outside the reach of the wards, opening himself to manipulation. The sheriff showed signs of reverting to his people's old ways and opening this town and community to invasion. We stopped the outrage."

"I'll meet you in town an hour before sunset. That's when Mac da Foe will come to wreak havoc in my town." I mounted Prospero and touched my heels to his sides. He needed no further urging to gallop headlong toward his paddock.

CHAPTER 33

Both Doc and Neil, from outside their respective offices, gestured to me to meet with them as I finally slowed Prospero to a walk. He needed to cool down. I by-passed both men and headed for the livery. One nod to Jed and he caught the reins as I slid off the stallion's back.

"Jed, please walk him back to his paddock, rub him down and groom him. Hay and water. But I may need him ready to go at a moment's notice. I'll pay extra."

"Resaddle him?" Jed asked. He looked a little star struck that I trusted him with such essential chores.

"Only when he and the blanket are dry. Then I suggest you hunker down in your barn and lock the doors."

I'd reached the gate when he spoke again.

"What about the horses? Pa says we have to protect the horses first."

Good lad.

"Turn them out in the pasture, leave the gates open. They'll run if endangered." Except Elinore. She'd stand her ground and fight with hoof and teeth and body weight. "I want Elinore at my side. Even if I can't ride her yet, she'll know what to do."

I whistled between my two fingers, two short and sharp signals.

Elinore lifted her head from grazing beside the creek. At least she wasn't *in* the creek. One snort and she walked quickly to my side. I scratched between her ears, and she nuzzled my side, eager to accompany me anywhere.

"What you expecting, Sheriff?" Jed didn't stammer or cower, just held Prospero's reins and looked me in the eye. *Good lad.*

"I hope we only have to contend with the usual crowd of rowdy cowboys. If it becomes more, hide."

"I'm a good shot," he protested.

"Then protect yourself and this pasture, but stay put so I don't have to worry about you."

I whipped around and walked rapidly back to the heart of town, Elinore keeping pace just behind me. The schoolhouse was quiet. The afternoon shadows had grown long. Without a school master, the children needed to stay home to help with the harvest or rounding up herds and flocks.

Then the sight of Jonquil hurrying from Doc's office back toward Rosie's, with her hand pressed to her injured side and her breath coming in short gasps, decided me. As much as I wanted to talk to Neil, to tell him my convoluted thoughts and let him help me find the logic in them, I paused at Doc's office first.

"Make it quick," I demanded.

Elinore paused. I recognized her stance as an alert and guarding posture.

Doc must have sensed our urgency. Gone was the relaxed and loquacious man who gently pried information from patients.

"Jonquil's given name is Jane. She claims she doesn't know her father's name. But I deduced from what she said that her stepfather— the man who beat and raped her, then sold her to Rosie—is Mac da Foe."

A pattern formed in my mind.

"The night of Rollie's birthday did Mac Junior ask for Jonquil to service the boy?"

Doc nodded. "Rosie changed things around so the boy got Lilly.

The family lust for perversion would have taken great joy at the coupling of half siblings."

Which made Mackenzie da Foe Senior the type of man vulnerable to manipulation and violence.

"Mac da Foe has an advisor with white-blond hair. Just like Marv Miller and the mummy."

Doc paused a moment, then nodded. "His foreman retired about a year ago to let young Mac step into his job. But he stayed on as Mac's business advisor. He's not very good at it. Can't say I've ever heard his name. Only seen him once or twice in the years I've been here."

"Rollie named him Sam Iamn. I don't know if the name means anything special."

I mused a moment longer, letting the patterns form in my mind while I followed connections. "Sam Iamn retired before Marv Miller had the circuit lawyer draw up his statement. If Marv was teetering on the edge of acting human or succumbing to his need to feast on human carrion, then the foreman had time to influence him. The foreman had time to push Mac's sons toward violence, to create the carrion the aliens needed to thrive."

The monsters were planning something big. Maybe their mother ship planned to land and take over the planet, turning humans into cattle.

But I suspected their numbers had declined dramatically over the years. *Maybe too many of them had adopted human lives, had families, and worked the land.*

What if this was a last-ditch effort to revive the mother ship?

"How far out of town is the da Foe ranch?"

"Ten miles east."

Most likely beyond the full effect of the wards. Maybe close enough to feel ripples of backlash as the magic began to wear thin.

We had to burn down the office and take control of the town. Backlash.

Fading magic was worse than no magic at all.

~

NEIL PACED. Josie had stopped to chat with Doc. While he couldn't see the details of her expression at this distance, her posture and restless hands constantly reaching for her guns told him that she worried.

He began to worry too.

At last, she dismissed Doc with a tip of her hat brim, flashing the flamboyant hawk feather still tucked into the band, and proceeded toward him.

"Does this town have anything resembling a posse?" she asked as soon as she stepped up onto the boardwalk from the alleyway running beside the bank building.

"Not really," he replied, not having to think about it. "We've been pretty peaceful until last month." His gaze kept drifting to that hawk feather. In his mind it symbolized authority more than the tin star pinned to her waistcoat over her heart.

"Who has the authority to station armed guards in every second story window or roof top with a line of sight to Rosie's?"

"You do."

"But do the townsfolk trust me enough yet to agree to that?"

Silence stretched between them. Too long. Too uncertain.

"Find Lucian and bring him to my office." She turned and moved to cross the street.

"I'll send him..."

"No. You come too. And all the other Pinkerton folk you can find. Madame Glissen and Esteban will be along shortly. I need to deputize every last man, woman, and teenager in town. Don't forget Rollie. He's probably still asleep in one of the single rooms at Rosie's. He ran away from home last night and told me his father's plans, and his delusions of grandeur. And we need to get everyone in place before the da Foe gang arrives. I expect them to come in shooting, and aiming for anything that moves, people, horses, dogs, even stray cats." Then she stomped away.

"I'm the mayor. I guess people will listen to me." But what would he do if his mother awakened from her drug-induced sleep and wandered into town as if she still owned it?

He stepped back into the bank and ordered Martin to close up and then ran to the Sanderson home to warn Rachel the maid, and Jack, his father's keeper, to arm themselves and stay inside.

~

"WHY NOT JUST SHOOT THEM OUT of their saddles as they come into town, leave the bodies to attract the monsters, then shoot them too?" Cutter Pine said. He sounded bored, at the same time eager to be the one to fire the first shots.

"Because, Mr. Pine, I am sworn to uphold the law in this town and the law says they have to shoot first, and I have to accept the surrender of those we don't have to kill," I replied, gritting my teeth against my anger. Cutter Pine had almost gotten me killed twice with that tactic.

"Since when have you allowed a little thing like the law stop you?" he sneered back at me. "We're Pinkertons. Our weapons make the law."

"I am no longer employed by Allan Pinkerton and I do not answer to Robert Brotherton." Every time I said it, tightened my resolve to stay in this town, made it more real. And right.

"Several hundred years ago a little document called *Magna Carta* decreed that no man is above the law, not even a king," Neil said, looking up from studying the town map. Of course he'd know an obscure detail like that.

My new, and I hoped temporary, deputies crowded my office to near overflowing. I'd asked for all of the best shots in town. Neil and Doc had found ten, including Rosie, and young Jed. But not Rollie. A dozen more men milled around outside, and a few people dotted the flat roofs of scattered buildings, hiding behind the false fronts and keeping their eyes peeled for any sign of rogue cowboys headed for town.

"And this country was founded on the principle of life, liberty, and the pursuit of happiness," Doc added. "I have seen and read copies of the *Declaration of Independence* and the *Constitution*. The da Foes and their hired hands deserve the protection of the law until they break it."

"I know men like da Foe." Pine said with a sneer. "He thinks that he makes the law to suit himself. If he wants to spray the town with bullets, not caring who he kills in the process, then he's right in his own mind. You willing to try and change his mind, *Sheriff* Blue?"

"Yep. That's what they pay me to do."

I decided to ignore him and returned to my study of the town map. I'd already walked most of the land, talked to many of the shop owners and a few inhabitants that lived within the roughly defined borders.

I marked key positions with a clear line of sight, some of them overlapping, to the trails that met the road and the alleyways that could be approached stealthily if you didn't care about rough and broken terrain. Two of the ravines were too rough and steep for horses, even a horse as savvy as Elinore. Those approaches had to be done on foot.

A strong tactician, like a half-breed alien would figure out those were routes most people wouldn't bother watching. I was a Pinkerton and an army scout. I saw impossible land as an invitation.

"You need someone with keen eyes and a steady hand on this roof." Rosie pointed to the square on the map that represented my office. "And in the belfry of the schoolhouse." She moved her finger to the spot for that building. We all knew how open and exposed that belfry was. Four posts and a roof to support the bronze bell with only half the mass of a small man.

Come to think on that, I'd never heard the bell ring, for school, or church services. Was it even still there?

We all stared at each other, assessing, waiting for volunteers. The shooters would be exposed to anyone creeping up the ravines.

What I had heard about Mac da Foe, told me that he plotted ahead. He'd think through his options before he succumbed to rage. His best men would walk up those steep and broken paths and take aim at any watchers before they sent signals to the rest of us.

"I wish your father was up to it, Neil. He used to have the best far sight and quickest trigger finger in town," Rosie said with a sigh.

"I may not remember my name but I can still shoot," A tall, gaunt man, wearing a suit that had gone out of fashion before the war, wandered into my office, followed by a shorter, but bulkier man who supported the old man's elbow.

"You must be Mr. Sanderson." I straightened and approached him with an outstretched hand in greeting.

"Pleased to meet you, Sheriff." His hazel eyes, so like Neil's that I'd recognize anywhere, fixated on the tin star pinned to my waistcoat above my heart. "I should know you..."

Neil moved as if ready to usher the old man out, but Jack, the keeper, held up his hand to stop Neil in his tracks. "Let him. His mind wanders but once set on a course he follows through. He needs focus. Give him one."

"Are you certain?" Neil asked.

The other man nodded.

"Got an extra rifle, Sheriff?" Neil called back to me.

I grabbed one from the long case behind my desk. While there I checked the people filling the space. They all had weapons. Except Cutter Pine. I weighed my options. "You up to guarding the overland approaches to town?" I asked him.

For the first time since I'd arrested him, Cutter's eyes cleared and he straightened out of his perpetual slouch. This was the man who'd rescued me ten years ago. He'd decisively handled the legal problems and led me into a different way of life. This was a man who got things done. When he wanted to. When it benefited him.

"I'll take this roof. Kinda feels like this building is home," he replied.

"LIKE A GOOD GENERAL, you have deployed your troops and now all you can do is wait," Esteban said from the back doorway while I stared out the front window of my office.

"I don't know where I am supposed to be," I replied. To my own ears, I sounded lost and forlorn. Alone.

Cutter Pine's clomping steps on the roof seemed distant and removed. He hankered for action. With nothing to shoot at, he paced.

"Show me this mysterious mummy," Esteban demanded.

I was reluctant to leave my observation post, though I couldn't see much.

"You demanded I come, so show me."

"Yes." I tore myself away from the window and touched the pressure latch on the top left corner of the obscure door. Strange how the shadows in the room lingered here. By design? One could not see the outline of the opening unless you knew how and where to look.

"If you were here for the original spell casting, you must know the way," I accused my old friend of I didn't quite know what.

"I need to know that you have ferreted out the secrets or if the shadows retreat of their own volition."

"A bit of both." I opened the door on silent hinges. They should have creaked. The metal should have rusted or at least been stiff after twenty-five years of neglect.

I'd been up and down these stairs enough to no longer cringe at the idea of what awaited me.

Two dead bodies. Between the war, the original massacre of my family, and my fieldwork for Pinkerton, I'd encountered death many times. I had nothing to fear from corpses. And yet I had difficulty forcing my gaze to examine them critically.

Something was different.

The decorated spear through the mummy's heart that anchored everything was no longer here. I searched the dark corners and recesses.

Empty.

Esteban spotted the absence immediately. "Who would dare?" he gasped, outraged.

"Pine! Get your sorry ass down here and explain yourself. *Now!*"

"He has ruined everything," Esteban growled. He pushed me aside as he stepped onto the floor, neck twisting right and left, up and down. "The spell lines are scuffed too." He stood in indecision, not like the man I had known for years.

"We must hurry," Madame Glissen said, coming up behind me. "All of the anger and lust for the taste of human flesh that has been contained within the geometry of the spell is rushing outward. I felt it as soon as I entered the office." She too pushed me aside to join her brother.

Esteban turned a furious face upon his sister.

"There is no time for old angers and hurts to interfere," I said sternly. "I do not know what to do to help, and you, Esteban, have no time to teach me. Work with your sister and settle your differences later."

"Mr. Pine," Madame called through the open trap door to the hidden room. By the amount of light coming through I knew that Pine had also opened the hatch to the roof.

"Yes, Madame?" He poked his head through the trap, looking all innocent, but triumphant too.

"We need the spear, now. Unbroken. With all the talismans intact," Esteban ordered. He drew himself up to his full intimidating height. His chest expanded impressively with his next intake of air.

"I... I thought it might be a more effective weapon against... against someone under the thrall of an alien." In all the years I'd known him, Cutter Pine had never cowered in the face of a powerful man or lost his authoritative voice.

Correction, he submitted to a powerful sorcerer.

"No. It will not make an effective weapon in your hands. It is a symbol only. Drop it down to me, gently."

Cutter obeyed without a squeak of protest.

"Sheriff Blue, take your post in the middle of the road at the center of town and await events. Do what you normally do in the face of a mortal enemy," Esteban said.

"Do not lose your focus for any reason, no matter what you see, even if this building catches fire," Madame added.

I decided to move Doc to the attic to keep tabs on Esteban and Madame. What little I knew of ceremonial magic, the procedures drained the participants of energy. If the two Basque practitioners grew too weak to move, and set the place on fire, they'd need help escaping.

Who else needed rearranging?

"Mr. Pine, please move your sentry post to the far end of the paddock," Esteban said politely, his gaze already on the mummy and his focus inward.

"You can see the ravine well enough from there. The roof is no longer safe for you. I suggest you exit by the ladder outside," I ordered him. "Don't make me come up there and force you!"

Esteban dismissed me with a gesture and a nod. A tiny smile tickled the corner of his mouth.

I retreated to the street carrying my Spencer repeater, both my pistols, two smaller guns in ankle holsters, three braces of knives, and my hat with the audacious hawk feather symbolizing my authority.

At the last moment, I took off my boots, needing to curl my toes into the soft mud of the street, anchoring me to the earth. That felt like something Madame would suggest.

CHAPTER 34

"Here they come!" Neil called from the bank rooftop, other than the schoolhouse belfry the tallest building in town. He and his clerk Martin stood tall between the brick crenellations.

All along the street a variety of hands waved to indicate they acknowledged the warning.

Elinore nudged me in my side. I reached my arm beneath her chin and scratched her opposite cheek. Our ritual. Prospero joined us on my other side. He didn't want cuddling. He'd rather bare his big teeth in warning to the enemy. We stood together against the outlaws, the aliens, anyone, any*thing* that stood between us and holding civilization together.

My mare snorted and pranced aside as she took her stance. Prospero maintained his usual aggressive posture.

I felt through my bare feet the vibrations of a dozen or more horses pounding the road before I saw the first dark hat as the wearer crested the hill by the livery stable. Too soon the figure of a middling sized, dark-haired man atop a cantering black stallion as tall and big muscled as mine, came into view.

MacKenzie da Foe led his pack, rifle barrel pointed skyward for the moment. A six gun in his dominant right hand aimed at my heart.

~

DOC SAT on the second to the top step of the attic. The two Basque magicians moved around and around the mummy in a complex dance that had no rhyme or reason. Sometimes they shook some flash powder at Marv Miller's corpse.

Stage magicians use chemicals in shows back east, he reminded himself. *Haven't seen anything as good since I left Boston behind me.*

He had to close his eyes tightly to clear his vision of the fire dazzle.

He sincerely hoped none of those sparks set fire to the dry timber building. He was pretty sure he could get out before flames engulfed the entire attic. He wasn't sure he could grab either or both of the Basques. If he had to make a choice, he'd rescue Madame.

Her mesmerizing allure from their first meeting had faded. But she was still a damned attractive woman in an exotic way, with her dark hair and eyes—she'd put the black velvet patch back on, the left eye this time—her lush figure, and her direct manner. No simpering miss this. She knew her mind and her worth and bowed in submissive blushes to no man.

Madame and her brother began chanting. Doc had not heard this language before. It resembled nothing in his experience.

But the melody line—more in the bass notes than the soprano— reminded him of the sonata (?) Josie had played on the piano. It begged for lyrics. It dove deep into his soul and twined itself into the very essence of himself. He sat there, on the uncomfortable step, jaw agape, as he became one with the music, felt incomplete without it.

Then Esteban, still chanting but in a louder and wilder tone, plucked the small feather talisman from the spear. A frisson of... of something trickled across the skin on Doc's arms and spread to his back.

Madame removed the next trinket. It looked like an eye tooth, pristine white despite its age and exposure to the elements and vagaries of the weather.

The frisson grew deeper, stronger, spreading along Doc's veins and delving down to his toes. He needed to flex his feet, move his legs up and down. Dance in place.

The third, fourth, and fifth tokens came away from the spear. The air inside the darkening attic grew thick with moisture, blurry with shadows.

He had to cover his eyes and ears so he didn't have to observe the next part of the ritual.

But he couldn't.

The snap of the spear as Esteban broke it over his knee sounded as sharp and loud as a gunshot.

Doc jumped to his feet, unsure where he belonged or if he should run blindly away from town and this grisly ritual.

Then he smelled smoke. The harshly sweet scent of burning flesh and decay.

Without thinking he grabbed Madame's hand and pushed her ahead of him down the steps. She had to lean against the wall to maintain her balance. Esteban followed her willingly.

With a mighty whoosh of sound, a massive shock wave pressed against his back, robbing him of air. He stumbled into Esteban and together they fell headfirst down the narrow staircase.

"Don't do it, Mackenzie da Foe!" I called to him, bringing my Spencer to bear. *Oh, please, God, don't make me kill another human being.* I'd done too much of that over the years. Monsters didn't bother me as much. People though....

"Pull that trigger and you'll be dead with a dozen bullets in you before you hit the ground. Kill me and you'll have the entire weight of the Riders of the Purple Sage and the Pinkertons coming down on your sons."

Mac blanched. His hand shook with the effort not to pull the trigger.

The white-haired man, Sam Iamn, behind his left shoulder—in the place where the Devil traditionally perched—moved his mouth.

But his words came out of Mac's throat. "When I am done with you and this town there won't be anyone left to report me to... to...."

I shifted my aim toward the white-haired man. His skin took on a lavender tinge. The wind shifted and blew his hair aside to reveal a budding horn.

A single note blew across the road toward me. Beautiful. Sweet. Mesmerizing.

I'd grown immune to that kind of manipulation.

The muzzle of a shotgun poked out from the false front on the roof of the "Last Chance" saloon.

We all heard the snap of the breech engaging.

Still the half alien man atop a smallish bay gelding mouthed words. His eyes glazed over. His personal magic enveloped him. Gibberish dribbled from Mac's mouth as he fought the need to parrot the threats coming from his companion.

Mac's sons began easing their mounts backward and to the side. Away from their father.

A crack as loud as the opening of a hellmouth near deafened me. The wind of the aftermath drove me to my knees and pulled my breath away.

Mac and Whitey flew to the ground as their mounts reared, pawed the air, and fled the scene.

My horses reared again and again, heavy hoofs coming perilously close to my head.

And above me, swirling and writhing in a column of fire, blue-green-white figures twisted in an arcane dance as lightning flashed from their hands back into my office. Preternatural flames of purple licked at the window from the inside.

Well, I'd told Esteban he could burn the place down.

I just hoped he and Doc had escaped. With my first breath, I whispered another prayer for the safety of my friends.

~

JOSIE WAS DOWN! Neil desperately wanted to cast aside his rifle, leap to the roof's overhang and then drop to the ground so he could run to her.

He needed to run to her, protect her from those lethal horse hooves stomping perilously close to her head.

Martin stopped him with a steady hand while pointing with his own rifle toward the ravine behind the schoolhouse.

Three hatless white-haired figures climbed the steep trail. Every yard of elevation they gained, they had to drop to all fours to keep their balance. Then at the next place wide enough to rest, one of them shrugged out of his jacket and flourished translucent pale purple wings and lifted free of the treacherous trail.

A single shot from the belfry pierced the creature's heart. He dropped, hit hard, broken ground and rolled, tumbled, and landed with a squishy splat atop his three companions.

As a tangled mass of limbs and wings they slid headfirst back the way they'd come. They came to a stop hard up into the prickly branches of a tumbleweed. Seconds later Neil heard the crack of dying plant limbs breaking from the impact. The intruders continued their chaotic journey downhill, until finally they smashed into a boulder.

None of them stirred.

If Father Xavier's shot hadn't killed the first one, the fall did.

Somewhat relieved, Neil turned his attention back to Josie. She'd made it to her knees and still gasped for air, just as Elinore and Prospero reared again, pawing the air in unison.

They had to come down. And when they did, Josie's head was in their way.

She began to crawl forward, toward the fallen Mac da Foe and his white-haired companion, right in the way of the dancing war mare and the angered stallion.

Doc dove for the ground taking Madame with him. Esteban followed suit. The street out the front door wasn't safe. He climbed to his knees and dragged Madame out the back into the paddock. He didn't know which direction the fire would burn. Fires were funny, unpredictable, and dangerous. On top of that, this one had started with magic. He chose the paddock because it had dirt. Lots of dirt and a pump with water to extinguish a normal fire.

Cutter Pine stood up from his crouch behind the limited protection of the split rail fence. He aimed his repeater while still only half standing and pulled the trigger three times before he came fully upright.

"It's safe now. Those white-haired aliens are all dead," Cutter said, opening the breach of his weapon. "Three fewer to harass us."

Doc wobbled to his feet. He wasn't supposed to be near the center of the violence. He received the aftermath in the surgeon's tent *behind* the battle lines.

"I should have known that nothing in the wild west is safe for anyone." He didn't know if he spoke out loud or not.

"Is life truly rewarding if we do not face challenges to our safety once in a while?" Esteban said. Gesturing beyond the fence. "Perhaps you should check to see if the invaders are still alive or not."

Doc had to breathe deeply to steady himself. But then he coughed on the smoke-filled air. A quick glance over his shoulder told him that retreat into the ravine might be safer.

Madame came up coughing as well.

Esteban ignored her.

Doc helped her up with one arm around her waist and the other holding her outstretched hand. He allowed himself to appreciate holding her body for just a moment. She smiled up at him in appreciation.

He could get lost in her deep, one-eyed gaze.

Never trust a one-eyed witch. Both Josie and Lucian had told him that.

Oh, what the hell. He didn't care. Briefly he kissed her, then set her aside as he climbed over the fence—Not as easily as just a few years and twenty pounds ago.

The white-haired men lay collapsed upon each other, purple blood puddling beneath them. If they weren't dead now, they would be before Doc could climb down ten yards over clusters of boulders.

"If you want your bounty, Pine, you'd best collect the horns now, before their compatriots descend," he called. He didn't know if the aliens ate their own carrion or not. He didn't care. He just wanted this day to be over so he could contemplate the wonders of holding Madame close. She reminded him a lot of Rosie, but not as bossy.

REVERBERATING bass notes clouded my thinking. Huge drums invoking the wrath of Thor and his thunder. I shook my head to clear myself of the numbness and the need to protect myself from the coming lightning bolt that must be part of the musical storm.

That was one hell of a shock wave. I'd heard of such things—like what preceded a cannon ball—but had never experienced it.

I deliberately swallowed, deeply. My ears popped. Some of the emptiness between my ears filled with sound. The deep roar of the magic tornado above my head, the harsh neigh of troubled horses, and the sharp crack of rifle fire.

Horses. Horses in distress.

Da Foe's boys fought their panicked horses. Half of them, at least, succumbed to their mounts' need to be elsewhere, as quickly as possible. The others were on the ground, chasing after the beasts that had thrown them.

My gaze sought Elinore and Prospero. The two horses pranced above their respective targets. The mare bared her teeth inches from Sam's ears. The stallion threatened Mac da Foe's midsection. Either animal could turn killer in an instant.

"Back off, Elinore," I ordered, as if we were back years ago when I'd first started training her.

Her ears swiveled and her nostrils flared. But she steadied her feet.

Sam continued to stare up at her in abject fear. Good.

"Yes, Elinore, I know he's one of *them*. That doesn't give us the right to execute him on the spot."

I could almost hear O'Toole tapping out the code of this news on his personal gossip-oriented messaging to the town's folk.

"Prospero, back off," I commanded my other horse. We didn't have years of working together to earn his trust or obedience.

My stallion had to think about it, but his feet stopped their restless intimidation.

I was losing strength in the aftermath of the shockwave of magic and the fear I'd carried for so long.

Then I took a moment to survey the situation. The da Foe brothers and their hired hands, the three left in town had backed off and stashed their rifles in the saddle holsters. I'd feel more comfortable if they'd move a little further away and grabbed their reins with both hands rather than letting them flutter restlessly near their handguns.

"Josie! Are you alright?" Neil ran toward me, sliding on his knees the last bit before wrapping his arms around me.

I allowed myself the luxury of resting my head against his. I could almost hear the gossip running the full length of town and back again. Another moment. I just needed another moment to borrow strength from him, let his warmth infuse me with new courage.

Using Neil's shoulder as a brace, I pushed myself to my feet. "Mac da Foe, I told you not to come into town again with your bully boys," I addressed the human on the ground, ignoring Sam, the source of his false courage. Both of their horses were probably halfway back to their home stable—where the sons were headed as they eased having abandoned their fallen father.

"By the time I'm finished, you won't have a town." Mac slurred his words, like there was a gap between his mind and his utterances.

"Not likely." I checked to make sure Sam wasn't giving Mac the words. His mouth moved while he kept his eyes closed. Feigning unconsciousness.

I side-kicked Sam in the ribs. He grunted and rolled to his side. His rifle now within inches of his three fingers. Elinore bared her teeth again.

Sam let out a squeak and pulled his hands back to cover his vulnerable neck.

"Tell him to stop his mind control," Doc said coming up beside me. He had an arm about Madame's waist. They supported each other. Cutter Pine strolled behind them, his rifle propped against his shoulder, barrel pointed skyward.

Esteban stood alone, almost transparent in the fading sunlight, eyes focused on the western horizon, shoulders slumped. Defeat or dejection?

Later. I'd talk to Esteban when I'd dealt with Mac and his cohort.

I signaled Lucian to join me from his position atop the post office. It looked like the invading roughneck cowboys had melted away. Mac had not prepared them for resistance, let alone an organized plan to repulse invasion.

"Hey, Whitey," I addressed the alien with the snowy hair and purple-colored eyes that seemed to be sliding together into one, over-sized organ the monsters usually sported. "How many were you planning to leave alive on either side of this conflict?" I shoved the muzzle of my Spencer into this gut.

His eyes widened and slid back into place.

"Yeah, you. I know you don't care which side wins or loses, just so you and your followers have enough to eat."

Fluttery movement around my peripheral vision sent shivers of fear up and down my spine. I'd been in similar situations, too many to count. But this time I had a whole town to back me up.

The slight breeze of flapping wings died, and new figures appeared behind Whitey. The aliens *ate* carrion. They did not create it. They left the job of murder to the humans they controlled.

In my experience, humans didn't need a lot of encouragement to kill each other. But in each one of us exists a tiny bit of empathy and the morals of our civilization. Somewhere in his befuddled mind, Mac fought Whitey's control.

I cocked my rifle.

Mac's eyes cleared. He swallowed again and again, not giving voice to Whitey's orders.

And then Jonquil/Jane marched forward with a shotgun aimed at Mac. Behind her five more of Rosie's girls spread out in a phalanx. Each carried a weapon, a butcher knife, a one-shot derringer, or a pitchfork, something that could kill or maim. They took aim at the fluttery things advancing up the road, on foot, wings folding tightly. Females, every one of them, wearing calico and homespun and clean, white aprons. Embroidery and ruffled edges made their costumes badges of honor.

"Time for a reckoning, Stepdaddy," Jane sneered.

"What are you going to do, little girl? I made sure you ain't good for nothing now. You've got no place to go. Go ahead and shoot me. They'll hang you for murder and that will be a mercy to you." He gathered a gob and spat into the dirt.

"Wrong. I've got a place here in this town. Sheriff Blue has given me a second chance. She's the only person who ever gave a shit about me. Something *you* don't deserve."

Gulp. So much for pretending to be a man in order to earn the trust of this town. On the other hand, now no one would consider my keeping company with the town mayor strange.

A quick glance around told me how few people *didn't* know my true sex. I guess my rough clothing and efficient manner of walking didn't fool many.

"So, what are you going to do, Stepdaddy?" Jane continued taunting the man who continued to scrabble backward, away from her shotgun and the lethal prancing feet of my horses. "Are you going to let someone else control you? You going to plead innocent to beating and raping me to within an inch of my life because someone else told you to?" Jane raised her weapon to her shoulder and positioned her index finger on the trigger. "Give me a reason to not shoot you and make you the first meal those teenaged monsters eat." She shifted her aim slightly to the few of Mac's followers still in town. Six or eight of them. They'd dismounted and tossed their guns aside.

They bared their teeth.

She was right. The salivating, white-haired cow hands still hovering behind Mac and Sam, hemming in the humans trying to flee, were young, in their teens. The female aliens walking into town along the road seemed to be aiming for those young men.

Teenagers. The time of life when the body is always hungry, and maturity had not yet given them any sense of responsibility or good judgement. Humans or aliens were alike in the uncontrollable appetites that fueled each growth spurt.

But another thing we had in common, teenaged boys tended to listen to their mothers for fear of not getting their next *cooked* meal.

"You... they would... you wouldn't," Mac choked out.

"Oh yes I would," I replied. "Whitey there doesn't care who he eats, as long as the body is dead, or at least mostly dead."

More movement, to the east side this time. This was getting confusing.

My senses reeled.

But Neil was there to hold me steady.

Lucian and Doc, and Madame, were also there to stop a massacre.

And O'Toole, and Rosie and young Jed, and... and young Rollie da Foe.

My town. My people.

"Excuse me," a new voice joined the murmurs of discontent rising among my town folk and Mac's ranch hands—his sons had disappeared or were at least lying low. The newcomer, a female leading a hoard of other women up the road, blasted a single note from the short, spiral horn in the middle of her forehead.

Silence.

"I have a few things to say to the one you call Whitey." A woman strode forward, folding her wings and retracting her horn. She wore a simple calico dress and apron like any other housewife, as did her companions. "You call yourself a shaman because you have the ability to mesmerize people with your gaze and your chants. But you have abused that title and your talents. Your predecessors healed our people and reduced our pain. For centuries we have sought a home. We have worked hard to blend in with the dominant creatures of each new planet. But our shamans have preached the old ways. For centuries your kind coerced our young to preserve our original culture. And each time we have been slaughtered and driven to seek a new home with ever reduced numbers."

The woman paused to breathe.

I could tell that her anger at Whitey might soon overcome her rationality.

"This man and the young people who follow him did not sing before entering town," I said. "I have battled many swarms, and always they raise a battle cry before descending upon their already dead prey. When they have finished feasting upon the dead of my people, they sing again, beautiful music, a prayer of thanksgiving. Whitey did not sing."

"And that makes him an outlaw among my people," the woman said. She looked up to me with pleading eyes. "I leave him to your laws to deal with. We have found you a race of people most compatible with our bodies. Three generations of interbreeding and most of our native characteristics are gone. We love your laws and your way of life. I, Gayia, as matriarch of my clan, leave this putrefying hunk of flesh to you."

"But we have to feed those on the mothership," Whitey protested. "If we do not provide them with meat, they will all die. We won't be able to find a new home...."

"We should not be nomads!" Gayia screamed at him. "We were once strong and proud, farmers, and ranchers, scientists, teachers, collectors of history. Centuries of wandering the stars stole all of our culture except the need to eat."

"We are done wandering," the female aliens behind Gayia shouted.

"But the mothership needs..."

"It needs to die along with all those aboard who will not adapt."

"How do we destroy a ship built to wander the stars?" I asked myself and anyone close enough to hear my musings.

"Easy," Cutter Pine said. "Next time they land and open a hatch we lob in sticks of lit dynamite on a short fuse and run like hell."

Logical. Could I do it? It was my job... it was my job to notify the Army and let them do it. I had too much to live for now.

Cutter rubbed his hands together in eagerness to get on with that adventure.

"Take the plan to Colonel Des Moines over in Wallowa, then do as you will, with or without his help." I turned my back on him.

"I approve your plan, sir." Gayia bowed her head and folded her hands in an attitude of prayer. "We have no need of them any longer. They do nothing but drain our resources and compel us to change from eaters to killers now that your war is over. We say *enough*. Dispose of them any way you can. Do the same to this false shaman."

"Don't quite know what I can do with him. I don't have a jail to put him in." Flames still licked the wooden walls of my office, casting an eerie light on the scene as the sun set. "Circuit judge and lawyer aren't due in town for another few weeks. We can't have a trial, let alone an execution until then."

"Then we will take him to our elders for judgement. But please, let us take our young home without prejudice and teach them respect and manners. We wish to continue living among you and making music with you." She bowed to me with weaponless hands at her side, palms open.

I returned her bow, setting my rifle on the ground.

Behind me, my people also retired their weapons.

"Take your young, raise them as best you can, send them to school among our children. Let them make friends and become part of our community," I replied.

"Please join us at church day after tomorrow," Neil called. "We'll have a picnic with games, and music. Bring food to share."

"We find buffalo and wild horse tastier than other... meats." Gayia smiled in reassurance.

"Whatever contribution you bring will be most welcome," Neil called as the other female aliens—no longer aliens, newcomers—gathered the shuffling and deflated youngsters to their breasts.

Forgiveness.

With the magic spell of repulsion, that had surrounded the mummy, gone, we could learn to care for each other, make two communities into one.

"Will they bring apples to the party?" a young newcomer asked.

"Spiced with cinnamon and sugar!" I planned to pick them myself.

CHAPTER 35

"How is Jane settling in at Blue's Hollow?" Neil asked me Sunday evening as I stretched from the top of a ladder to unhook the red, white, and blue bunting from the porch roof of the schoolhouse. He steadied the ladder for me, though I'd anchored and braced it securely before climbing.

"She's bossing the chickens and the obnoxious rooster around, and filling the whole valley with the aromas of her cooking. She wants a pair of goats for their milk and a side of beef to keep in the cold locker for winter dinners," I replied as I climbed down.

I pointedly adjusted the ruffled cuffs and front of my very feminine blouse, hoping he'd notice the compromise I'd made in my attire. The milliner had nipped in the waist line of my waistcoats to show off my figure a bit. Rosie wanted me to loosen my braid, maybe let my hair flow free and long. I wasn't quite ready for that yet.

Neil pulled me into a quick embrace. He'd noticed!

Father Xavier cleared his throat in disapproval, an unwelcome reminder that half the town lingered nearby clearing the schoolyard of the detritus of our impromptu harvest festival. "You two may be courting but there are moral limitations to how familiar you may be with each other until you've shared your wedding vows," the Catholic priest said with a grin on his face and a twinkle in his eyes. "Soon I hope, judging by the way you two can't keep your hands off each other."

Politely he turned his back. I took the opportunity to kiss Neil's cheek.

Courting. I hadn't thought about that phase of two people coming together and exploring the need to stay together.

"I haven't thought about courting and marriage since I was fourteen," I whispered. Then I rested my forehead against his, lingering long after a proper lady should do.

I was barely a lady let alone a proper one.

"Ah, 'tis a beautiful thing to see this town coming together in celebration again," Father Xavier rambled on, traces of his original Irish accent leaked through his speech. He continued to shield us from casual view of the people bustling about.

"Do you think we should continue to be known as Heller's Hole, especially if we are going to be on the maps?" the priest asked. He turned to face us.

"The survey crew for the new railway spur starts work tomorrow," Neil replied. He stepped away from me far enough that my entire front felt the chill of autumn air between us. But he stayed close enough to keep one hand on my waist. "We'll be a place on the map a year from now. What kind of name did you have in mind, Father?"

"Second Chance. We've a second chance at building a peaceful community."

"I'm hoping coming together in peace means I won't need to rebuild the sheriff's office and jail cells." I looked south, toward the still smoldering ruins of the old building. I thought we might salvage the stove and the cell bars. Not much else remained except the charred timbers framing the back door and a lot of ash. The afternoon wind portending the next rain squall stirred the fine grit and the smell of smoke. Strangely neither of the adjacent buildings had received so much as a scorch mark.

Doc and Maya Glissen wandered over, shattering our moment of privacy. They seemed joined at the hip. They'd spent the entire day within touching distance of each other, feeding each other samples of the many delightful dishes presented by the varied families.

"Neil, since you are the mayor, and the only legal authority about, would you be willing to marry us?" Doc asked, without preamble.

"Um…"

"A bit soon, Dr. Mathew Buchanan," Father Xavier interrupted. He placed his hands on his hips and stared at them sternly. "And I am a legal authority to perform a nuptial mass."

"Sorry, Father," Maya said in her rich and soothing voice. "Neither of us is Catholic, and we did not know if you would perform the rites."

Doc blushed. Then I remembered he hailed from Boston, the home of many Irish Catholic families.

"Coming back into the fold takes time and much repentance," Father said. He tapped his lips with one finger as if considering. "Were you baptized and confirmed in the true faith?" He addressed Doc.

"Long ago."

"Then the two of you meet me at the rectory tomorrow for supper. We'll discuss this in depth and make decisions. Otherwise, you will have to wait for the circuit judge to make his rounds in three weeks." He dismounted the porch steps and began helping three men dismantle a long trestle table.

Doc and Maya wandered off, arms draped about each other.

"Maya," I called after them. "I stopped by your brother's encampment this morning. The clearing was empty. I thought they'd planned to stay the winter." The memory of Esteban standing at a distance from the crowd Friday evening and how… translucent he looked, not casting a shadow, barely there in his thoughts or physical presence.

"We have not spoken," Maya replied. She looked down, twisting the lace edging on her black gown.

A wave of loneliness washed through me. I hoped I hadn't lost another friend.

"I know your people do not often mix with outsiders, but I'd hoped…"

"My brother makes his own rules, follows his own path. Working great ceremonial magic taxes the mind, body, and soul. He will return in his own time, if he can. In the meantime, look for bits of long grass twisted and braided into tiny wreaths. Leave them in place. They will protect the woman you left as housekeeper." She shook her head sadly. Then she clasped Doc's arm and urged him toward the back of the schoolhouse.

Neil and I folded the bunting into a neat square. I'd have just thrown it back into the storage closet where we'd found it, not my problem. Neil wouldn't hear of it. "My life used to be neat and tidy," he grumbled as he brushed a wrinkle out of a fold. Then you wandered into town." He looked at me with a smile spreading across his refined features. "Now I see too much of my mother's influence in my habits."

"She came to our party only for a few minutes," I replied.

"She disproves of any events she doesn't organize and preside over." Some of the sparkle left his eyes.

"But your father came and stayed until he started to fall asleep over his plate of beef ribs."

"He's not as ill as Jack's letters led me to believe. Perhaps he needed to be jolted out of his routine. Shooting those outlaws in the ravine reminded him of his youth when he protected this town and our family from marauders. He talked about riding your stallion in the spring races." His smile came back and his eyes twinkled again.

"Want to ride back to the orchard for some privacy?" I asked.

"Not yet," Lucian hailed us as he crossed the schoolyard. "Mr. Mayor," he addressed Neil in his most sophisticated and cultured accent. "I hear you need a new school master. I'd like the job. And I'd like Rollie to stay in the back room of the schoolhouse so we can finish his education. Then he'll take over running his father's ranch."

"I don't think there's much you can teach him, other than help him access the library in Pendleton." I had to giggle a little at the idea of the young man reading the entire law book, and understanding it, in one night. If I had my way, Rollie would go straight to Willamette University in Salem.

"I thought you had decided to buy the Dayton dairy farm. I have the paperwork ready for you to sign," Neil said.

"Oh, I do want the dairy." Lucian looked over to where Poppy awaited him a few yards away. "Priscilla loves milking and making cheese. Seems she did a lot of that in Wisconsin before she was brought here by... well, she came here and started working for Rosie. Now she wants something better." He grinned widely at the statuesque woman with café au lait skin and a mass of dark curly hair.

Like all of Rosie's girls, she'd adopted a floral name and left her birth name behind when she began working at the saloon.

Another person grabbing a second chance when it came her way.

"I was hoping to make you my deputy," I said.

"Maybe I can fill in once in a while if you get real busy at the orchard or we get a crime spree. Railway builders can create a lot of trouble on Saturday nights when they've got fresh pay for liquor and ladies." Lucian shrugged.

"A lot like cow hands," I muttered.

"But I'm done patrolling for the Riders of the Purple Sage." He paused, peering into the schoolhouse and the recent rumors of ghostly activity. "Mostly, I'm done."

Father Xavier came up to them again, this time leading a dozen or more men and women. "We think we should change the name of this place. We aren't a hellhole anymore on the arse side of the world. Second Chance sounds appropriate."

"We need a vote on that," Neil hedged. "A formal election presided over by a judge, someone who can register the change in the state capital and get us properly recorded on the maps."

"When's the judge due?" a man at the rear of the crowd called.

"Three weeks," Neil reminded them.

"That's time enough to rebuild the sheriff's office and have that as our official voting station," a woman added.

"State law, the saloon can't open until after all the ballots are cast and counted," I said.

A groan went around the crowd.

"Then we'll make sure we all vote early, no stragglers," Lucian added.

"And we pass a law at the same time that our duly elected mayor can perform weddings," Doc insisted. "Not that I plan on waiting so long."

"Me either," Lucian added.

"Shouldn't that be the sheriff's job?"

"Or we can find a new pastor who will build his own church and not depend upon the schoolhouse. Father Xavier can't do all the work of ministering to a growing town."

"A town where you can lose the world and find yourself," I whispered.

"And love," Neil whispered back, stealing a kiss on my cheek. The strength of his fingers digging into my waist told me how much more we both wanted.

"Let's do it! Let's do all of it," the entire town shouted.

"We are all getting a second chance," I murmured in agreement. "Even me."

The End...until the next crisis.

ACKNOWLEDGMENTS

Writing this book may have been a labor of love, but I couldn't have done it without a lot of help. Joyce Reynolds Ward came through with a broad knowledge of horses and tack and riding hats. I have to thank her above all others. She brought Elinore to life.

Sara Mueller and Maya Bohnhoff also contributed to my esoteric knowledge of the huge, wonderful, and quirky horses.

And, as always I have to thank my patient and supportive husband, Tim. He makes certain I remember to eat, kidnaps me for healing walks, and takes me elsewhere when I start throwing things. Fifty-four years together isn't long enough.

OTHER BOOK VIEW CAFÉ TITLES BY
IRENE RADFORD

http://bookviewcafe.com/bookstore/bvc-author/phyllis-irene-radford/

RIDERS OF THE PURPLE SAGE

The Barefoot Sheriff

TESS NONCOURÉ ADVENTURES

by Irene Radford writing as P.R. Frost

Hounding the Moon

Moon in the Mirror

Faery Moon

Forest Moon Rising

Family Bedrock

MERLIN'S DESCENDANTS SERIES

Guardian Of the Balance

Guardian of the Trust

Guardian of the Vision

Guardian of the Promise

Guardian of the Freedom

CONFEDERATED STAR SYSTEM

by Irene Radford Writing as C.F. Bentley

Harmony

Enigma

Mourner

TRANCE DANCER

Trickster's Dance

ARTISTIC DEMONS

Confessions of a Ballroom Diva

Confessions of a Piano Demon

Confessions of a Siren Singer

Confessions of a Changeling Dancer

PIXIE CHRONICLES

Thistle Down

Chicory Up

Dandelion Twist

WHISTLING RIVER LODGE MYSTERIES

Whistling Down the Wind

Whistle While You Plow

Whistling Bagpipes

Ghostly Whistles

Nine Nutcrackers Whistling (coming soon)

THE DRAGON NIMBUS NOVELS

The Glass Dragon

The Perfect Princes

The Loneliest Magician

The Wizard's Treasure

THE DRAGON NIMBUS HISTORY NOVELS

The Dragon's Touchstone

The Last Battlemage

The Renegade Dragon

SHORT STORY COLLECTIONS

by Irene Radford

Fantastical Ramblings

Speculative Journeys

Steampunk Voyages

Magical Meanderings

NON-FICTION

Magna Bloody Carta

Committing Novel

ABOUT THE AUTHOR

Irene Radford is a founding member of Book View Café. You can find many of her books, both reprints and original titles, at the Café, including her earliest books being released throughout 2023 and 2024. She has been writing stories ever since she figured out what a pencil was for. Editing, as Phyllis Irene Radford, grew out of her love of the craft of writing. History has been a part of her life from earliest childhood and led to her BA from Lewis and Clark College.

Mostly she writes fantasy and historical fantasy including the best-selling Dragon Nimbus Series and the masterwork Merlin's Descendants series. Look for her writing new historical fantasy tales as Rachel Atwood, a different take on the Robin Hood mythology in *Walk the Wild with Me*, from DAW/Astra Books and the sequel *Outcasts of the Wildwood*. In other lifetimes she writes urban fantasy as P.R. Frost or Phyllis Ames, and space opera as C.F. Bentley. Lately she ventured into Steampunk as Julia Verne St. John.

If you wish information on the latest releases from Ms. Radford, under any of her pen names, you can follow her on Facebook as Phyllis Irene Radford.

ABOUT BVC

Book View Café is a professional authors' publishing cooperative offering DRM-free e-books in multiple formats to readers around the world. With authors in a variety of genres, including mystery, romance, fantasy, and science fiction. The Café has something for everyone.

Book View Café is good for readers because you can enjoy high-quality DRM-free ebooks from your favorite authors at a reasonable price.

Book View Café is good for writers because 90% of the proceeds goes directly to the book's author.

Book View Café authors include New York Times and USA Today bestsellers, Nebula, Hugo, Lambda, Chanticleer, National Reader's Choice, and Philip K. Dick Award Winners, World Fantasy, Kirkus, and Rita Award nominees, and winners and nominees of many other publishing awards.

Book View Café's Newsletter includes new releases, specials, author news, and event announcements. Click here to sign up. https://bookviewcafe.com/newsletter/